JUMPERS

Book Four

Mother Trucker Book Series

Jumpers
Copyright ©2016 by CRLE Publishing
Mitchell, Robyn

This is a work of fiction. All names, characters, places, and incidents are the products of the author's imagination or are used fictitiously. Any resemblance to current or local events or to living persons is entirely coincidental.

Library of Congress Cataloging-in –Publication Data

                                                      p.   cm
ISBN: 978-0-9972129-5-2   PCN: 2016957471

I. Truckers—Fiction II. Trucking Industry—Fiction III. Adventure Fiction
Fic Mit   PS 3606.A775M46

Editor-in-Chief: Mindy Reed, The Authors' Assistant
Interior Designed by Danielle H. Acee, The Authors' Assistant
Cover Design by Douglas Brown, Album Artist

Printed in the United States

JUMPERS

ROBYN MITCHELL

PUBLISHING
Odessa, TX

Introduction

"Oh, Jack, it's just exactly what I wanted." Shelby walked slowly around her shiny new pearl black Pete. Shelby lifted the hood of the truck, which displayed a pink silhouette of an angel. Shelby ran her hands over the fine air brushed portrait. "You remembered. Jack, this is the most amazing birthday present ever."

Shelby put her arms around her husband's neck. Jack smiled and kissed his wife. "Now, all you have to do is find a sand hauling company you can lease on with, to go with the new pneumatic trailer that will be delivered here in about a week."

"What! Seriously, you bought me a new trailer too?" Shelby kissed her husband. "Thank you, Jack, thank you so much."

◊◊◊

"Jack, Jack! I got the job. I leased on with a sand hauling company out of Weatherford. I'm so excited. They are very reputable and have lots of work. They should keep me busy for a long time."

"Good, we need you working so that we can pay for those big pieces of machinery. When do you start?"

"I have to be in Weatherford on Monday for orientation. Do you want to go with me?"

"No, I think I'll let you do this on your own. I don't think you're going to get into too much trouble hauling sand. Besides, I can always call Angelica and she'll put you straight."

"Ha, ha, very funny. That reminds me, Angelica and Rex are getting married in June and I'm her maid…well..matron of honor."

"Really, where is the wedding being held? Pig's Ball Room? How about the honeymoon? I bet they have a special place reserved in Mexico."

"Oh, you're cute. No, they are getting married in Georgia, where she's from. They are honeymooning in Paris. I wish we could go to Paris some time."

"Well, get to work and pay off that truck. Then maybe I can afford to take you to Paris."

Shelby loved Jack more than ever. He had worked so hard over the last few years to make up for cheating. Shelby knew in her heart it was just a mistake. "I love you, Jack. I will work really hard so that we can go to Paris one day."

◊◊◊

Shelby held her cell phone between her ear and shoulder while she paid the cashier for her snack. "I just wanted my sweet husband to know that I just pulled a super good haul for my first job."

"Awesome, Shelby. Where you headed?"

"I'm headed to Pennsylvania. We're hauling several loads of specialty sand out of West Texas up there. So, I'll have time to come by the house and sleep with my husband tonight. I'll load tomorrow and then head to Pennsylvania. We'll deliver these loads and then there are several more loads out of Texas and Louisiana that I will be carrying up there. There's even some talk about hauling for some fracturing jobs in Oklahoma, West Virginia, Kentucky, Arkansas, and North Dakota, not to mention all the work in Texas that they cover. They are going to keep me really busy, sweetie, so you better take full advantage of me tonight when I get home. It might be a while before I make it home again."

"Wow, with that kind of work, you'll have that truck and trailer paid off in no time. You don't need to worry, baby. I'll take great advantage of you tonight. Maybe you'd better hurry your pretty little ass up and get home."

"I will, darling. I have to finish getting my fuel card authorized in the office. I'll put fuel in the truck and head home. I miss and love you, baby."

"I miss and love you, too. See you tonight."

◊◊◊

"Hey, sweetheart, just thought I would give you a call. I guess I have to leave a stupid message on your voicemail. I am headed back to Odessa tonight. I have to pick up another load for Pennsylvania, but I will be home for a couple days. Call me when you get this message." Shelby pushed the end button on her Bluetooth. Twinges of suspicion ran through her mind. Jack hadn't given her any reason over the last few years for her to suspect that he was cheating again, but every time he wasn't able to answer his phone, Shelby wondered.

Shelby hated feeling this way, and hoped that over time those feelings would disappear completely. They had diminished but had not completely left her thoughts. *Will I always suspect Jack, or will I eventually trust him completely again?* Suddenly, her phone rang and she looked at the caller ID. It was Jack. Her feelings of mistrust faded for the moment.

"Hi Baby, sorry I didn't answer the phone right away. I have a bunch of employees in my office."

Several of the men sitting in Jack's office yelled greetings to Shelby. "Hey, Shelby, how's it going?"

"Bring that new Pete by and let me try her out. Jack has a big old picture of it and you on the wallpaper on his computer. Sure is a sweet ride."

Jack interrupted. "Get back to work. I'm on an important phone call." Jack returned to his conversation with Shelby. "Sorry about that, baby. What's up?"

"I left you a message, but I can tell you haven't had time to listen to it. I just wanted you to know that I'm on my way home for a couple days. I'm coming back for another load for Pennsylvania. I'm due for a break so I thought I would take it at home."

"That sounds great, sweetheart. When will you be here?"

"Well, depending on traffic in Dallas and Fort Worth, I should be home sometime tonight."

"Great baby, I can't wait. I do have to get going. I'm swamped, but I'll be waiting for you when you get in. Will you be home in time for dinner?"

"No, probably not."

"That's okay, I will take my darling wife out tomorrow night. I love you and I miss you."

"I love and miss you, too. See you soon."

◊◊◊

Shelby was tired when she pulled the truck into its parking spot in front of the house. Jack met Shelby at the front door. "There's my baby."

Shelby threw her bag on the floor before putting her arms around Jack's neck. "I'm so glad I'm home. I'm tired."

Jack kissed Shelby's lips. "Let me help you to bed, sweetheart." Jack locked the front door and walked with Shelby to their bedroom.

Shelby undressed for bed. "That sure is a long drive, but I love every minute of it. I'll probably make two or three more of these trips before next weekend. Are you going to meet me in Georgia for Angelica and Rex's wedding? Or do you want me to bring the load on into Odessa and we can fly there together?"

Jack was already undressed and in bed. "Why don't I just fly there and we can make it a nice romantic weekend away together. You won't be so rushed and maybe we can see some of Georgia while we are there."

Shelby jumped into bed and wrapped herself around her husband. "That sounds like a terrific idea. I will park my truck at one of the truck stops in Atlanta. You can rent a car at the airport and we can get a hotel near Angelica's place. We have the rehearsal dinner on Friday night and the wedding is on Saturday. I'm going to take off the entire weekend, plus Monday and Tuesday so we can spend time together."

Jack took Shelby in his arms. "That sounds like a great idea, baby."

◊◊◊

Shelby had made her delivery in Pennsylvania and was headed down highway 95 toward Georgia. She pulled into a truck stop outside Richmond Virginia for the night. "Hi baby, how are you doing without me tonight?"

"Well, I'm doing okay, but I'm sure missing my sweet little wife. Where are you tonight, my love?"

"I'm outside Richmond Virginia, sitting in this lonely truck stop, thinking about you."

"You keep thinking about me and remember we will be in Georgia in a couple days. Don't be looking for one of those truckers to keep you from being lonely."

"You're out of your mind, Jack. Why would I want beer when I've got champagne at home?"

"I don't know about champagne, baby. Maybe just an aged whiskey or wine."

Shelby laughed at her husband. "I love you, baby, and I will be in Atlanta on Thursday night. I will park at the local truck stop near Angelica's parents' home. I made reservations for a rental car and a hotel. I was going to wait until Friday to pick up the car when I met you at the airport, but I think I'll get it Thursday night before I go to the hotel."

"That sounds great, sweetheart. I can't wait to see you. I can't wait to have some time away from this office. It will be great spending time with Rex and Angelica, too."

"I talked to Angelica this morning and she's going crazy with all the arrangements. I told her I would be there soon to help. It reminded me of when I was getting ready for our wedding."

"I'm glad I married you, Shelby Mathews."

"I'm glad I married you, too, Jack Mathews. Well, I'd better get some rest. I have a good drive tomorrow into Atlanta. I want to get there early so I can get all dolled up for my honey."

"I can't wait, baby. You sleep good and dream of me."

"You know I will. Love you more!"

"Love you most! See you Friday."

Shelby ended her call with Jack. She snuggled her pillow close and fell asleep.

CHAPTER ONE

Honk! Honk!

"Amber Ellen Nichols, you get back here right now!" The screen door of the decrepit, wood-framed house slammed shut. "You never folded that basket of laundry I left on your bed. Gabe needs his dinner and a bath, and I'm pretty sure you haven't touched your homework."

The petite, teenager jumped off the porch's three steps, dashed across a patch of brown lawn, and put her hand in the handle of the black Mustang. Her mother's words reached her ears the same moment she reached the curb.

Amber turned to face her mother as she opened the car door. "Mama, it's my sixteenth birthday. I want to go out. I'll take care of the laundry and my homework when I get home." She slid into the passenger's seat, blew a kiss to her mother, shut the door, and waved goodbye through the open window.

Once again, Elsa Mae watched through the tattered screen door as her youngest daughter drove off into the night with her friends. She looked down and spotted her two-year-old grandson wobbling toward her legs. She picked him up and kissed his cheek. "Well, it looks like it's just you and me tonight for dinner, Gabe. How about some macaroni and cheese?"

◊◊◊

"Charley, I'm worried. She hasn't been home in three days. The school has called and she hasn't shown up for classes either. She ran out of here in such a hurry the other night, I never even got the name of the boy driving that black car." Elsa Mae poured her husband another cup of coffee and then sat down to feed Gabe who was busy with some Cheerios she'd put on the tray of his high chair.

"Don't worry, Elsa Mae. She'll be back. She always comes back home. Amber has the spirit of a wild horse running free in the woods. You know you'll never tame her unless you break her spirit. I know you won't do that to our child. She's been like this since the day she was born."

"Why does she have to worry me so? Why does she leave little Gabe? I know she was young when she had this precious child, but she's a mother now; she needs to take care of her responsibilities. Maybe we were wrong in expecting her to keep the baby. Maybe we should have let Josh and Katie take him from the beginning."

"Did I hear my name?" Josh walked into his parents' kitchen, opened the cabinet next to the sink, and pulled out a coffee cup. He poured a cup of black coffee from the carafe still being warmed by the coffee maker. He sipped the hot brew and then asked his parents, "What about me?"

Charley put down the newspaper and finished off his breakfast. "Your mother is worried about your sister—again." He took his final sip of coffee, gathered up his dishes, and took them to the sink. He grabbed his lunch sack off the counter and headed toward the door. "I have to go to work, Mama."

Charley kissed the top of Gabe's head and then planted a soft, loving kiss on his wife's lips. "Don't worry about her, Elsa Mae. She'll be home tonight. I almost guarantee it. I'll call you later and let you know what time I'll be home, or if I'll be home. I love you guys."

"Bye, honey."

"Bye, Dad."

Josh sat at the table across from his mother. "You want me to make you something for breakfast, sweetheart?" she asked.

Josh sipped at his coffee and played a little with Gabe. "No, Katie fed me before I left this morning. I just came by to check on you and Pops. We've been kind of busy this week and I haven't heard from you, so I thought I'd swing by before work."

Elsa Mae gently patted her eldest son's face. "You are such a good son. I love you."

Josh smiled. "I love you too, Mama."

"Mama." Oatmeal spewed from the toddler's mouth as he spoke.

"You too, my little Gabe."

Elsa Mae wiped the child's mouth with a washcloth.

"So, Amber is out running around again. Mama, I told you she was going to continue this behavior as long as you and Pops allow her to get away with it. The two of you need to either make her come live with one of us, or put her out on the street. She is never going to grow up and face her responsibilities until you do. You guys are too soft on her. She manipulates you and uses you to get what she wants. She's a spoiled brat and she runs over you guys every chance she gets."

"I know, son. She's young and has made some terrible choices in her life. We're just trying to help her find her way."

"Helping her find her way would be better accomplished with a stiff belt across her ass. She can't keep doing this to you, Mama. She needs to buckle down and take care of Gabe. She created him, now she needs to take care of him. The longer you guys keep doing everything for her, the longer she's going to keep running off and partying."

"It's her birthday, Josh. I haven't let her go out for several weeks. I haven't forgotten the last time she disappeared and skipped school. I've been cracking down. She's feeding and bathing Gabe, putting him to bed, and doing her own laundry, too. She's still in school, so we try to give her time to study."

"I know you guys are trying to help her, but you're not making things difficult enough for her. She still wants to be a teenager, but she can't be that anymore. She's a mother now."

The screen door slammed. Amber walked through the living room to her bedroom and shut the door.

"Amber is that you?" Elsa Mae handed the bowl of oatmeal to her eldest son. "Here, finish feeding him while I go check on Amber."

"Mama, let me go check on Amber."

"No, I'll be right back."

The door to Amber's room was locked. "Amber, let me in please. We've been so worried about you. Where have you been? The school called several times; you haven't been going to classes. What's going on, Amber? Why have you been gone so long?"

"Leave me alone, Mama. I'm tired; I feel sick. I'll talk to you later. Just let me sleep."

Josh came out of the kitchen. "Mama, I have to go to work. Gabe is playing with his Cheerios. We'll be here this weekend to celebrate Pop's birthday. The whole family's going to have a big discussion about Amber. It's time we do something about her behavior, all of us, not just you and Pops." Josh kissed his mother on the cheek and left through the screen door.

"Okay, son, see you later." Elsa Mae knocked again on her daughter's bedroom door. "Amber, you have to go to school. You have already missed too many days. The truant officer is going to come by if you don't go to school."

"I don't care, Mama. I don't feel good and I'm tired. I'll go to school tomorrow."

Elsa Mae shook her head as she reluctantly left the bedroom door.

◊◊◊

"Happy birthday, Pops."

"Oh, thank you, everyone." Charley blew out the candles on his birthday cake. The family was gathered around the dark maple dining room table—Elsa Mae's favorite family heirloom.

Charley hugged his grandchildren as each one came to his side. He sliced a piece of cake for each one. "One for you, and for you."

Elsa Mae looked around the table at her children—her family. She had been blessed with three boys and four girls, two daughters-in-laws, two son-in-laws, and eleven grandchildren. Everyone was present for Charley's fifty-fifth birthday—except Amber. Kami, her second to youngest daughter went over and took the cake slicing responsibility over from her father. The recent college grad had just been accepted into medical school at the University of Texas in Houston. Elsa Mae looked at her with pride, stood up and said, "I'll be right back."

Amber's door was slightly ajar. Elsa Mae opened it to find Amber lying on her bed. "Are you okay, Amber?" Elsa Mae sat next to her on the bed.

"What's the matter, baby?"

Amber turned to face her mother; her green eyes were red. Amber wiped the tears that had streamed down her face. "I'm okay, Mama, just still not feeling too well."

Elsa Mae moved Amber's brown hair away from her face. "Amber, you have been sick for several days now. I think I should take you to the doctor."

Amber turned away from her mother. "No, Mama, I know what's wrong."

Elsa Mae touched her daughters shoulder. "What is it, Amber?"

"Mama, I'm pregnant, again."

Elsa Mae pulled her hand back and covered her mouth. "Oh no, Amber, not again."

"Just go, Mama; I want to be alone."

Elsa Mae got off of Amber's bed and walked toward her door. She turned and looked at her daughter's back, two tears fell from her eyes. She quickly wiped them from her face before walking back into the living room. She forced a smile as she walked through the group of children wanting their grandmother's attention. "I'll be back in a minute, my babies. Granny needs to clean up the dishes."

Josh noticed the red on his mother's face and her quick exit to the kitchen. "I'll be right back, Katie." He paused for a moment and watched his mother busying herself with the stack of cake plates and bowls from the party. "Can I help you, Mama?"

She turned, startled by the voice. She wiped the few tears that had fallen away from her face. "Oh, Josh you scared me. No, I think I got this."

Josh walked to his mother, put his hands on her shoulders, and turned her so that she had to face him. "Mama, what is wrong?"

Elsa Mae couldn't hold it back. "Oh, Josh, Amber is pregnant again."

Josh let go of his mother and slammed his fist down on the counter. "Hell no! Not again. We are going to have a family meeting right now about her."

"No Josh, not now," Elsa Mae cried. Today is your father's birthday. I really don't want to ruin his party with all this drama. I just need your support right now. I truly don't know what I'm going to do. It's been so hard for me, taking care of Gabe. I just don't know how I'll take care of another child." She wept.

"You're not going to, Mama, she's going to take care of both of them or give them both up for adoption. Enough is enough, and I won't stand for this any longer. Where is she?"

"Josh, please. Not today. Let me talk to your father and tell him. He knows nothing about this. I don't want to disappoint him today with this news. You and Katie come over tomorrow and we will talk with Amber together."

"Mama, we need to talk with everyone about what is going on. Everyone needs to know how she's treating y'all."

Elsa Mae put her hand on her son's shoulder. "Please, Josh, not today. This is going to hurt your father so much. You know he has a deep bond with Amber."

"Fine, Mama, but Katie and I are coming over after church tomorrow and we will figure out what to do with Amber. We are going to make sure before we leave tomorrow that she understands—no more free ride."

"Okay, son, thank you."

Katie, Kami, and Trish entered the kitchen with dishes from the dining room. "Here, Mama. Papa really liked the new rifle the boys gave him." Katie could tell from Josh's face that something was wrong. Kami noticed that her mother was tense. "Everything okay, Mama? Josh, what's wrong?"

"Everything is fine, girls. Just put the dishes over there on the counter."

"Yeah, everything is just fine. I'm going to go check out that new gun."

◊◊◊

"Did you have a nice birthday, Charley?" Elsa Mae was brushing her hair, getting ready to climb into bed with her husband.

Charley flipped through the channels on the television. "Yes, Elsa Mae, it was a wonderful birthday. It is always so wonderful when all the children are home."

Elsa Mae cuddled up next to her husband. "Charley, we have to talk. I promised Josh I would discuss this with you tonight. Josh and Katie are coming over tomorrow so that we can all talk about what to do. Amber is pregnant again."

Charley didn't stop changing the channels with the remote. "When did you find this out?"

"Just today."

"Does she know who the father is?"

"I didn't get into details with her about any of it today. I didn't want to ruin your birthday."

Elsa Mae began to cry. Charley pulled his wife closer to him after finally putting down the remote. "Don't worry, it's all going to be okay. We will talk with her tomorrow and with Josh. We'll figure out something. What the hell, Elsa Mae? It's just one more baby to add to our big clan."

◊◊◊

"How could you do this again, Amber? Look at what you're doing to Mama and Pops. Mama takes care of Gabe all the time while you go out partying, skipping school, and doing God knows what else. It's time you take responsibility for yourself and your child, I mean children. If you can't settle down and pull your own weight, you need to take Gabe and leave."

Amber sat curled up in a ball on the couch, as Josh paced up and down the floor in front of her. Elsa Mae sat with Charley on the loveseat and Katie stood next to them with her arms folded. "Josh, you need to calm down. Yelling at her isn't going to accomplish anything."

Tears fell down Amber's face. She stared at her mother with disappointment in her eyes. "How could you tell him, Mama? You know he doesn't like me."

"Amber, that's nonsense. Your brother loves you."

"Yes, I do love you, Amber, but enough is enough. You have taken advantage of Mama and Pops long enough. I suggest that you seriously think about giving this baby up for adoption. Katie and I have talked; we will take Gabe. That way you can do what you want with your life."

Charley raised up in his seat. "Now wait a minute, Josh. No one is going to do any of that. Not in this house. We are family and we will deal with this like a family. That unborn baby is a part of us just as much as Gabe or even you. We will come up with something that will work for everyone."

Josh threw up his hands and leaned up against the wall near his wife. "Fine, Pops. You figure it out. You and Mama are the ones she's taking for granted. You're the ones who are not going to be able to retire and spend your golden years doing what you want. Because she's a screw up, everyone in this family has to suffer."

Amber stood up and pointed her finger at her brother. "I am sorry I'm such a disappointment to you, big brother. I'm sorry I didn't grow up to be just like you. You're an asshole." Amber fell back onto the couch and curled up in another ball. She buried her face and cried.

"I think you need to make her go out there and get a job, Pops. She needs to find out what it's like to have to take responsibility for her own life and the choices she makes."

"Josh, no more yelling. But I think you may have a good idea, though." Charley stood and walked over to his isolated, distraught daughter. He took his child in his arms. "Amber, Josh is right. It's time you stand up and take responsibility for your actions. Tomorrow, I want you and your mother to get to the doctor. Then, I want you both to check out that alternative school your mama was telling me about. It's supposed to be only half a day of classes. I want you to go and find a part-time job."

"A job? I don't have any skills. What kind of job can I get, Pops?"

Josh interrupted. "You are sixteen years old. If you're old enough to party and get pregnant, then you're old enough to get a job. You can work at the mall or a fast food place or at a restaurant, Amber. There are a lot of things you can do."

"Please, Mama, don't make me do this."

Elsa Mae looked with forgiving eyes at her daughter. "Your papa and I think that this will be best for you. I will continue to watch Gabe for you until the baby is born. Then we will look for daycare. The children need you to be a responsible mama."

Amber jumped from the couch in anger. "Fine! I'll get a damn job." She stomped off to her room.

Gabe walked to his mother's door and cried for her. "Mama. Mama." Amber ignored the child's pleading. Josh turned to the hallway where Gabe was crying at his mother's door. "See? She has no idea what it means to be a parent." Josh picked up Gabe and brought him back into the living room. "Pack him some things, Mama. Katie and I will take Gabe for a while. It will give you some time to get her straightened out, maybe."

Katie took Gabe from Josh. Elsa Mae agreed and went up to gather the child's things. When she returned she asked, "Katie, are you sure you want to do this?"

Katie smiled at Gabe and kissed his nose. "Yes, Mama, it will be nice to have a little one in the house again. He can play with the kids when they get home from school."

CHAPTER TWO

"**S**eriously, who the hell do you think you are, Paul? I can't just go off in your truck with you." Amber put a plate of food in front of her customer. "Eat your food, and stop screwing with me. You come in here every other week, and it's the same old pickup lines. You need to get some better lines if you want anything from me."

Paul salted his food. "Oh, come on, baby. We would have a great time out on the road together. I could teach you to drive my truck; you'll get to see a whole lot of the country, too. I heard you tell old Wanda over there, that you want to see the world someday. Well, that day is here, and I'm your chauffer."

Amber laughed, as she walked away from Paul. She picked up a plate of food out of the cook's window and placed it in front of another trucker sitting at the bar. "What, and give all this up, Paul? You're out of your mind. I have two kids, and my family will disown me if I take off and leave my kids with my mama."

Paul pointed his fork toward Amber. "Who takes care of your kids while you work?"

"My mama does. Why?" Amber filled several other customers' tea glasses while she continued to have her conversation with Paul. It was common for the waitresses to speak with regular customers. Amber's boss liked the open conversations; he said it made people feel like they were at home eating with their families.

"We'll see, your mama knows you need to get out of the house and work. She knows that you would go crazy if you had to stay at home all the time. She understands how you feel; she was young once. You're only young once, Amber."

Amber put the tea pitcher under the tea brewer and started another batch of tea. "So? That doesn't mean she or the rest of the family understands anything about me. If fact, none of them even really understand me at all. They have no idea that I want to see the world. Most of all, none of them care. They just want me to be responsible and take care of my children. Especially, my older brother, Josh, who I hate. I am young, but what would you know about it Paul? You're old."

Paul laughed. "I'm old enough to teach you a lot of wonderful things, little girl."

Amber laughed. "I'm not a little girl."

"Prove it."

"Shut up, Paul, and eat your dinner before it gets cold. I'm not going anywhere with you in your truck."

◊◊◊

Amber reached for her purse under the counter. "I'm going home, Wanda. I'll see you tonight. I think Frank has me scheduled for the ten shift again."

A chunky, red head came out from the back of the restaurant, carrying a bus tub full of clean dishes. "Okay, sweetie, I think I'm working the same shift. I'll see you with bells on tonight.

The cool air of the early morning hit Amber as she made her way through the glass double doors. She adjusted her purse strap on her shoulder and slipped her hands into the pockets of her hoodie. Amber tightened the material closer around her small-framed body.

Her mother's four door Impala sat in the parking lot. As she walked slowly to the car, she played with the pack of cigarettes hidden in one pocket and the keys to the car in the other. She was cold as she walked across the parking lot, but that didn't matter at the moment. She had to go home. She was tired from working all night, but instead of going to sleep, which she desperately wanted to do, she'd be greeted by a barrage of cries from her four-month-old.

Once home, she would have to pull the crying child from her crib to change, bathe, and dress her. Then she would have to change the crib linens from the leaky diaper from the previous night. After that, she would take her little girl to the kitchen, warm a bottle for the hungry infant, and feed her in the rocking chair next to the bed she longed to be in.

Amber knew the routine, just as Annie would be falling back to sleep, Gabe would raise his little head from the pillow on his toddler bed. Excited, to see his mommy rocking his new little sister, he'd loudly run to them, startling the almost sleeping baby awake again. Amber would then shush the little boy, and encourage him to play quietly with his blocks scattered around the bedroom floor, all the time attempting to calm the now crying baby in her arms. The baby would eventually fall back to sleep, Amber would gently lay her in her crib and put her finger to her lips to let Gabe know that he still needed to be quiet. Amber would gather a few clothes for her eldest son before tiptoeing the two of them out of the room.

After quietly closing the bedroom door, Amber would escort her son to the living room. There, she would undress Gabe, remove his wet pull-ups and pajamas (potty training was not going well), and dress him again with clean clothes for the day. Gabe would then grab his mommy's hand and lead her toward the kitchen for breakfast.

After a quick stop at the trashcan and laundry room, Amber would help Gabe into his booster seat. She would grab a bowl from the cabinet, a spoon from the drawer, a box of Fruit Loops off the counter, and the milk from the refrigerator as her two-year-old sat impatiently in his highchair. She'd pour a small amount of the sugary cereal, drown it in milk and sit next to Gabe. He would talk with milk and cereal in his mouth, which he would spill on his clean clothes, and scatter all over the table and floor. All the while, Amber would yawn and yearn for the peace, and the silence of sleep that she hardly got any more. Eventually, Elsa Mae would enter the kitchen, grab a cup of coffee, and relieve her from Gabe's persistent chatter. Amber would get a few moments of rest before Annie cried for another bottle and some attention.

Amber would sleep on and off throughout the morning, until Elsa Mae woke her with just enough time to take a shower, throw on clothes, and go to school in the afternoon. Amber would do her best to stay awake during class, but her ability to sleep while sitting straight up had become well perfected.

Most of her teachers had become accustomed to Amber's inability to stay awake and knew of Amber's responsibilities. Her grades revealed the truth; she got nothing out of her half-day alternative educational program. Amber had argued with her mama several times over the fact that making her go to school was a waste of time. But her mama insisted that she needed to complete high school. It was clear to Amber and her teachers that she was never going to accomplish that goal.

The routine only varied on the weekends when Amber wasn't required to go to school. Her mama would kindly give her the two days a week to catch up on her sleep. This was one of those days, and Amber looked forward to the sleep.

Amber slipped inside the car, put her purse on the floor, and started the engine. She sat sideways with the door open, pulled out her pack of cigarettes from her pocket, selected one, tapped it a couple times on the box and placed it between her lips. She put the pack back in her pocket and rummaged for the lighter. She lit the cigarette and took a deep drag. Her mama allowed Amber to drive her car to work, but forbid her to smoke in it. She blew the smoke out of the car while waiting for it to warm up.

Startled by a knock on the passenger side window, Amber jerked to see who the hell was interrupting her smoke time. "Amber, it's me Paul. Open the door." Amber rolled her eyes, pushed the automatic door, button and allowed Paul to sit inside her mama's car. Without changing her position Amber continued smoking her cigarette. "What do you want, asshole?"

Paul reached over the console and rubbed her upper arm. "Well, I just thought I would come and say goodbye to you. I have to leave this morning and I wanted to see you."

Amber wasn't impressed with the older man's sentiment. She felt all men, especially this one, wanted only one thing, and she wasn't interested. "How nice of you, but why would you want to see me before you go home, Paul? You are headed back to your nice house, to your lovely wife, your two beautiful kids, and fabulous Georgia. I'm just a screwed up, single mother of two babies, slinging hash in a rundown truck stop in the middle of a dirty and stinky oil patch in West Texas. A no-brainer if you ask me, Paul."

Amber bent over and put the half smoked cigarette out on the ground beside her car. Paul reached up and rubbed her jean covered thigh. Amber quickly swung her right arm around toward Paul's head. "Asshole, get your filthy hands off me!"

Paul caught Amber's small arm, pulled her close to his face, and kissed her. "I've been wanting to do that for months."

Surprised by the passion she felt coming from the kiss, Amber jerked her arm from the grips of the man who had been pursuing her for the last year. "Get out of my car, Paul. Go home to your family and leave me alone. I know that the only thing you want is an out-of-town bootie call, and I'm not interested. I got two kids and no daddies, which proves all men are nothing but dogs."

Paul wouldn't leave the vehicle. "Amber, yes, I want to fuck you more than I can say, but I also really want you to go with me out on the road. I've fallen in love with you over these last few months. You're all that I think of when I'm not here, and when I am here, all I want is to be with you. My marriage is terrible; my wife has her life and I have mine. When I go home, it's like going home to strangers. I'm gone so much that they live their lives around my income. I'm nothing to any of them but a paycheck. My wife won't even consider riding with me anymore. The kids are busy with school, their friends, and sports. I'm lonely, Amber, and I really want you to come with me. We would have so much fun on the road together. Please think about it. I'll be back in two weeks, I really hope when I leave here next time, you will be rolling out with me."

Shocked by the confessions of the person who occupied her passenger seat, Amber took a hard look at the face of the man that had just stolen a kiss from her. *He's not that bad looking for an older guy,* she thought. He had been nice to her, leaving her large tips, flowers, Christmas presents, and gifts for Annie during her maternity leave. He was faithful in his constant visits to the restaurant when he was in town. That kiss, that passionate kiss still lingered on her lips—the biggest surprise of all.

She realized she had been daydreaming; her reality was still here. "I can't go with you, Paul. What about my babies? What about my job and school? My family would disown me if I take off with you. Besides, what are you going to do with me when you have to go home? Leave me in the truck, in a truck stop near your house? You're out of your mind, and I'm out of mine for even thinking about this crazy scheme of yours." Amber shut her driver's side door. "Now get out of my car."

Paul knew that it was time to go, but he also knew that he had got Amber to at least think about his idea. "We will work that all out along the way." He opened the passenger door and began to leave the car. "Can I have another kiss?"

Amber released the brake and put the vehicle in reverse. "Get out, Paul, I have to go home."

He slipped out of the seat, stood on the pavement, and put his arm on the frame of the door. He leaned back into the car. "Think about it, Amber. I know you already are. I will be back in two weeks. I want you to go with me all over the country. I want to show you beautiful places and buy you beautiful things. Please think about it."

She rolled back, making Paul move away from the car. "Goodbye, Paul. I need to go. Get away from my car."

Paul backed away, closed the car door, and allowed Amber to back out of her parking space. He waved at Amber as she headed out of the parking lot. Amber half-assed waved back, which gave Paul the impression that perhaps he had not accomplished as much with her as he had hoped.

CHAPTER THREE

The weeks had been nothing but the same old life that Amber had resigned herself to since Annie had been born. Her sister Kami had come home for a few days to visit, bringing with her the tales of the long hours she spent studying to be a doctor, stories about a new boyfriend that was also studying to become a physician, and descriptions of the abundant night life and entertainment that Houston had provided to her.

Not wanting to seem rude or show her anguishing pangs of jealousy, Amber broke away from the table of family that had gathered to hear Kami's stories. Tory and Traci, her two older sisters, Roger and Alex, her older twin brothers, and of course, Josh (whose visits she dreaded) had all come for the homecoming of their well-accomplished, soon-to-be wealthy younger sister. Brothers and sisters in-law and a slew of nieces and nephews were scattered throughout the Nichols's domain.

"I'm so glad you're home, big sister, but I have to get a little sleep before going to work tonight. I'm so happy everything is going so well for you in Houston. Maybe someday, the kids and I can come for a visit. I've never been anywhere but this old town. So getting to see all those wonderful things would be awesome."

Kami took the hug that Amber offered without getting up from her chair. "Okay, little sister. I'll hold you to that. Get some rest, and maybe I'll come to the restaurant this weekend and see you. I've been hungry for some of Frank's famous pancakes. I love you."

Amber walked toward her room. "That would be great. I love you, too."

In her room, Amber flung herself onto her bed, then turned over on her belly. She pulled her pillow under her chin, moved the bottom slat of the shade that covered her window and looked out into the street that ran along the front of her parents' home. She longed to see what was beyond the streets and buildings of the town she had been born into almost seventeen years ago. Who was she kidding? She was never going to leave this town.

Being a free spirit and the youngest of seven children, Amber had willfully engaged in activities that had been forcefully forbidden by her parents toward her older siblings. She had taken full advantage of the slow movements and mellowing attitudes of her aging parents.

However, her carefree attitude along with raging hormones, curiosity about drug culture, and the influence of older, more experienced friends had also led her to her current situation. Tears fell as Amber realized that she hated her life. It wasn't what she had dreamed it would be and she wanted out.

Sleep wouldn't come as Amber heard the inaudible hum of voices and the occasional clear yell of a child beyond the walls of her room. Gabe and Annie had been gratefully taken from the room for the afternoon by her mama. Kami wanted to enjoy the children's company during her visit. It was a rare opportunity for Amber to really get some rest, but her mind was racing.

One particular thought pressed through the rest—the words that Paul had spoken to her over two weeks ago. The echoes had entered her mind numerous times since his departure. He was due back into town either today or tomorrow. Amber found herself actually anxious for his return. She had even entertained, with some reservations, the thought that she might accept his offer. Paul wanted to take her away from her present prison of a life and introduce her to a life she had only dreamed of.

Tossing and turning, Amber gave up on sleep. She sat up in her bed and looked toward her closet. There on the floor of the opened door was her backpack. There above the bag hung some of her clothes. All she had to do was grab the bag, put clothes in it, and include a few incidentals from her dresser and jewelry box.

Her eyes then scanned the crib and toddler bed that lined the walls in her room. What would happen to Gabe and Annie if she left? Would they stay here with her parents in the home they had known all their life? Would

Josh and Katie take them? Or, would they end up in the custody of the state? No, her father would never allow that. If they did go live with Josh and Katie would they be kind and good to them? Josh was a hard and difficult man when it came to his younger sister, but he and Katie had always been good with her children. Gabe had spent many nights over at their home and he loved them. Katie always held Annie when she came to the house, telling her several times that she and Josh had thought about having another baby. Yes, they would be okay. Daddy would see to that if nothing else.

Looking for justification for the action she knew she was about to take, Amber began reasoning with herself. She was right in doing what she had finally decided to do. Gabe and Annie would be happier without their preoccupied and sad mother. She was always tired, never at home for them during the night and half of the days. Her mother was raising them anyway, and even though she hadn't turned out very well, the rest of her siblings had done well in their lives. Just look at Kami. Maybe Annie will become a doctor like her aunt one day, without her mother around.

Amber sprang from her bed, putting what she could from her closet into her backpack.

She sobbed as she put a few cosmetics and a special necklace that her grandmother had given to her when she was two into the bag with her clothes. Why was she crying? This was the best thing she could do for Gabe and Annie. She wasn't any good for them. She never liked playing with them or reading to them, even though she had tried to do that daily. She was a screw up, a failure, and she wasn't going to be anything but a damn waitress at the local truck stop if she stayed here.

Why shouldn't she try to reach out and grab her dreams? She was young, she had her whole life ahead of her. She would go with Paul, he would marry her, buy her a house and then she would come and get Gabe and Annie. They would live together in a pretty little house, she would go back to school, and maybe become a rich businesswoman. She would prove to her whole family she wasn't a screw up. With Paul loving her, and helping her, she could someday make her daddy smile. She would bring her new husband through the front doors of this crummy little house to meet him.

If that was all going to happen, Amber was going to have to leave. She was going to have to get started on her plan with Paul. She had to do it. She had to just go and get things rolling. Staying would only delay the inevitable. It would hurt leaving her children and her family, but it would be worth the pain once she achieved the ultimate goal—proving she was worth something and she was somebody.

Slipping her stuffed backpack into the bottom of her closet, she closed the closet door. Just as she sat down on her bed, Traci her older sister quietly opened the bedroom door. She had Annie in her arms. Expecting her little sister to be asleep, Traci stopped. She whispered, "Oh, I'm sorry, Amber. I thought you might be sleeping. Annie fell asleep and I thought she might be more comfortable in her crib."

Amber whispered back, "Oh, it's okay. I couldn't sleep."

Traci proceeded forward toward Annie's crib and gently placed the child beneath her favorite blanket. Traci noticed Amber's red tear-stained cheeks. She found a place next to her on the bed and hugged her. "Are you okay, sweetie? I know I haven't been around much with us living in Dallas and all, but you know I'm just a phone call away."

Amber let a couple tears fall but quickly wiped them with her hands. "Yeah, I'm okay. Just a little tired. It seems like all I do is work, sleep, go to school, and take care of the kids. I miss my friends and getting to do things like Kami does."

Traci cuddled her little sister. "I know, sugar. You haven't had much time to enjoy your life. All these responsibilities are tough on a young girl. Maybe you should think about bringing the kids to Dallas for a little while. Get away from all this and especially Josh. I know he has been extremely hard on you. I'll talk to Hal and see what he thinks. Maybe you just need a change of scenery for a little bit."

"Oh, I appreciate that Traci, but with still having one more year of school, my job, and everything else, I kind of doubt I'll be able to do any scenery changing anytime soon. Especially with our older brother on my case."

"Well, the offer is there if you ever decide you want to take it. I'm sure Hal won't mind in the least having y'all around for a visit."

"Thanks, sis, I appreciate that. I guess I'm just feeling a little sorry for myself right now."

Traci hugged her little sister again before getting up off the bed. "Well, I'd better get back to the clan before someone comes looking for me and wakes up that baby. You lay down and get some rest. Remember, little sister, I'm just a phone call away."

"Okay, I'll remember."

◊◊◊

Amber managed to get a few hours of rest before her mama came to her room—again. First, she came in to get Annie when she woke up from her nap. Then, she came in to get the kids' pajamas. Gabe was with her her now and climbed on Amber's bed. Amber kissed him and Annie before her mother took them from the room. "I love you, my babies."

I love you too, Mama," Gabe responded.

Now, Elsa Mae was there to get her up for work.

Amber stayed in bed for a couple more minutes. She finally got up and dragged herself to her closet, looked at the clothes, picked out some jeans and a shirt and threw them on the bed. She looked at the backpack that she had packed a few hours earlier and picked it up. In her sleepy state, she wondered if she was going to have the guts to go through with her plan. She threw the bag onto her bed, grabbed the clothes, and went to the bathroom for a shower.

After Amber finished getting ready for work, she grabbed the bag off her bed and threw it over her left shoulder. She hoped that it would be somewhat invisible to anyone as she walked out the door. "Well, I'll see y'all tomorrow after work." Gabe came running as she walked out into the living room. "Hey, sweet boy. You be good for Granny tonight."

Elsa Mae brought Annie to her mother from the kitchen. "Don't forget this one, honey."

Amber touched the baby's head and kissed her cheek as she sat up in Elsa Mae's arms. "I could never forget my sweet little pumpkin." Amber looked at her mom. "Thanks, Mama, for taking such good care of them for me. I love you."

"I love you too, Amber. You have a good night at work. We will all be here tomorrow and your daddy is barbecuing." Elsa Mae noticed the bag. "What's the backpack for, Amber?"

"Oh, I have some stuff I need to finish for school by Monday. Frank wanted me to work a few extra hours in the morning, so I thought I could get in a little studying when it slowed down."

"That's a good idea. I'm proud of you for thinking about school. It won't be long before you have that diploma." Elsa Mae kissed her daughter.

Amber grabbed the keys to her mother's car off the key holder on the wall and blew a kiss to her father who sat across the room. She left the house through the front door. A pang of regret went through Amber as she started the car and drove off to work for the last time. *Will I ever see my family again? Will I ever kiss my babies again? Yes, I will. Pops will see to it.*

The excitement of seeing Paul again overtook any doubt she may have had digging at her heart. She had no guarantee that Paul would even show up tonight, but she hoped that he would. Once inside the restaurant, Amber stored her purse and backpack behind the cashier counter and put on her apron. She looked in the mirror that had been strategically placed behind the register to make sure her hair looked good and her makeup wasn't smeared.

Wanda noticed her coworker's unusual behavior. Wanda and Amber had shared shifts for the last eighteen months. "What the heck is up with you, sunshine? You expecting a man friend tonight? Oh, wait, I know, Paul. Isn't this his weekend to show up?"

Amber did not care for Wanda's banter.

"Wanda, I don't put my nose in your personal business and I would rather you left your nose out of mine. I have no idea when Paul is expected to show his old face in here, nor do I care. I'm not waiting for anyone. You know me well enough to know, this girl waits for no man. I was simply checking to make sure I looked nice, so that I can make some extra money tonight. I'm saving up for something special."

Wanda wasn't convinced, but since Amber had become so defensive, she decided to drop it. She had raised five girls and could sense a girl waiting for a man from a mile away. Without a doubt, Amber was waiting for some-one. Wanda knew that she just had to watch and wait to find out who it was.

The night dragged, and the time when Paul normally came into the restaurant had come and gone. Amber busied herself with side work and customers, believing that Paul might come the next day. Just as she was plac-ing her last order on the order wheel for the night, Amber turned and saw a huge bouquet of red roses had been placed on the counter. She covered her mouth with her hand and blushed—Paul suddenly appeared and was on one knee before her. He held a small box that he presented to her as if proposing marriage. "Will you be my angel?"

Wanda and the few customers who were present in the restaurant applauded. Most thought Paul really was proposing. Amber was too shocked to speak as she took the small box from Paul's hand. She opened the box and saw a beautiful bracelet with an angel charm set with what appeared to be diamonds. Amber took the bracelet out of box. Paul got off his knee.

"It's beautiful."

"Can I put it on for you, my lady?"

Amber handed the bracelet to Paul. "Yes," she giggled.

"Yes, you'll be my angel? Or, yes, I can put on the bracelet?"

Amber whispered, "Both."

Paul almost fell over from her response. "Really?" Paul latched the bracelet and then he turned to his small audience. "She said 'yes.'" The roomed roared in applause and "yahoos."

Paul placed a small kiss on Amber's cheek before going to the food counter. He shook a few hands of fellow truck drivers who mistakenly believed he had just asked Amber to marry him.

Amber played with the bracelet while she waited for her order to come through the window. Wanda came to the window and placed an order on the wheel. "Not waiting for a man, huh? Let me see what he brought you."

"I wasn't waiting for him." Amber showed the bracelet to Wanda. "Isn't it beautiful?"

"Yes, it is."

As the women reached for food out of the cook's window, Wanda asked, "Amber, isn't Paul already married?"

Amber looked seriously at Wanda as she carried her food away from the window. "Yes, Wanda, he's already married. He gave me a bracelet, not a ring. He didn't ask me to marry him. We are just friends."

Wanda nodded. "Oh, just friends. I need a friend like that."

Paul hung out in the restaurant until Amber finished her shift. He then waited by the door as Amber went behind the cashier counter to retrieve her belongings. Wanda was taking money from a customer. "So, you going out on an early morning date with Romeo over there?"

Amber put her backpack over her shoulder and walked toward Paul. "No, Wanda. Paul is just going to walk me to my car. I'll see you tomorrow."

Wanda didn't believe Amber, but Amber had made herself clear earlier. It wasn't any of Wanda's business. "Well, have a nice time, anyway."

Paul opened the glass door for Amber. She held the roses that he had given her firmly in the hand where her new bracelet now sparkled. Paul reached for Amber's backpack. "Here, let me carry that heavy thing for you. What's with the heavy luggage this morning?"

Amber had not told Paul that she had decided to leave with him. She didn't want Wanda or anyone in the restaurant to know. The less anyone knew, the less they would be able to tell her family once they came looking for her. "A girl can't really travel without some clothes."

Confused, Paul stopped in the middle of the parking lot. "Travel? Are you going somewhere?" Amber had refused him on so many other occasions that he thought she was never going to leave with him. Paul had not brought up his wish the entire morning. He had still wanted her to go with him, but he had become content with the idea that she was just going to be his friend, at least for the time being. He planned to still pursue her, on the off chance that she would cave to the idea. But he hadn't thought of it much this morning.

"With you, silly." Amber continued toward her mama's car.

Paul stood stunned while holding her bag in the middle of the parking lot.

"I just have to put my mama's keys under the seat in her car. They will probably come by tonight, after I don't show up at home. I wrote her a little note so she won't worry." Amber looked at his perplexed face. "Come on, old man. What's wrong with you?"

Paul moved toward Amber, still awestruck that she had finally agreed. *Amber's going go with me on road? Am I ready? What's it going to be like? Did I remember to straighten up my truck for her? Is this really happening?* The words came from his lips with an air of disbelief. "You're coming with me?"

Amber handed the bouquet of roses to Paul and fished for her mama's car keys in the pocket of her hoodie. "Yeah, you did ask me to go with you." Amber opened the car door, but then stepped back, thinking about how Paul had just questioned her. "You still want me to go, right?"

Paul knew he had to give her an affirmative and forceful response. He had a slight nag of reservation, but the thought of losing her was stronger. "Yes, yes, of course. I'm just surprised that you really want to go now."

Temporarily convinced by the fluctuation in his voice, Amber returned to her chore of placing the keys under the driver's seat. She put the note that she had written to her mama on the dash. She turned toward Paul and shut the car door. "Well, I thought about it over the last two weeks, and decided that I needed to change things in my life. I need to change them for me and for my kids." She took the roses from Paul and waited for him to lead her to his truck.

"What about school, your job, your kids? Are you going to be okay leaving all that? Them?"

Amber was puzzled. *Does Paul really want me to go, or is he just another bullshitter?* "Sounds to me like maybe you are having second thoughts. Are you worried about *me* being okay with those things, or you? Have you just been pulling my chain all this time, or did you really mean it when you asked me to run away with you?"

Paul felt himself drowning in his own stupidity. He believed that he had meant everything he had said to Amber, but now that it was happening, he was beginning to worry about the consequences of their actions. *I have to decide now if I'm going to go through with my offer or be labeled a liar. Is she really sure?* There was only one way to find out.

Paul placed his hand behind Amber's neck and pulled her to his face. He kissed her with a deep, long, passionate kiss. If the kiss produced the same feelings that he felt the first time he kissed her two weeks ago, then he would go through with his offer. If it didn't, then he would apologize, give Amber her bag, leave her standing by her car, and never return to the truck stop.

For Amber, the kiss was much more than she'd ever felt from any boy she had ever been with since she began kissing. With her young sensual and soft lips, Amber responded in kind to the kiss.

That kiss reaffirmed Paul's feelings. Whether they were feelings of love or lust, he didn't care. He felt them, and that was what he wanted. He wanted to feel that way every day, and Amber did that for him.

Slowly, Paul pulled his lips from Amber's. "I told you I want you with me, and that is what I meant. Doesn't this prove that I'm serious about spending every day with you? Now, come on and let's get out of here. There is a great big world out there, waiting for me to show it to you." He took Amber by the hand, and escorted her toward his blue Pete parked in a truck line, behind the restaurant. "Here she is. My baby." Paul found his keys in his pocket and opened the passenger side door for Amber.

Amber had never been inside a big rig and looked inside without climbing the steps. All she could really see was the bottom part of a seat and a floorboard which was currently occupied with an old Wendy's food bag and a discarded styrofoam coffee cup without a lid. Paul quickly moved in front of Amber and removed the forgotten trash from her vision. "Oh, sorry. I meant to throw that away earlier. Go ahead, climb up the stairs and have a look."

Once inside, Amber sat in the passenger's seat and looked out the huge windshield. It reminded her of the front window that adorned her parents' living room. She felt like she was sitting up high above things. The truck was so big, bigger than any car she had ever been in. The dashboard was over-whelmingly complicated with all the gauges, knobs, and buttons.

Amber turned to see a bed, halfway concealed by some kind of leather curtains. The bed was about the size of her bed at home. It had been made, but the wrinkles in the top blanket and disorganization of the pillows showed that someone had recently been resting on top of them. She pulled back the curtain behind the passenger's seat, which revealed a door that had been left open slightly. She could tell from the exposed view inside the door that it had clothes hanging in it. Directly across from the closet, was a small refrigerator-like door and a microwave stuffed nicely in its own little space. A couple of drawers and a cabinet door filled the space to equal that of the closet. Above and below the bed were several more cupboards. The space was like a mini house glued behind the front seat of a big car. "Wow, this is some set up in here."

Paul was pleased that Amber found his work and portable living quarters acceptable. "I'm glad you like it." He handed Amber her flowers and backpack. "Here, put these on the bed, and let me get in on the other side. I will move things around so you'll have room for your stuff."

Amber took her things and did as Paul requested. There was so much room inside the truck that Amber was able to stand up in between the seats and walk to the back behind the curtains. Amber liked the inside of Paul's truck.

Paul got in on the driver's side of the truck and sat behind the steering wheel. Amber appeared through the curtains. Paul had turned himself toward the passenger seat, with his long legs in the walkway between the seats. Amber easily stepped over them and sat comfortably in her seat.

"So, what do you think?" Paul put his hand on Amber's leg. "Does my modest little home please my little angel? I will show you the drop deck trailer and my extra storage compartments outside later on today."

Amber nodded in agreement and yawned. "I really like it, Paul."

In the excitement of the morning, Paul had forgotten that Amber just finished the night shift at the restaurant. "You must be tired, sweetie. Why don't we take a little nap before we take off? I don't have to leave here for a few more hours."

The reality of the word "we" suddenly struck Amber as she looked out the windshield into the parking lot. The bed wasn't going to just be hers, it was going to be for the both of them. She had thought about what Paul would naturally expect from her when it came to sharing his bed. But right now, while she was exhausted from work, emotionally and psychologically on overload from her current and past life choices, she was, without warning, being forced to make yet another decision.

Amber turned and looked into Paul's eyes. They appeared to be kind eyes, gentle and soothing toward her, not mean or greedy. *Will he understand? Will he think I'm just a tease? Will he throw me off his truck in anger if I expose my honest feelings?* There was still time to leave, to get out, and drive her mama's car home.

"I am really tired, Paul, but I think we need to talk about just what you are going to want from me. We've just talked about sex jokingly over the last months. I'm not a prude, but I'm not ready to just give it up to you right off the bat. I don't really know you all that well, even with all the times you've visited me here at the restaurant. All my past experiences with boys has left me hurt, so I'm afraid to be with anyone else. I know you want me, that if I go with you, it will eventually come down to sex, but can we just take things a little slow for right now? I'd like to make our first time together mean something, if that's even possible. If not, well, I think maybe I'd better just go home."

Paul was taken aback by Amber's frank speech. "I appreciate your honesty, Amber, but to be honest with you, I wasn't even thinking about that at the moment. I do want you, and I can be a selfish prick when it comes to sex. But I'm not a rapist, or an uncontrolled sexual demon looking for my next piece of ass. I respect you. I've fallen in love with you. I don't expect you to give yourself to me just because you're in my truck. I want our first time together to be special, too. I just thought maybe you would like to sleep, just sleep, together for a while before we leave. I promise, I won't be with you until you're ready. I just want to hold you, to fall asleep with you in my arms. You have no idea how lonely it gets back there, when all you have is a pillow to hang on to, especially during the times we are forced to shut down these trucks."

Paul took a hold of Amber's hand. "I'm tired and I know you're tired. I don't want you to go. I want you to take off your shoes and coat, and cuddle with me back there in my sleeper. The rest will happen when it happens. You have a big world to see and I want to show it to you."

Amber leaned forward and let Paul kiss her, she believed him.

"Now, let's put your stuff away and get some rest, my little angel."

CHAPTER FOUR

"Caroline, you know very well that I won't be home for a few weeks." Paul waited for his wife to respond. "I've had some extra added expenses this month. Besides, we're talking about the money that I make, that's my money. You have a job, I don't use your money, but you think you can use all of my money." He waited again as she talked in his ear. "What am I supposed to use?" He paused. "We've talked about this already. You have your bank account now, and I have mine. I put half my check into your account every month to pay bills. I'm not giving you any more. If you can't pay the bills, feed the kids, and buy all the crap you buy all the time, I have no idea what to tell you. I'm not giving you more."

Paul pushed the button on his bluetooth ear piece. "Stupid bitch hung up on me."

Amber came from behind the curtains and sat in the passenger seat. "Hey, sorry I slept so long. I guess I was really tired."

Paul touched Amber's hand. "No problem. I'm glad you got some rest. I just hope that little conversation I just had with my wife didn't wake you."

"No, I had already started getting up. I didn't want to intrude, so I just stayed back there 'til you were finished. Is everything okay?"

Paul rolled his eyes and put his hand back on the wheel. "It's the same thing every time I get paid. She wants everything I make and I won't give it to her. Money has always been an issue with us. I make it and she spends it, mostly on herself. It would be different, I think, if she was spending it on the boys or on me. She's a compulsive shopper. She ran up so many credit cards a few years ago, that I had to get my own bank account. Our marriage had been going downhill for years before that, but when she did that, our marriage was over. Now, we are just waiting for our two boys to get through high school. Kyle is sixteen and Randy is fourteen. I'm so ready to end that story."

"You don't enjoy your children? You don't like kids or want any more?"

Without thinking Paul snapped out with what was really in his head. "No, I love my boys. I'm just gone all the time. I don't spend much time with them. I really didn't want kids when Caroline got pregnant and I had to marry her. I don't know, I guess I like kids. I'm just not really good with them."

"So, you really wouldn't want anything to do with my kids?"

Paul realized what he had just said. "No, I'm not saying that, exactly. I'm just saying I've almost raised my kids. I'm ready to just enjoy you and me."

"But what if my mama decides she can't or won't keep my kids anymore? What will we do about them?"

"Let's don't think about that right now. We will deal with that when and if it happens. I'm more interested in our next stop—San Antonio, Texas. I have a two-day layover there. We are going to have a great time checking out the sights in this town. I have a big surprise waiting for you there."

Amber was not sure how to take what Paul had just disclosed about himself, but decided to let it go. She watched out the window as Paul maneuvered the huge eighteen wheeler through traffic with ease. "I doubt I would ever be able to drive this big thing. I'm scared just watching you drive it."

"Oh, don't be scared. I'm a professional driver. Or at least that's what my driver's license tells everyone." Paul laughed. "Seriously, don't be afraid. It's just like driving a big car. You're longer, you have to make wider turns, and you watch out for stupid people who don't respect that you have those issues. I will teach you. I know you can do it."

Paul pulled off I-10 and into the Petro fuel island. "I'm going to get some fuel and then we'll get us each a shower. We have our first date tonight, and I have something really spectacular planned." Paul handed Amber some cash. "Here, go inside and get something to drink and grab me a soda, if you don't mind."

Amber took the cash and leaned down to gather her shoes off the floor. "Okay."

After purchasing the drinks, Amber went to the driver's side of the truck. She sipped on her water and watched as Paul finished filling both tanks of his truck. "Wow, that's a lot of gas." She looked at the pump. "That's a lot of money for gas, too."

Paul put the fuel hose and nozzle back into its rightful place and laughed. "Yeah, it costs a bunch to keep one of these little babies on the road. But we don't use gas, Amber. We use diesel fuel."

Amber giggled. "Oh, I didn't know. So where do we take a shower? Are they like the ones at the truck stop I worked at near home?"

Paul walked with Amber back to the store and opened the door for her. "Yeah, they are all pretty much the same. Some are nicer and cleaner than others, but these here are not bad."

At the counter Paul talked to the clerk. "I need my fuel ticket, please."

"What was your pump number?"

"Pump 24."

The clerk tore the slip from the printer and put it on the counter. Paul signed the document. The clerk tore off the perforated sides, separating out the yellow copy for herself and handed the rest to Paul. "There you go, have a great evening."

"We need to get a shower ticket, please."

"Certainly." She reached beside the resister and produced a slip of paper. "Here you go. I gave you a team shower ticket. You both can have the same shower, and you won't have to pay for an extra one."

"Thanks, I appreciate it." Paul took the ticker and reached for Amber's hand. "Come on, let's go get parked and cleaned up. I have a night planned for you, my little angel."

◊◊◊

"What do you mean, my daughter isn't here? She came here two nights ago to work, and she hasn't been home since."

Frank, the manager of Warrior Truck Stop tried to calm Elsa Mae. "I'm sorry, Mrs. Nichols, but Amber left here Saturday morning around four a.m., and she never showed up for her shift last night. I can't help you; she's not here. I can ask the night shift waitress, and the other staff, when they come in tonight at ten to see if they know anything. But I don't know where she could be. I don't keep track of my employees after they leave."

Kami grabbed her mother's hand and pulled her toward the door. "Come on, Mama, let's go out and check on your car. Remember, we saw it when we came into the parking lot? Maybe there is something in it that will tell us where she might be. If not, we will call the police and file a missing person's report."

Reluctantly, Elsa Mae followed her daughter to the parking lot. Kami tried the driver's side door. It was unlocked. She opened the door and sat in the driver's seat. She looked around the car for anything out of the ordinary while her mother stood and peered inside the car next to her. Kami found the note on the dash. It was in Amber's handwriting. "Here, Mama, it's addressed to you. Do you want me to read it?"

Elsa Mae took the note from her daughter. "No, I'll read it." She leaned back against the door, opened the letter, and read:

Dear Mama,

I love you, Pops, and the kids so much. But I can't do this anymore, I feel like I'm inside a trap and I can't get out. I know, I've made some mistakes in the past, and I know you think I'm making another one. But I don't. I met someone nice, and he is going to take me all over the world with him. He is going to show me the life I was meant to have. I love the kids, but I'm not good for them like this. All I do is work, sleep, go to school, and go home. I want to be more for them, more for me. I want to prove to you and Pops that I'm not a screw up. I know you love the kids and will take good care of them for me. I hope that you won't let Josh separate them, or give them to the state. I plan to make my way in this life, and come back for them, if you will let me. I don't want you to be angry with me. I'm doing what I think is best. I will be okay. Paul is a really nice man. I will call you in a few days and let you know where I am. Please understand that I had to go. I was dying inside. I'm not ready to die yet, Mama, I want to live. I want to see the world, and eventually show my kids the world. I love you. I will be okay. I put the keys to your car under the driver's seat.

All my love,
Amber

Tears ran down Elsa Mae's cheeks as she read Amber's words. She placed the letter over her face and burst into deep sobs when she was finished. "How could she do this to her children? How could she do this to me? How could she do this to her papa?"

Kami was out of the car, hugging her mother as she cried.

"Oh, Kami, this is going to kill your papa. He has always had a special place in his heart for Amber. This is just going to kill him."

Kami took a tissue from her pocket and handed it to her mother in exchange for the note. "Here, Mama, let me read it." Elsa Mae handed the note to Kami. Kami read the note before giving it back to her mother. "That sounds like Amber, only thinking about herself. Come on, let's lock your car, and I will drive you back to the house. Roger and Alex can come get it later."

"No, I'm okay to drive. I want to just take it on home. Kami, this is going to be so hard on your father. He's going to be heartbroken when he finds out that she has run off for good."

Kami helped her mother get into the driver's seat. "It will be okay, Mama. Pops is strong, and with all of us here this weekend, he will have comfort in knowing we are all here for y'all."

Elsa Mae patted her daughter's hand that was resting on her shoulder. "Oh, I know, Kami. Without the rest of you, we would have already gone crazy with all that girl has put us through."

"I know, Mama, she's a selfish little brat. Always has been and always will be. Let's go home; follow me." Kami shut her mother's car door and then went to her own vehicle.

◊◊◊

Paul led Amber to the showers and played a video game in the trucker's lounge while Amber got ready, and then he took his turn. That had made Amber feel much better. She thought she would have to take a shower with Paul. Several drivers came into the lounge to watch TV and talk while Amber waited for Paul. They smiled and exchanged pleasantries with her as she sat in the chair. Paul finally appeared. "You ready to go, baby? I called for a taxi and it will be here in a few minutes. We need to go put our stuff in the truck."

One of the drivers spoke out. "Fine looking woman you got there, driver. Y'all have a nice time in this beautiful city."

Paul escorted Amber from the lounge. "Thanks, driver."

"Is every truck driver that friendly? I've met a bunch of them at the restaurant, but a lot of them seem kind of grumpy."

Paul hurried Amber through the side door of the building and smiled. "Most of them are nice, like me, but there are a few crazies out here, like that one. You stay here for a minute, and watch for our taxi, so we don't miss it. I will run our stuff to the truck and be right back."

"Okay, hurry."

Paul kissed Amber's cheek. "Be right back, my angel."

The taxi was waiting with Amber safely tucked inside. Paul jumped in.

"Where to, sir?" the driver asked.

"To the River Walk, please, near East Market Street."

"Yes, sir." The taxi driver pulled the lever on the mileage box. "Sounds like y'all have been in our fair city before."

"Yes, I have several times, but this will be her first visit. I want to make it a surprise so please don't say anything that will blow it, okay?"

"No problem, sir. Mums the word."

Paul took hold of Amber's hand and kissed the top of it. "You really look pretty tonight. I like your hair down."

Amber blushed and smiled. "Thank you. Now where are we going?"

"We will be there in a few minutes. You are going to love your first night out on our great adventure, I promise."

◊◊◊

"Look, Pops, I know you're upset, but you've got to except that Amber has done it again. She's not coming back this time. Those kids need stability. I think you should let Katie and me take Gabe and Annie. Mama is exhausted. Give her a break."

Charley got out of his easy chair and walked toward the kitchen. "Gabe and Annie will stay right here. Katie can come over and help if she wants to. Those children will be here when their mother comes home. She just needed to get away for a while, read her note."

Josh was furious with his father's stubborn attitude. "How can you still feel this way about her? She's done nothing but run off, drink, get drugged up, fuck everything that comes near her, and she's a terrible mother."

"You will not talk about your sister that way! Yes, she's made some mistakes and been wild, but she's still a part of this family. She's still a part of me, and I won't stand for you to be so disrespectful or talk about her that way." Charley walked over to the back door and opened it.

"There is no reasoning with you, Pops. You can't see beyond the fact that she's still your little baby girl. She's going to keep doing these things to you and Mama until you stop her." Josh grabbed his head in frustration.

Charley pushed open the back screen door and stepped down to the patio. "It's over, Josh. The kids stay here until their mother comes back for them. I will help your mother with the children, and I expect the rest of you to help when you can." He let the screen door slam shut.

"Katie, get the kids and let's go. I can't stay here, watching these two dig their own graves while Amber runs around the country living it up."

Katie did as her husband demanded.

"I'll come by and check on you, Mama. I love you and I love Pops, but he's crazy if he thinks that Amber will ever change, or come back for her kids." He kissed his mother on her cheek.

Elsa Mae kissed each of her grandchildren and Katie as Josh escorted his family from his parent's home. "We love y'all."

◊◊◊

Once the taxi dropped Amber and Paul off, Paul guided Amber to a concrete staircase that lead to a river under the street.

"Oh, wow. This is totally awesome, Paul."

Paul took her hand and they strolled along the sidewalk that traced both sides of the San Antonio River. The couple weaved in and out of dozens of people enjoying the cool evening stroll. Passenger boats loaded with tourists passed. She could hear the guides explaining the special buildings and cultural interests. Paul gently led Amber into a quiet riverside restaurant.

"How many?" the hostess asked.

Paul put up two fingers.

The hostess took two menus and escorted the couple to a table. It was romantically hidden away in a corner of the dimly lit restaurant. Green leafy plants with brightly colored flowers adorned the walls. Flickering candlelight came from the vase in the center of the table. The table was covered with a white linen table cloth, sparkling silver, and crystal stemware. "Will this be okay, sir?"

Paul waited as the hostess pulled Amber's chair out. He sat across the table from her while the hostess presented each of them with a menu. "Can I get you anything from the bar?"

"We will have a bottle of White Zinfandel, please," Paul said.

"Very well, sir, your waiter will be with you momentarily."

Amber looked at the menu after taking in the room. "Oh wow, she said, 'momentarily.' This must be some fancy place."

"Nothing is too good for my angel." Paul looked at the menu. "What would you like?"

"I don't know, I don't understand some of the words, they are in Spanish or something."

Paul laughed. "Don't worry, I'll help. What do you like to eat? Chicken, fish, beef, pork…snails?"

"You've got to be kidding me, people really eat snails? Count me out on that one. Yuck. I like chicken and beef with French fries or mashed potatoes, maybe a salad. I'm not a real big eater, and I've never eaten anything fancy, so keep it simple. We could have gone to a KFC and I'd have been happy. I didn't grow up with a silver spoon in my mouth. I had lots of brothers and sisters and my parents are middle class. We just lived simply." Amber looked around at the restaurant. "Boy, if my mama could see me now."

Paul was amused with his new conquest. He was proud of the fact that he was going to get to show her things she had never experienced. "I will gladly order you something I know you will enjoy."

The waiter came to their table with their bottle of wine. He poured a small amount into each of their wine glasses. He then poured them each a glass of iced water. After placing the water pitcher on a tray nearby, he pulled out a long black notebook. "May I take your order?"

Paul eagerly ordered the same meal for each of them while Amber sipped at her water. "We will have the grilled chicken breast with seasoned potatoes and two salads with the house dressing, please."

The waiter wrote down the request and left the table.

Paul lifted his wine glass, and sipped at his wine. He noticed that Amber had not touched hers. "Do you not like wine?"

Amber smiled. "I don't know. I've never had any." Then she leaned forward and whispered. "I'm not twenty-one."

Paul laughed with surprise. "Oh really? Well, I guess you'd better tell me just how old you are."

"I'm seventeen," Amber boasted. "I've had beer with my friends, and even had some of my papa's, but I've never tasted wine."

Shocked, Paul almost choked the wine he had just taken into his mouth. He tried not to sound too surprised when he uttered. "Seventeen? When will you turn eighteen? I figured you were older, with two kids and all."

"Oh, I'll turn eighteen on September twenty-eighth, only a few months away. I had my little Gabe when I was fourteen."

"Your parents didn't go after the boy who got you pregnant?"

"Well, they would have if I had wanted them to, but I told them to just leave him alone. I suppose I should have. I guess I could have gotten some child support or something, but he was only fourteen, too. Not going to get much help out of a jobless jerk like that."

"No, I guess not." Paul poured himself some more wine. He wanted to change the subject. "I don't think you have anything to worry about here. They would have carded you if they thought you were too young. Being with me makes you look older. Go ahead and try it."

Amber took her glass of wine and tried it. "I like this." Just as she took another sip, the waiter brought salads and bread. Amber put the glass of wine down, not wanting the waiter to notice she was drinking it. The waiter however simply poured more wine into her glass. "Anything else right now, sir?"

Paul nodded. "No, I believe we will be fine for now."

The evening dinner went on for a couple of hours, two bottles of wine and lots of talking between Amber and Paul. After Paul paid for the meal, he took Amber for another walk along the River Walk. They stopped in and looked around several stores where Paul bought Amber several articles of clothing. Once they finished their shopping, Paul bought tickets so they could enjoy an evening riverboat ride.

Amber felt like a princess. No one had ever spent time with her like this. She kissed Paul, passionately on his lips. "This is the most wonderful night of my life. Thank you."

Paul smiled. "It's not over yet, my little angel. I have more surprises in store for you tonight and tomorrow."

"This is so awesome, I still can't believe that you want to be with me. That you want to show me all this stuff." She placed her head on his chest as they floated along the river and listened to the tour guide.

Once the ride ended, Paul grabbed Amber's hand and her packages. They left the River Walk and walked along some of the city streets. They soon came to a large market area still bustling with busy shoppers. "Come on over here." Paul pulled Amber toward a line of waiting horses and carriages. He picked out the carriage like one that Cinderella might have taken a ride in to the palace of her prince. "Climb in, Princess Amber. Tonight is your night."

Amber had only seen such a thing on television. "Oh, Paul, this is beautiful."

"Take us to the Hilton, please. I thought you might like to see what it's like to sleep in a huge king-size bed, and have breakfast brought to you in bed."

Amber smiled at Paul. She cuddled close to him as the horse and carriage trotted through the cobbled streets and finally stopped in front of the Hilton hotel. The driver helped the couple from the carriage. Paul handed the man money. "Thank you."

Amber smiled at the man. "Thank you, it was really fun."

Paul escorted Amber into the hotel. He had already made a reservation, so after checking in at the front desk, Amber and Paul took the elevator to their waiting room. Paul opened the door.

Amber gasped. "Oh wow, this is the most beautiful room I have ever seen." She put her packages on the bed and went to the sliding glass doors. She opened the door and went out onto the balcony. "Look, Paul, the river is right below us."

Paul joined her on the balcony and put his hands on Amber's arms as he looked over her shoulder at the river. "I like staying here when I come to San Antonio. Everything is so gorgeous, just like you."

Amber turned and allowed Paul to kiss her deeply as he held her in his arms. After the kiss, Paul remembered the bottle of wine he had delivered to the room before their arrival. "Let me get us a glass of wine and we can sit out here on the balcony and watch the river."

Amber let him go. She turned back to the view of the river. As she stood there, she thought about their kiss and she knew without a doubt that she wanted to give herself to Paul tonight. Was it because of all the wonderful things he had done for her, because she just wanted to, or was it the wine? *Maybe I'm beginning to have strong feelings for Paul.* She didn't care anymore, she was starting her life over, and she liked the way it was going so far.

CHAPTER FIVE

"**G**ood morning, beautiful." Paul kissed Amber's lips before getting out of the bed.

Amber stretched underneath the sheets. "Good morning."

"You need to get your beautiful body showered and dressed. I have a wonderful day planned for us."

Amber sat up in the bed. "Really? Last night was terrific. I had a really great time."

Paul bent over and kissed Amber again while putting on his shirt. "I think last night was pretty terrific, too. Especially the surprise you gave me in this bed."

Amber blushed as she thought about the love that she had felt for the first time while having sex. "So that's what 'making love' means."

Paul was a little surprised that Amber had never experienced love-making. "You have two children. No one has ever made love to you?"

"No. Most of the guys I've been with were just there to get their rocks off. No one has ever touched me or loved me in that way before."

"Wow, I guess you really have been sheltered. Baby, I'm going to show you the world and everything it has to offer." Paul's phone rang. He looked at it and then walked toward the balcony. "I need to take this, you get ready."

Amber got out of bed and walked naked to the bathroom. She could hear Paul's voice fluctuate in loud and soft tones, but she couldn't make out the words. She knew that it was not a pleasant conversation and that it was probably his wife. Guilt swept through her as she turned on the bath water. She had just made love to another woman's husband and she didn't feel all that bad about it. Her mama would think she was a terrible person for doing such a thing. Her brother, Josh would have just called her a slut, and the rest of her family except her papa. He would have thought she was whoring around again. The water seemed to calm her feelings of guilt as she showered off Paul's scent.

◊◊◊

"After breakfast, we are going to do a little more shopping. I want to take all your new things back to the truck before we head to SeaWorld. Does that sound like fun?"

"Oh, Paul, I've never been to any place like that. I told my little Gabe one time that I would take him there, once I'd saved up enough money. Of course, I doubt I would ever be able to do that."

"Well, we will spend the day at SeaWorld, then we have to go back to the truck tonight to sleep. I have to deliver that load we have on the truck now, and then pick up another one early in the morning. You don't mind sleeping in the truck do you?"

"Not at all. It's nice."

"Great. You're my kind of girl."

◊◊◊

"Hey, Mama, how you doing?" Josh kissed his mother's forehead before going to the cupboard for a cup. "How is Pops doing? Is he still upset with me?"

"No, Josh, he's not upset with you. He's just worried about Amber and the children."

"Why won't he let Katie and me take at least one of them?"

"He's afraid you will give them to CPS. He has very strong feelings about this family taking care of its own members."

"I know, Mama. I really wouldn't turn those kids over to the state. I was just pissed off at Amber and it makes me crazy the way you guys let her take you for granted. Katie and I would never do that to Gabe or Annie."

"I'm glad, son, and I guess your father knows that, too. He's just concerned. You two are so much alike, it's scary. I will talk to him and get him to let you and Katie take the children from time to time. Traci and Tory have offered to help as well. Roger is having to deal with his divorce situation right now, but he said he would take Gabe every once in a while when he gets little Drake for the weekends. Alex and his wife are working and finishing college so they are busy, but they offered to look after Annie or Gabe every once in a while. Kami is too far away and too busy to help, but she said she would come home on her breaks. So, everyone is doing what they can just like he wanted."

"We are a lot alike aren't we?" Josh snickered.

"Yes, you are." Elsa Mae got up from her chair at the table. Gabe was dropping his food onto the floor. "I see you are finished eating, my little man. You always start throwing it on the floor when you're finished, don't you?"

Josh put down his coffee. "Let me get him, Mama. I think I hear Annie crying."

Elsa Mae moved toward the bedroom where Annie had just woken from her nap. "Thank you, son. Just put his bib in the laundry basket and wipe him off with those wipes on the counter."

Josh lifted Gabe out of the high chair. He sat him on the counter and removed his bib. He gently wiped the child's face and hands. "Where is your mama, little one? I'll bet you miss her, don't you? I'm sorry this is happening to you, Gabe. I love you, little man. Your Uncle Josh will always be here for you. I promise."

CHAPTER SIX

I t had been almost a week since Amber had left the only place she had ever known. Now, she was about to return to that town, but only for the night.

"Are you sure you don't want to go and see your kids?" Paul was backing their truck into a truck parking spot at the Love's Truck Stop.

"No, I'm pretty sure if I go home, my mama will never let me leave again."

"Well, I still have plenty of country left to show you." Paul's phone rang. He looked at the caller ID. "Shit." He finished parking the truck and then opened his driver's side door. "I'll be back in a minute. It's my wife again. You know what that means."

"Yep, she needs money."

"Sit tight. I'll be back in a minute and we will get a shower and dinner."

"Okay." Amber looked out her passenger side window and recognized the landscape of the town that she'd once called home. It had only been a few weeks, but she felt like it had been a lot longer.

She went over in her head all the amazing things that Paul had already showed her. After their night in the fancy hotel in San Antonio, Paul had taken her shopping for more clothes. Then they went to SeaWorld, where she saw amazing animals she'd only seen in books or on TV. They'd finished their day making love again in his truck. The next day, they went and dropped their load and then picked up another one headed for Amarillo.

They took I-35 through Austin and into Dallas. Dallas was huge. They ate lunch at a truck stop before continuing on to Amarillo by way of Highway 287. Once they arrived in Amarillo, Paul took her to The Big Texas

Steakhouse. It was the craziest restaurant Amber had ever seen. They drank some beers at the bar, ate a lot of food, and even did some target shooting before returning to the truck where they once again made love.

The next morning before sunrise, Paul went and delivered the load and then got word on his quell-com that they had a load going to Denver. Paul and Amber were headed to Colorado.

It had been dark when Paul rolled their truck down I-70 into the interior of Denver. "Wow, Paul, this is beautiful. I thought the place would be covered in snow though."

"It's late spring, silly. There isn't much snow this time of year, except on the mountaintops. See? Up there."

Amber looked at the mountains that seemed to surround the city and stretch into the clouds. She had never seen mountains before, either.

They'd arrived just in time to unload and find a place to park at the truck stop. "I'm tired, but I want to go for a walk and get some fresh air. That was a long ride. I want to breathe," Amber said.

Paul understood. "That was only a little over four hundred miles, baby. Wait 'til we have to do seven hundred miles."

"Seriously? How often does that happen?"

"Often. I'll come with you."

◊◊◊

The next day, they had to wait for several hours for Paul's next load. Amber was disappointed that there wasn't time to visit the mountains, but they did go to the beautiful botanical gardens and the aquarium. While they were at the aquarium, Paul got a call from his company's dispatcher. They had a load going to Casper, Wyoming.

Although it was late spring, the mountain caps of northeastern Colorado and southeastern Wyoming still held visible patches of white snow. They found a small, clean truck stop in Casper. The woman in the store who provided her with her shower key that night had been so nice to her. She reminded her of her mother. Paul told her they'd been lucky to find a spot after dark.

The next morning, they delivered their load. Paul was scheduled to take another load, but it wasn't ready, so they went to the Historical Trails Center in the meantime. Amber had never been one to care about history, but Paul had opened her eyes to a big world. She had a newfound interest in how people of earlier generations pioneered the beautiful states she was getting to see.

She thought about how hard it must have been to ride in a covered wagon across land that had no highways—not even dirt roads. Most of the migration across the Oregon Trail went through Casper, Wyoming and other states. Some folks had no wagons and went on horseback or walked. Amber couldn't imagine herself doing anything that difficult.

Paul got the call from the dispatcher that the load was ready, so they'd left without seeing half of the exhibits. Amber was disappointed. "I'll bring you back another time," Paul promised.

They were headed to Jackson Hole, Wyoming. "You'll really enjoy the scenery," he assured her. "Besides, I have another surprise for you."

"What is it?" she asked, amazed at all the surprises she had received over the past week. Paul relented to her constant, "Tell me, tell me, tell me," and revealed that he'd arranged for them to stay in a log cabin for the night. Just the thought of the trees, mountains, and the cabin made her smile. When they arrived, Paul had been right. It was gorgeous. Amber wished she could have stayed there forever.

The next day, Paul dropped off the load and Amber could see he wasn't happy. She hoped it wasn't something she had done or said and asked him, reluctantly, if he was okay. Paul explained that he was going to have to drive unloaded miles to get another load. "I don't make any money for the "out of way" miles. Then his mood lightened. "You know what? It doesn't matter. Let's go see Yellowstone National Park."

They dropped the trailer at a truck stop near the park, and then went to the grocery store where Paul spent a few dollars on fruit, sandwich fixings, and some wine. They enjoyed the remainder of the day exploring the park. She even got to see Old Faithful. Although they were tired, Paul insisted that they have a quiet dinner before returning to his truck.

Amber had given herself to Paul several times during their time together on the road, but at that moment, she found herself wanting him with a deep passion she had never felt before. She'd been so young when she first experienced sex, and didn't associate that raw act with love. What she was beginning to feel for Paul was something quite different—in fact, the feeling was there even when they weren't having sex.

Paul was dispatched to pick up a load sooner than he'd anticipated in Missoula, Montana. Montana had proven to be another beautiful place to see from the windows on Paul's truck. There was no time for sightseeing, though, they had to get to Spokane, Washington. They'd only been able to stop once, in Lewiston, Idaho for fuel and food. Once they arrived in Spokane, they found a truck stop parking space and slept until early the next morning.

After Spokane, they dropped their load in Seattle, had a nice lunch, and then picked up a load for Portland, Oregon. They drove to Portland, delivered the load, and then found a quiet place to park. Paul had reached his weekly driving hours and had to shut down for thirty-six hours.

Portland turned out to be a beautiful place to spend their down time. Paul took Amber to the Pacific Ocean, St. John's Bridge, Portland's Japanese Garden, and the Columbia River Gorge. By the time they left Portland and headed to Sacramento, California they'd been together two full weeks.

Once they arrived in Sacramento, Paul took Amber to a place called the Firehouse Restaurant. They enjoyed dinner and then slept in the truck. The next morning, they delivered a load before heading to Reno, Nevada. In Reno, they picked up a load for Las Vegas.

Paul decided that it was time for Amber to spend a night in a hotel again and selected The Mirage. Amber felt so special in that beautiful hotel where Paul treated her to a fabulous dinner and some dancing. They even went to the slot machine area, but because Amber wasn't old enough to gamble, they took a walk along the Vegas Strip instead.

Las Vegas turned out to be one of the best parts of her trip with Paul. Amber had to admit that after spending two nights in the lights of Vegas, and all that she had seen over the last couple weeks, that there couldn't possibly be much more to see. She was wrong. After they unloaded and loaded again in Vegas, they headed to Flagstaff, Arizona where Paul introduced Amber to the Grand Canyon.

After Flagstaff, they took a small load to Albuquerque, New Mexico. There wasn't time to do anything in that beautiful city, but Amber saw the mountains. Their load from Albuquerque was headed to El Paso. They'd change loads and then spend the night in Odessa.

"Do you want to go home for the night?" Paul had asked her.

"Nope," she replied. She had been with him almost three weeks and felt her life had changed for the better. She liked the traveling with him. Her mind recalled all the wonderful things she'd seen so far.

Amber's thoughts were interrupted when Paul climbed back into the truck. "You ready for a shower and some dinner?"

Amber smiled. "Yes. Did you settle things with your wife?"

"That bitch is going to be the death of me. Once we get back to Georgia, I'm going to get my stuff out of the house and find us an apartment. I'm done with her only wanting my money. I've got you now and that's enough for me." Paul reached over and kissed Amber. "Are you sure you don't want to go by and see your kids?"

Amber moved to the back of the truck to gather a few things for their shower. "No, I think I'll leave that situation alone for a while."

"Okay, whatever you want, baby." Paul's phone rang again. "Shit, it's her again. I'll meet you inside. Be sure and grab me a set of clothes, please."

"Sure. Oh, we need to do the laundry." Paul didn't respond. Amber looked at the driver's seat, he was already out of the truck arguing with his wife. "That figures," she mumbled.

◊◊◊

"Are you ready to go Amber?"

"Yes, I think I got everything put away," she said. She had done laundry for the both of them. "Where are we headed next?"

"Dallas.

"That's where my sister lives."

"Yeah, I remember you saying that when we went through there the first time. Why don't you call your sister while we're there and talk to her?"

"Maybe, but I doubt I will. My sister Traci is a lot like my mama. She'll just want me to go home."

"She might not. Maybe she'll just want to talk. You really need to keep in touch with them Amber. I suspect they are pretty worried about you. At least let them know you're okay."

"I might give her a call. Let's just wait and see what happens when we get there."

"Okay, that's fair enough."

Seven hours after leaving Odessa, Paul and Amber arrived in Dallas. After dropping off the load Paul said, "Let's sleep in the truck tonight and I'll get us a hotel in the morning for tomorrow night. If you decide to call your sister, she can meet with you there or you can meet her somewhere else."

"Okay, but I'm not sure I want to do that yet."

"It's cool, my little angel, you just do whatever you want." Paul's phone rang. He looked at the caller ID. "It's her again. I'm going to go into the truck. Stop and find us a table for dinner. Can you get us some clothes together for a shower and meet me in there?"

Amber crossed her arms and looked out the window. "I thought you were finished with her, Paul. You said you were going to leave her, but you keep taking her calls."

Paul could tell that Amber was becoming more impatient with his relationship with his wife. Paul reached for Amber's arm. "I'm leaving her, angel, but I still have to talk to her until I get my things out of the house and hire a lawyer. I have to keep the peace or she'll burn all my stuff. That's why I try and talk to her when I'm not around you, so you don't have to listen to all the fighting. I'm yours, sugar, all yours."

Amber was glad that Paul felt that way, but she still hated that he was talking to his wife so much. "Okay, I'll see you inside in a little bit."

◊◊◊

The next morning, Paul woke Amber up with a soft passionate kiss. "Time to wake up, my little angel. I have a whole day planned for us." He climbed over Amber who was asleep on the outer side of the bed.

Amber turned over and covered her head with the blanket. "I'm tired. We drank coffee and talked to every trucker in the place till after two o'clock in the morning."

He pulled the blanket back slightly from Amber's head and kissed her cheek. "I know, sweetheart. Wasn't that fun? We got all the latest road gossip in one sitting. Now come on, angel, grab some clothes and anything else you think you'll need at the hotel. We're going to the zoo and aquarium right after we get our hotel and some breakfast. I was thinking pancakes and sausage sounded good this morning."

Amber forced herself out of bed. "Oh, all right, but I want eggs, too."

Paul was busy putting on his shoes while Amber paraded about in the truck in just a t-shirt as she gathered her things. "Where are we headed after we leave Dallas?"

"I'm going to try and get loads back to Atlanta. I really need to get my stuff out of my house and find us an apartment. I figure after we get an apartment, we can run a few loads and then I'll have enough money to hire an attorney. I also want to spend time teaching you to drive this big rig so we can team drive."

Amber stopped in her tracks. "Drive this big thing? Really, you think I can handle it?"

"Of course you can drive this truck. There are dozens of women out there driving big rigs these days. Most of them are team drivers with their husbands. You can make great money with two people driving."

"I guess, but I'm not sure I want to learn to drive a big truck. I'm kind of scared to." Amber continued packing.

"I know you can do it. I've been planning on us being team drivers after I get my divorce."

Amber finished gathering their things and plopped down in the passenger's seat. "Well, maybe you should have asked me if I wanted to drive a big truck before making plans like that."

Paul watched out the windshield for the taxi he had ordered. "Well, I sure hope you change your mind. I've invested a lot of time and money into this plan of mine."

Amber looked at Paul, horrified. "What? You've been doing all this with me so that I'll want to be the other half of your driving team? I thought you were doing this because you wanted to show me the world, because you loved me. Or was that just a bunch of lies?"

Paul realized his mistake. "Look, angel, I didn't mean it like that. Of course I've been doing all these things with you because I want to show you the world and I love you. I'm thinking of the future, once we get married. We're going to want to provide a good life for your kids, won't we?"

Amber relented. "Yes, I do want to give my kids a good life. But it just sounds like you've planned it all out without even asking if it's what I want."

"I'm sorry, sweetheart. I guess I just assumed that we would do this together forever. What do you want to do?"

Amber thought for a few minutes. "I'm not sure. I do like being in this truck with you and I do like seeing the world. Right now, I can't think of what I would like to do. Maybe truck driving would be a good occupation. I want to think about it for a while. I really just don't want anyone telling me what I'm going to do."

"Let's let it go for now; the taxi is here. Let's go visit the zoo."

CHAPTER SEVEN

Amber flopped down on the hotel bed. "Wow, the zoo was great, but I sure liked the aquarium. All those pretty butterflies fluttering around in all those trees. Thank you, Paul, for taking me there. My sister, Traci told me all about it one time when she came home for a visit, but seeing it for myself was much better. I hope we can bring the kids here some time."

"We'll try and bring the kids here when we get a chance. With us on the road like this, we will have to take some vacation time to do it, but we will." Paul picked up his cell phone from the table. "How about pizza tonight for dinner?"

Amber stared at the ceiling. "Yeah, pizza will be fine. I've been thinking, maybe I will call my sister. Just to check in on the kids and see how they are doing."

"I think that would be a great idea." Paul listened to the lady on the phone from the pizza delivery place. "What kind of pizza do you want, Amber?"

"Doesn't matter. I like any kind, except the fishy kind."

"We'll take one large meat combination pizza with original crust, please." Paul listened. "Yes, we're in room 275. Yes, it will be cash. Okay, thank you." Paul hung up. "It will be here in about an hour. Do you want to go down to the pool?"

Amber looked at the phone on the table next to their bed. "Can you make local calls from that phone?"

Paul got up and grabbed his bag. He opened it and looked for his swimming suit. "Yes, sure you can. I'm going to get my suit on and go down to the pool. Why don't you stay here and wait for the pizza and call your sister? Then when you get done talking to her and the pizza gets here, put on your suit and bring the pizza down to the pool. We can enjoy it and some of that beer we bought."

Amber sat up on the bed. "Okay, I think I will call her. I really want to know how the kids are doing."

Paul dressed and went to the pool. Amber found her sister's phone number in her purse. She fiddled with the piece of paper for a while before picking up the phone. She dialed the number and waited for someone to answer. "Hello?"

"Hi Traci, it's me."

"Amber, is that you? Where are you? Are you all right? Mama and Pops are so worried about you. Where are you? Why did you leave?"

"Look, Traci, I'm fine and I didn't call to get a lecture. I called to see how you're doing and if you know how the kids are doing."

"Well, little sister, I'm doing okay, and I talked to mama last night and the kids are doing okay. Annie is spending a good amount of time with Josh and Katie, and Gabe has been spending time with Tory, Roger, and Alex. Where are you? Everyone is really worried about you."

"I'm in a hotel in Dallas right now. I'm glad to hear the kids are doing alright. How's Mama and Pops?"

"They are fine, Amber, but they are worried to death about you. In a hotel? We thought you ran off with a truck driver."

"I am with Paul, but we had to shut down for his restart. Something to do with truck driving logs, I don't understand it all, but he's been really good to me. I've been all the way to California and Washington. He even took me to Vegas, Traci. I've seen the mountains and all kinds of beautiful things. When we get back to Georgia, he's getting us an apartment and I'm going to come get the kids. I know I should have told Mama what I was doing, but I knew she wouldn't have let me go. I just had to go, Traci. I was about to die at home. I miss you, big sis, and I was hoping I could see you tomorrow."

"Sure, Amber, I would love to see you. I'm glad Paul is such a great guy, but don't you think you should have introduced him to Mama and Pops? I'm sure they would have been willing to let you go with him if they thought he was a good guy. The waitress at your old job told Kami that this guy is married. Is he married Amber?"

"Yes, but he's getting a divorce and we are getting an apartment together. He really loves me. Traci. You can meet him tomorrow."

"Okay, but you know married guys aren't very dependable, Amber. They say a lot of things they don't really mean. Why don't you let me come get you and take you home?"

"No, Traci, I'm not going back home. I'm happy with Paul and he's going to take good care of me. I really want to see you tomorrow, but if you're going to try and make me go home, then I will just end our conversation now."

"Wait, Amber. I won't make you go home. I really want to see you and meet Paul. I just want you to be happy and be safe. Please, let's meet tomorrow."

"Okay, I'll call you in the morning and we can meet for lunch. Please don't call Mama and Pops."

"I won't, Amber, I promise. I can't wait to see you, baby sister."

"Me too."

"I love you."

"I love you, too, Traci. I'll call you in the morning."

◊◊◊

The next morning, Amber and Paul met with Traci at a local restaurant. "Well, it sure has been nice meeting you, Paul. I'm glad to see that you've been taking care of my little sister and it sounds like you have been really nice and showing her a bunch of really beautiful places."

"Thank you, Traci. I love your sister and plan to make a good life for her." Paul kissed Amber on the cheek.

Traci hadn't heard too much from Amber or Paul about how the children would fit into their lives. "The children will be really happy to have a father and have their mother taking care of them again."

Paul squirmed a little as he took his arm away from around Amber and took a drink of his tea. Amber interjected. "I think he's going to make a great papa."

Traci noticed Paul's behavior. It was clear to her that Amber was the only one interested in raising her children. She also knew that Amber was going to have to find that out for herself. "Well, I'm sure Paul will make a fine father to Gabe and Annie. They are precious little ones and anyone would be a fool not to fall in love with them the minute they meet them."

Paul gulped at his tea. His phone buzzed in his pocket. He quickly pulled it out, glanced at the Caller ID and looked relieved. "Work. I've got to take this, ladies." Paul left the table.

Traci wanted to tell Amber her suspicions about Paul, but she didn't want to alienate Amber, fearing that she might run and she would never see her again. "Well, he seems like a nice guy, Amber. I hope everything turns out just like you want. I know you don't want me to tell Mama and Pops that you were here in Dallas, so I won't, but I really need to let them know you're okay."

"He has been really good to me, Traci, and when we get settled in Georgia, I'm going to come get the kids."

Paul came back to the table from his phone call. "Well, Traci, it has been great meeting you, but I have to leave and go pick up our load for tomorrow. Amber, you are welcome to stay here. You can get a taxi to bring you to the truck when you're finished."

Amber gathered her things. "No, I'll go with you now so that we don't need to pay for two taxis." Amber reached over the table and kissed her sister on the cheek. "I love you, big sis." Paul picked up the check off the table.

"It was nice to meet you too, Paul. Amber, I love you. Please be safe. Call Mama and Pops soon. They love you too and worry about you so much."

Amber nodded her head. "Okay. I will." She grabbed Paul's arm and waved goodbye to Traci as they walked out of the restaurant.

Once Amber and Paul were in the parking lot, Paul motioned for the taxi he had called while he was away from the table. Amber piled into the taxi before Paul. "Where are we headed?"

"To the hotel to get our things." Paul gave the address to the driver. "Then we'll go to the truck stop and get the truck. The load is headed for Little Rock so I was kind of wanting to wait a few hours at the truck stop until

I can catch up to my log hours. I'd like to leave for Arkansas tonight if that's okay with you."

"I don't mind driving at night. Did you like my sister?"

"Yes, she was nice. I don't think she likes me too much."

"Oh, yes she does."

◊◊◊

"Hi Mama, it's Traci."

"Hey, honey. How are you guys doing in the "big D"? I'm so glad you called. I've missed you."

"I've missed you too, Mama. We are doing okay, busy of course. Mama, I called to let you know something."

"Okay, sweetie, what is it?"

"Well, I saw Amber here in Dallas yesterday. She called me and we had lunch."

"Is she okay? Did you meet the man she is with? He's not hurting her or anything?"

"She looked okay to me, and the guy she's with seemed alright."

"Did she say if she was coming home? Why she hasn't called me?"

"No, Mama, she's not coming home anytime soon. I think she's afraid to call home. I told her not to be afraid and that everything would be fine. I don't think she believed me, but maybe she will call soon. Just be patient. How are you and Pops doing? How are the babies?"

"Oh, we're doing fine. The babies are a handful of course, but the others are helping out when they can."

"I'm glad, Mama. I wish I was closer so I could help more, but I do want to take the kids soon."

"I think that will be wonderful, sweetie. Just let me know when. Let me know if you hear from or see Amber again. I sure hope she's going to be okay."

"I will, Mama. I'm sure she will be. I love you."

"I love you and miss you, baby. Hope you come home again soon."

"I will, Mama. I miss you, too. Bye."

"Bye, baby."

◊◊◊

Paul backed his truck into the dock in Little Rock. "Stay here; I'll be right back. They are going to unload this load and put another one on the trailer headed for Nashville." Paul's phone rang as he jumped out of the truck.

Amber hopped into the driver's seat. She looked in the mirror. Paul answered his phone quickly and then hung up. Amber knew in her heart it was Paul's wife. She had been calling the entire way from Dallas to Little Rock. Amber had climbed into the sleeper to sleep, but she heard every word of their conversations. Paul seemed to be softening his stance on leaving his wife with his words and Amber was worried.

Watching out the mirror, Amber shadowed Paul as he talked to the men on the dock about the loads. While Paul helped unstrap the load and went into the building, Amber counted four phone calls that Paul had received and quickly quenched. *What could that woman possibly want?* Paul had been extremely distant since their meeting with Traci in Dallas. Amber wondered what Paul was thinking, but was afraid to ask when he came back to the truck.

"Ready to go, baby?" Paul patted Amber on the leg. "We are headed to the city of country music."

"Sounds fun." Amber turned toward the passenger window and watched as Paul disembarked from the dock with their new load.

Paul could tell something was wrong with Amber. "What's up, my angel?"

Amber just kept looking out the window. She wanted to talk to Paul, but was afraid he would get upset with her if she questioned all the phone calls. "Nothing, I'm fine. Maybe just thinking about my kids, that's all."

"I understand that. You've been away from them for almost a month now. Do you want to go home?" Paul sounded like maybe he was trying to get Amber to leave.

"No, I can't go home, Paul, and you know that. Do you want me to leave?"

Paul was a little taken aback by Amber's tone. "Leave? Well, no, I don't want you to leave. I was just thinking about you and your feelings. What's the matter with you?"

Amber let a few tears fall down her cheeks as she sat quietly and looked out the window. It was cloudy and a drizzle of rain danced across the glass. "Nothing is the matter."

"Okay, but there is usually something wrong when a person has tears running down their face." Paul patted Amber's leg while trying to focus on traffic. "Come on, baby, what's wrong?"

"I heard you talking to your wife last night and all the phone calls today. You sound like you're going to go home as soon as we get to Georgia. What's going to happen to me? Are you just going to leave me in some truck stop?"

Paul found a place to pull over along the highway. He put on his hazard lights and took off his seat belt. He turned in his seat and forced Amber to turn in her seat to face him while he talked. "Of course not, silly. I have to talk nicely to her until I get my stuff out of the house. I am not leaving you at a truck stop. I may have to get you a hotel for a few days while I find us an apartment, but I will be leaving her the first chance I get, I promise."

Paul pulled Amber to his chest and held her tight. "I didn't bring us all this way for nothing. You're my angel and we are going to make a life on these highways together."

Amber found comfort in Paul's words. She hugged him back and kissed him when he drew her close. "Okay, I was just thinking you had changed your mind."

"Never, baby. Never."

The ride to Nashville was quiet except for the constant phone calls from Paul's wife. Paul finally put his phone on silent when Amber made it clear with several unpleasant sighs that she was unhappy. Paul was having second thoughts about what he was doing with Amber, but he didn't want Amber to know that until he had time to think things through completely.

They pulled the truck into a truck stop in Nashville to rest for the night before making their delivery.

CHAPTER EIGHT

"Okay, sleepy head, it's time to get up. We need to get this load delivered. I have two other loads to pick up, one is going to Louisville, Kentucky, the other one is going to Atlanta and it needs to be there tomorrow."

Amber stretched. "So we won't have any time to see Nashville?"

Paul was lacing his shoes. "No, angel, not today. We need to get to Georgia before my paycheck reaches the bank. I'm about out of money and although my old lady can't get into my bank account, I still want to get there and get us a place."

"I need to use the restroom." Amber moved toward the front of the truck while she brushed at her hair.

Paul started to pull the truck out of the parking spot. "Okay, angel, you can do all that while I get fuel." Paul handed Amber some cash. "Grab us a couple of cups of coffee and a donut or something."

◊◊◊

It took Amber and Paul most of the day to unload and reload in Nashville. They arrived late in Louisville, but early enough to drop the load they had for one of Paul's regular customers.

Paul's wife had called him continually during the two days it had taken them to find their way to Atlanta. "Well, this is it, angel. Atlanta, Georgia."

Amber checked out the city as they drove along the highway to the truck stop. "Wow, this is a really big place. How do you live here? I would get so lost."

"Oh, I don't live in Atlanta. I live in a little town outside of Atlanta called Mason. At least that is where my family lives. Do you think you'll mind living here in Atlanta?"

"Oh, I think it will be great living here. Look at all those huge buildings and all the people. Yes, Paul, I think I will enjoy living here very much."

"All right, the first thing I'm going to do is get you a hotel room. I have to take care of things with my wife, get my stuff out of the house, and get my check cashed. I'm going to go by the truck stop for fuel and get you some things for the hotel. I'll book us a room and have a taxi come get you. I have a pickup at the house. I'll get my buddy to follow me back to the truck stop and then I'll join you later tonight or tomorrow. Do you think you will be okay?"

"Yes, I'll be fine as long as you're not gone too long."

"I won't be gone too long. I promise."

Paul pulled into the truck stop and maneuvered his truck into the fuel line. "I'm going to fuel up the truck; you need anything?"

Amber looked out the window. "No, I'm fine."

"Okay, I'll be back in a few minutes."

Paul went into the truck stop and gave his credit card for the fuel. Just as he was heading back to the fuel pumps, a friend from the company he was working for put his hand on Paul's shoulder. "Paul, how you doing, old boy?"

Paul turned. "Ralph, how ya doing?"

"I'm doing great, you staying busy?"

"Yes, been gone for a whole month this time. I usually just stay out a couple three weeks at a time. Come on out to the pumps with me, I need to get fuel."

"Okay." The men walked out the door. "How's your wife and the boys ?"

Paul put the nozzles into the fuel tanks on the truck. "Doing okay, I guess. Like I said, haven't been home for a few weeks. The only time I ever hear from them is when they want money. You know how that is."

Amber decided that she needed to use the restroom. She slipped out the passenger side door where Paul and Ralph were talking. "I'm going to use the restroom, Paul."

Ralph looked surprised at Paul when he watched Amber walk into the store. "Who's that, Paul? She's kind of young, isn't she?"

Paul tried to brush it off. "Oh, she's just a hitchhiker I picked up out on the twenty a few miles back. I'm giving her a ride down to Mason."

Ralph wasn't buying it. "Be careful, Paul. I know that wife of yours, and she will have your head on a platter if she finds out you're messing around. Especially, with something that young, brother. I know a bunch of guys who've been caught, and they've lost their asses in court. You want to be paying out your ass 'til your kids are out of college for a young piece like that?"

"She's just a hitchhiker, Ralph."

"A hitchhiker that knows your first name and tells you where she's going? Right. You'd better listen to me, Paul." Ralph shook Paul's hand. "Well, I'd better get going. You take care of yourself, and think about what I told you."

"Okay, Ralph, been nice talking to you. See you later."

As Paul finished pumping his fuel Ralph's words played over in his head. *What if Ralph's right? What if my wife finds out about Amber before I get divorced? Will I pay for it forever?* He knew his wife, and he knew the answer was yes. *What am I going to do with Amber? I brought her all this way from Texas, and I like being with her, but is she really worth all the trouble I'm going to have to face?* Paul had to ask himself if she was worth the money he would have to keep spending to be with her. *Maybe I should just cut my losses and stay with my family.* He thought about it some more, and made a decision.

He would leave Amber at the hotel. He figured that once she realized that he wasn't coming back for her she would call her family and they would come get her. She'd be all right. He liked Amber and had fun with her, but it was time to face reality and get back to his life.

Amber touched Paul on the back. Paul jumped. Her hand on his back brought him out of his thoughts. He stared at the nozzle he still had in his hand.

"Sorry, I didn't mean to startle you. Who was that man?" she asked.

"That was just a guy who works for the same company I haul for here in Atlanta." Paul reached into his pocket and pulled out some money. "Go inside and grab you a few snacks for the hotel."

"Oh, I don't think I'll need anything. You'll be back tonight or tomorrow and I can wait 'til you come get me to eat."

Paul didn't like the response. "You really should get a few things, it might take me a little while to get everything moved. That wife of mine might be a real problem when she finds out I'm leaving."

Amber crawled back into the passenger side of the truck. "I'll be fine."

Paul finished fueling. He parked the truck, called to reserve a hotel room, and then called a taxi for Amber. Amber packed what she thought she would need. "You'd better take everything, baby. I don't know if my wife will get into my truck or not, but I don't want her to know about you until after the divorce."

"Okay, but I don't have enough room in my backpack for all the clothes and things you bought me."

Paul reached up into a cabinet above the bed. He had two cloth laundry bags and a small backpack stashed away. "Here, use these."

Amber took the bags and packed the rest of her possessions in them. She sensed something was wrong with Paul but decided not to make an issue of it. "Well, I can wash and iron these things while you're gone. I'll look beautiful when you get back."

"I know you will. The taxi will be here for you in a few minutes. I made the reservation at the hotel for the whole weekend. I'm going to take a few days off so we can look for an apartment."

Amber put her arms around Paul's neck and kissed his cheek. "It's going to be so wonderful being together forever."

Paul pulled away slightly. "Yes, it is, but we have got to get you ready. That taxi will be here any minute."

By the time the taxi pulled in, Amber believed Paul was telling her the truth about their new life together. Paul helped her into the cab and told the driver, "Take her to the Holiday Inn." Amber rolled down the back window and Paul leaned in to kiss her. He took several bills from his money clip and handed them to her. "This should be enough to keep you for a little while."

"Aren't you coming to the hotel tonight or tomorrow? You said—"

"I will, but I want to make sure you have plenty of money for anything you need just in case it takes me longer than I anticipate."

"Okay, I'll miss you."

"I'll miss you, too."

Paul waved at Amber as the taxi pulled away. *Poor girl*, he thought, knowing what he was about to do. Her fairy tale was about to come to an end. *Amber's nice, but she's too young. Besides, I'm done raising kids.*

◊◊◊

Shelby parked her rig in an Atlanta truck stop. She called the car rental company to let them know she was ready for them to bring the car she'd reserved. After signing the papers and getting the key, she left the truck stop and headed to the Holiday Inn. She had just dropped her bags by the door and flopped down on the bed when her cell phone rang. She looked at the caller ID and smiled.

"Hi, Angelica. I'm here at the hotel. Give me a couple hours to unpack and take a shower, then I'll join you for dinner. I can't wait to see you, girl."

Angelica gave her the address to the restaurant and they ended the call. When Shelby hung up she realized she was thirsty and grabbed the ice bucket and her key card and left the room. She walked down the hallway and saw a young woman standing in front of the machine.

The girl looked over her shoulder when she heard someone behind her. "I'm almost finished," she said.

"No hurry, sweetie." Shelby's husband always said his wife never met a stranger. She would strike up a conversation with anyone nearby. "I'm having dinner with my friend tonight," she told the girl. "She's going crazy trying to get everything ready for her wedding this weekend. My hubby won't be here 'til in the morning. I'm looking forward to having a few drinks with her and her fiancé. I know she's nervous about tomorrow and wants everything to be perfect for her special day."

"Wow, sounds like my sister and sisters-in-law when they got married. They were all basket cases by the time the wedding day came. I don't understand it, really. Why go to so much trouble just for a few minutes of words? I think when my boyfriend and I get married, I just want to go to the county courthouse." The young girl finished with her bucket of ice and made room for Shelby.

"Oh, I know it seems silly to go to all the trouble. But, believe me, if you're planning to get married, you won't ever regret having a wedding, especially having your family around you. It's a special time. You don't want to deny anyone you love the pleasure of watching you walk down that aisle. You're so pretty; you'll be a beautiful bride someday."

Amber liked this friendly woman. "Oh, my boyfriend hasn't even asked me yet, so I'm sure it's going to be awhile before all that happens. Besides, my mama and daddy are a little upset with me right now. The last thing they want to do is throw me a wedding."

Shelby finished filling her ice bucket and walked back down the hall with Amber. "Well, mamas and daddies get that way sometimes, but they always want to see their babies take those big steps in their lives. You're young and have plenty of time. I'm sure the minute that boy of yours asks you to be his bride, and you tell your family you're getting married, they'll come like flies to honey to see you say, 'I do.' I've got three boys and two of them are already married. My youngest is in his last year of college in Odessa, Texas. He has a girlfriend, but hasn't asked her to get married yet. I suspect he will as soon as he finishes college."

"You're from Odessa?"

"Yes, I am. Do you know where that is?"

"Of course, that's where I'm from. My boyfriend is from a little town just south of Atlanta, but he's having some family issues. He's a truck driver and as soon as he gets his family stuff straight, he's coming here to get me. Then we're going to get an apartment together."

Shelby could tell the young girl was frightened about being alone in the hotel. "How long has he been gone? When did he tell you he would be back?"

"Oh, he just put me up in this hotel today. He's supposed to be back tonight or tomorrow."

"I'm sure he'll be here tonight. He'd be an idiot to leave his best girl alone for long. I think it's cool that you're from Odessa; it sure is a small world. I'm a truck driver, too. I drive sand all over the country for fracking companies. Do you know what that is?"

"I've heard my daddy and big brothers talk about fracking. They all work in the oil fields, but I don't really know what it is."

Shelby reached her door and took out her key card. "Well, this is me,. Maybe tomorrow, if you're still here, we can talk down by the pool and I'll telling you all about fracking."

Amber kept walking down the hallway. Shelby was concerned about how young she was. "Take care of yourself and let me know if you need anything," she called to her.

"Thank you, I will. It's good to know that someone else from home is in the building. Have fun at your dinner." Amber reached her door and slid in her key card.

"You too and, by the way, my name is Shelby."

"My name is Amber."

"Nice to meet you Amber from Odessa."

"Nice to meet you too Shelby from Odessa." Both women entered their respective rooms.

Shelby couldn't help but wonder about Amber as she got ready for her dinner date with Angelica and Rex. She felt sorry for Amber. *She's so alone—and so young.*

◊◊◊

"There's the blushing bride." Shelby hugged Angelica as soon as she reached the table.

"Oh, Shelby, it is so good to see you again." Rex pulled the chair out for Angelica to sit next to Shelby. "I'm so glad you're here. I've been a wreck trying to get everything together. My mom has been a great help, but all these last minute details are driving me crazy."

"I have to agree with that observation." Rex laughed as he motioned for the waiter. The waiter approached the table. "I'll have whatever you have on tap. Ladies, what can he get you to start the night off?"

Shelby laughed. "Angelica, I figured you would need a drink tonight. You must really be putting Rex through hell if he's the one needing to drink. I'll have a tap beer, too, thank you."

CHAPTER NINE

Amber held out the remote and thumbed through the TV channels. She kept checking the time, wishing Paul would call her. *He did tell me that he might not be able to make it to the hotel until tomorrow,* she reminded herself, trying not to worry. She pulled the money that he had given her out of her pocket. It was about two hundred dollars, more many than she would ever use in one evening. *Why did he give me so much? Why isn't he here with me?*

Amber turned off the TV, slipped under the covers and tried to go to sleep. *Paul will wake me when he gets here,* she tried to convince herself. She had a hard time shaking the feeling of abandonment. She tossed and turned, unable to fall asleep. She got up, grabbed the ice bucket and her key card and headed for the door.

Shelby was walking down the hallway as Amber came out of her room. "Hey, Amber from Odessa. How're ya doing? What are you doing out so late? Did your boyfriend ever show up?"

Amber held tight onto the ice bucket, willing herself not to cry. "No, he hasn't shown up yet. The ice melted," she said and held out the bucket. "Did you have fun with your friends?"

"Yes, I had a really good time." Shelby could tell from Amber's expression that she needed a friend. "Hey, would you mind if I walk with you down to the ice machine?"

"Sure."

"Let me just grab my ice bucket." Shelby popped into her room, dropped her purse and jacket onto the bed, and emptied out the half melted ice into the bathroom sink. "I sure like this city—it's beautiful and has a lot of character. When your boyfriend shows up tomorrow, you need to get him to take you to see some of the Civil War history in this town. My husband Jack will be here tomorrow. If we had the time, that's what we'd be doing."

"Paul has showed me a bunch of stuff since we've been on the road together. I don't know if he'll have time since we need to be on the road again soon. But, I'll definitely tell him I'd like to see that stuff. I hope he gets here early tomorrow; it's kind of lonely here especially since I don't know anyone."

"Well, listen, if for some reason he doesn't show up tomorrow, why don't you just plan on going with us to the post-rehearsal dinner party tomorrow night? I know my friends won't mind and it will get you out of this hotel for a little while."

"Oh, I'm sure he will be here tomorrow, but I appreciate the offer."

"I'm sure he'll be here, too. In fact, if you don't have to get back on the road, you should both come with Jack and me."

Amber brightened a bit. "I'd like that. Of course, we'll will have to wait and see what Paul says."

"Okay, then it's a date—if Paul agrees."

"Thank you, Shelby from Odessa."

"You're welcome, Amber from Odessa."

◊◊◊

Shelby wrapped her arms around Jack's neck. "Hi sexy man, I have my car outside. Would you like a ride?"

Jack kissed his wife. "Well, what would your husband think about you picking up a strange man at the airport and giving him a ride?"

Jack and Shelby laughed and held hands as they walked out of the terminal. "I'm sure glad you're here, baby. It was getting lonely without you. I felt like a third wheel last night at dinner with Angelica and Rex."

"I'm here now, sweetheart. How are the newlyweds holding up?"

"Same as all couples about to get married. Like you and I were when we got married."

"Poor Rex, Angelica must be driving him crazy."

Shelby laughed. "Yep, she sure is."

Jack opened the door of the rental car for Shelby, then he got into the passenger side.

"Take me to the hotel, little lady. I need a nice lunch and maybe a roll in the hay with my old lady."

"Well, sir, I think I can get you to your hotel and maybe even get you a nice lunch, but that 'roll' is going to cost you."

"I've got lots of money."

Shelby laughed with Jack. "More than money, honey. More than money."

"Oh, no. She wants the shirt, too."

Jack kissed his wife on the cheek as they drove to the hotel.

Jack followed Shelby into the hotel. As they passed the door that led to the swimming pool, Shelby said, "I think we need to go for a swim. The rehearsal dinner isn't until seven o'clock tonight."

"That sounds like fun. I hope they have a hot tub, too."

Shelby pulled Jack down the hall toward their room. "This way, handsome. Room 456." Shelby stopped in front of their room and swiped her key card. She looked down the hall to Amber's room. "I met a young lady on this floor from Odessa. She's in that room down there. Her boyfriend is a trucker, and he put her up here for a few days while he took care of some family business. I haven't seen her today, but she seemed really nervous and upset yesterday because he hadn't showed up yet. I feel kind of sorry for her. I sure hope he doesn't turn out to be a real asshole and abandon her here. I invited them to the party after the rehearsal dinner tonight."

"Shelby, you shouldn't have done that without talking to Angelica and Rex first."

"Oh, Jack, Angelica and Rex aren't going to care if I bring a couple of extra people to a bar. Besides, I haven't even seen her today. He boyfriend probably showed up and they're already gone."

"You are something else, my love—always taking care of strays. Now, I understand how you always get into so much trouble. You just can't help yourself when someone is in need. I guess that's one of the reasons I love you so much." Jack wrapped his arms around his wife and kissed the back of her neck. "Let's put on our suits and go for a swim, and then come back here and pretend we're on our honeymoon."

"Sounds good. Maybe we should pretend we're on our honeymoon and go swimming later." Shelby turned around in her husband's arms and kissed him.

"I like that idea."

◊◊◊

"I'm sorry, sir, but he works for your company and I really need to get in touch with him. He's not answering his cell phone and I really need to talk with him, it's an emergency." Amber waited while the man on the phone looked for the information.

"I'm sorry, Miss, but the only phone number we have for Paul Gibbs is the cell phone number you have. My boss says I can't give you his address. I suggest you call the local police in Mason and have them go by his house and give him that emergency message."

"When is he supposed to come back to work?"

"Well, I'm not supposed to give that information out either, but he's due back on Sunday. He took some personal days according to the paperwork."

"Okay, I really appreciate it. I'll try and get the police to go by the house." Amber hung up the hotel room phone. She kept thinking that maybe she was wrong and that Paul was just trying to get things straightened out at home. *If I call the police, that might upset Paul and make things worse with his wife.* She laid back on the bed and looked at the ceiling. *I'll wait until Saturday night; if I don't hear from him by then, I'll call the cops and have them contact him. Or maybe I'll get a ride from someone and go to his house myself.*

It was getting late and Amber hadn't eaten in two days. She decided that it was time to find something to eat. She didn't want to use much of the money that Paul had given her in case they needed it later. It had been nice of Shelby to invite her to that party, but she was too embarrassed to tell her Paul hadn't come for her. She stayed hidden in her room until after seven o'clock. Once she was sure Shelby was gone, she slipped out her of her hotel room and headed to the elevator. She had noticed several places that had food near the hotel when the taxi driver had dropped her off two days earlier. The restaurant near the hotel looked good. She made her way across the parking lot. She could sit in a booth and drink some coffee after she finished eating.

When Amber entered the restaurant she was quickly taken to a small booth at the back of the room. "Will this be okay?"

"Yes, this will be perfect. I can see the front of the hotel in case my boyfriend shows up tonight." She would eat something and then sit and drink coffee until she saw Paul.

The waitress handed Amber a menu. "What can I get you to drink?"

"I think I want coffee and a glass of water, please."

The waitress left while Amber looked at the menu. Everything seemed to be so expensive, but she was hungry. When the waitress returned she had decided. "Here you go, coffee and water. What can I get for you?"

"I want the roast beef dinner with mashed potatoes and salad with ranch dressing, please." Amber felt a little uncomfortable ordering such a big meal, but she hadn't eaten since coffee and donuts on Thursday morning.

"I'll get it for you right away."

Amber sipped at her black coffee. "Thank you."

"We'll take that big booth over there." Three young guys about Amber's age rushed past Amber's table. One of the men jumped over the back of the booth next to the seat they had requested.

He plopped down hard into the booth, which caused the table to shake as the condiment caddies shifted toward the edge of the table. The young man grabbed for the caddies and laughed. "Oops."

The waitress frowned at the rambunctious boy.

"Sorry about that, Miss, he's a little on the excited side today." The other two men piled into the round booth.

"Please be a little more careful. What can I get for you, guys?"

Amber had been staring out the window, hoping Paul would arrive. Her thoughts were abruptly interrupted by the noise of the young men. Amber watched as the waitress did her best to make the men settle down.

The man in charge of the group caught Amber's stare. Amber quickly turned her attention back to the window she had been looking through.

"Hey, guys, look at that pretty little thing siting over there. I think she likes me."

Both of the other men looked over at Amber. "She's looking at me, Zeke. Why would she be looking at an ugly asshole like you?"

"Shut up, Frankie. She was looking straight at me."

"No, she was looking at all of us because Jess was acting like an idiot."

"She was looking at me, Zeke. She liked the way I cleared the back of this booth."

Zeke looked at Amber. "I'll bet you a hundred dollars, Jess, that I catch that one for myself. I've never seen her around here before, I wonder if she's from Atlanta?"

"I'll take that hundred dollars because I'll bet she's probably waiting on a husband or a boyfriend."

Zeke got out of his seat and headed straight toward Amber. "Only one way to find out."

Zeke slid into the seat across from Amber; his smile made his dark brown hair and green eyes stand out. "Hey there, beautiful. I was wondering if you would like to join me and my friends."

Amber put her coffee cup down and smiled back at the forward actions of the man dressed in jeans and a hoodie. "I don't think so. I'm waiting on someone."

"Well, I don't see a ring on your finger, so it can't be a husband. Boyfriend, maybe, but he's a fool letting you out of his sight."

Embarrassed by the compliments, Amber blushed. "He's my boyfriend and he's going to be here any time."

"Well, he's an idiot."

The waitress brought Amber's dinner and placed it in front of her. "Can I get you anything else?"

"No, this is just fine."

"Zeke, you need to go back over to your table and leave this poor woman to eat in peace."

Zeke slid out of the booth and sneered at the waitress. "Fine, Teresa, but you're messing up my game."

"Go play your *game* on someone else Zeke, or I'm going tell Ike, and you know he'll kick you out of here for bothering the customers."

"It was nice to meet you, Miss. My name is Zeke. If your boyfriend doesn't show up, or you get lonely, come join us."

"Okay." Amber picked at her food until Zeke left her table. She nodded at Teresa in a gesture of thanks. The waitress winked and waited until Zeke was back at his seat before returning to her other tables. "She's putty in my hands, boys."

"Bullshit, Zeke. I heard everything; she's waiting for her boyfriend."

"A boyfriend that isn't here—and she's all alone. Wait and see; that guy isn't going to show up. He's either a real loser or he's stupid. You already owe me a hundred dollars, want to make it two hundred?"

"I don't owe you a dime, you owe me a hundred dollars and you haven't got two hundred. Besides, you haven't closed any deal with her."

"Yet! The night's still young."

The waitress picked up Amber's empty plate, and then poured her another cup of coffee. "Can I get you anything else?"

"No, I've had plenty. Is it okay if I sit here and enjoy my coffee?"

"Of course, sweetie. Stay as long as you like."

◊◊◊

"Come on, baby, we'd better get some rest tonight. We have a wedding to attend tomorrow," Jack said as he stood outside their hotel room.

"I know, but I think I'm going to put on my bathing suit and use the spa to relax before I call it quits for the night. Why don't you join me?" Shelby put her arms around her husband's neck. "It could be fun."

Jack put his arms around his wife. "That might be a good idea; then we could come back here and finish the fun." Jack gently put his wife against the wall and kissed her passionately. "You are so beautiful, Shelby."

Shelby smiled. "You're my baby always and forever."

"Come on, sugar. Let's get sweaty in the hot tub." Jack let Shelby go so they could get into their room. "I guess standing outside our room making out like newlyweds isn't something two mature adults should be doing."

Shelby giggled and put her hands around her husband's waist. She pulled herself close to his back while he inserted the key card. "Probably not, but who says we have to be mature?"

"Better quit, Shelby, or we will forget about the hot tub and get sweaty in bed."

◊◊◊

It was almost midnight when Amber pulled her jacket closed to protect herself from the cool evening air. After several hours sipping coffee, she got up, left two dollars for a tip, and walked slowly back to the hotel. Paul hadn't called and she didn't see him return to the hotel. *I've made a terrible mistake. This last month has just been a big lie. What am I going to do now?*

"Hey, beautiful. How about I walk with you? I wouldn't want anything to happen to your pretty little ass—the rough part of town is just a few blocks in that direction." Zeke interrupted Amber's thoughts and pointed south of the hotel. "Never know when one of those criminals might decide to walk over into this neighborhood."

Amber laughed. "Oh, I think I'll be okay. I only have to walk across this parking lot."

"Oh, come on. Give me a chance to be a gentleman; although, I'm not a very good one." Zeke stepped in front of Amber and walked backwards in front of her. He almost tripped on the uneven pavement. He wobbled and Amber instinctively let go of her jacket in order to keep Zeke from falling. "Wow, thanks. I think they should fix that crack." Zeke quickly composed himself and put Amber's arm into his. "Now, you have to let me walk you to the hotel. You just saved my life."

"You're crazy. If you hadn't been walking backwards, your stupid ass wouldn't have tripped." Amber laughed and removed her arm from Zeke's and wrapped her jacket around her body again. "I really think I can make the last forty feet alone, thank you."

"Well, okay, but since your boyfriend stood you up tonight, I was wondering if you might be interested in having breakfast with me in the morning?" Zeke opened the front door to the hotel for Amber.

"He just got busy. He'll be here in a little while. I don't think he would like me having breakfast with a strange man who walks backwards and trips over cracks in concrete."

Zeke snickered. "Everyone has to have a talent." Zeke put out his hand. "My name is Zeke. The offer to buy you breakfast over at the restaurant at nine o'clock is still open—just in case that boyfriend of yours doesn't show."

Amber left Zeke at the door without telling him her name. "He will." Amber walked to her room. As she opened the door, Amber decided that a dip in the pool would help her forget her problems for a while.

Just as Amber turned into the hallway to go to the pool, Shelby and Jack came toward her. "Amber from Odessa, how are you? This is my husband, Jack. Where is your boyfriend? We figured he showed up and you guys decided to stay in for the evening."

"Nice to meet you, Jack." Amber shook Jack's extended hand. "No, Paul hasn't shown up yet and I didn't really feel like going anywhere without him. I'm hoping he will be here soon."

Shelby wrapped her wet body up tighter in her towel.

"I see you guys have been to the pool. I thought a nice dip in the pool might take my mind off of Paul. How's the water?"

Jack grabbed Shelby by the waist and pulled her to his side. "It was terrific. You'll really enjoy it."

Amber continued her path to the pool. "It was nice meeting you, Jack. See you later."

Shelby could tell that Amber was bothered about something as she watched her disappear down the hall, but Jack had opened their hotel room. "Are you coming in, baby?"

"Yeah, coming." Shelby let her concern for Amber rest for the moment. Jack wanted her attention and he was more important.

CHAPTER TEN

"Hurry up, baby, it's almost nine and we are supposed to be there by ten to help Angelica's mother with the last minute stuff." Shelby put on her high heels and earrings. For the first time in their marriage, she was ready to go out before her husband.

Jack was in the bathroom combing his hair. "I know, Shelby, but you took forever in the bathroom this morning so I haven't had enough time to get ready."

"Sorry, honey. I just wanted to look extra special for the wedding." Shelby removed her dress from the closet. The plastic from the department store was still over it. Jack came out of the bathroom half dressed. He grabbed his tie and coat off the bed. "You said you were ready—you're still in your jeans."

"I'm taking my dress so I won't mess it up on the way over there."

"Well, Rex asked if I would help him get ready since his best man got kind of loaded last night. I guess I can finish getting ready over there, too. Do you want to stop somewhere and get some breakfast?"

Shelby held the door with her foot while Jack grabbed her makeup bag and his clothes off the bed. "No, Angelica said her mother has lots of food for the wedding party. I'm sure we can find something there. I really just want another cup of coffee."

◊◊◊

Amber paced in her room anxiously waiting for a phone call from Paul's employer. She had called them two hours earlier, and a different young woman had promised to contact Paul and have him call her. Amber couldn't wait any longer. She picked up the phone and called them again. "This is Amber Nichols and I called earlier, are you the lady I talked with?"

"No, that probably was someone from the night shift and they go home at seven. Is there something I can help you with?"

"I am looking for my boyfriend, Paul Gibbs. He left me here in a hotel in Atlanta and told me he was coming back two days ago after he took care of some family business. I haven't seen him and I'm worried something has happened to him. The lady I talked to earlier said she would contact him and have him call me, that was two hours ago."

"Well, I'm not sure who you talked to, but we are not allowed to give personal messages to drivers unless they are emergencies. But I do see here on my computer that Mr. Gibbs left town last night with a load. I'm sorry, dear, but it looks like your boyfriend has left you at home this time. Perhaps you'd better just go home and wait for him to call you?"

Tears fell down Amber's face. "Okay, thank you."

Amber threw herself face down on the bed and cried. Thoughts ran through her mind as she wept. *What am I going to do? I can't go home—not now. I left my family and my children for Paul. Where am I going to go?* Amber sat up in the bed and realized that she needed to find out when her time was up at the hotel. She wiped her tears and phoned the front desk. "Yes, this room 459 and I was wondering when my checkout date and time might be? Okay, thank you."

Amber hung up the phone. She didn't cry this time. She didn't have time. She had to figure out where she was going to go and what she was going to do. The front desk had told her that she only had till noon tomorrow.

She took the money out of her pocket and the money she had left in her purse. She had about three hundred and fifty dollars. She knew it wasn't much, but it might be enough to get by for a few days. *What I need is a job.* Her thoughts went to the restaurant she had visited last night. *Maybe that nice waitress I met yesterday could recommend a cheaper place to stay—and maybe recommend me for a job at the restaurant.*

Amber quickly washed her face and replaced the makeup that had washed away with her tears. She wanted to get to the restaurant soon and then find another place to stay. "Paul screwed me over just like every man I've been involved with," she mumbled. But she didn't have time to think about that right now. She grabbed her purse and key card, left the room, and headed across the parking lot.

"How many today?"

Amber looked around the restaurant for the waitress who had served her last night. She couldn't see her anywhere. She gave up on looking for her and responded, "Just one—and can I get an application? I need a job."

"Sure, but I don't know if we are hiring right now. Come on. First I'll get you a table, and then I'll bring you the application. What can I get for you to drink?"

"I'll have a cup of coffee, please."

"Okay, be right back."

Amber looked around the room again, hoping to spot the waitress who had been so nice to her last night. Her search was abruptly interrupted. "Hey, sweet thing. I see you showed up for our breakfast date."

Annoyed, Amber continued looking around the room. "I'm not here for breakfast with you. I'm looking for that waitress I had last night."

"You mean Teresa? She only works evenings and nights around here."

"You mean she won't be here until tonight? How do you know that?"

Zeke slid into the booth across from Amber. "I know everything about Atlanta. I've been here my whole life. I know everybody, too. This here is one of my favorite hangouts. I know all the staff here."

"Here you go, honey." The waitress put the application in front of Amber and then poured her a cup of coffee.

"Thanks, Shelly. Put this and anything she wants to eat on my bill."

The waitress rolled her eyes before walking away from Amber's table. "Whatever, Zeke. Why don't you go home, or get a job, or do something instead of hanging around here so much? Watch out for this one, sweetie. He's bad news."

Zeke ignored Shelly's comments. He looked at the application in front of Amber that she had started filling out. "I see you're looking for a job, and your name is Amber. You forgot to give me your name last night."

"I didn't forget. I just didn't want to tell you." Amber put the application next to her on the seat. "You don't need to buy me anything, and my business isn't any of your business." Amber looked around the room while she sipped at her coffee. "Aren't your cronies around here somewhere? Why don't you go sit with them? I appreciate your interest in me, but I'm not interested in you."

Zeke laughed. "I like a woman who speaks her mind. You might not be interested in me right now, but you wait a little while. Come on, finish filling out that application and I'll talk with Michael the manager and get you on right away."

"I'll finish it later, and I don't need your help finding a job. I don't need any man doing anything for me."

"I guess your boyfriend never showed up and that's why you're looking for a job?"

"I told you my business is my business and you need to butt out."

Zeke poured himself a cup of coffee and settled in. "Well, if you're not from around here, I can be a real help to you. I told you I know everything and everybody in Atlanta."

Amber was irritated. She took one last sip of her coffee, grabbed her application, and scooted out of the booth. "I don't need your help. Thank you for the coffee."

Amber left the restaurant, but before she could get back to the hotel, Zeke caught up to her. "Come on, Amber. I'm not such a bad guy. I won't run out on you like your boyfriend just did."

Amber couldn't stand that Zeke had figured out her personal life so quickly. "Shut up, Zeke, and leave me alone. You have no idea what you're talking about." Amber went into the hotel. "Go away. I don't need your help. I will figure things out on my own."

Zeke followed Amber into the hotel and down the hallway. "So it's true; he's left you here in this hotel. Where are you from?"

Amber stopped in the hallway. She was angry and got right in Zeke's face. "Look, I don't know who you are or what you want from me, or how much plainer can I be with you. Leave me alone!"

Amber turned and walked to her room. Zeke realized he had probably pushed Amber a little too far for now. "Okay, baby. I know you're upset right now. When you settle down and want someone to talk to, I'll be at the restaurant."

Amber ignored Zeke and went into her room.

◊◊◊

"Oh, Angelica, you were the most beautiful bride ever."

Angelica hugged and kissed Shelby and Jack. "Thank you both for being willing to help with my wedding. Shelby, we have to stay connected. I consider you my best friend."

"We are best friends for life, Angelica. You guys have a wonderful and safe trip to Hawaii. I will help your mom finish cleaning up after this dance clears out."

Jack shook hands with Rex after helping him load their luggage into the trunk of the taxi. "Thank you, Jack, for everything."

"Thank you, Shelby." Angelica gave her friend another hug. "We are going to have a wonderful honeymoon, I'll send you some pictures." Rex opened the cab door and helped Angelica into the seat.

"Take care of that little lady," Jack said as he pulled Shelby away from the curb.

Rex slipped in the cab beside his new bride. Through an open window he and Angelica waved goodbye. "I will, Jack, thanks again."

Shelby held onto Jack and kept waving until the taxi was out of sight. The crowd of people that had been there to send the happy couple off soon dispersed back into the reception. The couple the party had been for may have left, but the party wasn't over.

"Wasn't the wedding beautiful, Jack?"

"Yes it was, baby. It reminded me of ours. Only I think I got the prettier bride."

"Oh, Jack, you're terrible. Angelica was stunning today and you know it."

Jack put his arms tighter around his wife. "I know she was, but so were you."

Shelby kissed her husband. "You're amazing, I love you. Let's go inside and help Angelica's mother clean up a little bit and then go back to the hotel.

I think we need to continue that hot, steamy 'roll in the hay' we've been doing the last couple days."

"I'm for that, sugar." Jack took his wife's hand and walked her back into the building.

◊◊◊

After waiting all day, Amber decided that it was time to go back over to the restaurant and talk to Teresa. She hoped that Zeke wouldn't be there, but was afraid it probably couldn't be avoided. She walked into the restaurant and was relieved when Teresa met her at the door with a menu. "Welcome back, sweetie, another booth tonight?"

"Yes, please, and I was wondering if you could give this to your boss for me." Amber handed Teresa the application she had filled out in her room.

Teresa was a little shocked. "Looking for a job, sweetie? Coffee?"

Amber sat down in the booth. "Yes, I'll have coffee and yes I really need a job. My boyfriend, ex-boyfriend, left me in that hotel over there. I'm going to run out of money soon and I have to leave the hotel in the morning. It's really a long story, but if you could talk to your boss I sure would appreciate it."

"I'd be glad to, sweetie, but I never see Michael much since I work nights. I will try and talk to him when he comes in to check on things first thing in the morning. He always comes in early on Sunday morning to make sure that the Saturday night crowd didn't destroy things for the Sunday morning rush."

"Okay, I sure appreciate it. I'm not sure what I'm going to do. I only have a few dollars left and I know I can't afford the price of that hotel another night. You don't know of a cheaper place I could get, do you?"

"I do, but they aren't any place a nice girl like you would want to stay. Most of them are drug-infested, with whores running in and out of the rooms all times of the night. You'd be better off going home with that money, sugar."

"Oh, I can't go home. My family will never accept me back, especially after I ran off with Paul."

"Well, let me go get you some coffee, I will think about it and ask some of the other people here at work. I'm sure someone will know of at least a halfway decent place you can get for a while."

"Thanks, Teresa, I really appreciate it." Amber stared at the hotel through the window of the restaurant. She had enjoyed staying there, but now she had to find something else quick.

"Hey, baby, I see you couldn't stay away." Zeke slid into the booth across from Amber again.

"Look, get out of my booth and leave me alone. I don't want any help from you and I'm not interested in anything else you might want from me." Amber turned away from Zeke and stared out the window.

"Look, baby."

"Stop calling me baby."

"Look, Amber, I don't want anything from you. I just want to be friends. I just want to help you while you're in Atlanta. Come on, I'm a really nice guy." Zeke put his hand on top of Amber's folded hands.

Amber jerked her hands away and put them under the table. "Get your hands off me! Leave. Me. Alone!"

Teresa came back to Amber's table with the coffee. "Is this jerk bothering you, sugar?"

Amber shouted, "Yes!"

Teresa looked at Zeke. "Get out of here, Zeke, and leave this poor girl alone before I call the cops and have you removed." Teresa poured Amber her coffee while Zeke got out of the booth.

"I was just trying to be friendly, no need for everybody getting all bent out of shape." Zeke left the table without another word to Amber.

"Thank you again, Teresa, I've been trying to get rid of that asshole since last night. He even followed me back to my hotel."

"Oh, Zeke? He's pretty harmless really, just a pest."

Amber sipped at her coffee. "A pest is right."

Teresa laughed. "I understand. Hey, I talked to the night manager and to some of the other waitresses. The manager said he would talk with Mike in the morning for you, but he wasn't sure if they had anything open right now.

Maybe by the end of next week. A couple of the girls gave me these names of places that are fairly cheap." Teresa handed Amber a piece of paper with several names of apartments and motels. "I don't know anything about any of them, but they might be worth checking out."

"Oh, thank you. I will check them out first thing in the morning. I think I can afford another night where I'm at, but if not, maybe I can find a cheaper hotel close to here for tomorrow night."

"I'm sure sorry this is happening to you, sweetie. That boyfriend, ex-boyfriend, of yours was sure a jerk for leaving you like this."

"Yes, but it's my fault. I should have expected it; after all, he's a man. If I've learned anything in my seventeen short years, it's that's men are assholes. They only use women for one thing and then when they are done with them, they throw them away. Only exception would be my daddy. He has never thrown me away."

"Then why don't you call him, sweetie? I'll bet he would be here in a New York minute to get you if you asked him."

"I'm sure he would, but the rest of my family wouldn't let him. They are all mad at me for taking off with Paul. They will never let me back home."

"Listen, I have to take care of my other tables. But if I were you, I would call home. I'm sure it's not as bad as you think it is."

"Thanks, Teresa, but I can't go back there."

Amber ate a salad for dinner and sat in the restaurant until she got tired of coffee. Zeke hadn't come back to her table and she hadn't seen him or felt his stares, so Amber figured he'd either left or gave up on bothering her. It was chilly again as she walked back to the hotel. She wanted to soak in the spa again once she got back. She was so concerned with a job and living arrangements that she hadn't had much time to think about Paul. As she headed back to the hotel, what he had done to her crept back into her mind and a few tears found their way down her cheeks. She quickly wiped them with the sleeve of her jacket.

◊◊◊

"Come on, baby, I'm tired. We can go swimming tomorrow." Jack pulled Shelby away from the window of the pool room at the hotel.

"I'm tired too, Jack, but look—Amber is in there all by herself again. It doesn't look like that boyfriend of hers showed up yet." Shelby pulled away from Jack and continued watching Amber through the glass.

"Come on, Shelby, you can check on her tomorrow. I want to go to bed."

Shelby went with Jack to their room. "I know you're tired, Jack, but I'm going to put my suit on and go talk to her for a little while. You go ahead and go to sleep and I will wake you up when I get back. I just really need to go talk to her, I'm worried."

Jack took his wife in his arms and looked into her eyes. "I love you for the way you are, baby—always wanting to help people. You go down and talk to that little lady for as long as you want. We have until Monday morning together, plenty of time to enjoy each other."

Shelby began to take off her clothes and put on her bathing suit. "Thank you, baby, I won't be gone too long. I just really want to make sure she's okay."

"Take as long as you want. I'll be right here."

◊◊◊

When Shelby entered the pool area, Amber was still soaking in the hot tub. "Hi, Amber from Odessa, how are you? How's the water? May I join you?"

Amber moved over so that Shelby could find a nice spot in the spa. "I'm doing okay. The water is a little warm, but I like it. How are you, Shelby from Odessa?"

"Tired. I forgot how exhausting a wedding can be—but we finally got the newlyweds off on their honeymoon. How are things with you? Did your boyfriend ever show up?"

Amber really didn't want to talk about Paul but she needed to tell someone about what he had done to her. "Ex-boyfriend. No, Paul has not shown up, and when I called him at work again this morning they let me know that he took a load yesterday. The lowlife took me away from my home then he lied to me about loving me and about how he was going to show me the world. Here I am again, screwed over by another man. It's the story of my life."

"Wow, I'm sorry about that, Amber. I'm so sorry that men have treated you with such disrespect. You are so beautiful and do not, in any way, deserve that kind of treatment. Have you decided what you're going to do?"

"No, not really. I have to be out of this place by tomorrow at noon. I have a little bit of money, but I can't afford the rates here. I applied for a job at that restaurant across the parking lot today, but that might take a week to come through. The waitress over there gave me a few names of cheaper places, so I'm going to check them out tomorrow."

"What about going back home? I'm headed back there on Monday in my truck. I'd be happy to give you a lift."

"I really appreciate that, Shelby, but I can't go back home. I left my family without telling them I was leaving. I left my two kids with my parents and I'm pretty sure my older brother is working on taking them away from me. I just can't go back. I have to try and make things right before I try and go home."

"Oh, I'm sure if you go home things won't be all that bad, but I understand wanting to make things right. I didn't know you had children. You don't look old enough to have any babies."

"Yes, I have two—a little boy named Gabe and a little girl named Annie. I miss them, but I'm not a very good mother to them. When I was at home, all I did was work, go to school, sleep, and take care of them. It wasn't a good life for them or me. I was so tired all the time I never enjoyed being with them. Everything was so depressing all the time. I felt like the life was draining out of me."

"Yeah, children can do that to you. I have three boys, and I can totally relate. It does get better after they get a little older. Babies are very time con-suming. With school and work on top of the little ones, you really had your hands full. Did your parents help out?"

"Oh yes, in fact my babies are with my mama and daddy now."

"What do your parents do? Do they work?"

"My daddy is a driller for Slattern Drilling. He's been with them for forty years or more. My mama just works at home. My oldest brother Josh works at Slattern, too. He's a driller, but hasn't been there as long as my daddy.

They call him little Nichols. He hates it, but won't quit because he's too much like my daddy."

"Sounds like you have a fine family, Amber. A real West Texas oil field family. Are you sure you don't want a ride home?"

"No, I really don't, not right now."

"Well, I will probably be coming through here several times during the next few months. I'll give you my number and you be sure and keep in touch. Anytime, you want a lift home you just let me know."

"Thank you, Shelby, I will keep that in mind."

"Well, I guess I better get back to the room. Jack is asleep, but if he wakes up he might be worried if I'm not there."

"You're lucky to have someone that loves you so much."

Shelby had slipped out of the hot tub and was wrapping herself in a towel. "It hasn't been all gumdrops and lollipops. Jack and I have had our rough spots, but that's when the love for each other comes out. You have to really love someone to forgive them for whatever they do."

"Yeah, my mama and daddy have that kind of a relationship. I doubt I'll ever have love like theirs."

"Be patient, it will happen."

CHAPTER ELEVEN

"Here's my key card for room 459."

"Okay, let me just check you out and give you a receipt." The front desk receptionist scanned her computer. "Amber Nichols?"

"Yes, that's right."

"Well, was something wrong with your room; do you want a different room?"

"No, nothing was wrong with my room. I'd take another room, but I can't afford it."

"Okay. Well, you're paid up for another week, until next Sunday."

"Really? When I called you yesterday, you said I had to check out today by noon."

"Yes, but someone has paid for you to stay another week."

"Do you know who?"

"No, I'm sorry, it was paid for by an anonymous source with a request that we not reveal any information. It also says that you have an envelope in your mail slot, but that can't be released to you until tomorrow evening at six o'clock."

"Wow, that's great. I was just going to take a taxi to the closest cheap hotel on this list. Now, at least I have a week to figure out what I'm going to do here in Atlanta."

"Oh, sounds like your stranded here."

"You could say that, my ex-boyfriend put me up in this hotel and then never came back for me. Now, I have to figure out how to make it on my own in this place. This is the first time I've ever been in Atlanta—the first time I've been in Georgia for that matter. I'm from Texas."

"Well, it's kind of hard to find jobs here in Atlanta right now. But you might be able to find a job as a waitress or something."

"I've already put in an application at the restaurant across the parking lot. I was going to go over there as soon as I got checked out and talk with the manager."

"So, do you want to keep your room?"

"Yes." Amber looked down at her things. "I'll take my stuff back to my room and then go see the manager."

The desk clerk gave Amber back her room card. "You might check with our manager, we might have an opening in housekeeping."

Amber had gathered up her things and was headed back to her room. "Thanks, I'll check that out tomorrow."

"Sure, anytime."

Amber couldn't believe it. *Who could have possibly paid for me to stay another week? Had Paul paid for another week out of guilt? Maybe he's planning on coming back for me.* She realized how foolish that sounded. *No, he would have called and told me what he was doing. I have no idea who it could be, but I'll probably find out tomorrow at six*—if that was what the letter in her mail slot was about. She felt relieved that she had a place to live for one week, which would give her plenty of time to find a job and a cheaper place to live.

It didn't take Amber long to put her stuff away. She wanted to get over to the restaurant before the morning manager left for the day. When she saw the crowd at the door, Amber realized that it was Sunday. It was the after church crowd, something that all waitresses knew. Having nothing else to do, she decided to have a seat and let the manager know that she wanted to talk with him when he was available after the rush.

"What can I get for you?" The waitress poured Amber another cup of coffee.

"I think I'll just have the coffee. But I was hoping that I might be able to talk with the manager before he leaves for the day."

The waitress looked to the door where a man with a briefcase was leaving. "You'd better hurry if you're going to talk to him; he's leaving early today."

Amber looked at the waitress. "Can you hold my seat for me? I'll be right back, I promise. I just need to talk to him for a minute before he leaves."

"Sure."

Amber jumped out of her seat and ran through the front doors of the restaurant. Without realizing it, she nearly ran Zeke down in the foyer.

Just as Michael the manager got to his car, Amber caught up to him. Out of breath, she tried to explain. "Michael, I don't know your last name, so I'm sorry I have to call you by your first name, sir." Amber put out her hand for Michael to shake. "My name is Amber Nichols and I was hoping that you might have a waitress, or really any position, open for me in your restaurant."

Michael was a little surprised that someone would approach him in the parking lot, but he did recognize the name. "You must be the young lady that Teresa was telling me about this morning."

"Yes, sir, she told me she would try and talk to you if she got the chance."

"Well, Amber, I don't have any full time positions available at the moment, have you ever been a waitress before?"

"Yes, sir, I worked in our local truck stop back home in Texas. But I really need a job and I'll take anything right now. I'm a really hard worker and I will do a good job."

"Well, come see me in the morning about nine and we will see what we can do."

"Okay, thank you, Mr. Michael." Amber put her hand out for Michael to shake again.

Michael laughed slightly at Amber's enthusiasm over a possible part-time waitressing position. He shook her hand again. "Don't be late."

"I won't, sir. Thank you again."

Michael left the parking lot in his car and Amber went back into the restaurant to drink her coffee. She was pleased with the prospect of a job. *Now I just need to find a place to live.*

Amber looked out the window near her booth. She smiled. *Everything is going to be okay. I have a place to stay for a few days and at least a chance at a part-time job.* Paul may have knocked her down, but she wasn't going to stay down.

"I like the smile, it makes you look so beautiful." Amber looked up from her coffee. She couldn't believe it—Zeke. *Is this guy going to ever get it?*

"Oh. Well, I'll try and not smile when you're around so I won't distract you." Amber turned her smile into a frown.

"Don't do that; I like your smile. Why do you hate me so much, Amber? I just want to be your friend and you won't give me the time of day."

"What gender are you?"

"Male, why? You aren't one of those girls that like girls are you?"

"No, stupid. I don't like girls like that, but I don't like men right now, either, and you're one of those."

"Now, why would a pretty little thing like you not like men?"

"Look, Zeke. It is Zeke, right?" she spat.

"Yes."

"I don't want anything to do with you. You're arrogant, self-centered and loud. The reason I don't want anything to do with other men is none of your business. So, just accept the fact I am not interested and go away."

"But I can't just walk away, Amber. I find you to be a very special lady. Not like all the other women around this town. You are smart and witty, and to be honest, you're the first woman I have ever met who won't take my shit."

Amber smiled slightly. She wanted to believe that she'd outsmarted this jackass. "Right, and you have a piece of tropical land you'll sell me in west Texas. You must think I'm an idiot who'll believe anything you have to say."

"Please, Amber, give me a chance to show you what a nice guy I can be. I know I'm a jerk and you've been hurt by at least one bigger jerk than me. All I'm asking is that you let me walk you back to your hotel and maybe buy you dinner tonight. I promise I will be a real gentleman."

"Did you...? Never mind." Amber thought twice about asking if he might have been the one who paid for her extra days at the hotel. "If I let you walk me back to the hotel this afternoon and I agree to have dinner with you tonight, then you will leave me alone? Forever?"

"Yes, I promise. Forever. But you have to agree that if you have a nice time tonight, and I treat you like a real lady, that you will give me a chance to take you out for a while."

Amber knew she wouldn't want any more dates with Zeke. "Okay, I will let you walk me home and have dinner with you tonight. But, I promise, it will be our only date. Zeke the Geek."

Zeke smiled. *I'm winning her over; she already has a nickname for me.* "We will see, Miss Amber, we will see."

Amber sipped at her coffee and rolled her eyes at Zeke's arrogant behavior. *What an asshole. At least I'll get a free meal out of the deal.*

◊◊◊

Shelby put her arms around her husband's neck and kissed him. "Baby, this has been the best weekend ever. I'm sad that we have to leave this morning. I'm going to miss you so much."

"It has been terrific; I'm going to miss you, too. But you will be back in Odessa in a few days, right?"

"Yes, but it will only be overnight. I have to keep running loads to PA until winter. Then I'll be running more local stuff until the weather warms up."

"Well, one night is better than no nights. This is what you love—driving those big ass trucks up and down the highways."

"I know, but sometimes it's tough being away from you."

"I'm at home, sugar, waiting on you to get there. Now, come on, if we don't get checked out, I'm going to miss my flight." Jack pulled away from Shelby and started gathering the luggage. "You have to pick up your load in Odessa in a couple of days, right?"

"Yes."

"So you need to get on the road, too. We've had a great weekend, but now it's time to go back to work."

Shelby reluctantly gathered the rest of their things off the bed. "Okay."

When they reached the lobby, Jack continued on to their rental car. "I'll go ahead and take these things out to the car while you check us out."

"All right, baby, I'll be right out." Shelby handed the two key cards she had in her hand to the desk clerk.

The clerk looked over her computer. "Was everything satisfactory, Mrs. Mathews?"

"Yes, it was great. Can you tell me if the young lady in room 459 is still here?"

"Yes, she's still here and I will give her the envelope you left for her tonight at six."

"Good, I was afraid if she found out that I had paid for her room while I was still here she might try and refuse the help. Please make sure she gets that envelope tonight."

"Yes, Mrs. Mathews, we will make sure she gets it."

The clerk handed Shelby her receipt. "Thank you."

"Thank you, and we hope you will stay with us again."

◊◊◊

Amber was excited about opening the letter that had been waiting for her. "I'm Amber Nichols and I have a letter that I'm supposed to pick up at six o'clock."

"Yes, Miss Nichols, here it is." The clerk reached into the mail slot and handed Amber the long white envelope.

Why a letter? Why couldn't whoever just tell me to my face what they want me to know? Amber opened the letter. Inside she found five crisp one-hundred-dollar bills and a nicely hand-written note.

Dear Amber,

I was afraid if I handed you this money and you found out that I had paid for you to stay in the hotel for another week, that you might not accept my gift. I understand that you want to prove to your family that you can survive on your own, but sometimes we need a little help from friends. You are a special young woman and I support your ambition. Please except this gift with my best wishes and hopes for you. I still believe that if you went home, your family would gladly accept you back, no matter what you might think you have done to disappoint them. Family is all we have in this life and I think you need to go home to yours. But, I respect your need to at least try and make it on your own. I am always available if you ever want to talk or need a ride or need anything. Below you will find my contact information. I know that Paul has hurt you deeply, but don't let one bad egg spoil it for you. There are some really great men out there, you just need to find yours, if you want one.

Always,
Shelby Mathews

Amber was shocked that Shelby had helped her out. *Why would this stranger want to help me? Is it because we're from the same town?* Whatever the reason, she was glad she had met Shelby and was even more grateful that she had helped her and taken the time to write a letter that she would keep with her always.

Amber folded the letter and put it and the money into her purse. Between the money she had left from what Paul had given her and Shelby's money, Amber figured she had enough to get a place to stay after her time ran out at the hotel.

She hurried out of the hotel, and made her way across the parking lot toward the restaurant for her 6:30 dinner with Zeke. She had only agreed because she wanted to conserve her money. Now that she had cash, she was keeping the date because if he really did know Michael, she didn't want to lose her chance at a job.

Zeke attempted to give Amber a kiss on her cheek when he met her at the front door of the restaurant. Amber quickly turned her head and pushed toward the door. "Let's go in and eat. I'm starved."

Zeke then tried to grab Amber's hand.

Amber pulled her hand away to open the door. "Come on, let's get a good seat."

"Two please." Teresa looked surprised that Amber was with Zeke. Amber noticed. "Oh, he's just buying me dinner. I talked with Michael today;

I have to be here at nine in the morning. It's not full-time but part-time will work. I'm going to try and find another job, too."

"That sounds great, sweetie." Teresa escorted Amber and Zeke to a booth. "What can I get for you to drink?"

"I'll have coffee, please." Amber slipped into one side of the booth where she placed herself in the middle, not leaving enough room for Zeke to sit. He motioned for her to move over, but Amber pointed to the booth seat across from her. "Sit over there. I like my space."

Zeke reluctantly sat in the other seat across from her. "I'll have coffee, too."

Teresa handed each of them a menu. "I'll be right back with your drinks."

CHAPTER TWELVE

"Come on, Amber, we have been going out for several weeks now. I've bought you food and I even put up the money for some of the weeks at that hotel you call home. Don't you think it's time for us to move this relationship to the next level?" They were at the laundromat and Amber was busy folding her clothes.

"What the hell are you talking about, Zeke? First of all, I never asked you to help me with anything…you voluntarily gave me that money for those rooms and took me out to eat. As for us taking our relationship to the next level, I'm not aware that we are in a relationship—we're just friends." Amber went to the dryer and took out some more clothes.

"Seriously, Amber, you know we have more than a friendship going here. I can't afford to keep paying for your rooms anymore. I think you need to move into my apartment with me."

Amber laughed. "Move into your apartment? Are you nuts? We've never even held hands and now you want to live together? I don't need your help. I have my job at the restaurant. I can make it on my own."

"Yeah, I see how that's working out for you. I have paid at least half of your hotel bills for the last few weeks. You've gone through all the money you had and all the money you're making. Besides, you've had no luck finding a second job. Look, we don't have to be anything more than roommates. I have that three-bedroom apartment with Joe and Kyle. I'll make them move into one room together and you can have a room by yourself. It will be cheaper for all of us, and it's not far from the restaurant, so you can still work there."

Amber continued doing her laundry. She knew that Zeke was right about everything, but she hated the possibility of being "kept" by a man again. "Fine, but if I move in, I get my own room, we are just friends, and I take care of myself."

"Okay, I will make Joe and Kyle move into the same room tonight. Your rent at that cheap motel you stay at is due tomorrow. I will help you move your stuff in after you get off work in the morning."

"I'm not working tonight. Michael has cut me back to just the weekends. Things are pretty slow at the restaurant right now, and he doesn't need all that much help. I've been looking for other work, but there just isn't anything for someone like me. I haven't graduated from high school yet, and I have no skills to do anything."

"Well, don't worry about it. I will cover you for a few days 'til you get some tips."

"No you won't. I will take care of myself."

"Okay, whatever you say, but if you would just let me be your boyfriend, I could take care of you."

"Shut up, Zeke, or I'm just going to pack my shit and live on the streets. I am not going to let any man take care of me ever again."

"Fine, I'll be by later to help you take some of your stuff to the apartment."

Amber continued with her laundry. "Don't try anything stupid, Zeke. I mean it when I say we are not a couple. We are just friends and that's all we will ever be."

Zeke rolled his eyes and left the laundromat. *Amber's the most hard-headed woman I've ever met.*

◊◊◊

Shelby knocked on the screen door of the old wood-frame house. Elsa Mae opened the door with baby Annie on her hip. "Yes, can I help you?"

"I'm sorry to bother you. My name is Shelby Mathews. Is this the Nichols residence?"

Elsa Mae opened the screen door slightly in order to get a better look at the woman standing in her doorway. "Yes. What is it that you need?" she asked cautiously.

"Well, if I could come in, I would like to talk with you and your husband about your daughter, Amber. You do have a daughter named Amber, don't you?"

Elsa Mae opened the door wider and allowed Shelby to enter the house. "Come in, my husband is in the living room. You have news of Amber?"

Shelby followed Elsa Mae into the living room where Charley was watching TV. "I saw Amber and I thought I should talk with you about her."

"Please, Ms. Mathews come in and have a seat." Elsa Mae put Annie in a playpen that was set up in the middle of the living room. "Charley turn that thing off. This young woman has information for us about Amber."

Charley quickly turned off the television. He got out of his chair and pointed at the couch for Shelby to sit on. "Have a seat, please. You talked to our Amber?"

"Yes, sir, Mr. Nichols."

"Please, call me Charley."

"Well, Charley, I met her when I was in Atlanta, Georgia a few weeks ago. I would have come and talked with you earlier, but I'm a truck driver and I haven't been had time enough to track you down before now. I hope you don't mind me coming to your home. The only way I was able to find you was through the place where Amber told me you worked."

"What the hell is Amber doing in Atlanta?" Charley asked.

"Well, I was in Atlanta with my husband Jack for a wedding and I met Amber at the hotel we were staying at. She told me she was there waiting on her boyfriend to take care of some business and then he was supposed to come to the hotel and get her. We stayed there all weekend, and by the time we left on Monday, she was still stranded at that hotel. I asked Amber what happened to her boyfriend and she'd finally come to the realization that he was not coming back for her. I guess he had second thoughts about their relationship or something. She never did give me much of an explanation as to why she was with Paul. At least that's the name she gave me."

Elsa Mae sat in the recliner next to her husband's chair. "Oh no, Charley, that man left our little girl alone in a big place like Atlanta. Was she okay, Mrs. Mathews?"

"Please, call me Shelby." Based on their concern Shelby realized that Amber's parents were far from disowning their daughter. "She appeared fine, clean. I mean she's taking care of herself. She said she had gone to the restaurant near the hotel several times to eat and she had mentioned that she had applied for a job there."

"Why is she taking a job there? Why doesn't she just come home to her family?"

Charley spoke out. "Elsa Mae, she isn't coming home because she thinks the family doesn't want her back."

"That's correct, Charley. While I was talking with Amber, she told me in confidence that she didn't believe that her family could ever take her back because she'd run off with Paul. I tried to tell her that probably wasn't true, but I think she felt like she needed to prove something not only to you, but to herself."

"Oh, Charley, we have to do something, she's all alone in that big city. She's only seventeen years old and she's never been any place but Odessa."

"I figured that when I was talking with her and that is why I'm here. Atlanta is a nice place, but you're right, it's a big city. Someone like Amber… well…she could easily get swallowed up by the criminal elements of city life. I gave her some money and paid for a week at the hotel to help her out, but I'm sure by now that money has run out. I really like Amber and I'm just concerned that she might get mixed up with the wrong kind of people and end up doing things she wouldn't normally do if she were back here in Odessa."

"I agree with you, Shelby. I think I should go to Atlanta right away and bring her home," Charley said.

Elsa Mae wasn't sure that was the best idea. "Charley, don't you think Josh or one of the boys should go? After all, you haven't been feeling really well lately and they are younger."

"No, Elsa Mae, I'm fine. She wouldn't listen to the boys anyway, especially not Josh. No, I need to go and bring her home." Charley looked at Shelby. "Can you give me the name of the hotel she was staying at and the restaurant she said she was going to go to work for? I'm going to book a flight tonight and go to Atlanta and find her."

"Do you have a pen and some paper?" Shelby asked.

Elsa Mae went to the desk in the hallway and got the items Shelby requested. Shelby wrote down the information. "I put my name and phone number on there, too. If you need to contact me about anything, please feel free. Amber is a bright girl. I just don't want anything bad to happen to her."

Charley and Elsa Mae walked Shelby to the door. "Thank you so much for letting us know about Amber, we truly appreciate it."

"No, problem. I left my number with her as well, so if I hear from her I will let you know. Please, though, don't tell her that I told you where she is at; she might not trust me again."

Charley shook Shelby's hand. "You have our word, and please let us know if you hear anything more from her."

Shelby stepped down off the porch. "I definitely will."

◊◊◊

"Try this, Amber, it will make you feel so good." Zeke handed Amber the marijuana joint.

Amber had been drinking, but wasn't sure she wanted to smoke with Zeke. She had smoked marijuana with her friends back in Odessa; in fact, she had done a lot of different kinds of drugs, but she hadn't had the money for most kinds of drugs, so she had only done them when other people paid for them.

"Fine, the way things are going lately, I need something to help me forget everything." Amber looked at the joint, took it from Zeke, and puffed. As hard as she had tried, she just hadn't been able to make it on her own without Zeke's help.

"The dope will ease your stress." Zeke leaned over Amber and kissed her after she had passed the joint on to Joe. "Stop it, Zeke, you agreed we would just be roommates."

Zeke's persistence toward Amber had become excessive lately, especially since he had been paying a lot of her bills. "Look, Amber, I'm tired of you pushing me away. It's time you stop acting like such a bitch. I've been paying all your bills and taking care of you. It's time I get something in return for it."

Amber was on the couch, Zeke reached down and pulled Amber up off the couch and pulled her toward his bedroom. Amber tried to pull away from him, but he was too strong. "Leave me alone, Zeke. I don't owe you anything. You offered to help me out, and I told you I would pay you back when I got another job."

"Too late, Amber, it's time to pay up. I'm not waiting any longer for you."

Amber screamed, "Stop him, Joe; stop him; Kyle! He's going to rape me! Stop him, please!"

Joe and Kyle laughed as their friend dragged Amber away kicking and screaming. "Don't make too much noise in there, you guys. The game is on and we don't want to be interrupted by you two getting it on," Joe shouted.

Zeke pushed Amber onto his bed and ripped off her shirt. He tore away her bra and fondled her small breasts. Then, he pinned her down on the bed with her hands above her head while he removed her shorts, and pulled off her panties. Amber fought with all her strength against Zeke's strong arms, but to no avail.

Once he had finished using his mouth on her breasts and rubbing his hands all over her body, he undid his pants and forced his body between Amber's legs. Amber screamed and twisted on the bed as Zeke forced himself deep inside of her. "Now, doesn't that feel nice? I've been waiting to be inside of you for so long, and it's been well worth the wait."

He moved in and out of Amber's body with rapid force and deep thrusts, causing Amber's small body to jolt against his force until he found release. After Zeke gave way to his lust, he laid in relief on top of Amber. "Oh, baby, that was great. Wait a few minutes and we will do it again. This time I will wait for you to get off. See? I told you we were meant for each other."

Amber felt sick and wanted to vomit, but the weight of Zeke's body on top of her kept her from moving no matter how hard she tried to get away.

It was no use. She quietly gave up her fight with Zeke. He was twice her size and she had no way of keeping him from taking her again by force. She laid in silence under the monster that had just raped her. Tears streamed down her face as she realized that no one really cared about her, that her life wasn't worth anything, and that she was nothing but a piece of ass for men to use as they pleased. *How many times have I allowed myself to be used by men this way? I'm worthless; the world has no use for me. There's no use in fighting it anymore.* Right then and there she decided that she might have to exist, but she didn't need to feel anything ever again.

Zeke didn't notice the tears on Amber's face when he rolled off of her. He sat up on the bed for a few minutes and then removed the rest of his clothing. He turned to Amber and removed the rest of her clothing. This time he saw the tear stains on her face, but she wasn't fighting him anymore. "Oh come on, baby, don't cry. It was wonderful for me, and I'm going to make it wonderful for you. Look, he's already wanting you again."

Zeke wiped Amber's face with his hand. Then he took both of his hands and rubbed over every part of Amber's body. "Come on, sugar, doesn't that feel nice? Look, I can feel it, you want me again don't you?"

Amber just lay there while Zeke put his body between her legs again. He didn't have to force himself on her this time. He moved himself in and out of her without her participation. "Oh yeah, baby, isn't this good? Come on, baby, I can feel how much you want me. Come on, let it go baby."

Zeke took Amber over and over again for the entire night. Amber just let him do whatever he wanted to do to her and said nothing. Zeke might have control of her body but he didn't have control of her thoughts or her words.

When morning came, Amber woke on the edge of an empty bed. Zeke had left her alone finally. She gathered her ripped clothes and was about to leave his room when Zeke came back through the door with coffee. "Here, baby, I brought you some coffee. Oh, don't worry with those clothes right now. We are going to move your things into my room anyway. Joe wants his bedroom back and since we are sleeping together now, I figure he might as well have it back."

Amber threw her clothes on the floor and sat on the bed. "Whatever, Zeke. Can I go take a shower, please?"

Zeke handed Amber her cup of coffee and then kissed her on her cheek. "Sure, baby, but why don't you just drink this hot cup of coffee first? Oh, and if you have any intentions of telling anyone, like the police, that I raped you, remember Joe and Kyle were here, and you had been drinking, and well, one thing led to another. We just ended up in bed. No one will ever believe that we didn't have wonderful sex together."

Amber sipped at the coffee and felt like she wanted to die. Her whole body felt like she'd been hit by a truck. "Don't worry, I won't say anything."

"Good. Now after you finish your coffee, take a shower. I want you to meet some of my friends at a party tonight."

"I have to work at the restaurant tonight, Zeke."

"Not any more, baby. I'm going to take care of you from now on. No girl of mine is going to sling hash."

Amber went into the shower and let the water cascade on top of her head and over her body. She was numb, but the water from the shower head stung her body. She cried, but the falling water quickly washed the tears off her face. *Where am I? How did I get here? What does it matter? No one cares about me.*

She stopped crying and pushed all of her feelings deep down inside of herself. *I'll stay numb and not feel anything ever again. I don't have to do anything or prove anything to anyone ever again.* Her body might still be moving around in the world, but she wasn't there anymore. She was safe, in a quiet secluded place in her mind where no one and nothing could ever touch her again.

◊◊◊

Charley entered the lobby of the hotel and approached the front desk.

"Can I help you, sir?"

"Yes, I was wondering if a girl named Amber Nichols is still registered here?"

"We are not supposed to give out information about our guests; it's a security policy."

"She's my daughter and she's gone missing. We received information from someone that met her here, and I would like to find out if she's still here so I can take her home."

The clerk looked at her computer. "I understand. Is she a minor?"

"Yes."

"Let me see what I can find out." No. I'm sorry, sir. We don't have any-one by that name registered with us right now. Do you know what room she might have been staying in while she was here?"

"No, I don't know that information, but it was about a month or so ago."

The clerk looked again at her computer.

Another clerk came to the desk from the back office. "Hi, how are you, sir? Can I help with anything, Barbra?"

Barbra explained to the other receptionist what Charley wanted. "Oh, I remember that young lady. She was in room 459 and another customer who was staying with us paid for her to stay another week. But after that week was up she left, sir. I'm not sure where she went; she never said anything. I do re-member that she got a job at that restaurant across the parking lot there." The woman pointed toward the restaurant. "Maybe you can go over and see if she is still working there. I wish we could be more help, but that's all we know."

"Okay, well thank you. I'll go check with them at the restaurant." Charley tipped his hat to the ladies. "Thank you again."

"Sure, no problem. We hope you find her. She was a really nice girl."

Charley waved at the women as he walked out the doors of the hotel.

In the restaurant Charley looked around to see if he could see Amber. "How many in your party, sir?"

"Oh, I don't want a table. I was looking for a young lady who works here."

"Who's that?"

Charley pointed to the hotel across the parking lot. "Her name is Amber Nichols, and I'm her father. I was told by the people over at that hotel that she might be working here."

Teresa put down the menu she had picked up for Charley. "She doesn't work here anymore, sir. She was supposed to work last Friday night, but she never showed up. In fact, she hasn't been back since. Come to think of it, neither has the guys she's been sharing an apartment with the last few weeks. I told her to be careful with those guys, but she thought she could handle them."

"Do you know where they live?"

"No. But I do know that Zeke, the ringleader of the group, has been in trouble with the law. Maybe if you check with the police department, they'll be able to tell you where he lives."

"Okay, thank you."

"I'm sorry I couldn't be of more help, and if you find her, please tell her that Teresa has been worried about her."

"I will, thank you." Charley slowly walked out of the restaurant. He walked to his rental car. *Where is my little girl? What has happened to her?* He felt a twinge of pain go through his body. Something went wrong with Amber and he wasn't there to protect her.

◊◊◊

"Yes, my name is Charles Nichols and I'm from Odessa Texas. I need to speak with someone that can help me find my daughter." The police station was crowded—busy with police officers escorting prisoners to the back of the building, people waiting to talk with police officers in the front of the building, and others standing in line like Charley, trying to tell the desk sergeant what he needed from the police.

"How old is your daughter?"

"She is seventeen."

"Here take this number, sit over there with those people, and we will get to you when we can."

Charley took the number and sat among the large group of people.

CHAPTER THIRTEEN

Amber sat quietly on the couch at Zeke's friend's place. There was a crowd of people at this party, just like all the other parties he had forced her to attend over the last couple of weeks. Normally, Zeke left her alone while he drank and got stoned. Then, when they got back to the apartment he would force her to perform oral sex on him or have sex until he fell asleep on top of her. She would roll his limp body away from hers and then crawl to the closet where she would sleep on the floor in peace.

Tonight was different. Zeke and two of his buddies came to the couch where Amber was sitting. Zeke had a needle in his hand. Before Amber had a chance to resist, Zeke's friends grabbed Amber's arms and legs. "This won't hurt a bit, baby. You're going to love it, and maybe you will start acting nice instead of being such a cold fish."

"Don't, Zeke. I don't want that. I'll do whatever you want. I'll even enjoy it, I promise."

"Well, you already do everything I tell you. Now you're going to do everything I tell you and enjoy it.

"She's going to be a gold mine, Zeke. You keep her juiced up like that, and she'll make you a load of money," Kyle said.

"Shades better not find out what you're up to. He'll take it to Dante," Joe warned.

Zeke shrugged.

"Man, you are so lucky to find one that's pretty, young, and not fat," Kyle said.

"Yeah, and she has all her teeth, too."

Zeke and his friends laughed.

◊◊◊

Soon after Zeke and Amber returned to his apartment, they heard a knock on the door. "Shit," Zeke said, "who could that be?" He hoped it wasn't Shades. He dragged Amber toward the bedroom. "If it's Shades, I'm not here. Cover for me," he said and closed the bedroom door.

Zeke got up and looked through the peephole and then walked over to the closed door. "It's not Shades; it's some old man with a cop."

Zeke was shaken a bit that the cops were at his door, but right now he'd rather deal with cops than with Shades. "I'll get it."

Zeke went over to the front door and opened it slightly with the chain still on the door. "Yeah, what do you want?"

The police officer spoke for Charley. "This man is looking for his daughter Amber Nichols, and we've been told that she's staying here with you."

Zeke laughed. "There ain't no bitch up in here, old man. You got some wrong information."

Charley tried to reason with Zeke. "Have you seen her, sir? The waitresses at the restaurant near the hotel said you used to talk to her there. She is only seventeen years old, young man, and her family misses her."

"Look, I might have talked to her. I talk to a lot of women, but she ain't here. Now, you're interrupting my dinner."

Before Zeke could close the door the cop put his foot in the opening. "How about you let me have a look inside?"

"How about you get a warrant?" Zeke pushed the door shut and forced the cop to remove his foot.

"I'm sorry, Mr. Nichols, but if she's in there, we will have to try and get a warrant, and that's tough to do."

Charley leaned up against the wall in the dark hallway. "I understand, sir. I think I will hang around for a while downstairs in my car and see if I can catch her coming out of the building. I really appreciate your help."

The officer pushed the button on his radio attached to his shoulder. "Unit 415, 10-8."

Charley walked with the officer down to the ground floor of the apartment complex. "You can sit outside the building and watch, Mr. Nichols, but be careful around here. This neighborhood is rough, and I suggest that if you do spot your daughter that you give me a call and I'll help you make contact with her." The officer handed Charley a business card with his information on it. "I wish I could have done more for you, Mr. Nichols. I have two daughters myself and I would be doing just what you're doing if it were me."

"Thank you, sir. I will keep this handy."

Before the officer got into his patrol unit he warned Charley again about the neighborhood and the people he was dealing with. "Zeke is a bad character, Mr. Nichols, stay clear of him. He's been implicated in several possible murder and rape cases. He's a known drug dealer and pimp. If your daughter is involved with him, she's in a really bad situation. Don't try to save her by yourself; call me if you spot her. Okay?"

"Okay, I will."

Charley sat in front of the apartment building for several hours. He never saw Amber go in or out of the building. He saw several strange looking characters enter and leave the place but not his Amber.

When Charley couldn't keep awake any longer, he went back to his hotel. He slept for several hours and then went back to the apartment complex. Elsa Mae called him several times while he sat waiting to see if he'd spotted their girl. It was difficult for Charley to imagine Amber was in danger and he couldn't do anything about it.

Close to midnight, Charley was ready to head to his hotel when Zeke appeared at the front door of the apartment building with two other men. One of the men had his arm wrapped around a small figure of a person, but Charley couldn't tell if it was a woman or a small man. The person was wearing a hoodie over his or her head. Charley decided that he needed to find out if it was Amber. He got out of his car and walked toward the four subjects.

Zeke recognized the man and quickly blocked his path to the covered individual. He motioned for Joe and Kyle to put Amber into a waiting taxi. "Wait just a minute, old man. Just what do you think you're doing?" Zeke pushed at Charley's chest. "I thought I told you to take a hike. It would be in your best interest to leave my city and never come back. I don't know who your daughter is, and I don't care that she's missing. If you don't get out of here now, I'll make sure you never come back, ever." Zeke pushed Charley so hard that he ended up falling to the ground. "Go away, old, man. I mean it."

"I just want to make sure that's not my daughter."

"It's not, trust me. It's not your precious little baby girl."

Zeke got in the taxi with the others and left Charley on the ground. Charley picked himself up off the ground and called the police officer.

"This is Charles Nichols. Do you remember me? I'm the man looking for his daughter."

"Oh yes, Mr. Nichols. What can I do for you?"

"I saw her, sir, or at least I think it was her, and that Zeke character put her in a taxi with a couple of other men. The taxi number is 5876. Can you check and see where they took her?"

"Mr. Nichols, did you see her for sure?"

"Well, no. They had a hoodie over her head, but the body looked like her."

"I'm sorry, Mr. Nichols, even if you did see her, I have to have a reason to interfere with their activity. Did this person appear to be in trouble or appear to be injured?"

"No, but they surrounded her and it was hard to get close."

"Did you make contact with them Mr. Nichols?"

"Yes, but I had to, they were leaving."

"I told you not to make contact, you're just asking for trouble. Now, I can't make you go home and let us try and find Amber ourselves, but I'm telling you that if you aren't careful you could end up dead."

Charley was disappointed. "I'm already dead knowing that my baby girl is out here somewhere and that she might be in trouble."

He knew he didn't want to go home, but he was in over his head in this world that Amber had gotten herself mixed up in. Charley drove his car back to his hotel. He didn't want to leave Amber alone in this big city, but what else could he do? The police obviously weren't going to help, and he couldn't find her on his own. He had to go home; he had no choice.

◊◊◊

Over time, Zeke got Amber hooked on heroin and became her pimp. The drugs kept Amber from caring about what was happening to her body and under Zeke's control. As long as she was juiced she didn't think about her family or the life she once knew. Zeke was happy with the profits from Amber, and everything seemed to be working in his favor, until Shades met her.

◊◊◊

Charley's family had come to the house after Elsa Mae called to let them know that their father was home from Atlanta. "Pops, what were you thinking going to Atlanta without some of us? Mama said you came home with a big bruise on your back. How did you get that?"

Charley sat down in his recliner. "I went to find your baby sister and I slipped on the sidewalk. Your mother has a vivid imagination."

Josh continued to interrogate his father. "Did you find her, Dad? Why bother with her any more? She is exactly where she deserves to be, leaving her family and her children the way she did. Don't you think it's time to just let her go, Pops?"

Charley couldn't believe what he was hearing. "You have no idea what terrible danger she's in or what horrible things might be happening to her. You need to remember she is your flesh and blood, and we take care of our own, no matter what. When I heal back up, I'm going back there to look for her again."

Josh huffed and moved away from his father. He gathered with his two younger brothers at the table. "It's useless. He won't even listen to reason. We can't let him go back there by himself again. If he's determined to go back, some of us will have to go with him."

Roger fiddled with his fork. "I don't think we will have to worry about him going back there any time soon. Mama told me earlier today that he hasn't been feeling very well and that bruise on his back side isn't the only thing wrong."

"Seriously? Mama hasn't said anything to me about Pop's health."

"I don't know. She wouldn't elaborate. She said Pops doesn't want her talking to us about it. That he's fine and won't be treated like a sickly old man."

"This stuff with Amber has really taken a toll on him. It's no wonder he's having health problems, but Mama says he won't go to the doctor or slow down at work," Alex said.

Josh didn't know what to think as he sat with his brothers and drank iced tea. Amber had caused so much trouble for their family, and he felt it was time to leave her to her own demons. But his father couldn't let go of Amber, and now her behavior was causing his dad's health to fail. He wished he could get his hands on Amber and strangle her.

CHAPTER FOURTEEN

"Look, asshole, I've been bringing you loads of this shit for weeks and the price just went up. I don't know if you're using it or if you're selling it, but my bosses raised the price on me and now I'm passing it on to you. You know shit rolls downhill, and you're at the bottom."

Zeke was a low-level pusher who had overstepped his boundaries when he conned Amber into living with him. His handler Shades and his boss Dante were livid when they learned that their underling had ventured into his own business.

"Come on, Shades. Can't you give me a break?"

"You're lucky I don't break your legs. Do you think I'm stupid? You think I don't know about that girl?"

"She's a real moneymaker, but she can't perform without being loaded. I have to keep her high all the time. I wasn't trying to keep her from you," Zeke lied. "I was getting her ready, kind of a gift for Dante."

"You're an idiot, Zeke. Give her to me before Dante gets involved."

"No way, man. She's my goldmine. I'm ready for more."

"How the hell did you get a good looking girl to work for you? What did you do?" Shades grabbed Zeke by the collar and pinned him up against the wall. He pressed a switchblade to his throat.

Zeke still didn't answer Shades's questions.

Shades drew the blade across Zeke's jawline—a cut so fine the blood seeped out without dripping. It was enough for Zeke to tell Shades everything.

"Are you out of your fucking mind? If Dante doesn't get to you first, the cops will get you for trafficking a minor." He released Zeke and he slid down the side of the wall.

Out of Shades's grip, Zeke became defiant. "Fuck you, Shades. Fuck Dante. That asshole thinks he can run my business and raise the prices of things whenever he wants to. I'm done with him. I'm going up north. See how he likes losing my business. Son-of-a-bitch thinks he can come over here and use my property whenever he wants. That's not going to happen."

Shades pulled a handkerchief out of his pocket and wiped Zeke's blood off his hands. He put it and the switchblade back in his coat pocket and turned for the door. "We'll see about that."

◊◊◊

Shades waited for Dante to enter the room before he stood. He shook hands with his boss. "Sir, we have a problem in the district, and I think you should know about it before it comes down on us. It's Zeke."

Dante poured himself a glass of scotch. "Zeke—what has he done now?"

"Well, sir, he's got a minor—keeps her high. Thinks he can be a big time pimp."

"This is not a good thing. Do the cops have any idea about what he has done?"

"No, not that I know of so far. But that doesn't mean they won't find out, especially if this girl has a family that might go looking for her."

Dante ran his fingers around his glass. "This is definitely a problem. I suggest you take her away from him any way you can, even if you have to use some of my guys to break a few bones. Clean her up and put her on the truck circuit, don't work her too much at first, keep her wanting the shit so that she will have to work for it. Put some fear into her so she won't talk. We'll keep her working, but she won't be in our town."

"Okay, Dante. I will take care of it tomorrow."

◊◊◊

Zeke entered his apartment with a bag of Chinese takeout. He stopped dead in his tracks when he saw Shades and four of his men sitting in his living room. He put the food on the counter and noticed that the door to his bedroom was open. Joe and Kyle were nowhere in sight. He had a red bandanna around his neck in an attempt to cover the incision Shades had left at his last visit.

"What can I do for you, Shades? It would have been nice if you'd given me some notice that you were coming." He tried to sound nonchalant.

Shades smirked. "I don't need an appointment to visit, do I Zeke?" Shades stood and moved toward Zeke. "I have a message for you from Dante. You are to give me that girl without a fight so that I can get her out of this town."

"I have everything under control, Shades. Take a look for yourself. She is in that room and even with the door open she doesn't leave. I take her to her jobs every night and bring her home. She hasn't caused me any problems."

"Maybe not yet Zeke, but when she gets busted, and she will eventually get busted, then you will bring down the whole operation. No, Dante wants me to take her away and make sure she doesn't become a problem."

"No, you can't have her; she's making me a lot of money. I won't let you take her."

"Have it your way, Zeke, but she is leaving with me. Now, my boys are going in there and getting her and her things. If you try to stop them, they will start breaking your bones."

"Come on, Shades, you can't take her. I'm making good money. Everyone wants them young and pretty."

"That's the point, Zeke. Boys, get her for me, please."

Zeke moved in front of his bedroom door. One of Shades's men picked Zeke up and threw him out of the way. Zeke landed on the floor against the kitchen wall. Zeke tried to get up and fight against the men as they entered his room and removed Amber and what few things they could find that belonged to her. Shades went over to where Zeke had landed. He put his foot on Zeke's private area. "Stay down, Zeke, or I'll make sure you will never be able to rape another woman again."

Zeke realized that he could not stop Shades and his men from taking Amber away. "Fine, take her, she was costing me an arm and leg in heroin anyway. Now you can pay for her shit."

Shades and his men left Zeke's apartment with Amber. She was so strung out on heroin that one of the men had to carry her out of the building and put her in Shades's vehicle. Amber had no idea where she was or what was going on.

◊◊◊

Shades carried Amber into his house and laid her down on the couch. "Crystal, this is Amber. She's high as a kite on heroin. I want you to bring her down slowly and clean her up. She's been working for Zeke; he ganged her in and she's under age. When you get her straightened out, Dante wants her on the truck pipe or put out on service in another district. We don't want this heat coming down on the family."

"I got it, Shades."

Shades took off his suit coat. "I'm going to the apartment building for a while. I have some customers showing up in about an hour. Don't let her out of your sight. Dante doesn't want to have to kill her, but if she goes to the cops or her family before we have a chance to clean her up, it could come to that for her."

Crystal moved Amber's hair away from her forehead and looked at the young face. "Oh, Shades, she's so young. Why didn't you take Zeke out for doing this? You know he's bad news and always has been."

Shades went to his front door. "Just clean her up, Crystal, and let me deal with the business."

After getting a moist towel, Crystal sat next to Amber on the couch. She wiped her face with the towel and brushed her hair. "Poor little thing, how in the world did you end up in all this mess? You're so young and beautiful, with your whole life ahead of you. This is no place for a pretty little thing like you."

◊◊◊

"Where the fuck were you two while Shades and goons where here taking Amber from me? You two are supposed to be my bodyguards against people like Shades. What the hell good are you, and why are you living in my apartment if you're not going to take care of me? Maybe both of you need to clear your shit out of here."

Joe and Kyle both stood firm in front of Zeke. "Bullshit, Zeke. We pay to live here and we never agreed to guard anyone, least of all you," Joe said.

"Yeah, and if you think for one second we are going to stand up to Shades's or Dante's men, you're out of your mind." Kyle pushed Zeke out of the way and plopped down on the couch. "You can go to hell, Zeke. I paid my rent for the month and I'm staying right here."

Joe didn't push Zeke, but he found his way to a chair in the living room. He turned on the television. "You never should have brought that girl here, Zeke. I heard from some of Dante's handlers that Dante is really pissed at you. He thinks your little stunt with Amber is going to bring heat on the family. You'd better watch your back."

Zeke flew into a sudden rage and started throwing anything he could find at Joe and Kyle. "Fuck both of you! Fuck Dante and fuck Shades! They just wanted the money I was making with that whore for themselves!" Zeke went to the door of the apartment and opened it. "You're the ones that need to watch your backs, and the same goes for Shades and Dante! I promise, I will get every last one of you, then I will get Amber back!"

Kyle shook his head. "That asshole is completely out of his mind. He's going to end up getting himself killed."

Joe changed the channel on the television. "Yeah, I think maybe we'd better find another place to live. Do you want to be roommates?"

"I guess so."

CHAPTER FIFTEEN

"**C**ome on, honey, Shades wants you in his office right now." Crystal pushed Amber toward the bedroom door.

"Please, Crystal, I don't want to meet him. I want to go home." Tears streamed down her face.

Crystal grabbed Amber's hand. "Look, sugar, I know you're scared and everything, but you belong to Shades now. I'll be there with you, and you'll see that working for Shades ain't so bad. He's actually a really nice guy, as long as you do what he tells you."

Amber tried to resist again, at that moment Shades walked to through the bedroom doorway and over to Amber. "What seems to be the problem Crystal? I thought I told you to bring her to me?"

Crystal let go of Amber's hand to go stand by Shades. "I've been trying, Shades, but she wouldn't leave this room."

Shades moved closer to Amber and lifted her face so she was looking into his dark eyes. "I know you've had a rough time these last few weeks, coming down off that shit Zeke was giving you. I understand that you want to go home, wherever that might be. But you can't—not now."

Shades pointed out different areas around the room. "You see all this? This belongs to me, and I belong to a man named Dante. Since I've been taking care of you, you belong to me and by proxy to Dante."

Amber broke away from Shades's grip on her chin. "I appreciate you helping to get me away from Zeke, and helping to get me off the shit he was giving me, but I don't belong to anyone and I want to go home."

Shades crossed his large hands in front of his chest. "You do belong to me, and going home is out of the question—for now. I've been extremely patient with you, but it's time for you to understand what choices you have in this world you now find yourself in—my world. You will do exactly as I tell you. Right now you will work and be paid. You'll live comfortably, meaning you'll have food, clothing, and anything you need. You do as you're told and you may get a chance to see your family from time to time. If you disobey me, you will be shot and thrown into the St. Laurence River. The choice is yours. You have until tomorrow morning to decide."

Shades turned to leave the bedroom, then paused. "Crystal will explain to you everything that I expect and all the rules that will prevent you from taking that swim."

Amber didn't say a word, she fell to the floor and cried with deep sobs. Crystal decided to leave her alone for a while and let her decide what she wanted.

◊◊◊

Amber slept on the floor most of the night. Crystal woke her up the next morning. She helped Amber off the floor and into her bed.

"Thank you so much, Crystal, for helping me these last few weeks. You remind me of my sister, Traci," Amber said.

Crystal pulled back the blankets and Amber slid into the clean sheets. "Thanks isn't necessary, sweet little Amber. The first day you came into this house and I saw what Zeke had done to you, I knew that I would love you. I'm sorry you have found yourself mixed up in this dark side of the world. You don't belong here, I know that, but Shades really has no choice in the matter. Dante made it perfectly clear that you either worked for them or you had to die."

"But why? Why can't they just let me go home? I won't say anything to anyone about what's happened to me. I am so ashamed of everything that I don't want my family to know anything about any of it."

"Oh, I know how you feel. Shades pulled me out of a similar situation. I went to work for him. I became his number one girl and everything has been pretty good ever since. But I came from a poor family; I got mixed up with a guy like Zeke years ago. I was real ashamed about what I had allowed myself to get trapped into doing. He bought me things, took care of me, but then he turned on me. He shared me with his friends, beat me, forced me to take drugs, and then had his friend's gang rape me to break my spirit. After that, he forced me into prostitution on a full-time basis. He gave me just enough food, money, and clothing to keep me in indebted to him."

"That's exactly what was happening to me. So how did you get out?"

"Shades. He was just coming up with Dante and he was trying to get rid of some of the lowlifes that were causing problems for the family. The man I was working for was a monster, and when Shades tried to force him to clean up his act and to treat his working girls better, the guy threatened to kill him. Dante told Shades to make him disappear and Shades did."

"But if Shades is such a great guy, why won't he just let me go?"

"Because you know too much. You have been on the inside of Dante's organization, and that knowledge is dangerous to anyone that has it. Dante is a real high roller; he deals with government people, and has men inside various police forces. He deals with a lot of people from other countries, too. Most everything he does is black market or drugs. He doesn't deal with us working girls much, but he gets his cut of the profits from his boys."

"I promise I won't tell a soul about anything that I've seen or anything that I know."

"I know, sweetie, but they won't take that chance. You could bring the whole empire to its knees. So you either work for them or you die—there aren't other choices."

"What do I have to do? Do I have to continue being a prostitute?"

"No, Shades doesn't push being a "working girl" on anyone. He won't stop you from making money from being a "pro," and trust me, there is some big money in it. But your main job with Shades will be delivering his products to his customers. It's really not all that hard. You run with a small group of girls, and each of you is given a portion of the product. Then you each either hook up with a trucker, or find some other way to get the products to a certain location at a certain time. Most of the girls use the truckers because it's free, and they can make extra money "working" the truckers. See, if you decide not to be what we call a "jumper," then it's on you to pay for your way to the delivery point. So, you lose some of your money if you don't jump your way there."

Amber listened carefully as Crystal explained how things worked.

"You also have to be careful not to get busted with Shades's stuff. You see, they check bags everywhere now, especially public transportation, like buses. Shades will beat you to death if you lose any of his stuff. I've only seen him beat one girl the whole time I've been with him. But she was a real coke head, which made her careless and stupid."

"How do you 'jump'?"

"Oh, jumping is easy, you just go to the truck stops, wherever you are, and ask the truckers for a ride to the place you're going. It usually doesn't take long to get a ride, being a woman, most truckers are lonely and like the company. Then you take your ride with the trucker, meet up with the others in your group at the delivery point, hand your portion of the product to the lead girl, get a room or stay with a trucker and then wait on your next drop. It will usually be waiting for you, but sometimes you have to find something to do for a couple of days. That's it, you just keep doing that until Shades gives you two weeks off. He always gives his girls two week off about every three months."

"So, I don't have to prostitute myself? I don't have to take drugs? Will he let me go home for my two weeks off?"

"Well, you don't have to be a "working girl," but like I told you, it sure made me a lot of money when I was jumping. As for the drugs, you don't have to do anything you don't want to do, but if you do take drugs, you have to pay for them. I found that a little heroin helped me be a better "working girl," but it can become a habit and cost you a lot of your own money. So, if you can't control it, don't use it. As for letting you use your time off to go home, I really doubt that Shades will let you do that right away. He's going to have to learn to trust you. If you become a really good jumper, he will probably let you go home in a year or so."

"A year! I can't wait that long to go home. I miss my family and my kids."

"You got kids? You look too young to have kids."

"I have two; they are just babies. I was stupid and fell for a man that told me he loved me and wanted to show me the world. I left my babies with my parents and ran away with him like a total idiot. He abandoned me here in Atlanta; that's how I ended up meeting Zeke. I miss them so much. I just want to go back and pretend these last six months of my life never happened."

Crystal hugged Amber. "I know exactly how you feel, sweetie. We have so much in common. I don't have any children though. I got pregnant once and when the man that I worked for before Shades found out, he made me get an abortion. The abortion was done by a quack doctor and I lost my ability to have babies."

"I'm so sorry, Crystal."

"No need. With the profession I'm in, it has been a blessing not to have children. But I think I have become a mother to a lot of the girls around here. I will even be a mother figure to you, if you will give me a chance."

"Oh, I think you're a great mother, Crystal." Amber hugged her new friend. "Not to pry, Crystal, but do you still jump?"

"Oh, no way, sugar. I'm too old for that. I'm just Shades's girl now. I take care of things around his house and I take care of his girls. I even take care of him every once in a while. He's kind of like a husband to me, except I doubt he will ever marry me." Crystal laughed.

"So have you decided what you will tell Shades tomorrow?" Crystal asked. "Please tell me you will give jumping a try. I know it's not the life you want for yourself, but it's better than floating in the river face down." Crystal touched Amber on the cheek. "I couldn't imagine those beautiful eyes without life in them."

Amber thought about it for a few moments. "I really don't have a choice. How long do I have to stay working for Shades? Will he ever let me go home?"

"I don't know that, Amber. It's up to Shades. But he usually lets the girls go when they start showing their age. He kept me and several of the older girls living here for a while, but some of the girls also married into the family. You're real young, so don't plan on that happening for a while."

Amber didn't like that answer, but knew she didn't have any options. She was either going to work for Shades or she was going to die. She would have to work for him if she ever hoped to see her children again. "I guess I'll learn to be a jumper. Will you be able to teach me to be a good one?"

Crystal was happy with Amber's choice. "I'm so glad, sweetie. I will help you and give you all the advice I can to make you're one of Shades's best girls."

◊◊◊

"She's calmed down, Shades, and has agreed to work." Crystal crawled into Shades's bed and put her head on his chest. Shades had been looking over some papers that he put away when Crystal came into the room.

Shades kissed Crystal's head. "You are the best. I'm so glad you were able to convince her to jump instead of me having to take her out. She's too pretty to be a floater."

"I know, Shades. You were right about her; she has a family and she even has some kids. Zeke did a real number on her. I wish you would get rid of that guy. I really like this little girl and I feel sorry for her."

"I know you do, baby, but Dante was adamant about what he wanted done with this girl. I can't go against him or I'll become the floater. As for Zeke, his time is coming. Dante is agitated with his behavior. I'm sure he'll l do something that will cause Dante to hang him upside down by his balls soon enough."

"I hope so. Amber wouldn't be here if it weren't for that bastard."

Shades kissed Crystal and then covered her up with the blanket. They fell asleep until morning.

◊◊◊

Shelby pushed the button on the screen of the radio panel for her Bluetooth. She pushed Jack's number. "Hi baby, how're you doing without me?"

"I miss you, and wish you were here. Where are you? When will you be home?"

"Well, I'm on my way to location to deliver my load. Then they want me to head to South Carolina and pick up a load of sand I've never heard of

123

before. It's another type of manufactured ceramic sand. I should be home in about four days, depending on how long it takes to get this load off at location."

"I'm glad you'll be back soon. It's beginning to get lonely around here."

"I'm sorry, baby. I'll be home as fast as this little truck of ours will go. Well, maybe not that fast."

"Yeah, that might not be the best plan. You've been working so much lately that we already have half the truck paid off. We really don't need to pay for a ticket or add points to your driving record."

"Nah, wouldn't want to do that. Have you heard from the boys today? Jack Junior called me yesterday, and so did Mark, but I haven't heard from Steven in a couple days."

"Yeah, in fact Steven just left the house about fifteen minutes ago. We had breakfast together. He was wondering when you would be back. He and Jasmine want to talk to us about something when you get home."

"Are you thinking what I'm thinking? They've been dating a long time."

"Yep, I'm thinking they are fixin' to get hitched."

"Can you believe it, Jack? All three of our boys are going to be married. Jack Junior has given us six grand babies, Mark has four now, and I wonder how many Steven will bless us with in the next few years."

"I don't know, baby, but we are blessed, that's for sure. Not so good on the pocketbook during the Christmas holidays though." Jack laughed.

"Oh, Jack, think of how boring Christmas would be without our children and grandchildren. Remember what you told me years ago when we were struggling to make ends meet? 'Don't worry, babe, it's only money.'"

"Oh, I remember, and I wish I could take it back. Especially when my sweet darling wants to go shopping for all those rug rats."

"Too late, can't take it back. Don't forget you like buying for them, too."

"Oh, I know. Just hurry up and get your pretty little butt home."

"Alright, baby. I'll let you know when I leave location and head south. Miss you and love you."

"Miss and love you, too."

CHAPTER SIXTEEN

The air breaks on the truck hissed as Damian released them. "Here you go, little darling, we have arrived at our destination—Buffalo, New York."

Amber was resting in the sleeper of Damian's truck. She yawned, got up, slipped on her backpack and appeared from behind the leather curtain. She had her shoes in one hand and her socks in the other. "Thank you, Damian, for the lift. Are you going to be around for a couple days?"

"Don't know right now, have to wait and see what the quell-com gives me. But if you're asking me for a date, I'd be happy to stick around and go out with you."

Amber sat in the passenger seat and pulled on her shoes. She laughed. "Damian, you're a trip. I was just thinking that if you were going to be around in couple of days, I could pick up another ride from you, if we were going in the same direction."

Damian put on a sad puppy dog face, feigning disappointment. "So, all you want me for is my truck?"

Amber laughed as she reached for the handle on the door. "Like I said, Damian, you're a trip. I'll look for your truck when I get done with my job. If you're here, I'll ask you for a ride."

Damian stood between his seats and made a courteous bow toward Amber as she exited his truck. "I look forward to the opportunity of serving you again, my lady."

Amber rolled her eyes and smiled as she walked away from Damian's rig. "A trip, Damian, a real trip."

The year had gone by fast, Amber had quickly learned how to be a good jumper. Although Shades still owned her, controlled where she went, and what she did, she found working for him tolerable. She would spend her two weeks off from work with Crystal, who had become her surrogate mother, friend, and sister. But as time went on, Amber missed her real family more and more.

Amber's work had taken her to every place imaginable in the United States. She had even gotten a ride into Alaska once. Her favorite trips had been to those towns close to her own hometown. Shades had made it a point not to send her on jumps to Odessa, knowing she would have trouble not making contact with her family until he gave her permission.

As time went along, however, Amber found ways to call her family on the phone without Shades or any of the other girls on her team knowing. The first few calls Amber made to her family she just called and hung up. She eventually got up the nerve up to talk with her mother and sisters. They all encouraged Amber to return home, but Amber let them know that coming home wasn't possible yet. She never let them know why she couldn't come back, but she assured them that she would eventually.

"Here is my package, Cassie." Amber handed the birthday-wrapped package to the team leader.

Cassie took Amber's package and put it into a box with the other presents. "Great, I only have two more left and then we can get our new presents going to New Orleans. It might be a good idea to look for those rides now. I'll give you a call on your cell phones when I have your next gift."

Amber quickly found Damian's rig. She had liked hitching rides with him because he never asked for sex and she felt safe with him. Amber rapped hard on Damian's driver's side door. "Hey, Damian, it's Amber."

Damian came from his sleeper and opened the driver's side door. "Well, I know I've been sleeping, but I haven't been asleep for two days."

Amber laughed and pushed Damian out of the driver's seat so she could sit in his truck. "It's only been a couple of hours, but I already know where I'm supposed to go. Are you going anywhere near New Orleans?"

"Oh, just come in and make yourself comfortable." Damian sat in the passenger seat.

"Well, are you going near New Orleans?"

Damian turned his quell-com toward the passenger seat. "I'm not sure yet, Amber. I haven't checked with the office because I'm on my break. I won't know until morning, but I can put in a request going in that direction."

"Okay, good."

Damian put some information into the quell-com, then he leaned back in his seat. "You know, Amber, I've been giving you rides all over the country for the last eight months. You have never once told me what you do."

Amber thought about how could she tell Damian what she did without really telling him what she did. "I deliver gifts, presents, and packages for people all over the country for this friend of mine."

"Really, what's in the packages?"

"I don't know. I just deliver them."

"Well, why doesn't your friend use the mail system or FedEx or UPS, something like that, instead of you?"

"He doesn't trust the postal system to make the deliveries. He trusts me to get things where they need to go."

Damian shook his head. "You really don't expect me to believe that line of crap, do you?"

Amber took off her shoes and put her feet in Damian's seat. "Yes, because that's what I do," was her snarky reply.

Damian pushed the quell-com out of the way, grabbed one of Amber's feet, and started to rub it. "I want you to know that I have grown very fond of you over these last few months. I like you. I'm worried about you, too. I'm not stupid, Amber, and neither are you. We both know that you're muling drugs across the country for some dope dealer somewhere."

Amber pulled her feet away from Damian, she grabbed her shoes, and attempted to put them on. "I'm delivering presents. Gifts. It would be best for both of us if you remember that."

Damian put his hand on Amber's and tried to stop her from putting on her shoes. "Look, I'm not trying to upset you or make you mad. I just need you to be honest with me and with yourself. I like you too much to see you get hurt, jumping like you are."

Surprised, Amber looked at Damian. "You know about jumping?"

Damian rolled his eyes. "Amber, I have been driving a truck for five years now. Everyone in this industry knows about jumping and jumpers."

Amber pulled her hand away from Damian's and continued putting on her shoes. "Well, if you have known all along what I do, and you don't like it, why do you let me ride with you so much?"

Damian put his hand on hers again and used the other to gently pull Amber's face toward his. He looked at her with soft eyes. "Because I think I am falling in love with you, Amber Nichols."

Amber jerked away, opened the door and slipped out of the truck. "You're out of your mind. I'll find another ride to New Orleans. You can't love me! You can't fall in love with me, I'm no good!"

Damian didn't want to let Amber go, but he knew that he had to for now. When she was ready, she would find him again just like she had over the last eight months.

◊◊◊

"Look, I just need a lift to New Orleans, are you going that way or not?" Amber waited for the toothless, old driver to answer.

"Yeah, I'm going to New Orleans, but what do I get for the ride?" The old man smiled at Amber, revealing the gaps in his mouth between other rotting teeth that were barely left. She hated taking rides from drivers like this one, but she had asked almost every driver in the parking lot.

"Whatever you want."

"Well, hop in, honey. I could use a little comfort during the night." Amber hopped into the truck. She knew that she would have to shoot-up before giving this driver what he wanted, but she had to make the delivery. This was the cost of some of her rides, she used the heroin, as Crystal had taught her, to get through the bad ones.

◊◊◊

"Look, Pops, you need to relax and take care of yourself. Mama said that you aren't doing what the doctors have been telling you. She says you've been trying to go back to work."

"Yes, I need to get out of this bed and go back to work." Charley tried with all of his might to throw his legs over the side of the bed. He couldn't make them move like he wanted. He finally gave up in exhaustion and let Tori help him back under the covers.

"Pops, please, you have to take it easy for a while. The stroke you had was pretty bad. The doctor says you need to rest or you could have another one. You don't want to cause more damage to your body, do you?"

"No, but a man needs to work. I need to work. I'm going to go crazy lying in this bed."

Tori sat on the edge of his bed and combed what hair he still had on his head. "Just take it easy; let us take care of you for a while. Relax, watch some television, read a book, rest. We want you up and around again, but if you don't relax and take care of yourself you will be stuck in this bed forever."

In the other room, Elsa Mae was busy preparing dinner. The phone rang. "Hello?" Elsa Mae stopped cooking when she heard Amber's voice. "Hi, Mama. How are you?"

"I'm good, Amber. How are you?"

Amber couldn't tell her mother that she had just given a toothless, old truck driver sex for a ride to New Orleans. That the man had not only slobbered all over her, but made her perform several sexual acts during her time with him. Amber willed herself to hold back her tears. She replied with as much positive emotion as she could muster. "Oh, I'm doing okay, Mama. I'm in New Orleans right now. How are the babies? How is Pops?"

Elsa Mae hadn't heard from Amber in a few weeks. Since their last conversation, Charley suffered a stroke, and the children had to be farmed out to other family members so she could take care of her husband. "Oh, Gabe is with Terri in Dallas right now, and Annie is with Kerri and Josh. They are having fun and enjoying time away from their grandma."

"Oh, that's good, Mama. I'm glad they are doing okay. How are you and Pops doing? I bet you are enjoying the quiet."

Elsa Mae hesitated for a few moments.

"Mama, is everything okay?"

Elsa Mae finally let go of the news about Charley. "Amber, your daddy had a stroke."

"Oh my God!" Amber couldn't breathe. "Is he okay, Mama?"

"Yes, for now. He's at home, but he can't move some parts of his body. The doctors aren't sure he ever will. Tori is here helping out, and the boys come by every day to help me take him to physical therapy. But you know your daddy, he doesn't want to do what the doctors want. They are afraid he might do too much and cause another stroke."

Amber's face was stained with tears. "Mama, I'm going to do my best to get home as soon as I can. I don't know when that will be, but I'm going to try. Do you think Pops will be fine with me coming home?"

"Oh, Amber, your father would be thrilled if you came home. He went all the way to Atlanta looking for you over a year ago. Why wouldn't he be okay with you coming home?"

"He came to Atlanta looking for me?" Amber had never been told about her father's trip to find her.

"You never knew?" Elsa Mae stirred her sauce on the stove with the phone propped between her ear and neck.

"No, Mama, I never knew." Amber's tears flowed again.

"Well, I'll tell you about it when you get home or he will. Look, I don't want to hang up, but your daddy's supper is ready. I'm not going to tell him until I know for sure when you will be here. Be sure and call me back when you know when you'll be home."

Amber wiped her tears. "Okay, Mama, I will. Give everyone hugs and kisses for me. I love you."

"I love you too, Amber. Be careful out there."

"I will, Mama."

After hanging up the phone in the truck stop, Amber went outside and sat on the sidewalk. She found a spot away from the entrance and foot traffic of the drivers. She put her head in her lap and cried. Her daddy was sick and she was stuck running drugs around the country for a drug dealer who was going to kill her if she left. *What am I going to do? I have to go home.*

"Can I help you, little lady?"

Amber recognized the voice, but she wasn't in the mood for Damian's bullshit. She lifted her head out of her lap. Damian had squatted down in front of her.

"What the hell are you doing here? Are you following me?"

Damian didn't let Amber's smug attitude affect his concern for her. "No, I'm not following you, but when you came to my truck the other day and asked for a ride to New Orleans, I did put in a request for it and I got it. So, here I am, just like you wanted, but you took another ride. That kind of hurt my feelings, but I'm sure if you will allow me to buy you dinner tonight I will forgive you."

Amber wiped her face with her jacket sleeves, and with a small smile Amber let Damian help her up off the sidewalk. "Why are you trying so hard Damian? I'm no good for you. I'm a drug running whore."

Damian knew that what Amber was saying was more truth than he really wanted to think about. But his feelings for her wouldn't let him leave her alone. He looked at her face and wiped away the makeup that had been smudged by the tears. "I love you. I can't help it."

Amber broke down and let Damian hold her in his arms for the first time while she cried. "My daddy is sick and I need to get home to see him." Amber quickly pulled away from Damian. She realized that if any of the girls on her team saw her crying in the arms of this man, it could mean trouble for her and him. "Look, it's too dangerous for you to get too close to me. Shades will kill you and me both if he finds out that I have someone outside the family looking out for me."

Damian pulled her back to his arms. He then walked them both to the back of the truck stop store where they were out of the watchful eyes of anyone. Amber tried to pull away again. "Stop, Amber. I will protect us both, I promise. I don't know who this Shades is, but I know if you're out here on the truck circuit, he can't have as much control over you as he would like you to believe. Besides, what is this about your dad?"

Amber stopped pulling away. "Let's go somewhere. I can't take the chance that any of the girls on my team might see me getting cozy with you."

"Okay, let me take off my trailer and we'll take my truck and go get something to eat. I know this nice little seafood restaurant in town."

"Okay, I'll go around the backside of the building and you go get your truck. I'll meet you at the fuel island."

◊◊◊

Damian looked at Amber from across the table. "Did you enjoy your dinner?"

Amber sipped at the glass of sweet tea she held in her hand. "Yes, that was the best meal I've had in a long time."

"Now, tell me about your father. You said he was ill." He crossed his hands on the table and waited for Amber to reveal why she had tears in her eyes today.

"He had a stroke and my mama said it was pretty bad. I haven't been home in over a year. I really need to go home and see him."

"So, go."

Amber leaned back in her seat. "It's not that simple, Damian. Shades, my boss, won't let me visit my family without his permission. Crystal told me that he might not let me see them for up to two years."

The brow on Damian's forehead lowered slightly. "Won't let you go home. Why?"

"It's a complicated, long story. Just trust me when I say that I can't go home until he gives me permission."

"Then ask for permission. You do understand that this man can't own you. This is America, and it's against the law for one person to own another."

"Yes, I know that, but he will literally kill me if I break away from the family."

"Well, I don't know what kind of family you're talking about, but they can't hold you against your will like this. You give me the word and I will take you back to your family."

"That's just it, Damian, if I go back to my family and Shades finds out about it, he won't just kill me, but he might even kill my family."

"Then get permission from the asshole and let me take you home to your family."

"I have already put a call in to Crystal tonight before we left for dinner. She said she'd speak with Shades, and then she'll let me know if he'll let me go home."

"Where are you from, anyway?"

"Odessa."

"Oh, wow! Oil town, U.S.A. I know where that is, I've been through there a bunch on I-20."

"Yep, spent the first sixteen years of my life there."

"So, you have a big family?"

"Yes, my mama and daddy, uncles, aunts, cousins, three brothers, three sisters, four nieces, six nephews, one son, and one daughter."

"Wow, wait, you have a son and daughter?"

"Yes, Gabe and Annie."

"You need to go home, Amber. You need to be with your father and your children. How in the hell did you get mixed up with this Shades character?"

"Like I told you earlier, it's a long story."

Damian moved back in his seat. "I have all night. Why don't you tell me how a beautiful girl like you, with two kids, ended up jumping for a living?"

Amber wasn't sure she wanted to get into the entire saga of the last few years, but Damian seemed determined to know every last horrible detail of her miserable, messy life.

CHAPTER SEVENTEEN

Amber held on tight to her cell phone and waited for Crystal to answer. "Crystal, it's Amber. Did you talk to Shades? Can I go home to see my daddy?"

"He said no, Amber. He's still not sure he can trust you yet."

Amber broke down in tears. "Come on, Crystal. My dad is really sick. I need to go home and see him. What if he gets worse or something? You've just got to talk to him and get him to let me go. I promise I will come back, and I won't tell anyone anything about what I'm doing. I promise, Crystal. I put my life on it."

Crystal could hear the pain and desperation in Amber's voice. "I know, baby girl, but he won't change his mind. I know Shades and he doesn't go back on anything he says."

"Oh, Crystal, please, you've got to help me get home, at least for a week. Please, I'm begging you."

Crystal thought for a moment. "I tell you what, Amber, I have an idea. But if you double-cross me, you will be ruining everything I have right now."

"I understand, Crystal. Whatever you can do for me I will not let you down. I give you my word."

"Okay, I'm going to tell Shades that I'm taking you to the Florida Keys for a week. I will let him think that it will give me a chance to see how you behave away from the family. I will go by myself while you go home, but you have to return at the same time that I do. If Shades finds out that I did this, he will turn me out, or kill me. Do you understand?"

"Oh, thank you, Crystal, I promise I will be back exactly when you tell me. I won't let you down, I promise."

"Alright, do you have a ride home?"

"Yes, there's a trucker who often gives me rides. I know if I ask him, he will gladly give me a lift to Odessa."

"Okay, I'll set everything up. I'll call you in the morning and give you the details. You cannot let any on your team know anything about this. Once we're supposedly on the way to the Keys, none of the girls can spot you anywhere. Do you understand?"

"Yes, I understand. I'll stay completely hidden."

"Alright, I'll call you in the morning. Be ready to leave town."

"Thanks, Crystal, you're the best."

◊◊◊

Amber went into the truck stop and asked to use the phone. She never used her cell phone to call Damian or her family.

"Damian, it's Amber. I talked to Crystal and even though Shades won't let me go, she's going to help me get home. I need to find a ride. Do you think you'll be anywhere near Odessa tomorrow?"

"Well, I don't know, pretty lady, but I think maybe I can arrange that just for you."

"Oh, you're the best Damian! Thank you so much. Listen, I have to call my mama. I'll call you back here in a few minutes."

"Okay, sugar."

Amber hung up the phone and then dialed her mama's number. She waited for someone to answer at her parent's house. "Hey, Mama, it's Amber."

"Amber, baby, I'm so glad you called us back. How are you?"

"I'm fine, Mama. I just wanted you and Pops to know I'll be coming home for a few days."

"Oh, Amber, this is wonderful news. When will you be here?"

"I'll be leaving in the morning and I should be in Odessa sometime the next morning."

"Okay, baby. I won't tell your father until you get here, that way it will be a surprise. I will tell Traci to bring Gabe home this weekend so you can see both of your babies."

"Oh, Mama, that would be terrific."

"How long are you going to be able to stay?"

"Only until Monday, I have to be back to work in Georgia in exactly one week."

"Well, everyone will understand about you having to work. But a week is better than not seeing you at all."

"I can't wait to see everyone."

"We can't wait to see you, honey."

"Well, I'd better go. I'll call you tomorrow. I love you, Mama."

"I love you too, Amber."

Amber hung up the phone. She had a strange feeling. She hadn't been home in over a year. She wanted to go home and see her parents and, of course, her babies. But she wasn't sure about seeing the rest of her family, especially he older brother Josh. She could anticipate his reaction and knew he would make her feel like crap.

◊◊◊

"Hey, wake up, sleepy head. Your cell phone is going off." Amber quickly grabbed her phone next to the bed in Damian's sleeper.

"Hello?"

"Hey, sweetie, it's Crystal. I have everything set. You have to be back in Georgia on Tuesday night. You need to be waiting for me at the airport parking lot. I will be parked in parking space 1204. My plane will arrive at 5:15 p.m. Don't be late."

"Don't worry; I won't be late. I promise, Crystal. I really appreciate you doing this for me."

"Just be there and that will be thanks enough. Remember, my plane leaves at one o'clock this afternoon. Be sure and keep out of sight, especially at the truck stops you normally use."

"I understand, Crystal. I will stay hidden and be at the airport parking lot by five p.m."

"Okay, sweetie. Enjoy your visit with your family."

"Have fun in the Keys. Take care of you."

"Take care of you."

Damian had moved from the bed to his driver's seat. "So everything's a go?"

Amber climbed into Damian's lap. "Yes, everything is set." Amber kissed Damian on his cheek. "Are you sure you can take the time off and have me back to Atlanta by Tuesday? It's a long trip to Odessa, Texas."

"Look, Amber, if I didn't want to take you to Odessa and back to Atlanta, I wouldn't be here. Now, let's stop talking and get out of this truck stop."

"Okay, but I need to use the restroom."

"Can you wait until we get out of town? Remember Crystal wants you to stay out of sight."

"It will be okay for now. Crystal doesn't leave from the airport until one this afternoon. I just have to be careful after that, and until we get to Odessa. I haven't met any of the girls who work that area, so no one should know me out there. There is a big truck stop that I used to work at that we can stay at during the nights."

"Okay, so you mean you're going to let me snuggle with you like last night again?"

Amber giggled. "Yes."

Damian is the most wonderful man I've ever met, Amber thought.

All the time they had been together, he had not once requested, demanded, or took sex from her. In fact, Amber had never offered herself to him. Last night was the first time that they had ever shared his sleeper. Amber would have given herself to Damian if he had wanted her, but he never even tried. Amber thought it was kind of strange, but she figured when the time was right, they would know.

◊◊◊

When Damian and Amber arrived in Odessa it was early in the morning. Damian pulled into the local truck stop to get fuel. Damian had decided to get up around midnight and drive on into Odessa. He knew the cover of darkness would help keep Amber protected until they got into town. "Okay, baby, we are in Odessa."

Amber came out of the sleeper. "Wow, I must have been tired. I don't even remember going to sleep." She looked through the windshield and recognized the very place she hadn't been back to since she left with Paul. She had been back to Odessa once with Paul, but not here. The old restaurant where she worked still looked the same, and the parking lot was still stacked with trucks. "Welcome to the oil patch, Damian." She pointed at the restaurant. "I worked there for over a year before Paul asked me to ride with him."

Damian looked over the place; there wasn't much special about it. "Looks like most other truck stops, Amber. Why do you call it the oil patch? I see a few trees out back behind the trucks and some oil on the ground, but nothing that would make you think they're putting patches over the oil leaks."

Amber laughed and hugged Damian's neck. "No, silly, you know what I mean when I call my town "the oil patch." This is the place where oil is pulled out of the ground. My daddy used to work out there in those fields, drilling for oil. My three brothers all work out there, either drilling or doing some other job for the oil companies."

Damian kissed Amber's arm. "I know, baby, I was just messing with you. Let me get some fuel and we'll find a place to park. I'll drop the trailer and take you to your parents' in the truck. Then I'll come back here and rest while you visit with your family."

Amber moved to the passenger seat. "I want you to get some rest, Damian, but I also want you to meet my family."

"I want to meet them too, sugar, but I think you need to fix some of the damage first. If things don't go well, you can always call me and I'll come get you. But if things go all right, you can introduce me to them later."

"Okay." Amber looked at the store. "I need to go into the restroom and clean up a little before I see them. I think it will be okay for me to go into this truck stop. Even if Shades has some girls here, I'm sure none of them know who I am."

"Sounds good. I'll fill the truck. Then I'll come in and get you before we park." Damian got out of the truck.

Amber grabbed her things, and then she got out of the truck. She kissed Damian on her way past the fuel pump. "Be ready in a flash."

Inside the truck stop, Amber found the ladies' restroom. The old place still looked the same from when she worked in the restaurant that was attached to the rear of the store. She hoped that no one would recognize her as she slipped into one of the restroom stalls. It was so early in the morning that chances were no one would.

"Lada de, lada da." A woman sung as she entered the bathroom, taking the stall next to Amber.

Amber's face flushed, she knew that sound. Wanda, the woman she had worked nights with at the restaurant sounded just like that all the time. Trying not to attract attention, Amber continued to change her clothes and hoped that the woman would hurry and leave.

"It sure is going to be a nice day today, don't you think?" Wanda spoke out from her stall in the restroom.

Amber didn't respond.

Wanda waited for a moment for a response, but when she got none she continued to speak anyway. "Yep, going to be a bright, sunny day today." Wanda finished her business, flushed the toilet, left the stall, washed her hands, and left the restroom.

Amber let go of the breath that she had inadvertently been holding. "That was a close one," she sighed with relief. She finished dressing, but before leaving the restroom stall, she looked to see that no one else was in the room. Certain not one else was there, Amber quickly left her stall, washed her face and brushed her teeth.

She had wanted coffee, but decided that she better return to the truck. Just as she was reaching the exit door, Damian approached her with a tall cup of coffee. She smiled and took the cup as they walked out of the store and toward the truck. Amber sipped the hot brew and then told Damian about her experience in the restroom. "It was close, Damian. I didn't see her but I knew her voice and the smell of that cheap perfume she always wore."

"Well, you were smart not to respond."

Damian helped Amber into the truck on the driver's side. "Up you go. I spotted a nice place on the front line. It won't take too long to trailer down, then you can go see your family."

"I'm nervous." Amber threw her things on the sleeper, and then sat in the passenger seat next to Damian. He maneuvered the truck into the spot he had picked out.

"I know, but you have to do this. Don't you miss them? Don't you miss your babies?"

"I have missed them more and more every day since I've been gone. Annie will be almost two and my little Gabe is four. I can't believe it has been so long." Amber held back her tears as best she could. "I can't believe I left them in the first place. What was I thinking? I wasn't thinking—I was being selfish. I thought things would be better for them and me if I saw the world. I saw the world all right—just not the kind of world I wanted to be involved in. Now, I'm stuck in it and can't get out."

"Don't say those things. You're a good person. You're your own person, and I'm going to help you get away from Shades, if you'll let me. I want to help you get back to being the person you really are."

"Those are wonderful thoughts, Damian, but Shades isn't someone you want to mess with and you know that. He would sooner kill you than look at you for taking one of his girls. They start out telling you that you are free to do what you want, but as time goes on, he's just the same as Zeke was to me. The only difference is that Zeke did things to my face and Shades does things behind my back to keep me in check. No, I'm stuck doing this until he lets me go. I don't want you or anyone in my family to be hurt because of me. I'll just wait it out."

"What? You're going to wait until your children are grown or your parents are gone before you decide to get out of this? That is crazy. You know Shades isn't going to let you go any time soon. By the time you are in your forties…maybe. I'm sorry, but I want to be with you now. I want to be with you and your babies right now. I don't want to wait for Shades to let go of you. I'm going to get you out of this and that's final."

"Come on, we can talk about this later when you have had some sleep and are thinking clearly," she said. "Let's get dollied down so you can take me to face the music I've got coming from my older brother."

CHAPTER EIGHTEEN

"I'm coming."

Amber stood at the door, waiting for her mother to open it.

Elsa Mae stood silent for a moment trying to recognize the child that now stood before her as a grown woman. "Amber? Amber, my sweet girl! Come in, come in! Why did you knock? This is your home and always will be. There is no need to knock. You should have just come on in the house."

Amber hugged her mother. Elsa Mae's gray and course hair swept across Amber's tear-stained face. "Oh, Mama, I've missed you so much." Amber pulled away and wiped the wetness from her cheeks. She hadn't wanted to show any emotions.

Elsa Mae grabbed Amber by the hand and led her down the all too familiar hallway to her parents' bedroom. They passed Amber's old room, but the door was closed. She missed being in that room, with her children and all of her belongings that she had left so many months ago. "I didn't tell your daddy you were coming. I wanted it to be a surprise for him. Come on, he will be thrilled to see you. I know he'll feel better just having you here."

"Charley, look who's here!"

Charley laid a book down that he was reading and propped himself up higher on the pillows behind him. He stopped mid-movement when Amber passed through the threshold of the bedroom. A tear fell from his eye as his hand stretched out to gather his little baby girl. "Amber? My Amber! Where have you been?"

Amber sat on the bed and took the long embrace that her father had been saving for her. "I'm here, Pops. I'm here."

Elsa Mae wanted to sit with her husband and her daughter, but she left the room. She knew that Charley needed the time with Amber alone. Amber had always had a special piece of Charley's heart—a piece neither she nor any of the other children shared. She believed that with Amber's departure, that piece of Charley's heart had been left void. She hoped with Amber back, Charley would heal and grow strong again.

"Why did you leave me, Amber? I would have done anything to make you happy here, you know that, my sweet little girl."

"I know, Pops. I just had to see if I could do things on my own. I wanted to see the world. I wanted to see what I was missing. Or at least that is what I thought I wanted."

"Was it like you thought it would be? Are you home for good?"

Tears fell like rain from her eyes. "No, Pops, it wasn't anything like I thought it would be. I saw a lot of the states, mostly from the windows of big trucks, and I have been in all of them—except for Hawaii. It's nothing like what I had pictured in my mind, nothing at all."

Charley hugged his child again. "So you will stay then?" He waited patiently for her answer.

"No, I have a job and I have to get back to it. I live in Atlanta most of the time, but my job takes me all over the country."

"But, you can move home and still do your job can't you?"

"Not right now. Maybe in a few years, but for now I have to keep doing what I'm doing to survive." Amber patted his hand.

"Well, what is it that you do? Can you at least stay awhile with us? See the babies? See your sisters and brothers? Everyone is expected to be here tomorrow. I think your mama said something about making wedding plans for Kami."

"Yes, I can stay for a few days, but I have to be back in Atlanta by Tuesday." Amber didn't want to feel the way she did about her older sister Kami, but she'd hoped that her homecoming wasn't going to include a visit with Kami. There had always been so much unspoken comparison between Kami's success and Amber's failures in her family. Amber always felt she could never live up to their expectations, especially since her sister was so good at everything. "Kami is getting married? She's going to be here tomorrow, too?"

"Yes. You know Mama; she wants a big wedding. I think they should just go to the church, say 'I do,' and be done with it like we did." Charley laughed, but didn't wait for the answers to his questions, he just hugged his daughter again. "I'm so glad you're here. You know I came to Atlanta to find you, sweetheart. I went to the restaurant where you worked, but they said you had quit. Then with the help of the police department I found a man that the lady at the restaurant said you might be with—a Zeke somebody. But when the policeman and I went to his apartment, he said you weren't there. I staked out the place for a while and I thought maybe I saw you leave with him and a couple of other men, but when I tried to check and see if it was you, that man Zeke pushed me away and threatened me. Please tell me you weren't with that man. I would hate to think that my sweet little girl was keeping company with the likes of him."

Amber couldn't believe that her father had been at Zeke's apartment and she hadn't even known it. *That bastard put his hands on my daddy?* She hated to tell her father the truth about what had really gone down with Zeke. She was afraid the truth would impact his health. "I stayed with him for a while, but I wasn't there when you came by, they would have told me. I just rented a room from him for a while."

"Good, that's good, Amber. I was so afraid that you were being harmed. I have had you on my mind from the day you left. Mama thinks that's part of the reason I've taken ill. I told her she was imagining things. My poor old body is just falling apart. It's just one of those things, you start to die the minute you're born, you know."

"I know, Pops, I know. How did you find out that I was in Atlanta?"

"Oh, a friend of yours, her name was Shelby Mathews. She came by to let us know that she had seen you and that she was a little worried about you."

"Shelby came here?"

"Yes, she was really nice."

"Yes, she was good to me as well." Amber decided not to discuss Shelby any further with her dad. She just sat with her father for a long time talking, until Elsa Mae interrupted them.

Elsa Mae brought a tray of food into the bedroom for Charley. "Lunch is ready. Amber I thought you might like to have a sandwich with us, so I made your favorite, tuna salad."

Amber hadn't had one of her mama's famous tuna salad sandwiches in forever. "Oh yes, Mama, that would be terrific. I'm starved. I only had a cup of coffee with Damian this morning before he brought me over here."

"I was wondering who that man in the big truck was." Elsa Mae said. "Is that the man you left with from the restaurant?"

Amber nibbled at her sandwich. "No, Mama, that's not Paul. That's Damian. He's just a good friend of mine. He's been helping me with my new job. He's really a nice guy and I would like both of you to meet him tomorrow if that would be all right?"

After a drink of tea Elsa Mae responded. "Well, everyone will be here tomorrow. Kami and her fiancé are coming so we can discuss the wedding. I asked Traci to bring Gabe back this weekend since they were coming as well."

"Oh, I'm so glad she's bringing him. Annie is with Katie and Josh?"

"Yes, since your daddy has been sick, the others have been taking care of the babies for me. They are growing so fast and I just can't keep up some days."

"I'm sorry, Mama. I shouldn't have ever left. I'm working on getting a place that will be big enough for them."

"You're going to take them to Atlanta?"

Charley knew the conversation was going to lead to trouble. "Elsa Mae, these sure are good sandwiches. Can I have another one?"

"Sure, but…"

"I think I'm getting my strength back, I sure am hungry."

Elma got up to fetch the sandwich Charley had demanded. "Be right back. Amber can I get you another one?"

"No thanks, Mama."

Elsa left the room

"Thank you, Pops. I really don't want to fight with Mama about the kids."

Charley patted his daughter's hand. "I know, baby. Josh is coming this weekend and I suspect things aren't going to be that easy for you. You stick with me this weekend and I'll take care of you."

"I was kind of worried how I was going to handle everyone—especially Josh."

"Don't worry about him, baby."

"Okay."

Elsa Mae came back with Charley's sandwich. Charley, Amber, and Elsa Mae spent the rest of the afternoon talking. Amber went into her old bedroom and looked through the things her children had while Elsa Mae helped her husband with a shower. Her old things still occupied the same space as when she was living at home and reminded her of a life she wished she had back.

After Charley finished with his shower, Elsa Mae helped him to the living room where he sat and talked with Amber until dinner. Amber enjoyed a calm dinner with her parents before deciding that it was time to call Damian.

"Hey, Damian it's me. Can you come and get me in about an hour?"

"Sure, sugar. Sounds like things went pretty good today."

"Yes, but it was just Mama and Pops. Tomorrow is going to be a little more difficult. My brother Josh will be here. I'm not looking forward to that meeting at all."

"You can do it, Amber."

"Well, I already told my folks you were coming with me tomorrow. You're going to be my back up."

Damian laughed. "That bad, huh?"

"Yeah, he doesn't like me very much."

"I'll be glad to be there with you, sugar."

"Okay, well, see you in about an hour."

"No problem. I just want to say, I've been thinking about you all day."

"You're crazy." Amber hung up her parents' landline phone. She walked back into the kitchen and helped her mother with the supper dishes.

She dried the last pan. "Well, that does it, Mama. Can I help you do anything else?"

"No, I believe that's it. Why don't you go talk to your daddy again for a while? I can already see a change in him since you've come home. We will need to change the sheets on your bed if you're planning to spend the night."

"Oh, I'm not spending the night here, Mama. Damian is coming for me. I think I will go talk to Pops for a little bit before he gets here. Thank you for the food and everything. What time would be a good for me to come tomorrow?"

"Oh, maybe sometime after lunch would be good. That way I can have your daddy bathed and ready for everyone."

"Will it be all right if I bring Damian tomorrow?"

"Sure. I guess that will be fine."

Amber put down the dishtowel and hugged her mama. "Thanks again for everything you've done for me."

"You're our child, Amber. We love you. We'll do all we can to help you."

"Love you too, Mama."

◊◊◊

The hum of the truck mesmerized Amber as Damian rolled the bobtail down the highway back to the truck stop. Her mind was flooded with thoughts of her daddy and how ill he looked, about how things would go tomorrow with her family, and especially how the children would react to seeing her again. *Annie was just a tiny baby; she might not even know me. Gabe might remember, but he's not really old enough for that kind of recollection.*

"You okay, baby?" Damian asked.

"Yeah, I'm okay. A little nervous about tomorrow, but I'm okay. Thank you for coming to get me. I'm really tired; I think I just want to take a shower and go to bed."

Damian continued to watch the road and Amber at the same time. "Sounds like a plan. Are you sure you want to stay at the truck stop where I parked the trailer?"

"Yes, I think it will be safer than any other. It's an older one and Shades's girls don't hang too much at the older places."

"What about that woman, Wanda?"

"Oh, she works nights. I have to remember not to go in there during the night shift. I don't think anyone else will even remember who I am. Wanda was kind of a friend at work."

"Well, we are almost there if you want to get your stuff together. I'll drop you off at the door and then park the truck. I'll wait for you. Do you need money for a shower?"

Amber had slipped into the sleeper for her things. "No, I have money. I've been saving as much money as possible, Damian. I really want to get my babies a house someday. A place for them to call home."

Damian pulled up to the door so Amber could get out and take a shower. "Can I help you with that dream?"

Amber smiled and laughed slightly as she opened the door and stepped down onto the steps. "You're still crazy."

Damian laughed. "You keep telling me that, but I don't feel crazy."

Amber shut the door, shaking her head. Damian smiled and drove the bobtail to the parking spot in front of his trailer.

Inside the store, Amber realized she was out of shampoo. She walked through the rows until she located some. "You know, that cheap shampoo really isn't good for beautiful hair like yours, Amber."

Amber looked up shocked that anyone in the store would talk to her, let alone know her name. The fear that had been triggered inside of her body was soon squelched with a smile. "Shelby?"

Shelby reached for a hug from her small, young friend. Amber hugged Shelby. "How are you, Amber? I see you made it back to Odessa. I'm so glad. I have been worried about you. Have you seen your family?"

Amber put the shampoo in her arm. "I'm doing okay. Yes, my daddy had a stroke, so I had to come back and check on him. He told me you visited them a few months ago."

"I'm so sorry to hear about your father. I hope he's going to be all right. Yes, I did go visit with them. I was very worried about you and thought they might be able to help. I hope you're not upset with me for talking with them."

Amber walked to the cash register. "No, I'm not upset. I know you were only trying to help. My daddy is recovering slowly, but he seems to be in good spirits."

"That's great. So, are you back here for good?"

She put her purchase on the counter and pulled some money from her back pocket. "No, I have a job back in Atlanta and I have to be back by Tuesday."

"So things have worked out for you there?"

"Well…not really. In fact, things went kind of crazy for me there. But I survived, and I'm trying to get back here for good. I've even met a really nice guy; his name is Damian. He's trying to help me get home, too. Maybe you would like to meet him, he's out in his truck. He's nothing like Paul or even any of the men I've met over the last few months. He doesn't want anything from me; he's been really kind."

"Well, sure. I would love to meet him."

Amber grabbed her shampoo. "Come on, he's out on the front line. It's not far. I'll come back for my shower later."

Shelby followed Amber out of the store. "All right."

Amber and Shelby walked together across the parking lot. Several of the trucks on the front row flashed their lights at the two women. Shelby laughed. "Nothing ever changes."

"Nope, and it never will. They think because you're a woman and you're walking across the parking lot that you're trying to sell something."

"They are some horny boys, aren't they?" Shelby laughed.

"Yep, always looking for a little company."

"Too bad they can't afford us, huh?"

"Most of them can't afford the free stuff they've got at home."

"I know you're right, sweetie. I know you're right."

They arrived at the truck and Amber knocked on Damian's driver's side door. Damian came from the sleeper and opened the door when he saw Amber. "I thought you were going to take a shower?"

"I will in a minute. Come out here; I have someone I want you to meet." Damian came out of the truck and stood in front of Amber and Shelby.

"Damian this is my friend Shelby." Amber pointed to Shelby and then to Damian. "Shelby this is my friend Damian."

Damian shook Shelby's hand cautiously. "Nice to meet you. Do you work with Amber?"

Amber laughed, knowing what he was thinking. "No, silly. Shelby is an owner-op. We met at the hotel Paul left me at in Atlanta. She helped me out."

Relieved that Shelby wasn't part of Shades's organization, Damian eased up on his suspicion of Shelby. "Owner-operator, huh? Me too. I haul a little bit of everything, but my specialty is cattle and heavy equipment when they are available. I own a drop deck, a poor boy, and a cattle trailer besides my refrigerator box on the back here."

"Well, I only have one trailer, and it's a sand hauler. I haul sand for the fracking companies. I find the money is the best in sand."

"Yeah, I've heard sand hauling is pretty profitable. You live around here?"

"Yes, I think that's why Amber and I connected so well in Atlanta."

Amber interrupted. "Hey, you guys keep talking truck talk. I'm going into the store for my shower. It was good to see you again, Shelby. I still have your card. I'll give you a call sometime." Amber gave Shelby a hug.

"It was good to see you again, Amber. Take care of yourself. I look forward to hearing from you."

Amber disappeared into the building for a shower. Shelby and Damian continued talking. "So, you helped her out in Atlanta?"

"Oh, just a little money and a few nights in a hotel. I tried to get her to let me give her a ride home, but she wanted to prove to her family she could make it on her own."

"Well, some pretty shady stuff happened to that little lady after you left. I'm trying hard to get her out of it now. She's a jumper. Did you know?"

"No, I had no idea she was doing that."

"How did you get involved with her?" Shelby and Damian moved to the front of his truck to talk.

"Well, I gave her a lift to one of her destinations. She wasn't anything like the other girls that are in that business. She was careful and unsure about what she was doing. I felt sorry for her, so whenever I saw her at the trucks stops I frequented, I'd give her a lift. That way she didn't have to deal with the weirdo truckers out there."

Shelby looked at Damian. "Sounds like you have feelings for this girl."

"I do, but I have to get her away from Shades if I'm going to do anything about changing her future with me."

"Who's Shades?"

"He's this scumbag from Atlanta. I think he works for some high-roller named Dante. Regardless of who these guys think they are, they're using women to deliver their drugs across the country. From what Amber has told me, they will kill her, or even worse, if she tries to get out."

"How do you know so much about these guys?"

"Amber has been really open with me about what she has to do to survive out here."

"Have you met any of these guys? Do you know their real names or last names?"

"No, I have no interest in that world. Why would I want to know their names? I just want to get that girl out of their nasty grip."

"I understand that. The reason I'm asking is because I have some connections with the DEA. In fact, the reason I was in Atlanta when I met Amber was because I was maid-of-honor for an agent in the DEA."

"Seriously?"

"Yes, maybe I can give them the information, and they can do something about getting Amber out of there."

"That would be awesome, but she's really scared. She had to hide in my truck on the way here. I guess they run in packs and if anyone from the organization saw her, there would have been trouble for the girl who's covering for her."

"So there is someone else inside the organization that wants out or is willing to help Amber?"

"Well, yes, sort of. The woman is supposedly, Shades's girlfriend or madam or something. I have no idea what she is, really, but her name is Crystal and she likes Amber. She told Shades that she was taking Amber to the beach in Miami for a week, so I could bring her here to see her dad. Bastard wouldn't even let her come see her sick dad."

"I see. I'm not sure what I can do right now, Damian, but I can tell you care about Amber. I will talk to my friend Angelica and see if there is anything she can do. Do you have a number where I can get in touch with you?"

Damian pulled out his wallet and handed Shelby his business card. "It's kind of bent, been in my wallet for a while."

Shelby took the card and looked at it. "I can read the name and number, that's all that matters." Shelby reached into her back pocket. "I always carry a few. Never know who might want to hire a sand hauler. I gave one to Amber, but call me if you ever need anything, and I mean it. Sounds like our girl is into some really bad stuff."

"Yeah, she gets pretty mad at me when I push her to just leave and come with me. She says I'm crazy."

"Well, if she's in as deep as it appears in this drug organization, she could be right about you being crazy to get involved."

"Doesn't matter. I care a lot about Amber and I want to get her out."

"I hear you. Let me talk to my friend and see what I can do."

Shelby shook Damian's hand. "I need to get going, but I'll be in touch. Take care of our girl."

"I will, and thanks, Shelby."

"No problem. Oh, probably best to keep this conversation between the two of us for now. Amber has enough to worry about."

"I agree."

CHAPTER NINETEEN

The house was noisy and crowded when Amber and Damian arrived at her parents' home. Damian had opted for a taxi this time. He wasn't sure he would be able to find a place to park his bobtail near Amber's folks' place.

Elsa Mae greeted them when they walked through the door. "Come in, come in."

Traci was sitting at the table, but jumped up to greet Amber. She hugged her little sister. "Oh, Amber, we are so glad you're home." She looked at Damian. "Who is this handsome young man?"

"This is my friend, Damian."

Damian shook hands with Traci. "Damian Adams."

"Nice to meet you, Damian. Amber, I'm going to take this guy around to meet the others. We will talk later about where you found him." She mouthed toward Amber as she took Damian by the hand, "I like this one better than Paul."

Amber had been sidetracked by the appearance of her eldest child Gabe. He had come to her without any coaxing. "Mama! I've missed you, Mama."

Amber took the child in her arms. She hadn't held her baby boy in over a year. Tears welled up in her eyes when he hugged her back. "I've missed you too, my baby boy."

Damian finally managed to get away from Traci. He found Amber seated next to her father on the couch. Gabe was glued to her lap. "Come sit with us, this is my son, Gabe and my dad."

Damian put out his hand and shook Charley's hand. "Nice to meet you, sir."

"Nice to meet you too, Damian. Please, call me Charley."

"Okay, Charley."

Amber looked around. Kami was at the table with Traci and Tory and Alex's wife Trisha. Most of the men were in the kitchen with Elsa Mae. Except for Elsa Mae and Traci, none of the others had made their way to see Amber. Amber didn't care. She was going to do her best to stay right next to her father, just as he had told her to do. Josh and Katie hadn't arrived yet, which wasn't unusual. She wasn't looking forward to the reunion and hoped they wouldn't come. Just as the thought crossed her mind, Josh, Katie, and their clan came through the door.

Katie had Annie in her arms. The moment Josh saw Amber he took Annie from Katie and went straight to the kitchen with the child. Katie came over to where Amber was sitting and hugged her and Charley. "Good to see you, Charley, how are you feeling?"

"I'm doing okay, Katie. How are you? We haven't seen you in a while."

"Been busy, Charley. You know what it's like raising Josh."

Charley, Amber, and Katie laughed. "Amber, I'm so glad you're here. How are you?"

"Okay, Katie. I'm just trying to survive. I can see that my brother hasn't changed much."

"No, Amber, you know he won't. He'll get over whatever bur is up his butt. I'm just so glad you're okay. I've worried about you a bunch."

"How is Annie doing?"

"Oh, Amber, she is such a smart little girl. She's growing like a weed. I've enjoyed having her around. With all the boys, a little girl around is wonderful. I'll go get her here in a few minutes from Josh. He's just trying to be a jerk. You know he has a hard time forgiving."

"I know, Katie. Thank you so much for taking care of her for me."

"Anytime, Amber. She's a joy."

Amber moved Gabe slightly and pointed toward Damian. "This is my friend Damian."

Gabe got off of Amber's lap and went to play with the other children in the room.

"Nice to meet you, Damian. I'm Katie, Josh's wife."

Damian stood up and shook hands with Katie. "It's a pleasure."

Katie looked at Amber. "Well, I better go see what the kids are into, and if Elsa Mae needs my help with anything. Amber, I like this guy, he's a keeper."

Amber smiled at Damian. "I know."

◊◊◊

"Hi, Angelica, this is Shelby."

"Well hello, stranger. I haven't heard from you in a few weeks. I thought maybe you fell off of the earth or something."

Shelby laughed. "Nope, not yet. Still kicking and trucking."

"That's my girl. What're you up to these days?"

"Oh, still hauling sand and looking after strays."

"Only you, Shelby. What kind of stray have you taken under your wing this time?"

"You remember that girl I told you about at your wedding who I met at the hotel?"

"Yeah, I remember, but that was months ago."

"I know. Well anyway, she's from Odessa and I ran into her and her friend yesterday. I got to talking to her friend and he was telling me about some really interesting stuff she's gotten herself mixed up with in Atlanta. Have you ever heard of 'jumping' in the trucking circle?"

"Yeah, we've heard of it, but it's not that big a deal."

"I don't know about that, Angelica. From what this guy was telling me, it's a pretty sophisticated means of trafficking drugs with hardly any detection."

"Are you sure we are talking about the same kind of 'jumping,' Shelby."

"I don't know. I just know about the one where girls, mostly girls, ride the truck circuit with truckers. They prostitute themselves out to the drivers for the rides and to pay for their drug habits. I know because I have had several ask me for rides."

"Yeah, that's the same jumping, but I don't know where you got the trafficking idea?"

"Well, according to what this guy was telling me, Amber is assigned to a small group of jumpers. They are each given a package of drugs—most of them are wrapped as gifts and put in their backpacks. Then the girls hitch rides with truckers going to their destinations. They hand the drugs off to their connections when they arrive and then they get another package."

"Wow, they must be moving a lot of stuff across the country. Did he give you any names besides this girl?"

"Yes, and from what he said they are both in Atlanta. One of them is a character named Shades…no last name. His boss is apparently a guy name Dante."

"Dante Ramsey? Oh, wow. This is big. Dante Ramsey is a real big fish in the drug world. He's connected all over the place—from the Mexican cartels to the bigger fish in Central and South America. Wow, Shelby, what have you stumbled into?"

"I don't know, Angelica, that's why I'm calling you. This friend of Amber's is a real sweet kid, or seems to be, and he's trying to get Amber out of the organization. I thought I'd better call and ask you what to do."

"The first thing you need to do is tell that kid not to do anything right now. Tell him to be cool. Dante is vicious. He's even worse than those guys we played road tag with in Mexico. I need to talk this over with Rex and see what we can do to infiltrate this drug ring. This is serious, Shelby. Tell whatever his name is to just stay out of it for now. We are going to need some time to figure out how to expose the ring without getting anyone killed."

"Okay, Angelica, I will do my best to keep him calm. He did mention a woman named Crystal who likes Amber and is on the inside. She's supposedly Shades's girlfriend. Shades is the one who controls the girls."

"Well, I'm not personally familiar with that Shades character, but if he's involved with Dante, some of the guys that have kept an eye on Dante will know who he is. I really appreciate the information, Shelby. You are quite a lady."

"Right back at you, sweetie. Let me know what you find out. I'm going to be in Atlanta in a few weeks again. I will try and find some time for lunch with you."

"Sounds like a plan, my friend."

"Talk at you later."

"Okay, sweetie, I'll keep you informed. You be careful out there and try not to pick up any more strays."

"Not in my DNA."

"I know."

◊◊◊

Katie handed Annie to her mother. Annie looked at Amber's face, then she put her head into Amber's chest.

"Hi, my little angel." Annie looked again into Amber's face. "Do you remember me?"

Annie turned away from Amber and reached for Katie. She whimpered until Katie took her from Amber.

Damian could tell that Amber was having trouble with her baby girl's reaction to her. "Don't worry, Amber, she's just little. She hasn't seen you for a long time. You need to give her time to get to know you again."

Amber brushed away the tears. "I know; it's my fault. Oh, Damian, what have I done?"

Damian held Amber's hand and let her cry softly for a few moments. Amber wiped her tears away before anyone noticed.

Katie held Annie and touched Amber's cheek. "It will be okay, Amber. She's just a baby and doesn't remember things yet. The more time you spend with her, the more she'll remember."

"I know." Amber's regret hurt more than she could handle. "Pops, I need to go outside and sit on the porch for a little while."

"Okay, baby. I'll keep Damian company—go ahead and take some time."

Amber stood up.

Damian reached for Amber's hand. "Are you sure you don't want me to go with you?"

"No, I just need a few minutes alone."

"Okay."

Katie went to the table with the other women. Josh came through the kitchen door into the living room and sat near his dad. "So, how you feeling today, Pops?"

"I'm feeling a whole lot better. How are things at the office?"

"About the same; we sure miss having you around." Josh looked rudely at Damian, but spoke to his father. "Who's this, Pops? Another one of Amber's buddies?"

Charley moved in close to his son with some difficulty. "I know you have a problem with your sister and I can understand it. But I don't like the way you treat her and this is my house. So, until I'm dead and buried, you will respect my home and be polite to my guests, or you can go home."

Josh backed down and did as his father asked. "Yes, sir, I'm sorry. I will do my best to show respect when I'm in your house."

Josh looked at Damian and put out his hand. "I'm sorry, I shouldn't have been so rude to you. I have no right to judge someone without cause. I'm Josh Nichols."

Damian put out his hand and shook Josh's hand. "Damian Adams. Nice to meet you, Josh."

"Oh, I'm sure my sister has already told you about me."

Damian smiled. "Yes, she mentioned that her older brother Josh doesn't like her very much."

"Oh, I love Amber. I just don't like her behavior. But you seem level-headed enough, how'd she find you?"

"I met Amber in Atlanta, we met through her job."

"Well, what exactly does my sister do in Atlanta?" Josh folded his arms waiting for Damian's answer.

"She delivers packages to businesses for a company called, 'Don't Mail, Deliver.'"

"Really, she has a real job? I figured she was slinging hash, or other stuff."

Charley moved forward again. "Enough, Josh, and I mean it."

Josh backed down again. "Sorry, Pops, that just slipped out. I am glad she's doing better. When does she plan to come and take her kids to live with her?"

Before Damian could answer Josh's question, Amber came back into the room and sat next to her father. She immediately responded to her brother's question. "As soon as I have enough money to buy a nice house for all of us. I've been saving everything I can, and I think I'll have enough in about three more months."

Josh was a little impressed that Amber was doing so well, but he still wasn't buying her success. "So why haven't you come home before now, Amber, if everything is going so well?"

Amber was annoyed. "Because I was afraid of you, Josh. I was afraid of what you would say and what you would do if I came home." Amber got up from the seat next to her father. "Pops, I'm going to the bathroom, and then Damian and I are going to leave. We'll come back tomorrow and see you before we head back to Atlanta. I have to be back to work on Tuesday and it's a long drive."

Charley looked crossly at Josh.

"What Pops? I didn't tell her to leave. I wasn't rude. I just asked a very important question. We are all sitting here, raising her children while she is off doing God knows what."

With those words, Damian got off the couch and shook Charley's hand. "We will see you tomorrow, Charley."

"Nice to meet you, Damian. We'll see you tomorrow."

Damian didn't shake Josh's hand; he simply went to the front porch and waited for Amber to come out of the house. He used his cell phone to call for a taxi.

Josh came out to the front porch after Damian finished his call. "Look, you seem like a really nice guy, but you don't know my sister. She's poison and she will ruin your life if you let her. I'm sorry I'm so hard on her, but she just won't grow up and take responsibility for her actions."

Damian didn't make eye contact with Josh. He simply stared out into the yard. "You're right, I am a really nice guy and right now I don't feel like I want to be a nice guy. You are wrong about Amber. I know your sister. Regardless of what you think you know, or what you make yourself believe you know, Amber is a wonderful woman. She has made some mistakes, but she's trying to fix them and make things right. You have no idea what your sister has gone through or her current struggles. I suggest you go back into the house and leave me alone, before the 'nice guy' in me whips your ass."

Josh looked at Damian's body and decided to comply. He really didn't want anything to do with the six foot four, two hundred and forty pounds of muscle standing next to him. Josh went back into the house. A few minutes later, Amber appeared.

"I'm really sorry about my brother. I told you he was an asshole."

Damian hugged Amber. "No need to apologize. I think our little talk out here put him in his place for now. Our ride should be here any minute."

The taxi arrived just as Elsa Mae came to the porch. "Don't leave, Amber. Josh will behave himself, I promise."

Amber gave her mother a hug. "We'll come back tomorrow Mama and see you and Pops and my babies. I love you."

Elsa Mae watched once again as her youngest daughter left. "I love you, too."

CHAPTER TWENTY

Amber kissed Damian on the cheek. "Thank you so much for taking me to see my daddy. Mama says he is doing much better now that he knows I'm okay. I also wanted to thank you for standing up for me in front of my brother. It's going to take him some time to forgive me, but I think you set him straight. I really appreciate you, no one has ever done that for me but my daddy."

"It was my pleasure, little lady. I love being your knight, and I will be happy to take you anywhere you need to go."

◊◊◊

Damian went to the sleeper and brought back a gift bag. "Hey, sugar, I'd like us to stay in contact when you're working."

Amber was bent over, tying her shoes. "That's really difficult. First of all, I never really know where they are sending me. Second, I can't always use the phones in the stores. Some of those old bitches in them stores aren't very nice. I can't use the cell phone Shades has given me. He watches our phone calls."

"I know; that's why I bought you this." Amber stopped putting on her shoes and took the pretty bag from Damian. "Wow, thank you." She pulled two small boxes from the bag. "Damian, you shouldn't have done this."

"Why not?" He took the smallest of the boxes from her hand and opened it. "I got this one for you because I love you, Amber. I know you have to do what you're doing until I can figure out how to get you out of it." He took a ring out of the box and put it on Amber's hand. "Once we do get you away from Shades, I want you to marry me."

"But it might be a really long time, Damian." Amber looked at the ring on her finger. It sparkled in the sunlight that came through the windshield.

"It's beautiful, Damian."

"I'm willing to wait as long as it takes, Amber." He kissed her. "So, will you marry me?"

Amber looked at the ring again and then at Damian. "Yes." Amber kissed Damian.

Damian took the ring box and removed the protective cushion in the bottom. He pulled out a gold chain hidden beneath the cushion. "I got this for you so that you could put the ring around your neck. That way Shades will never see it and it will be close to your heart."

Amber took the ring off and put it on the chain. Damian put the necklace around Amber's neck. "It's perfect, thank you. I hope it won't be too long before we can be together forever." Amber put her hand over the ring that was now under her shirt and next to her heart. "I will keep it there until you can put it on my hand for good."

Damian smiled. "Open the other box," he said.

"Damian, this is too much." She opened the box. "A cell phone?"

"Yep, now you can call me whenever you want to without having to use those stupid phones at the store. It's in my name and I'm going to pay the bill. You can call me and we can try and work out your deliveries around my loads."

"This is terrific." She kissed him again.

"Now, be sure and keep it hidden. I'm sure Shades will take it and destroy it if he finds out you have it."

"You're right. I'll keep it on silent and hidden. Can I use it to call my folks and check in on my kids?"

"Of course."

"You're the best fiancé ever. I can't wait to call my mama." Amber looked at the time on the phone. "Is this time correct?"

Damian looked at the cell phone and then his watch. "Yep. Oh, shit, Amber. I'm sorry." He moved into the driver's seat. "Hold on, baby, we have twenty minutes to get you to that car parked at the airport."

◊◊◊

Crystal walked out of the airport elevator and into the parking garage. She spotted her car and saw Amber standing next to it. "I'm so glad you didn't let me down, sugar."

"I told you I'd be here." Amber lifted Crystal's suitcase into the trunk.

"Thank you. You have no idea the trouble I would have been in if you flaked on me." Crystal opened the driver's door and got into the car.

Amber got into the front passenger seat of the car. "Oh, I think I know."

Crystal started the car and backed it out of the parking spot. "How is your father doing?"

"He's doing much better now that he knows I'm okay." Amber liked Crystal. She was a tall, thin woman in her mid-forties with long blonde hair. Amber knew that she would never be as tall as Crystal. She did hope, however, that she would be able to hold onto some of her God-given beauty as Crystal had over the years.

"That's good. Did you enjoy the visit with your family?"

"Yes, especially my two little babies. Broke my heart that my little girl doesn't remember me, though. My oldest brother was an asshole, as usual. But the visit was great. Thank you so much for making it happen for me."

"Oh, you're so welcome, Amber. I haven't seen any of my family in years. I'm not even sure any of them are alive anymore. When I became Shades's top girl, I just never thought about home anymore."

"You never wished you could go home?"

Crystal shrugged. "Oh, I guess I did some, but I just didn't come from a very stable home. My dad was an alcoholic, and my mom was doped up on anti-depressants all the time. The state came in while I was in school one day and took my younger brother and sister. I took off before they came back for me. I ended up on the streets and that's where I met Jessie. He's the one that Shades took me from, and I sure was thankful to Shades for it. I think that's why I never went back home; there just wasn't anything there."

"You ever think about marrying Shades?"

"Oh, sometimes I wish he would ask, but I know that's never going to happen. Shades just isn't the marrying kind. Why all the talk about marriage and family?"

"Oh, my sister is getting married in about three months. I just can't figure out why a beautiful, smart woman like you is with someone like Shades."

The conversation came to a close when Crystal pulled into the driveway at Shades's house. "Well, he's not a law abiding citizen, but he's always
been good to me."

"I understand."

"Now, remember, you were sick most of the time we were in Miami,
that's why you didn't spend much time on the beach," Crystal told her. 'We
were in room 640. I don't think he will ask many questions, but just in case
he does."

"All right, I got it."

◊◊◊

"Amber, I need you to get up. One of my girls got arrested last night. I need
you to take this package to Maryland with her team."

Amber stretched. "Okay, but I'm still on my time off."

"I know. I'll make it up to you later. This delivery is really important."
Shades put the package on Amber's bed. "Crystal is going to take you to the
truck stop so you can find a ride. Make sure you get it there by tomorrow
night."

"Okay, Shades. Maryland is a tough ride to get, but I'll do my best."
Amber was up and dressing before Shades left the room.

"It's important, Amber. Get it there."

"I understand."

Shades left and Crystal came into the room. "You ready to go, sweetie?"

Amber grabbed the package and put it into her backpack. "Yes. I don't
think I know any of the girls on this team. Can you give me a couple of names?"

Amber and Crystal got into Crystal's car. "I'll call you in a little while
and let you know who your contacts will be. Be careful with this team, Amber.
These girls are rough and very cliquish. They don't like it when someone new
is put on their team."

"This isn't going to be permanent, is it? I really like running with my
team."

"I don't know, Amber. The girl that got busted has been busted before. Shades will have to transfer her to another team on the other side of the country. He may keep you on this new team, but you may work on the other team too, maybe…I'm not sure. But you'll be closer to the house this way."

Amber didn't let Crystal see her disappointment. *Damian's loads are mostly in the Midwest. How will this effect our connections?* Hiding her thoughts, she said, "Yeah, that will be nice. I just hope they aren't too hard to get to know." Amber looked out the window as they entered the parking lot of the truck stop.

"You'll be all right, Amber. Just be a loner and make your deliveries. Don't try and make friends with them. They know you're one of Shades's top jumpers, so they shouldn't mess with you too much."

"I will. Thanks for the ride, Crystal. Text that connection as soon as you can." Amber got out of the car and put on her backpack.

"Be careful."

"I will."

Crystal didn't wait for Amber to enter the store before she left the parking lot. Amber went directly to the restroom and found an empty stall. She pulled her new phone out and called Damian. "Hey, it's me, I can't talk long, but Shades has transferred me to another team."

"Why?"

"One of the girls on this team got busted last night. They are a very profitable team and he can't afford for the team to be down a girl. Most of their turf is on the East Coast."

"So, where are you headed?"

"Maryland, but I'm not sure where in Maryland yet. The team is already on their way and my package has to be there tomorrow night. I have to meet up with the team connection the next morning."

"Do any of the girls know you?"

"Not really, but they know that I'm one of Shades's top girls. Crystal warned me that they are rough and mean to new girls."

"You're my girl. I haven't found a load yet out of Atlanta, but I see one on the board for Oklahoma City from Maryland. I'll take that one and I'll take you to Maryland tonight. What truck stop are you at?"

"I'm at the Love's."

"Be there in a few minutes."

"Okay, thanks, Damian. See you soon."

Amber ended her phone call. She placed the phone in a secret pocket on the inside of her bag before she left the stall.

Amber went into the store to get a cup of coffee for herself and one for Damian, then went to the register to pay for the coffee.

"Well, well, well, look who we have here boys." Amber looked up from getting her change from the clerk. The blood drained from her face.

"Zeke!" Amber grabbed her coffees and headed toward the table next to the window. "You leave me alone, Zeke or I'll call Shades."

Zeke followed Amber to the table. "You belong to me, Amber, and I want you back." He pulled on Amber's backpack. "You need to come back with me to our little place."

Amber pulled away from Zeke. She spotted the two new guys who were with Zeke now. "You and your goons need to leave me alone."

"What you going to do, Amber, call the police? You know Shades will have your ass if you do that." Zeke laughed and grabbed Amber's arm.

"You're coming with me." Amber fought with Zeke as he pulled her outside the store by one arm.

"I'm not going anywhere with you, Zeke. You let go of me or I'll scream." She tried to twist out of his grasp. "Let me go!"

"I suggest that if you want to keep that arm, mister, you let her go." Damian was directly in Zeke's path.

"Who the fuck are you? This isn't any of your business, just get out of the way before my men here put you on the ground." Zeke's two new guys moved forward in front of him and Amber.

Damian didn't move. Zeke's new guys attempted to throw punches at Damian to make him move. Damian blocked both men's punches and landed direct fist blows to both men's abdomens. As both men folded forward, Damian hit both of them in the back of their heads with his fists, sending them to the ground in pain.

Zeke realized his two new bodyguards were worthless. He attempted to force Amber around the fight, thinking that Damian was too occupied to notice what he was doing. Amber took her free hand and hit Zeke in the face as hard as she could.

"Bitch!" Zeke let go of Amber's arm and grabbed her hair. He lifted his fist to hit her in the face.

Damian grabbed Zeke's fist and pulled his arm behind his back.

Zeke let go of Amber's hair.

Amber ran toward Damian's truck.

"You fucker, let go of me."

Damian pulled Zeke's arm back further until he heard a crack. Zeke screamed in pain. Damian let go of Zeke's arm and he fell to the ground, grabbing his broken arm. "You son of bitch! I'll get you for this."

Damian got into Zeke's face. "I doubt that. Now leave Amber alone or suffer the consequences."

Damian walked away from the mess of bodies laid out in the truck stop parking lot. He went straight to his truck and quickly pulled away from the scene.

"I'm so sorry, Damian. He just came out of nowhere. That was Zeke, the one who got me into this mess in the first place. He shot me up with heroin and ra—" She began to weep.

Damian stopped the truck. "That's the bastard that raped you?" Damian put on the air brakes on his truck and got out.

"Damian, come on. Don't do this—the cops are going to be here any minute. Come on, he's not worth it," Amber yelled out the window.

Damian found Zeke and his guards nursing their wounds near Zeke's car. Damian grabbed Zeke by the arm that wasn't broken and swung him around. "So you're the motherfucker that raped my girl?" Damian threw the hardest fist he could throw into Zeke's face. Zeke went flying over the hood of his car. Damian went to the other side of the car. He lifted Zeke's now bruised and bloody face up so that Zeke could see Damian's face. "Remember this face, because I will remember yours. If I ever see you again, or if you ever mess with Amber again, I'm going to kill you." With those words, Damian shoved Zeke's head into the wheel rim of his front passenger side tire.

Damian went back to his truck. He pulled out of the parking lot and they were down the highway before the police even arrived at the truck stop. No one, including Zeke and his boys told the police anything about what had happened.

Tears fell from Amber's eyes. "Oh, Damian, thank you for being there. I don't know what I would have done if Zeke had gotten his hands on me again. Damian, I want out of this mess so badly." Amber put her head on the dashboard and sobbed. "I just want out!"

Damian rubbed Amber's back as she cried. "I know, baby. I'm working on it."

CHAPTER TWENTY-ONE

Shelby's phone rang and she pushed her Bluetooth button on her earpiece. "Hi, Shelby, this is Angelica. How're you doing?"

"I'm doing well, Angelica. Just rolling this big truck toward Oklahoma City on the I-40."

"I miss running a truck. I need to come out there and run with you one of these days."

"That would be awesome. You just let me know when and I'll make it happen."

"Well, I may want to come out on the road with you sooner than you think. That's the reason I'm calling. Rex is going to put me in a truck pretty soon so that we can work on busting that jumping ring. You have no idea how big this thing is, Shelby. Dante has girls delivering all over the country, and he's using the truck circuit to do it. Rex and the agency feel that the best way to take it down is to get involved with it. We are going to put out a couple of young female agents to infiltrate the jumpers. A few other agents and I will with be running some trucks."

"That sounds great. What can I do to help?"

"Do you still have contact with that young guy Damian?"

"Well, I have his number, but I haven't talked to him much since we first met."

"How about the girl?"

"Same thing, I haven't seen her in a while."

"Give me any contact information you have on them. Better yet, call them and let them know we need to speak with them."

"Sure, I will text Damian's number to you."

"Great. I can't wait to get back out there with you. I told my boss to get me into a sand hauling company so that I can haul with you. He's going to try."

"That would be terrific, Angelica. The two wild girls riding the open road together again."

"Yeehaw!"

"Yeehaw!"

Shelby and Angelica laughed and talked for a few minutes before Shelby had to go.

"Well, Jack is calling me, so I'd better call him back. Can't wait to see you out here again."

"Can't wait to be out there again, sweetie."

Shelby hung up with Angelica. She pushed buttons on her screen until she found Jack's number and called him. "Hey, baby, I'm sorry I missed your call. I was talking to Angelica."

"So how are the newlyweds?"

"They are doing great. Angelica wanted to let me know that she would be out on the road again soon."

"Really, why?"

"Well, you remember that girl Amber who I was telling you about?"

"Yeah, the one you met in Atlanta."

"Yes, well, the other night, when I was at the truck stop off exit 236, I ran into her and her boyfriend. Turns out, after talking to the boyfriend, that Amber is messed up in some really bad stuff out here on the highway."

"Oh no, Shelby, not again."

"No baby, I'm not involved in any of it. I just passed the information on to Angelica. She talked with Rex and now there is a full blown investigation going on over it."

"But you're not involved?"

"No, not at all. That's why I told Angelica about it."

"Good, I'm proud of you for staying out of it. Please, no matter what happens—you let Angelica and Rex handle things."

"Of course, Jack. I'm so busy with work that I really don't have time to get involved."

"I hear the words coming out of your mouth, Shelby, but I know you. Now you stay out of it and I mean it."

"I will, Jack, I promise."

"You'd better. I love you, but it never fails, if there is trouble out there, you will find it."

Shelby laughed. "Seriously, baby, I'm too busy. I will call you here in a little while. I need to work through traffic in Oklahoma City right now. I think I'll stop and get a bite to eat before I take my break here."

"Okay, sweetheart. Be careful."

"I will."

◊◊◊

"What the hell happened to you, Zeke?" Shades opened the door to the apartment where he conducted his business.

"Shut up, Shades, you know what happened to me. It was one of your henchmen who broke my arm and messed up my face."

Shades laughed. "I have no idea what you're talking about, Zeke. None of my men would have done that to you—my men only do what I tell them to do. You piss me off, I'm just gonna have you killed. I'm done messing with you."

"This guy told me flat out that Amber was his girl and that I'd better stay away from her."

Shades didn't like Zeke and really didn't care that he was busted up, but more than that, he especially didn't like someone else claiming his property as their own. He leaned back in his desk chair. "Have you ever seen him before?"

"Nope, never, but he's a trucker. Amber ran straight to his truck. And when he finished beating the hell out of me and my men, he got in his truck and left."

"Did you get a name off the truck, a color or a type of truck? What kind of trailer was he pulling? What did he look like?"

"I don't know… he was big…really big. I think the truck was blue…I don't remember much more. He came out of nowhere. Look, I didn't come over here to talk about that son-of-a-bitch. I came to get my street shit."

Shades let the subject drop, but he wasn't about to forget what Zeke had just told him. "Fine. Put your money in the box and it'd better be right or I will send my boys after you. Remember, they won't break anything, they will finish you."

"Whatever." Zeke took the baggie of white powder, put his cash in the box on Shades's desk, and left the apartment.

Shades sat back in his seat and thought about what he'd just learned. He picked up his cell phone and called Crystal. "Hey, baby, did Amber mention anything to you while you were on vacation about having a boyfriend or someone taking care of her out there?"

"No, not a word, Shades. Why?"

"Oh, it's probably nothing, but when she calls in, tell her I want her to come back to Atlanta and finish her time off. I need to find out about something."

"Okay, I'll tell her."

◊◊◊

"I'm going to miss you so much, Damian. I wish I could go with you to Oklahoma City."

"I wish you could, too, but I can't get a load going to North Carolina right now. And you need to keep making deliveries until I hear from that DEA agent Shelby was telling me about. You just call me and let me know where you'll be going next. I will do my best to get a load going to wherever you're going. You just keep in touch with me and I will make sure I find you. Shelby talked really highly of that friend of hers. She said that we just had to pretend that everything is normal. She doesn't want us to make Shades suspicious about anything."

"Okay, I'll keep jumping, but I really wish I could just leave with you. I know I can't, but I really want to. I'm so scared about going back to Atlanta. Zeke is an animal."

"Well, if you go back to Atlanta, you stay away from that truck stop where you saw Zeke. I don't think he's going to bother you again, but if he does, I promise you, his time here on earth will be done."

Amber kissed Damian. "I love you."

Damian was surprised by Amber's words. "I love you, too."

Amber lay next to Damian while he held her tight, and they fell asleep together.

◊◊◊

Shantia's cell phone rang. "Hi Shades." Shantia sat up in her bed.

"Hey, Shantia, I want you to do me a favor."

"Sure."

"Tomorrow, when you go to the truck stop and pick up the packages, I want you to keep a close eye on Amber, the new girl on your team. I want to know who she's seen with and who she takes a ride with. I want to know everything. Crystal already texted all the girls that they are headed to North Carolina with that other delivery, so I want to know who she catches a ride with. Can you do that for me?"

"Sure, boss, I will let you know what I see."

"Good girl. There will be an extra couple hundred dollars in your pay this week."

"Awesome. Thanks, Shades."

◊◊◊

Damian hugged and kissed Amber by his driver's side door. He wiped the sleep from her eyes. "I'm sorry I have to leave you here. The sun isn't even up yet, but I have to go get my load. I will find a load going to North Carolina when I get to Oklahoma City, I promise."

"I wish I could go with you, but if I do, Shades will just hunt me down and kill us both."

"He's going to have a hard time doing that, Amber. I'm going to do everything I can to protect you. As soon as Shelby's friend calls me and we have a plan in place, I'm getting you out. I want to marry you and no one is going to stop me."

Amber kissed Damian again. "I love you."

"I love you, too. Now, keep that phone charged and call me often."

Damian took a piece of paper out of his pocket. "Here, this is a list of some of my trucking buddies. I've talked to most of them, and they are going to help when they can with rides for you."

Amber looked at the long list. "This is great. I won't have to do anything for the rides?"

"Nothing. They are doing it because I asked them to help me keep you safe."

"Thank you." Amber kissed Damian again.

"Now, Durango is in town here somewhere, I don't think he's here at this truck stop, but he's close. Go into the store and get some coffee, give him a call when you're ready to roll; he's headed down to Florida. He said he would give you a lift to North Carolina. I want you to try and get rides with these drivers when you can. Most of them know you're my girl, they won't expect anything from you."

"Okay."

Damian looked at his watch. "I have to go, or I'm going to be late picking up that load."

Amber moved away from the driver's side door of Damian's truck. Damian opened the door and climbed into the seat. "I love you, Amber Nichols. You go get some coffee. I'll see you in a few days."

"I love you too, Damian Adams." Amber watched as Damian pulled his rig out of the parking lot before she went into the store.

After getting a cup of coffee, Amber sat at one of the tables inside the store. She sipped at her drink and waited for the sun to rise and her team leader to arrive. Amber had only met Shantia once; she was an African American woman, about twenty-five. Amber hadn't had many dealings with Shantia, but she knew from the rumors that she was very dedicated to Shades. She was known to be very strict with the girls on her team. She handled her business by any means necessary. Amber wasn't looking forward to working with her.

"Hey, Amber, I didn't expect to see you in the store so early. You made it here before any of the other girls, and you were bringing in Trisha's package. How did you get here so fast?" Shantia stood over Amber for a moment before she slid into the booth across from her.

"Oh, I just got lucky, I caught a ride with one of my regulars in Atlanta and he dropped me here a little while ago. He was headed somewhere else, so I thought I would grab some coffee."

"A regular, how many regular rides do you have?" Shantia asked, her tone serious.

"Oh, I have a few. I find it easier to catch rides when you know the drivers, a lot safer, too." Amber could tell that Shantia was pumping her for information and felt uneasy in the fact that she'd taken a sudden interest in her.

"Safer. I understand that. I've found myself in a few situations where I wish I'd had some backup. You ever been in anything like that?" Shantia sipped her coffee. "You know, where you wished you had a boyfriend or someone watching your back?"

Amber knew something was up. "No, not anything like that, so far. I just like to be safe out here."

"So who'd you get a ride from? I might want to use him sometime," Shantia continued to pry.

"Oh, he's one that runs in the Midwest most of the time. I doubt he will be on this side of the country for a long time." Amber sipped at her coffee and then moved to get out of the booth. "I need to use the bathroom. Are you going to be here or outside when we exchange gifts?"

"Oh, I'll be outside. I sure wish you'd give me his name or his trucking company. I could really use a nice guy to ride with every once in a while. Some of these drivers stink."

Amber wanted to end the conversation. "I've really got to go pee. I don't know his name and all I know about his truck is that it's red and a Pete."

"A red Pete." Shantia sipped her coffee. "I'll see you outside in twenty minutes."

"Okay."

Amber nearly fell into the empty stall in the bathroom. She slammed the door, locked it, and put her back to the door. She put her hand on the ring that hung from her neck. *Something is going on. Shantia is asking too many questions about Damian and his truck.* She hoped her lie about the color of his truck coupled with not giving away any pertinent information about Damian would keep him out of trouble.

Breathing hard, Amber opened her bag and took out the phone that Damian had given her. She wanted to talk to Damian right then, but she then decided against it, and put the phone back in its special pocket. With all the team members possibly in the truck stop parking lot, it might not be safe. She would find a safe place after the exchange. Once she was with Durango she would call Damian. She forced herself to calm down and waited several minutes before she headed out to the parking lot.

A few of the team girls were waiting to exchange gifts with Shantia. Amber quietly waited her turn by the wall. When it was Amber's turn, Shantia smiled. "So, you got a ride with another of your regulars taking you to North Carolina?"

"No, I'll have to look through the lot and see what I can find." Amber said.

"Wow, a popular girl like you shouldn't have any trouble finding one of her regulars out here."

Amber was annoyed. She grabbed her package out of her bag and handed it over. Shantia took it and then handed her a new one. Amber grabbed it and walked away without answering any more of Shantia's questions. "Oh, come on, Amber. Friends share."

Amber hated Shantia and now she was worried about Damian. *I'd better be careful. Shades knows something and he's watching me.* Amber left the parking lot of the truck stop on foot.

After walking several blocks, Amber stopped at a local fast food restaurant. She went into the restroom and called Durango. "Hi, is this Durango?"

"Yes, who's this?"

"This is Amber, a friend of Damian's; he told me I could call you for a ride to North Carolina."

"Sure thing. I'm almost finished with my break. Where would you like to meet up?"

"Well, I'm at the Sugar Shack on the ninety-five. I don't know exactly where everything is, but I really don't want to meet at the truck stop near here, if that's okay."

"Not a problem. Give me about an hour and I will swing by and pick you up on that service road next to the ninety-five. Do you see it?"

"No, I'm in the bathroom, but I know what you're talking about. I'll be waiting. Thanks so much."

"Any time. Anything for my buddy, Damian. See you soon."

◊◊◊

"I tried, Shades, but she was already at the truck stop when I got there. The only things she told me was that her ride from Atlanta was a regular, and that he rolled mostly in the Midwest. She said his truck was red, but she didn't give me anything more, I guess she didn't know anything more. I watched her leave, but she walked away from the truck stop. I couldn't follow her; I had to take care of the exchanges."

"It's cool, Shantia. I appreciate the information—be sure and keep an eye on her for me. Let me know if you see or hear anything, okay? The extra money will be in your pay."

"Thanks, Shades. I'll keep my eyes open."

Shades sat back in his chair. Crystal came into the room with a glass of iced tea and handed it to him. She could tell he was deep in thought about something. She sat on the arm of Shades's chair. "What's up?"

Shades took a gulp of his tea and then put it on the desk. "Why would a guy who normally rolls in the Midwest be rolling on the East Coast? Then he just so happens to be at the same truck stop when one of my girls is being roughed up by a former pimp. Then he beats the hell out of the pimp and mentions that one of my girls isn't my girl at all, but his girl."

"What the hell are you talking about, Shades?

"Amber, I'm talking about Amber. Apparently, our little Amber has a regular and he's claiming to own her."

Crystal felt uncomfortable when Shades brought up Amber's name. She hoped that he hadn't got wind of the fact that Amber had not been in Florida with her. Crystal got up from the arm of the chair and sat on the desk. "Shades, you know that it isn't that hard for some of those drivers to get attached to your girls."

"I suppose you're right, but you know it bothers me when the girls get attached to the drivers."

Crystal gently touched Shades's face.

Shades pulled Crystal toward him on the chair and kissed her hard on the lips.

"I know, baby," Crystal said, "but she lives right here and I haven't seen any signs that she has the slightest interested in anyone. She never said a word while we were away in Florida. I wouldn't worry about it."

"You're probably right. Will you keep an eye on her and let me know if you hear or see anything different with her?"

Crystal kissed Shades. "You know I will."

Shades tried to let it go, but he had a feeling something was going on with Amber and he was determined to find out more about it.

CHAPTER TWENTY-TWO

"Look, Damian, I'm fine. I'm with Durango and we are headed to North Carolina. I really think we'd better cool it for a while though. Shades knows something is up, and I don't want him to find out about you."

"I'm not afraid of Shades, Amber, and I don't see any reason why we need to stop seeing each other. That will kill me."

"I know. I feel the same way, but we need to. At least until you hear something from Shelby's friend. Have you heard anything?"

"No, but I do have an unknown number on my phone and a message on the voice mail that I haven't listen to yet. It's probably some kind of salesperson or something. But I will let you know when I hear from them. Shelby said it might be a couple of weeks before she contacts me, so that should be soon."

"For now, I want you to stay away from the East Coast. Let things calm down. I'll use your friends for rides so you won't worry about me. I just know Shades, and I'm pretty sure that asshole Zeke told him something. I can't take the chance that he might find out about us. It's not only you I'm worried about but also my family. Shades knows where they are, and it wouldn't be too hard for him to find them. Please, pretty please, for us, for our future."

Damian didn't like the idea of not seeing Amber for a while, but after hearing about Shantia, and all the questions she was asking, he figured Amber was probably right. "All right, but only until Shelby's friend at the DEA comes in and helps us get you out. You have to promise to stick with my driving buddies and call me at least once a day."

"I promise, Damian. I will call you once a day. If for some reason you don't hear from me, wait two days and then you can worry. I might not always be able to call you."

"Okay. I love you, Amber. You're my girl forever."

"I love you too, Damian. We will be together soon."

Amber hung up the phone and looked at Durango. "He's really upset about all this."

"I can tell, but I think you're doing the right thing, Amber. I don't know this Shades character, but he sounds pretty dangerous."

"He is, but his boss, Dante—he's the one who is really dangerous. Thank you for the ride."

"Oh, it's not a problem. You can crawl back there and get you a nap if you want. I'll wake you up when we get to your truck stop in Raleigh."

◊◊◊

"This is Damian Adams. I had a message to call and speak to a lady named Angelica Dillon; her extension is 3792." Damian waited while the receptionist put his call through to Angelica's office phone.

"This is Angelica."

"Angelica, this is Damian Adams."

"Oh, yes, Mr. Adams."

"Just call me Damian, please."

"Okay, Damian. I received a phone call from my friend Shelby Mathews and she told me about your situation and a woman named Amber Nichols."

"Yes, Amber is my fiancé and she is in really big trouble. She's a jumper for this guy named Shades. Amber and I just got engaged a few days ago. She's in real danger working for Shades. I wanted her to just leave and marry me, but she says that if she does, Shades will kill her and her family. In fact, I can't even see her right now, because someone has said something to Shades and now he's got his radar on her."

"Okay, calm down, Damian. Let's take this slow for a minute. I've done some investigation into the names you gave Shelby. I won't go into any of the details, but we are currently working on a plan to infiltrate that organization."

"That's great! When do you think it will be safe for me to go and get Amber?"

"Slow down, Damian. It will take us some time to gather evidence on the organization. We have very little information on Shades, but we know a lot about his boss Dante. Dante isn't an idiot, and it won't be easy getting people close to him. But we are working on it. We need you to be patient and wait for us before you do anything."

"Well, I'll wait, but I'm not going to wait forever. Amber means a lot to me and she needs to get away from those drug dealers."

"So you are aware that Amber is trafficking drugs for her boss, Shades?"

"Yes, and if she doesn't she will find herself in the Mississippi River or a Louisiana swamp as food for the fish and alligators. That Shades doesn't play games, but I'll tell you now, I'm not afraid of him or any of his goons. I took care of three of them just the other day, when they tried to put Amber in a car."

"What?"

"You heard me. Some asshole named Zeke, who used to be Amber's pimp, tried to kidnap her in Atlanta. If I hadn't been there, God knows where she would be right now. Amber told me that Shades took her away from Zeke and now Zeke is trying to take her back. Shades may be a drug dealer, but Zeke is a rapist."

"So, you have seen this Zeke guy?"

"Yes, ma'am. We need to hurry and get her out of there as soon as possible. She is in danger, and I don't know how long she will be able to hang in there. I gave her a list of my trucker friends, and she is going to make contact with them so she won't have to hook her way to her deliveries. This jumping business is really bad."

"Yes, I agree with you, Damian. They aren't just breaking the law by trafficking drugs, but they are engaging in sex and human trafficking as well. I can't wait to get my hands on those scumbags."

"I can't wait until your agency takes them out, either. Just remember, Angelica, my Amber doesn't want to be doing what she's doing. They are making her do it."

"I know, Damian. Now, I will be in touch with you in a few days. I want you to be patient and try not to do anything on your own. It will cause problems for us. Do I have you're word that you won't act without my permission?"

"Yeah, but don't take too long. I can't see her right now and it's killing me."

"I understand, Damian. Give me a little time, please. I promise I will get her out of that organization safely if you let me do it."

"Okay, Angelica, I will try."

◊◊◊

"Hey, Crystal, I'm done delivering in Raleigh, what's next?"

"Well, Amber, Shades wants you to come back to the house and finish your time off. We need to have a private talk when you get back, too. I'm not sure what's going on with you, but he's all up in arms over something that happened at a truck stop here in Atlanta."

"That was Zeke, Crystal. Zeke tried to take me back."

"We'll talk about it when you get back here. You need to be careful. Shades is keeping a really close eye on you. Do you understand?"

"Yes, I understand. I'll be there as soon as I can get a ride."

"There is a package for you to pick up from Shantia coming back here for Shades. It's a very special package, so don't lose it."

"Okay, I'll be there soon." Amber sat down on the curb next to the store of the truck stop. She wanted to cry, but the tears just wouldn't flow. *What the hell am I doing in this world? I made some major mistakes in my life and now I'm paying dearly for them.* She missed Damian and she missed her babies and she missed her parents. She wondered if she would ever see any of them again.

Amber's thoughts were suddenly interrupted. "Amber."

Amber turned to see Shantia standing over her.

Amber got to her feet.

"Here, you need to take this package directly to Shades, and don't lose it."

Amber took the package. "Okay."

"I looked for you after I got all the packages collected and you were gone. Where did you go?"

"I went to get something to eat."

"How'd you get here so fast?"

"Just hitched a ride."

"How'd you do that so fast? You must have a bunch of drivers waiting in line to give you a ride. You seem to find them anywhere you are."

"I guess." Amber walked away from Shantia and toward the highway. She wanted to get as far away from that nosy bitch as possible.

It wasn't long before she found a gas station near the ninety-five. Amber quickly found her way to the restroom. The restroom door was locked, so Amber waited for the party occupying the bathroom to finish. Once inside the restroom, she removed her list of drivers and started calling to see who might be near. After about ten calls Amber reached Willow.

Amber was a little taken back when it was a female voice on the phone. "Hi, my name is Amber and my boyfriend Damian gave me your number. He said you might give me a lift from Raleigh to Atlanta, if you were in the area."

"Well, hi Amber, my name's Willow. I'm not in Raleigh, yet. I'm about an hour out. I will have to take a break when I get there. I have to deliver in the morning, but I do have a load going in that direction tomorrow. Will that be okay for you? Do you have somewhere to stay until we leave tomorrow?"

Amber didn't have to think long—she needed a bath. She decided she would rent a cheap hotel room for the night. "Yes, I do have a place, can I call you in the morning to arrange to meet?"

"Sure, that would be fine."

"Thank you so much, Willow. When would be a good time to call?"

"Oh, probably around seven."

"Great, I'll call you in the morning. Thanks again, I really appreciate this."

"No problem. Damian and I have been friends for a long time. I'd do anything for that kid. See you tomorrow."

Amber put her secret phone away. She took Shades's phone out of her pocket and called Crystal. "Hey, it's Amber."

"Hi sweetie, did you find a ride?"

"Yeah, but the driver has to finish her break before we leave. I will be in Atlanta sometime tomorrow. Is that okay?"

"Yeah, Shades just said he wanted you back here to finish your break."

"Okay. Well, I'll call you when I get in. Can you pick me up or should I just get a taxi?"

"No, just call me; I'll come get you. We can go get a bite to eat or something if it's not too late."

"All right Crystal, see you tomorrow."

◊◊◊

"I don't know anything, Shades. She took the package and left the parking lot just like all the other times. I followed her down the highway a little ways, but she went into a gas station. She stayed there for a little while, but then when she came out she started walking down the highway again."

"Did you follow her down the highway?"

"No, I didn't follower her any further. I have my own deliveries to make. If you and I don't want Dante on our asses, I have to do my job, too."

"Oh, I know, Shantia. I just don't know what's up with that girl."

"All I know is that she has no trouble finding a ride."

"Well, I just can't shake this feeling that something is up with her and I'm going to find out what it is."

"Okay, boss. Well, I need to get going."

"All right, I'm going to send one of the West Coast girls in to help you out while Amber is in Atlanta."

"Okay, whatever you need to do. I think the girls and I can handle things, but you're the boss."

"More girls, more product."

"I know. Talk to you later."

◊◊◊

Amber crawled into Willow's truck. She had been waiting at the truck stop since seven a.m. The gray-haired woman was dressed in a tie-died muumuu and reminded Amber of her grandma. "I sure appreciate the ride, Willow."

"No problem, Amber. I tried to get here earlier, but the idiots at the dock where I was unloading couldn't read, I guess. They tried to take part of my load that's headed for Georgia. I caught it before they unloaded every-thing, but they had to reload what they took off by mistake."

"Oh, that's okay. I'm just glad for the ride."

"Well, anytime, sweetheart. Any friend of Damian's is a friend of mine."

Amber watched as the lady driver pulled her big truck out of the truck stop and onto highway ninety-five. She could handle the big rig as well as any man she'd seen. "You've known Damian for a long time?"

"Oh, I'd say so. I sort of took that little boy under my wing when he first came out here. He was as green as a greenhorn can get." Willow's laugh sent a small shrill into the truck's cab. "Honey, let me tell you, that poor baby boy couldn't back a truck into a dock to save his neck." Amber and Willow laughed. Amber hadn't felt like laughing in so long, it felt good.

The trip to Atlanta seemed to fly by with Willow at the wheel. "I have to say, Willow, this has been the most amazing truck ride I've ever taken. Now I know why Damian was so drawn to you. You have the most wonderful stories about your life out here on these roads."

"Well, thank you, little Amber."

Willow pulled her big rig into the truck stop that Damian had asked Amber to avoid. She didn't want to ask Willow to go to another truck stop. "This be okay, sweetie?"

"Sure Willow—this will be just fine."

Willow pulled into the fuel island. "Well, I'd better give the old girl some go-go juice."

Amber got out of the truck and gave Willow a big hug. "Thank you, Willow. I hope we meet again."

"We will, little Amber, if not on these highways, then we will meet one day on the golden roads of heaven."

No one had ever been so kind to her. "I know we will."

Amber left Willow pumping fuel. She waved goodbye and disappeared into the truck stop store.

Amber headed straight to the restroom. She hadn't talked to Damian in two days. She couldn't wait any longer. "Hey, it's me."

"Baby, I'm so glad to hear your voice. I've been going crazy without you."

"Me too, Damian." Tears welled up in Amber's eyes. She stopped speaking and tried hard to hold back the emotions that were flooding out of her soul. She didn't know why she was acting so crazy. Maybe it was being with Willow or maybe it was that she was just plain tired of the life she was forced to live. She didn't care anymore; all she wanted was to be with Damian.

"Amber, are you okay, baby? Amber, where are you? I will come and get you right now."

Amber took in a deep breath and spoke as clear as she could through her sobs. "I'm fine, Damian…I'm fine. I just really miss being with you. I miss my family, and I miss my babies so much Damian." Amber couldn't control her tears any longer. "Oh, Damian, I can't go on like this anymore. I want to go home. I want to be a mom to my kids and a wife to you. I love you, and I miss you so much."

Damian had never heard Amber speak so deep from her heart. "Amber, baby, where are you? Tell me, baby, I'll come get you right now."

Amber couldn't stop crying. "No, Damian…not right now." She cried. "I'm in Atlanta," she sobbed. "I have to take this package to Shades." She continued to cry. "But, I just want to be with you." She sobbed uncontrollably.

"I'm coming there, Amber; I'm coming to get you right now." Damian's head was spinning. He was in a truck stop parking lot in Michigan. He was hours away from Amber. He was pacing the parking lot with his phone in his ear. *How am I going to get to her? She needs me now.* "Amber, can you hear me, baby?"

"Yes."

"Amber, I'm in Michigan, but I'm putting my truck in overdrive. I'm coming for you, baby." Damian went to his truck; he had a load on that needed to be delivered in the morning, but he didn't care, Amber needed him more. Amber worked to control herself. She couldn't put Damian in danger. Shades would kill him and she couldn't live with that. "No, Damian, no! Don't come here, I'll come to you."

"Amber, my dear sweet Amber. Don't cry, baby, please. I can't stand to hear you hurting." Damian put his hands through his hair in frustration. "How are you going to come to me, Amber?"

"Just be waiting for me, okay?" Amber brushed away her tears with the palm of her hand. "I will get to you in a few days. I have to take a package to Shades and then I'm going to get out. I'm going to run. I'm going to run to you, Damian."

"Amber, I love you. I would wait for you until the end of the world." Damian wanted Amber with him, but he didn't want anything to happen to her. "Amber, I know you want out; I want you out more. But maybe we'd better wait for the DEA agents. I don't want you hurt."

Sniffing Amber composed herself. "I'll be okay. I'll be careful, I promise." Uncontrolled sobs escaped as she spoke. "Just don't give up on me, promise you won't leave me or give up on me."

"I will never give up on you, Amber. I will never leave you. You are my girl forever. I love you with all my heart."

Amber had composed herself. She was ready to get her life back—or die trying. "I know what to do, Damian; just remember that I love you and I will call you in a few days."

Damian wasn't connected to Amber anymore. "Amber! Amber!" As he hung up his phone Damian knew what he had to do. *I'll call Angelica and Shelby.*

CHAPTER TWENTY-THREE

Amber washed her face, as she wiped the water off, she saw herself in the mirror. *Who am I?*

She hadn't really seen herself in a long time, and had not seen who she'd become. The mirror revealed more than puffy eyes and red cheeks. Amber Nichols was a woman with someone who loved her for who she was—she was a mother, a daughter, and a sister with a beautiful family.

She wiped her face once more, threw the paper towels in the trash, and gathered her things. She had carefully put Damian's phone back in her backpack. *I'll deliver the package to Shades, and then I'll get the hell out of this town.*

She placed the phone call to Crystal. "Hey, it's me. I'm at the truck stop off the twenty. I'll be waiting for you near the side doors."

"Okay, Amber, I'll be there in a few minutes."

Amber hung up the cell phone and put it in her pocket. She walked out into the store and grabbed a cup of coffee.

"Amber, Amber, Amber."

Amber lifted her head up when she recognized the voice—the voice that sent chills through her body like nails on a chalkboard. Amber sipped at her coffee, turned around, and saw Zeke standing in front of her with his arm in a sling. His two goons stood poised behind him with faces bruised and hands bandaged. "What do you want, Zeke?"

Zeke smiled. "You know what I want, Amber. I want you, and I'm going to have you."

Amber pulled her backpack up onto her shoulder and walked away from Zeke and toward the register.

Zeke couldn't believe what had just happened. "You can't just walk away from me! I own you." He followed Amber to the register. He forcibly turned her around, causing her backpack to fall on the floor.

Amber rolled out of Zeke's grip and threw her coffee in his face.

Zeke screamed. "Bitch! Get her."

Amber grabbed for her backpack but the goons got to it first. Amber was afraid now. Shades's package was in there and Damian's phone was in there as well. Two things she didn't wasn't Zeke to have or find. Amber went at the goon who had her backpack. "Give that back! Zeke, you don't own me. I don't work for you anymore. I will never work for you again. You have to give me back my pack. Shades will kill you if you don't. I will tell him."

The other goon grabbed Amber and held her back from the one who had possession of her backpack. Zeke wiped what he could of the coffee from his face with napkins off the counter. The clerk grabbed for the phone. "Put that phone down, or I'll do to you what I'm about to do to her." Zeke pointed toward the door. "Take her outside."

Amber was easily overpowered by Zeke and his men. "You let me go, Zeke! Shades will have your ass for this."

Outside, Amber fought as Zeke and his men pushed her into his car. Zeke took the backpack from his man. He unzipped it and spotted the package. Amber couldn't see what Zeke was doing because Zeke's two men had their backs against the doors. Quietly, Zeke spoke. "Look at what we have here, boys." Zeke laughed with his men. Then he took the package and put it in the inside pocket of one of his men's jackets. "Shades will never know what happened to his little gift."

Amber slapped at the back windows of the car. "Let me out of here, Zeke! Shades will kill you for this and you know it."

Zeke zipped the backpack, and then opened the passenger door of the front seat. "Let's get out of here before the cops show up."

"Not so fast, Zeke." A woman's voice broke through Amber's cries for help. With a gun in her hand, Crystal approached Zeke and his two men. "Let Amber out of that car and give back her bag. Now! I've already called Shades and he's on his way. You really don't want to be here when he gets here."

Zeke laughed. "Crystal, oh man. We were just giving little Amber a ride home."

"Shut the fuck up, Zeke, and let her out of that car or I will shoot you in the balls."

"Okay, okay! Take it easy." Zeke lifted up his arm that was not in the sling as if he was under arrest. He motioned with his head for his men to let Amber out of the car. "Let her go guys."

The men moved away from the door and opened it for Amber. Amber crawled out of the car and ran to Crystal. Crystal pointed her gun at Amber's backpack. "Give her back the bag. Now!"

"Okay, Crystal, don't bust a gut. Zeke threw the bag on the ground in front of Amber. Amber picked it up.

"Now, get the hell out of here you piece of shit, unless you want to wait for Shades." Crystal and Amber backed toward Crystal's car that was parked in the middle of the parking lot with the driver's side door open. "Leave, Zeke. Leave now."

Zeke and his men got into Zeke's car and backed out of the parking space they had occupied. Without looking at Crystal and Amber, he burned rubber as he peeled out of the lot.

Amber and Crystal climbed into her car. Crystal drove as fast as she could out of the parking lot.

Amber couldn't believe that Zeke had tried to kidnap her again. "Crystal, thank you. That bastard won't leave me alone. I don't know what I would have done if you hadn't shown up. That's the second time he's tried to take me."

"I know; he's crazy." Crystal rubbed her hand over Amber's head. "You're safe now. I've told Shades a bunch of times that he needs to get rid of Zeke. Maybe now he will do something."

Crystal called Shades. "I got her. Zeke took off with his men. You have to do something about that asshole, Shades. He's losing it, and he's going to cause problems for Dante."

"I will deal with him shortly; bring Amber and the package to the house. I was leaving the apartment when you called. I sent Leo and Arnold to help you, but I can see you didn't need any help. That's why you're my number one girl."

"Thanks, baby. I'll see you at the house."

◊◊◊

"Look, Shelby, I really need to talk to Angelica, but it's too late to call her on the office number. Do you have her cell number?"

"Well, sure, I have her cell number, Damian, but I have to call her and ask her if I can give it to you. I'm sure she won't mind, but it wouldn't be right to give it to you without asking her first. What's going on?"

Damian walked up and down the small space in his sleeper. "Shelby, this is really important. Amber called me just a little while ago and she's losing it. I think she's going to try and run away from Shades. Angelica told me that we shouldn't do anything until they got things in place to take Shades and the Dante guy down. I tried to talk to her, but she hung up on me. I haven't been able to get her back on the phone. She turned it off."

"Oh damn, Damian. Here, call Angelica at 555-677-7156. That's her cell number. I'm sure she won't care that I gave it to you. Please keep me informed about what's going on and if I can do anything to help."

"Thanks, Shelby. I'll let you know."

◊◊◊

"I don't know what happened to it, Shades; it was in here when I was in the bathroom." Amber stood in front of Shades's desk; her backpack had been poured out onto the floor.

Shades came from behind his desk—Crystal was between him and Amber. Shades pushed Crystal slightly out of the way and sat on the corner of his desk. "It's not here, Amber, and that package was very important."

Shades quickly raised his hand and slapped Amber across the face. The force sent the petite teen stumbling backward and she fell on her butt.

Crystal went to Amber and helped her to her feet. "Shades, Amber has never *not* delivered a package. Maybe Zeke or his goons took the package from her backpack. He did have it in his possession when I got there."

Shades got off the desk and grabbed Amber by the face. "Did he take my package, Amber?" Shades slapped her again, this time making her mouth and nose bleed.

"Shades!" Crystal again went to Amber's side. "Stop! I'm sure Zeke must have taken it."

Amber felt Shades slap her again. "Did he take my package, Amber?"

With blood and tears mixed across her face Amber tried to talk. "I don't know, Shades. It was there when I was in the bathroom."

Shades slapped her again.

"He must have…he must have taken it," she cried.

Shades's blows made hamburger out of Amber's face.

Crystal did what she could to stabilize Amber who was about ready to fall over.

Shades moved back to his chair. "Help her clean this mess up off my floor and get her out of here. I don't know what I'm going to do with this one, but she's becoming a real problem."

Crystal made Amber steady herself while she picked up the items from Amber's backpack up off the floor. She noticed the bulge at the bottom of the bag but didn't bring it to Shades's attention. Amber had suffered enough. After gathering Amber's things, Crystal walked her toward the door. "This was totally unnecessary, Shades. This isn't like you. You need to find Zeke. I'm sure he and his men are the ones that have your package."

Shades didn't like Crystal talking to him like that, but he loved her and let her get away with more than any girl ever could. "Get her out of here, Crystal. I have to make sure she understands there are consequences to not making a delivery. Especially *this* delivery."

Shades got on his phone. "Leo, get the car and meet me out front. We have a problem that needs to be taken care of immediately."

◊◊◊

Zeke jumped around his apartment like a child who just gotten a new bike for Christmas. He had a fist full of hundred dollar bills in his hand. Zeke's guys were at the coffee table counting the remaining bills that had scattered about. "Shit, boys, we hit the motherlode; can you believe we landed one of Shades's payoff bundles?" He laughed. "I bet he is about ready to shit his pants. I bet Amber is getting the hell beat out of here. This is payment enough for that bitch." He continued to run around the apartment. "We're rich, boys. We're rich!"

The doorbell rang.

Zeke stopped mid-stride in his jubilation. One of the men went to the door and opened it. One of the four men with Shades grabbed Zeke's goon before he had the door all the way opened. He quickly pulled Zeke's man close to his body and twisted his neck. The man fell to the floor dead.

Shades and the rest of the men walked into Zeke's apartment. Zeke dropped the money that was in his hand.

Shades walked over to Zeke. "I see you found my money. Pick it up and hand it to me."

Zeke bent down, picked up the money, and handed it to Shades. "I was going to bring it to you tomorrow, Shades."

Shades took the money from Zeke and put it in his pocket. He nodded at two of his men to pick up the rest of the money on the table. They grabbed the cash and then walked to the door. Shades and his last man pulled out revolvers with silencers. Seconds later, Zeke and his other goon were dead on the floor.

Shades kicked Zeke's bleeding body out of his way as he and his men walked from the apartment and closed the door.

◊◊◊

Crystal wiped at Amber's face.

Amber mumbled softly to her mother figure, "I swear, Crystal…I didn't take that package."

"I know, baby girl, I know. Shades had to do this so that we remember who's in charge." Crystal lifted Amber's chin up and looked at her face. "It's not too bad. I can remember when I got my beat downs from my other pimp. Be glad it was Shades and not that guy."

"It hurts, Crystal," Amber cried.

"I know, sugar." Crystal gently hugged Amber. "I know."

◊◊◊

"Angelica, I know it's late and I'm so sorry I had to call, but Amber is in trouble I think. Or, I think she might try and do something before you're ready."

"Calm down, Damian; what's going on?"

Damian went into details about his conversation with Amber earlier in the evening. "She was really upset, Angelica. I thinking she's at her breaking point. She's going to do something soon; she kept telling me to be ready and wait for her. What do I do?"

Angelica thought for a moment. "Where was she when she called you?"

"She's back in Atlanta."

"What did she say she was going to do?"

"All she said was that she was going to give Shades his package and then take off. She didn't give me any details of how she was going to do it or anything. She just told me to wait for her call and be ready."

"Where are you right now?"

"I'm in Michigan, but I can be anywhere you think I need to be, fast."

"No, you just keep working and wait for her call. I'm going to try and see if I can get down to Atlanta by tomorrow. We don't have everything set up yet, but I'd think I better move things along. I think you're right—she's probably going to try and get out of her situation now. Did you tell her that we were working on getting her out?"

"Yes, I even told her that maybe she'd better just hold on and wait for you guys. I don't think she wants to do that."

"I don't think she does, either. I wonder what has happened to make her want to get out right now?"

"I don't know; I just think she's done with it all and wants her life back."

"You're probably right."

"It might have had something to do with that old pimp of hers trying to kidnap her, too."

"Yeah, you could be right. I've been looking into that guy, Zeke, but the Atlanta Police haven't gotten back with me yet. I will definitely look into that when I get down there."

"Do you have any idea where she stays when she's in Atlanta?"

"Not really. She talks to Crystal, and I think she lives with her, but she hasn't shared much about that with me."

"Okay, Damian. I appreciate your call and I totally understand your frustration with this thing. But for now, you must stay calm and let us do our jobs. Keep my phone number handy and let me know right away if you hear from her."

"Okay, Angelica, I will. Thank you so much."

"It's all good, Damian. We will get her out."

Damian hung up his cell phone and put his head in his hands. "Oh, Amber, where are you? What is happening to you?"

A sense of helplessness consumed him as he collapsed onto his bed in the sleeper.

CHAPTER TWENTY-FOUR

mber sat up in her bed. Her head hurt. Crystal had given her some drugs to help her sleep and to dull her pain. But now that the drugs had dissipated she felt like she had been hit by a truck. She went to the bathroom and looked in the mirror. Bruises encircled both eyes and her lip was split and swollen. Amber touched her face. "Bastard."

She undressed and got into the shower. She was determined that before the day was out she would be on her way to Damian.

As she let the warm water cover her head and body, Crystal's voice came from the bedroom. "Hey, sweetie, I brought you some breakfast." Crystal put the tray of food on the nightstand next to Amber's bed.

"I'm in the shower," Amber called out.

Crystal entered the bathroom and sat on the toilet. "Well, I'm glad you're up. I was hoping that you'd be feeling better this morning."

"I feel like shit. My face looks even worse." Amber pulled the shower curtain back so that Crystal could see the damage that Shades had left.

"Ouch! I'm so sorry—and so is Shades."

"Yeah, I can feel how sorry he is."

"He really is…I promise…he told me last night. In fact, he told me he found the package and you were right. Zeke and his goons did take it."

"I told him I didn't take it."

"He knows, and he wants to make it up to you. He wants you to go shopping with me today. He wants you to buy some new things for yourself. He gave me a thousand dollars to spend on you."

Amber pulled the curtain back. "I can't go out looking like this Crystal. I don't want to go anywhere today." Amber went back to her shower. "I just want to take a shower and then go back to bed. You can give me some more of those pain pills, though."

"Oh come on, Amber—we can put some makeup over those bruises and you'll look fine. Don't you want to go shopping? A whole thousand dollars!"

Amber turned off the water, pulled the shower curtain back, and grabbed the towel from the towel rack. She wrapped herself in the towel. "You can spend the money on yourself, Crystal. I really don't want anything from Shades. I don't want to go anywhere, either."

Crystal didn't like Amber's response to Shades's attempted apology, but she understood it. She followed Amber into the bedroom and sat on Amber's bed. She spotted Amber's bag on the floor. "It's okay. Maybe you'll feel better tomorrow and want to go."

Amber pulled some clothes out of a drawer and sat on the bed. "I doubt it."

Crystal wasn't sure that what she saw in the bottom of Amber's bag was an extra phone but she figured it was. She felt like she had to warn Amber about what would happen if Shades found out she had another phone. "Look, Amber, I didn't say anything to Shades, and I won't, but I saw something in the bottom of your bag yesterday when I was picking your stuff up off the floor."

Amber jumped off her bed and grabbed her backpack. She dumped everything out of the bag and found that Damian's phone was still safely hidden in the pocket.

"It's still there, sugar. I didn't take it and I won't tell Shades you have it, but if you think he messed you up yesterday, just let him find out you have another phone. Amber, he will beat you to death. Just like if he finds out you went to see your folks. You and I are soul sisters and we need to protect each other. Don't get caught with that thing, you understand?"

Amber held her backpack to her heart. "I understand. I have to be able to talk to my family, Crystal. I miss them so much."

Crystal got off the bed and walked over to Amber. She pulled out the money that Shades had given her. "I know you do, Amber." Crystal put five hundred dollars next to Amber on the bed. "Maybe someday you can be with them. Here, hold on to this and maybe in a couple of days when you feel and look better, we can go do some shopping."

"Okay, thanks for not ratting me out."

Crystal touched Amber's cheek. "Like I said, we are soul sisters. Be careful…I like having you around."

After Crystal left the room, Amber continued to hold tight to her bag. The phone contained in the bottom of the bag was her only connection to the world that she loved. She wished she could share with Crystal her plans to take off, but she didn't want to put her in any danger for knowing too much.

◊◊◊

"Look, Chief Hill, I know you're busy and Atlanta is a big city. But I need some help here, and the director of the DEA isn't asking you for that help—he's demanding it."

Angelica stood with her hands on her hips, staring at Atlanta's Chief of Police.

"I just can't spare the manpower," he said.

"Then I guess you want me to go over your head and have my boss talk to your boss."

The chief of police stood up from his desk, went to his door, and opened it. "Sergeant Nepal, come in here."

A man seated at a desk some feet from the chief's office, rose to his feet and made his way to the chief's office.

"Sergeant Nepal, this is DEA agent Angelica Dillon."

The two law enforcement officers shook hands.

"Sergeant, Agent Dillon is here investigating a possible jumper drug ring that is involved in sex and human trafficking. Now, I haven't seen any reports come across my desk that leads me to believe that we have anything like that going on in Atlanta, but she says otherwise. I want you to help Agent Dillon find her way around the station and help her with anything she might need. You will get approval for any extra man hours and all expenses that might be incurred before you incur or use them. Do you understand?"

"Yes, sir."

"Now, Agent Dillon, if you do find the evidence through your investigation that these crimes are being committed in my town, you will come to me before you expose anything to anyone else. You owe me at least that courtesy, so I can get ahead of any media fallout."

Angelica shook the chief's hand. "Thank you, sir. I will keep you posted."

The chief looked at his officer. "You're dismissed."

Sergeant Nepal left the chief's office with Angelica. They went to the sergeant's desk. "Sorry about the chief, Agent Dillon. He doesn't realize that there is a lot that goes on in this town right under his nose."

"So, you know about the drug ring? You know about the trafficking? Why doesn't he know?"

"Well, we just have suspicions, and cases that have been pointing in that direction. We have a few open cases, and some names, but not really a whole lot else. A lot of the guys in the detective division have been working to put things together." Sergeant Nepal pulled a file off his desk and put it in front of Angelica.

Angelica looked it over.

"This case just hit my desk today, the beat cops did the preliminary report, but the detective's haven't finished the crime scene investigation yet. In fact, if you want, I can take you to the location. These guys were executed and the detectives already know that at least one of the men murdered was connected to a drug ring they have been investigating."

Angelica picked out Zeke's name from the list of victims. "Yes, this is one of the names that my informant mentioned." She pointed out Zeke's name to the officer.

"Yep, that's the guy. He was a known drug dealer and small time pimp around Atlanta. He's been connected to several other people that our detectives have had their eyes on, too."

Angelica thought for a moment. "Would you guys happen to be looking for someone who goes by the name of Shades? Or his boss, Dante?"

"Sure, those are household names around here. We just haven't been able to tie them to any of the crimes they have been committing. Dante is a really big fish with South American and Mexican Cartel connections. You want to go to the scene?"

Angelica closed the file. "Yes, I do." She followed the officer out of the station.

◊◊◊

Amber picked at the food on the tray that Crystal had left behind. She had gotten dressed, packed her bag, and was ready to leave. She just didn't know if Crystal was in the house. She decided to find out. She opened her bedroom door and called out, "Hey, Crystal, I was wondering if I could have a couple of pain pills?" There was no answer.

She moved into the kitchen. Crystal was nowhere around. She picked up the cellphone Shades had given her for the package deliveries and called Crystal's cellphone. "Hey, Crystal, I wanted some more pain pills."

"Oh, I forgot you wanted those, Amber. I'm in town shopping. I guess Shades is out, too. I'll be back later tonight. Shades and I are going to meet for dinner. Can you wait 'til tonight?"

Amber was thrilled with the information. "Sure, Crystal, I can wait. I'm going to take some over-the-counter stuff I saw in the medicine cabinet and go back to sleep. I think I just want to sleep for a couple of days."

"I understand that, Amber. I'll check on you when I get back and give you the pills."

"Okay, thanks Crystal."

"No problem. Get some rest."

"Hey, I was thinking about going out on the back patio for some fresh air before I lay down. Will that be okay?"

"Sure, I didn't set the alarm when I left. Shades gets annoyed when it sets his phone off and he's doing business. Just make sure you lock the door when you go back to your room."

"I will. Talk to you later."

"Feel better."

When Amber hung up, she knew that this was her chance. She took all of the money she had saved and the money that Crystal had just given her and put half of it in her pocket and half of it in her backpack. She made her bed look like she was asleep in it, and then she took Shades's cellphone and put it in the toilet bowl. She grabbed her backpack, opened her bedroom door, and looked down the hall to make sure no one was around. She made her way to the back door that was off the kitchen. She opened the door and walked out into what she hoped would be her new life.

My first order of business is to get out of Atlanta and head to Michigan, she thought. She opened the gate in Shades's backyard, looked down the alley, and then slipped out of the yard. Amber didn't want to go to any of the local truck stops for fear of seeing any of Shades's girls. She walked to a park not far from Shades's house and took out Damian's phone and list. She called almost all the driver's on the list. The second to the last name on the list answered his phone.

"Yeah, this is Yuma."

"Yuma, my name is Amber and I'm a friend of Damian's. Damian gave me your name and said you might be able to give me a ride if I ever needed one."

"Sure, sugar. I'd be happy to give Damian's girl a ride. Where are you at and where are you going?"

"I need a ride out of Atlanta, are you anywhere near Atlanta?"

"I just got to Atlanta yesterday, been waiting for a load. The load just came through about an hour ago, and I was just leaving the truck stop to go and pick it up. "Where you at? I can wait here at the truck stop for a few minutes."

"No, I can't come to a truck stop. I can't explain right now, but do you think you can pick me up at a park on the north side of Atlanta?"

"Sure, if you can give me a couple of cross streets. Are you okay?"

Amber was nervous, she wasn't that far from Shades's house and she was exposed in the park. "I'm fine, I just really need to get out of Atlanta. The cross streets are Elm and 69th."

"Okay, I've got it in my GPS. I'll be there in about fifteen minutes. Since I've never met you, Amber you need to tell me what you look like so I don't pick up the wrong girl."

Yuma's sense of humor helped Amber feel a little less scared. "I'm sorry, I guess that would help. I have shoulder-length brown hair, and I'm wearing blue jeans with a yellow shirt. I'm the only one at this park right now."

"Well, I'm on my way."

"Thanks, Yuma. I really appreciate it."

"No problem."

Amber climbed into a plastic tube that was on the playground in the park. She wasn't completely protected from exposure, but it was better than just standing out in the open.

◊◊◊

Angelica walked out of the elevator near the crime scene with gloves and covers over her shoes. Sergeant Nepal led Angelica to the apartment but stopped short of entering the crime scene when Detective Olson emerged. "Detective Olson, I need to introduce you to DEA Agent Dillon."

Angelica and the detective removed their rubber gloves in order to shake hands. "What brings the DEA to a murder scene in Atlanta?"

"The chief told me to help her fill in some of the gaps in a jumper drug ring case she's working." Sergeant Nepal left Angelica and Detective Olson to talk. He leaned into the apartment to scope out the damage. "Well, whoever took out these guys didn't make much of a mess."

Detective Olson looked at his notes and then at Angelica. "What can I help you with, Agent Dillon? I just finished up in there, the coroner is fixin' to bag and tag those guys, and I have a report to file."

"I don't want to keep you from your work, Detective Olson, but one of those victims in there was on a list of suspects I've been checking out." Amber took out her notepad from her pocket. "One, Zachariah Hampton, aka, Zeke. White male, aged 26."

The detective looked over his notes. "Yep, that's one of the DBs in there, the one with a bullet in the front of his head. He was dead before he hit the floor. Walk with me, I really need to get back to the station."

"Sure, maybe I can ride with you. Give me just a minute to tell Sergeant Nepal."

"Okay, see you downstairs." The detective disappeared into the elevator.

Angelica turned to find Sergeant Nepal who was still watching as the M.E. finished putting one of the victims on a gurney. "Sergeant Nepal, I'm going to ride back to the station with Detective Olson. Thank you for the information you have provided so far, you've been very helpful."

"No problem, I'll be back at the station in a little while if you need anything."

"Okay, thanks again." Angelica hurried back to the elevator.

◊◊◊

Amber moved deep into the plastic tube every time a vehicle passed by. When a big truck with a flatbed rolled up to the corner of Elm and 69th, Amber got out of the tube and ran to it. She climbed onto the passenger side step and opened the door. "Are you Yuma?"

"Yes, I am. Are you Amber?"

Amber crawled into the cab of the big truck. "Yes, I am."

"What's with all the hide and seek, Amber?"

Amber didn't want to get into specifics, but she knew Yuma needed a little explanation. "My ex-boss is not happy that I'm leaving him. I'm going to marry Damian."

"I can see from your face why you're hiding from him."

"Yeah, he's kind of a mean person. I really want to stay alive long enough to get married."

"Man, if I were Damian I would have already shot that guy."

"Don't give him any ideas; it's been hard enough keeping him away from Atlanta."

"I believe it; Damian isn't one to run from a fight."

"Well, this fight is my fight and I don't want Damian hurt because of me. Please, if anyone asks you anything about me, you haven't seen me and you know anything about me."

"You got it, baby girl, my lips are sealed. By the way, where are you going? I mean besides with me—I'm headed toward Kansas."

"Oh, that will be perfect. I will call Damian and see if he can get a load going toward Kansas." Amber took Damian's phone out of her backpack. "I really appreciate this, Yuma."

"No problem, but we have to go and pick up my load. It's going to be a while before we hit the highway, but it will be mostly night riding tonight."

"That will be great." Amber called Damian. "Damian, it's me."

"Amber, are you okay? I've been so worried."

"I'm fine now, Damian. I've left Shades. I called just about everyone on the list to get a ride out of Atlanta. I finally got one with Yuma. We are going to pick up his load and head to Kansas. Can you get a load going there?"

"Yes, I'm sure I can find a load going there, but the agents didn't want you to do anything yet."

Amber was angry. She went to the sleep area of Yuma's truck and closed the leather curtains for some privacy. "Look, I have had it, Damian. I couldn't wait any longer on those stupid agents. I had a chance to escape and I took it. In the last week and a half, I have been across five states, Zeke has tried to kidnap me twice, Shades's package went missing, I've been beaten, and now I'm on the run. I am not going back, I'm done. If you don't want me, then I will go home and try and change my life on my own." Tears burned Amber's lip as they reached the split in her mouth.

"No, baby, no. That's not what I meant. I want you with me—we will figure this out on our own. We don't need those agents. I love you. I want you with me right now. What do you mean you've been beaten?"

Amber cried. "Oh, Damian, it doesn't matter. I will tell you all about it when I see you. Are you going to meet me in Kansas or not?"

"Of course, Amber, I will meet you anywhere."

"I'll have to call you in a little while, Yuma has to unload and then I will know exactly where we are headed. It won't take too long for them to figure out that I'm gone. I think I left things to where they might not notice until tomorrow, but if not, Shades will send out the word tonight. I will be well out of Atlanta by the time they figure anything out. I just have to stay out of sight. I'm worried about my family, Damian. I know I haven't done things the way that those agents wanted me to, but can you at least ask them to protect my family? Shades will do anything to get back at me, including hurting them."

"I will call Agent Dillon right away. She was supposed to be in Atlanta today anyway."

"Okay, I have to go. I'll call you back when I know where we will meet."

"Be careful, I love you."

"I will, I love you, too."

Amber ended her phone call and returned to the passenger seat in Yuma's truck. "Sorry about that; I just needed a little privacy."

"It's fine, but privacy in this little space is kind of hard to come by. I didn't mean to overhear everything you guys were talking about, but it was hard not to. This guy must be really bad."

"Yeah, he's going to try and kill me."

"Kill you, what kind of work were you doing for him?" Yuma realized the question was stupid. "Never mind, I don't want to know. I think I just figured it out."

"Don't worry, you won't be in any danger as long as no one sees me with you."

Yuma pointed to the sleeper. "I'm not worried about me, but if you would feel more comfortable, you can climb in the back and rest while we are getting on the load and leaving town."

Amber gathered her things and moved to the sleeper. "I think that would be the smartest idea." Amber touched Yuma's arm. "Thank you, you are very kind."

"My pleasure, Amber."

◊◊◊

"So, what exactly are you looking for here in Atlanta, Agent Dillon?" Detective Olson drove his cruiser through the streets of Atlanta back to the police station.

"Well, I have a young woman, her name is Amber Nichols. She has been forced into prostitution and jumping by a man who goes by the name Shades. Do you know anything about him?"

"I know the name and once we get back to the station I will check the computer. If it's who I think it is, he's second in command in the Dante family."

"Yep, that's the man I'm looking for. I need to take that man, and anyone else who's associated with him, down. They are trafficking drugs, sex, and humans across the U.S. and using the trucking industry to do it."

"I know what you're wanting to do, Agent Dillon, but that's going to be a hard order to fill. Dante and this Shades guy are very well insulated, getting to them is going to be difficult."

"Well, that's what I'm all about, Detective Olson—getting to the ones that think they are untouchable."

"I'll give you everything we've got on them, but I doubt our chief will approve any man hours on a case that's not going to be easy to prosecute."

"I have plenty of resources through the DEA to tackle this case. I just want your information."

"No problem, I'll give all of it to you."

CHAPTER TWENTY-FIVE

Crystal opened Amber's bedroom door, Amber appeared to be sleeping. Crystal quietly shut the door, deciding not to bother her resting friend. She went into Shades's bedroom and put the pills she had in her hands on the nightstand. She took off her robe before getting into the bed. "She's asleep. I didn't want to wake her up. I'll give her the pain medicine in the morning. Shades, you shouldn't have hurt her so bad. She looks terrible."

Shades moved the papers he was looking at in bed to the side. He was slightly angered at Crystal's insistence. "Look, Crystal, maybe I was a little tough on her, but she needed to understand what happens when you lose something that belongs to me. Now, I gave you both money to buy new things and this will be the last time I hear about this, do you understand?"

Crystal knew when to leave something alone. "I understand. I'm sorry, I won't mention it again."

◊◊◊

"Everything is coming together really well, Kami. Your wedding is going to be so beautiful, sweetheart." Elsa Mae moved the phone from one ear to the other while she stirred the chili on the stove.

"Oh, I know Mama, you have always managed to pull off some of the most beautiful weddings for folks. I wish I was there to help more."

"Nonsense, I have everything under control. We only have five weeks left. When do you think you guys will be here?"

"Well, we were planning to be at the house the weekend before the wedding. Will that be okay for you and Pops?"

"Of course. That will give us plenty of time to have the bridal shower and the rehearsal dinner. You guys can go to the church and speak with the priest before the wedding, too."

"It sounds great, Mama. How is Pops feeling?"

"He's actually doing a lot better. I think it's partly because he saw Amber and he doesn't have to worry so much about her. The doctor just thinks it's because he a strong old cuss."

"Well, I'm with the doctor on this one. Pops really is a strong man. Speaking of Amber, have you heard from her, will she be coming to the wedding?"

"Oh, I don't know, Kami. I haven't heard from her since she left. I wouldn't plan on it. I think she's really busy with her new job."

Kami paused. "To be honest, I just really don't want her at my wedding. I know she's my sister, but it seems like the whole family is unhappy when she's around. I don't want my wedding to be interrupted by those feelings. I want everyone to be happy on my special day."

"I understand that, Kami, but she is your sister and part of this family. We have to forgive, especially those closest to us. I don't think she will be there, so you won't have to worry about it. But if she does show up, let's all just try and be happy, okay?"

"Okay, Mama. I love you!"

"I love you, too. Well, I'd better go and get your daddy in here for supper."

"All right, Mama, I'll let you go. Give Pops hugs and kisses for me."

"I will, Kami. We love you."

"I love you guys, too. Talk to you soon."

Elsa Mae poured two bowls of chili and put them on the table. She walked into the living room and reached for Charley's hand. "Sweetheart, your dinner is ready."

Charley woke with a start. "Okay, Elsa Mae. Smells good."

Elsa Mae helped Charley out of his chair. "Well, it's your favorite chili."

◊◊◊

Yuma pulled the truck into a truck stop near Nashville. "Hey, Amber, I have to get some fuel. We are in Nashville, you want to get out and use the little girl's room or get a cup of coffee?" Amber had been asleep since Yuma had offered the sleeper to her in Atlanta.

Amber came out from behind the curtains. She rubbed her face and tried to brush down her messy hair. She looked out the window and saw that the truck stop was not a normal chain. Yuma had taken them to a place off the beaten path. "Well, I haven't ever been in this truck stop, I doubt any of Shades's girls have either. Yes, I really need to use the restroom, and I'm starved."

Amber put on her shoes and grabbed her phone. "Can I get you anything, Yuma?"

"I'll be in there in a few minutes. I think I'll get a cup of coffee and a sandwich."

Amber looked into the parking lot and near the store. There wasn't anyone hanging around outside. Everything looked good, so Amber exited the passenger side of Yuma's truck. "I'll be inside waiting for you."

Yuma continued to fuel his truck. "Okay, Amber."

Inside the store, Amber found the restroom. She then got coffee and sandwiches for both her and Yuma. She paid for it at the register and found a small table in the corner. Yuma came in to pay for his fuel. Amber spoke out, "Over here, Yuma."

Yuma turned to see Amber at the little table. After paying for his fuel, he pointed to the restrooms. Amber knew what he meant. She took another bite of her sandwich and sipped at her coffee. She looked out the window and for the first time in a long time she felt free…truly free.

"So, what kind of sandwich did you get me?"

Amber's thoughts were interrupted by Yuma. "I got you a ham and cheese, with a package of mayo and mustard because I wasn't sure which one you liked."

Yuma was a semi-bald man, with a potbelly and slight limp. He slid into the chair across from Amber. "Well, I love ham and cheese, but only with mayo. Thank you for the sandwich and coffee. I didn't mean for you to buy me supper."

"I wanted to buy it for you. It was the least I could do since you gave me a ride to Kansas." Amber took another bite out of her sandwich. "By the way, since I managed to sleep through everything since Atlanta, where are we going to land in Kansas? I really need to call Damian and let him know where to meet us."

"We will be stopping in Kansas City and then I have a delivery in Wichita. You can ride with me as long as you need to. We will meet up with him where ever he needs."

Amber pulled out her cell phone. "Hey, sugar, it's me."

"I've been on pins and needles waiting for you to call me back. You still with Yuma?"

"Yes, in fact he's sitting across the table from me right now, eating a sandwich and drinking some coffee."

"Are you safe sitting in a truck stop, Amber?"

"Well, I'm safe in this one. It's really out of the way and there isn't anyone in here."

"Good, tell Yuma thank you for taking care of you." Amber handed the phone to Yuma.

"Hey, bud, how's it hanging?"

"Yuma, it's hanging. Thank you so much for giving my girl a ride. I'm so relieved that she is out of that city. Where you headed with your load?"

"Well, like I was telling your little lady here, we will be taking part of it to Kansas City and part of it to Wichita. You got a load going anywhere near either of those places?"

"I got a small one going to Kansas City, but I can't pick it up 'til tomorrow. Maybe you can get her near a hotel and she can wait for me there?"

"Okay, you talk to her about that and you guys decide. She's welcome to stay in the truck if she needs to, I can sleep in my driver's seat."

"Oh, hell no, Yuma, we can't have you doing that. She can stay in a hotel until I get there. You have already done more than we could ever ask. Let me talk to her, Yuma. Thanks again so much for all your help."

"We are drivers, Damian, we help each other out when we can. Brothers and sisters of the road." Yuma handed Amber back her phone.

"Baby, Yuma is going to leave you at a hotel in Kansas City. I can't get there until tomorrow night sometime. I have to pick up my load in the morning. Will you be okay by yourself?"

"Of course, baby. I've been out here on these roads by myself for almost two years. I'm pretty sure I can stay in a hotel by myself. I can't wait to see you."

"I love you, Amber Nichols."

"I love you too, Damian Adams. Hey, did you ever get a hold of that agent and to ask her to keep an eye on my family?"

"I left a message on both Agent Dillon's phone and Shelby's. I've been really busy and haven't checked to see if they called me back yet. I will check as soon as I get off the phone."

"Yes, please, Damian. Someone needs to watch after my family."

"I know, baby. I'm going to hang up right now to check to see if they called back. If not, I will keep at it until they do. I love you, and can't wait to be with you tomorrow."

"Me too, I love you, too." Amber ended her phone call with Damian.

"Sounds like our Damian is head over heels in love with you."

Amber smiled and sipped on her coffee. "Yeah, and I'm head over heels for him, too."

"You'd better finish your sandwich; it's about time to go."

Amber folded up what was left of the sandwich, gulped down the last of her coffee, and got out of her seat at the table. "Let's go, Yuma. I'm ready to roll."

Yuma gathered his sandwich paper and got up as well. "Put it in high and roll on down the road, baby girl."

◊◊◊

Damian listened to his messages, both Angelica and Shelby returned his calls, but now it was way too late to call them. He set his alarm for six a.m. He would call them in the morning to let them know that Amber had left Atlanta.

◊◊◊

Crystal knocked on Amber's bedroom door. "Amber, are you awake?" When no answer came from Amber, Crystal opened the door and looked into the room. "Amber, wake up, you've been asleep all morning." Crystal went into the bedroom and stood near Amber's bed. "It's almost noon, sugar. You'd better get up."

Still no answer.

Crystal put her hands on the figure that was beneath the covers on Amber's bed. She shook it slightly.

Realizing that Amber's body was not under the covers, Crystal pulled at the covers to verify what she already knew. Amber was gone. Crystal sat on Amber's bed. "Oh, Amber, Shades is going to kill you."

Crystal got up and looked around the room. Amber's backpack was missing as well as several of her personal things. She went into the bathroom and found Shades's cell phone in the toilet. She pulled the phone out of the water and laid it on the counter. Then she pulled out her cell phone from her back pocket and called Shades. "We've got a problem…Amber is gone."

"What do you mean she's gone?"

"I mean she's not here. I think she's taken off, Shades. Her cell phone is here and a few of her things are missing. She made her bed look like someone was sleeping in it, that's why I thought she was asleep last night."

"Shit, Crystal, it's your responsibility to keep an eye on the girls. I knew something was up with her. I knew it."

"I'm sorry, Shades, it looked like she was asleep."

"I have something I need to take care of with Dante. I'll be home in a little while. I knew something was up with her," he said again.

Crystal knew that Shades wasn't going to be happy when he got back to the house. She left everything just as it was—she even put the cell phone back into the water. She had mixed emotions about Amber being gone. On one hand, she was angry with Amber for leaving her alone with Shades. On the other hand, she was glad that Amber was at least trying to get out. Crystal knew from experience that Shades always found his girls when they ran off. If they didn't die from the beatings he gave them, they wished they were dead.

Crystal waited in the kitchen for Shades to get home. She shook when he and six of his men busted through the front door. Shades didn't say a word to her—he and his men went straight to Amber's room. "Tear it apart, check everything. There has to be something in here to give us some idea of where she went."

Shades went into the bathroom and saw his phone in the toilet. "Get that out of there. I'm sure there won't be anything on that phone since it's been drowned." Shades waited until his men were finished tearing Amber's room apart.

"There isn't anything here, boss."

Shades went into the kitchen where Crystal was sitting. He grabbed her by the arm. "Do you have any idea where she went, Crystal?"

Crystal was shaking with fear. "I have no idea, Shades. She never said a word to me about wanting to leave. I swear it."

Shades looked into his girlfriend's eyes. She was scared, but she was truthful. She knew the consequences if she lied to him. "If you hear anything, or if any of the other girls know anything, you'd better be the very first one to tell me. You might be my top girl, but you're still just a whore, and I'd throw you away in a heartbeat if I couldn't trust you anymore."

The words Shades spoke stunned Crystal to the core. She began to cry. "I know, Shades. I know I'm just a worthless whore to you, but I've never lied to you and you know that."

Shades pulled Crystal close. He was angry and knew that he had just hurt the only person he had ever been able to get close to. But he couldn't let himself care. "Never lie to me—I don't want to kill you."

He released her and looked at his men. "I want a complete city search. If she's not here in town then she must have gotten a ride out of town. Check all the truck stops and see who saw her. I know she is from Odessa, Texas. If we can't locate her in the next few days, we will search for her there. The birds always return to their nest. I want her found. No one leaves the family and survives."

◊◊◊

"This is Agent Dillon," Angelica said into her cellphone.

"Agent Dillon, this is Damian. I heard from Amber yesterday. She has left Shades's organization and she is on her way to meet up with me."

Angelica moved away from the desk that she had been using at the Atlanta police department. "Oh, Damian, that's so dangerous. She got away safe, then?"

"Yes, for now she's safe. I'm sure not for how long, but I will do my best to keep her safe. She is really smart, and knows most of the girls working for Shades, so she's avoiding the normal trafficking routes. But that's only part of why I'm calling."

"What is it?"

"Amber is afraid for her family. They live in Odessa, and she's afraid that Shades might try and hurt them to find her. Can you have someone keep an eye on the family?"

"We can try, Damian, but a twenty-four hour detail is very expensive and we have to have proof that it's justifiable. I'm in Atlanta right now working with the Atlanta Police. I'm trying to build a case against Shades and his boss Dante. I have truck drivers out working in the field, gathering evidence of the jumping going on."

"Okay, but can you protect them? Amber is really scared that Shades is going to hurt them."

"I'll call the agency and see what we can do. Don't worry about it; I'll make it happen somehow."

"Thanks, Agent Dillon. I will let her know."

"Where is she, Damian?"

"I'm not going to tell anyone where she is right now. She's safe and that's what's important."

"Okay, Damian, but if you run into any problems, please let me know if we can help."

"I will, Agent Dillon. Thanks again."

Detective Olson looked at Angelica. "Trouble?"

"Well, not right now, but I'm sure eventually all hell is going to break loose. Amber has just escaped from Shades's custody. She took off some time yesterday and now she is somewhere safe, or at least Damian thinks she's safe."

"Angelica, from everything we know about Shades and Dante, she won't be safe forever. Dante's reach is long and Shades is the silent, evil type who won't allow anyone to do anything he doesn't permit. That poor girl has a big target on her back. Shades won't stop until he takes her out for betraying the organization."

"I know, but I'm going to do my best to try and protect her from him. Let's get busy and see what we can come up with to take these guys out."

CHAPTER TWENTY-SIX

Damian knocked on the hotel room door. Amber went to the door and looked through the peephole. Her last experience in a hotel had not turned out well, and although Yuma had used his credit card to reserve the room, she still worried that Shades might track her down there.

She opened the door, relieved, and threw her arms around Damian. "Oh, I'm so glad you made it."

The sky was full of stars and it was almost midnight. Damian pulled Amber out onto the balcony. He kissed her passionately. "Oh God, Amber. I was so worried about you. I'm so glad you're safe and here with me."

Amber kissed Damian and held onto his neck. Damian held her with a gentle strength.

"I'm never going back," she said.

Damian pulled away from Amber and looked at her face. "That bastard did this to you?"

Amber hid her face in Damian's chest. "It's not as bad as it looks. I'll be all right."

Damian was furious, his heart raced as he caressed Amber's hair. "That son-of-a-bitch is going to pay for this, I promise."

Amber lifted her head. "Come on, let's go inside and get some rest. We can talk about this in the morning."

Damian followed Amber into the room and locked the door behind them. Amber kissed Damian and pulled him toward the bed. "I love you, Damian. No one has ever cared for me like you have. You have never asked for or taken anything from me since the moment we met. I want to give my-self to you. I want you to make love to me."

Damian looked at Amber with all the love he had for her, and he wanted her. He wanted to know every inch of her body; he wanted to be with her in every respect. But he couldn't, not now. He kissed her and lay with her on the bed. "Amber, I love you, but I can't make love to you. Not right now, I want you to be my wife first. I want you to know in your heart that I want you, not your body."

Amber sat up, confused. "You don't want me?"

Damian sat up next to her. "Of course I want you." He pointed to the bulge in his pants. "It's obvious that I want you. I just want our first time to be as man and wife. I love you so much and you have had men treat you like a piece of meat. I don't want you to ever think or feel that I am like them. I want you, not what I can get from you."

Amber didn't know how to react. "But, you love me, don't you?"

Damian grabbed Amber and kissed her. "I love you more than I love myself. I would die for you. I want you to know that. I want to prove it to you by waiting for you until we get married, which, if you agree, could happen really soon. Like in the next few days, you know, find a justice of the peace at a courthouse somewhere and get hitched."

Amber hugged Damian. "You mean it, just go and get married now?"

"Yeah, just go and get married. Why not? We love each other don't we?"

"Yes, but what about my family, what about your family? Shouldn't they be there too?"

Damian held Amber. "I've been thinking about that, and yes, they should. But with everything that's going on right now, people looking for you and trying to kill us and all, well…I think maybe we'd better hold off on a formal church wedding until things calm down a bit. Don't you?"

"Yes, but that could be a while," she sulked.

Damian kissed Amber, got off the bed, and took off his shirt. "That's why, we go get hitched somewhere in the next few days. Then, when Agent Dillon and her team eliminate Shades and Dante and their gang, we'll go to your parents' house and I will properly ask your father if I can marry you again. We can have another, more appropriate wedding with our families. I will call my family and we will just make it one of the best wedding days ever."

Amber smiled. She moved over to her side of the bed. Damian jumped onto his side. Amber cuddled into Damian's arms. "That sounds wonderful, but why get married now if we will just get married again then?"

Damian laughed. "Because neither of us want to wait that long to be together. You said so yourself just a minute ago. You saw how much I want to make love to you. Let's just get married and then get married again."

Amber snuggled into Damian's arms, as he wrapped her in them close to his body.

"Let's do it. Mr. and Mrs. Damian Adams. I think that sounds wonderful." Amber had no doubts now that Damian loved her. Amber held her ring that was still attached to the chain Damian had given her. She pressed it softly into her chest next to her heart.

◊◊◊

"Boss, we have looked everywhere in this city for that little bitch. We've checked out all the truck stops, rundown motels, crack houses, and abandoned buildings. We checked with the working girls down on the strip and with all our girls. No one has seen her; it's like she just disappeared."

Shades sat back in his chair. "She didn't just vanish, boys, she's out there. I'm thinking her little trucker friend that saved her ass a few weeks ago at the truck stop has her. If we can find out who he is, we will find Amber."

"How do we find him, boss? The only thing we got right now is that he was driving a red Pete? I guess we can look at all the red Pete's we see, but that's a bunch."

"Go back and talk to the girls in the Midwest section where she ran most of the time. I want you to find out everything you can about who she ran with. Anything that will help us locate her.

"Yes sir, what about her family?" one of his henchmen asked.

"Leave that to me for now. We will use them as a last resort. We don't want to attract too much attention—it could get messy bringing in the family."

"Yes, sir."

"She drowned my cell phone, so I'm pretty sure she has a new one. Maybe she's had another one for a while. This little girl isn't an idiot. I should have gotten rid of her when she first showed up. Regardless, Dante wants her found and eliminated. He does not want the cops or the Feds to take notice of anything, so be surgical about things."

"We are on it, boss."

Another of Shades's men looked at his cell phone. "I just got a text from Shantia. One of the other girls told her the truck Amber was always getting into isn't red…it's blue."

◊◊◊

"There it is, Angelica, Dante's headquarters, mansion, hideout, whatever you want to call it. That's where the majority of all Atlanta's drug traffic ends up." Angelica and Detective Olson sat on the street across from the massive gate and fence that protected Dante's estate.

"Yeah, Rex gave me the run down on old Dante. What I can't figure out is why we haven't been able to nail the son-of-a-bitch yet. I mean, come on, we know where he lives, we know he's in bed with the cartels, and yet we haven't been able to touch him. Why?"

"Well, that's a pretty complicated question. The best I have been able to come up with is that the people he's got working for him are keeping us so busy dealing with the crap on the streets that we don't have time to deal with the supply chain for the shit. When ninety percent of your caseloads are small drug busts, drug-related assaults, overdoses and other petty crimes, you can't concentrate on the bastards that are causing it all. They insulate themselves with patsies who treat their leaders like gods because they've been showered with lots of money to buy their loyalty. These guys use vicious killings of non-compliant victims to keep the others in line."

"Yeah, it's the common situation in most American cities these days. It's "tesectonderugism" at its finest."

"Te-secton-derug what ism?"

"Tesectonderugism. It's a word I made up, it describes exactly what these cartels or families are all about. The secret of bondage, terror, and drugs, I just added the -ism for color."

Detective Olson laughed. "You are nuts, Agent Dillon."

"I'm pretty sure, Olson, that I'm not the only one in this car that's nuts. I think it's a prerequisite to being a cop."

Detective Olson smiled. "How about I show you the house and apartment complex Shades has been known to occupy? Then we can go to the truck stops and meet some of the girls who work for Shades."

"Sounds good. Let's go."

"You understand that none of these girls will ever talk to you about what they do?"

"I know they might not talk to a cop, but will they talk to a driver?"

"What? You have a CDL?"

"Yeah, I'm an truck driver." Angelica took out her driver's license. "All neat and proper."

"Why the hell do you need a CDL, don't you work in a cozy little corner office?"

"I'll have you know I'm an agent, not a paper pusher. Most of the cases I work are in the field. You ever hear about the Pig case down in Louisiana?"

"Yeah, that was a pretty big drug case, wasn't it? It affected almost every major city in the country. They took down hundreds of cartel connections in the U.S. We even had several connections here in Atlanta taken into custody. Dante wasn't one of them, unfortunately."

"Well, that was my case. I worked undercover for Pig as a truck driver and then took him down."

"Wow, that's pretty impressive, Dillon. You can drive a big truck *and* take down a pig."

Angelica and Olson laughed. "Shut the hell up, Olson, and drive. Unless, of course, you would like a professional driver to show you how it's done."

"No, I don't want to have to explain that back at the station."

Detective Olson pulled the car through a crowded parking lot of a high rise apartment complex. He pointed up in the direction of an apartment near the top floor. "We think he does most of his drug business out of an apartment on that floor. But he won't deal with anyone he doesn't know. If you want to buy drugs from Shades, you'd better know someone he knows, or you can forget it. We've tried repeatedly and failed. A lot of the girls and people working for Dante live in this complex, and in several houses around town." He drove on through the parking lot, moved back to the streets and steered his police unit toward Shades's house.

"It's tough breaking into some of these organizations. It takes a lot of time and patience. I never would have busted Pig if I hadn't gone undercover in his organization."

"So what, you're going to go undercover and work for Shades?"

"I wish it was me this time; but no, we're using a new, younger female agent. In fact, she's already inside. Our agency has been working on Dante for months. I wasn't aware of the ongoing investigation until my case with Amber crossed over into it. The agents working on the Dante case didn't want me to interfere. They were afraid my case would cause Dante to get nervous and pull up stakes. They weren't real forthcoming with information either, that's why I had to come to you."

"So, the young woman they have inside is a jumper?"

"Yeah, in fact, I think she's been in your custody recently. She was busted for drug possession, but I think one of Dante's men has already bonded her out. I sure could use some of the information those agents aren't sharing."

"It sounds like a favor is in the air. Am I right?"

"Yeah, you've been great giving me all the information you guys have on Dante's organization. With your help, I've been able to piece together a lot of what I need to use in order to track Shades and his girls. But what I really need is faces with names."

Olson slammed on the breaks and then pulled to the curb. "There, the house over there is Shades's residence. That's where Amber probably lived." He pointed to another house down the street. "She might also have stayed in that house, but we aren't sure about any of the specifics on living arrangements." The detective put his car in drive and pulled back out onto the street.

"Do you have any pictures of Shades or the men who work with him?"

"I've showed you most of the case files we have on these clowns. They have been pretty hard to photograph unless they've been arrested. When we get back, let me pull that girl's file you were talking about, and see what we can find."

The detective moved into the parking lot of one of the big truck stops in Atlanta. He turned into a parking spot. "Let's go in here and get a cup of coffee. I'll try and point out some of the jumpers who hang out in here."

When they got inside the store, Angelica looked around, using her surveillance skills. Detective Olson went straight for the coffee without looking around the room at all. Angelica was soon standing next to the officer, pouring a cup of black coffee into a paper cup. Detective Olson had flavored his coffee with several packages of sugar and cream. He stirred it and then took a little sip. He poured more cream in and continued stirring his concoction. He turned around, and leaned against the coffee counter while Angelica finished stirring some sugar into her coffee. "To the right of you, near the restroom, two girls talking…both of them are Dante's girls. The three near the front door when we came in are also jumpers, and the man approaching the girl standing near the outside back door are all involved in Dante's organization."

Angelica turned around. "So, if you know these people are involved with trafficking why don't you bust them?"

"Proof. They are very good about their exchanges. We haven't figured exactly how they do it." We think it's carried in the girls' bags and then transferred to a leader, but we haven't been able to catch them." Olson moved toward the registered and paid for the two coffees.

"Thank you for the coffee," Angelica said and the two returned to the police car. They sat in the front seat, talking. "How many girls do you think Dante runs?"

Olson sipped at his coffee. "Hard to say, but I suspect he has scores of them just here in Atlanta. They call these girls the Eastern Team. They usually traffic the drugs just along the East Coast."

"I did learn that much from the not-so cooperative agents in my office. They said there were three or four teams, Eastern, Western, Central, and Midwest. How do I find out which team Amber might have been involved with?"

"I don't know, like I told you before, these girls are really tight-lipped. Did you notice that man approaching the girl near the rear entrance?"

"Yeah."

"I think that guy is probably one of the handlers, or a guard for one of the handlers. She knew that guy, and she was talking to him. He was in there asking all those girls questions. I could tell from that one girl's body language, that she was scared answering those questions, too. Normally, those girls don't dare talk to anyone unless they know who they are. If they do, they'll suffer the consequences. How much you want to bet they are interrogating the girls here for information on your girl, Amber?"

"You really think so?"

"Yeah, I do. In fact, look right over there." Olson pointed toward the girls standing outside the building. "He's questioning them, too."

"You think she was running this area?"

"Don't know, but it's possible at least for a little while, maybe just lately. You said Damian runs his truck mostly in the Midwest, and that she's from the Central area. If she has only been out for the last year or two, chances are she was working the Midwest area, and then got moved to the Eastern area for some reason."

"Yeah, that makes sense. Damian told me that he beat up those three guys here at this truck stop. That Zeke was an ex-pimp trying to take her back from Shades. I'll bet he was either waiting for her, so he could give her a ride, or he had just dropped her off."

"That would explain why she ran, too. Dante doesn't like complications with his employees. If they cause problems that get him noticed, then he eliminates the problem. I'm not sure how many open murder cases we have that might be connected to this guy."

"Wow. Well, I guess I'll just have to become a trucker again. Maybe some of these girls will want a ride."

"Probably going to be your only way to get answers. Just remember that the Eastern Team is a really loyal, extra tight-lipped group. You will probably have more luck working the Midwest or Central Teams. From what I know about these teams, their handlers start them off in a Central or Midwestern

Team. There is less product being moved there, so Dante has less to lose in those areas if the girls make mistakes. That's where I would start."

"Okay. My main goal at this point is to keep this Shades character from killing Amber, and her boyfriend. I really want to take him down so that he can't hurt any more of these girls, but I guess we'll see how that goes."

"It's going to be tough. I wish I could be more help, but I got my hands full with all the crap going on right here in this city."

"Don't worry about it. I appreciate all the help you've given me, thank you." Angelica sipped at her coffee.

"No problem. Let's head back to the station and see if we can hunt down a picture or two of these creeps."

CHAPTER TWENTY-SEVEN

"Amber Ellen Nichols, do you take this man to be your lawfully wed-ded husband, to have and to hold, for richer, for poorer, in sickness and in health, 'til death do you part?"

Amber looked deep into Damian's eyes. "I do."

"By the power vested in me by the state of Nevada, I pronounce you husband and wife. You may kiss your bride." Damian took Amber in his mus-cular arms and kissed her.

"I love you, Mrs. Amber Ellen Adams."

"I love you too, Mr. Damian LeRoy Adams."

Damian grabbed his new wife and lifted her small frame into his strong arms. "Come with me, my beautiful wife. I have a night of food, dancing, and lovemaking waiting for you."

Amber laughed as Damian carried her out of the Little White Chapel. She waved at the minister and the woman that stood up with her. "Thank you."

The woman and the man waved and watched the happy couple leave their place of business. "Congratulations, have a wonderful life together."

Amber giggled.

Damian put his new wife down when they reached the street. He kissed her again and then whistled for a taxi. Damian spun around and shouted into the air. "I just married the most beautiful woman in the world! Her name is Amber Ellen Adams, and she's my wife! I love her more than life!"

Amber smiled and couldn't stop giggling. She felt like nothing in the world could ever match the way she felt at this very moment. Damian shouting to the whole world his unconditional love for her made every-thing perfect in her life at that moment.

Damian grabbed her hand when the taxi came to the curb. He kissed her again. "I love you so much it hurts, baby."

Amber kissed Damian back. "I love you more, baby."

"You guys going to ride or just stand there and kiss? Meter's running."

Amber and Damian got into the cab and disappeared down the street.

Two girls who were standing nearby looked at each other. "Wow, I wish I had someone that would shout to the whole world how much he loves me."

"Right and I have a piece of beach front property I'll sell you in the Mohave Desert. Ain't going to happen, girl, we are slaves to this trade until we grow old."

The girls continued to walk along the strip. "I know. Hey, what was that girl's name?"

"I don't know. Amber, something, I think. Why? You going to look her up and ask her what her secret is to catching a man with such devotion?"

"No, look." The girl pulled her cell phone out of her pocket and showed the picture to her friend. "Shades sent this out today, didn't you get it?"

The other girl looked at the picture and then pulled out her phone. "Yeah, I got it but I didn't pay much attention to it. That girl worked the Midwest turf; I've never seen her before."

"I know, I just kind of blew it off too, but that girl that just got married sure looks like the girl in this picture, and both are named Amber."

"Maybe, but are you sure? I didn't get that close a look at her."

"No, but Shades is paying three hundred extra dollars for any information. I think we get paid even if the information doesn't pan out."

"Might be worth sending a text to Joey. I think they list marriages in the newspaper or something. Joey should be able to find out if it was the Amber they are looking for or not."

"Yeah, you could be right." The young woman stopped along the street and sent a text to her handler with the information about the couple, the girl's name being Amber and the Little White Chapel. She also told him that they left the chapel in a taxi going to the south end of the strip. "There, maybe I'll get an extra three hundred this week."

"Yeah, and if you're right about that girl, she's going to get a bullet."

◊◊◊

Damian gathered Amber in his arms again after they exited the taxi in front of the restaurant. He had booked a private table in a secluded corner of the restaurant for their wedding dinner and had arranged for a cake. "This is all for you, my beautiful bride. This whole night is just for you."

Amber smiled. "It's for *us,* Damian; we are one now." Damian led Amber into the restaurant. "We have a reservation for two, Damian and Amber Adams."

"Right this way, Mr. and Mrs. Adams. Your table is waiting for you." The waitress led her to the special place decorated and prepared exactly as Damian had requested.

Amber was amazed.

The table was decorated in the colors of the dress she had picked out for the wedding. A small two-tiered cake, also decorated in the same colors, sat in the middle of the table. Two wine glasses, two small plates with forks, and a cake spatula was waiting for the couple to toast their nuptials.

"Oh, Damian, this is beautiful."

Damian pulled the chair out for his wife. "All for you, my sweet love. All for you."

The waiter appeared. "Good evening, my name is Tony and I will be serving you this evening." He reached for the bottle of champagne that was chilling in ice next to the table and popped the cork.

Amber jumped slightly at the sound of the bottle opening. With poise and grace the young man poured Amber and Damian each a glass of the sparkling beverage. No one asked her age. "Would you like to cut the wedding cake together and then I will serve it for you?"

Amber nodded. "Yes, please."

"Good," said Tony. "Life is short, you should eat dessert first."

Damian and Amber both held the spatula and cut their wedding cake. The couple put the first piece of their wedding cake on a plate. Damian took a corner of the cake and fed it to Amber. Amber took another corner of the piece of cake and feed it to Damian. The waiter clapped. "Beautiful.

Congratulations to both of you." Then the waiter served a piece of cake to the couple. "When you have had time to enjoy your cake and champagne give me a little wave and I will bring you the first part of your four-course wedding meal."

"Thank you."

"You're welcome."

Damian lifted his champagne glass to Amber. "Shall we make a toast to our future—to our life together?"

"Yes." Amber lifted her glass and Damian interlocked his arm with her arm.

"To us, Amber and Damian Adams, may our life together be full of joy, happiness, and love."

Amber spoke. "To us, Damian and Amber Adams, may we love each other until the end of time."

With their arms still locked, the couple took their first sips of the champagne.

Amber coughed slightly and tapped her chest with her hand. The chain was still around her neck, but the ring was now sparkling on her left hand. "It's a little bubbly."

The couple unlocked their arms. Damian hadn't stopped smiling the entire evening. He held Amber's hand. "You are so beautiful. I'm so glad we decided to do this here in Vegas." He suddenly let go of Amber's hand to retrieve a small box from his jacket pocket. "I have something for you." He handed Amber the box.

"Damian, we discussed this. The wedding is our gift to each other. I didn't get you a gift."

Damian tapped the box. "I already had this one from when I gave you your ring."

Amber opened the box. Inside was a silver heart on a bed of felt. Amber reached into the box and retrieved the heart. "Oh, Damian, it's beautiful."

Damian touched the heart. "It open up."

Amber opened the heart. Four small, heart-shaped picture frames unfolded from it.

Damian got up from the table and moved Amber's hair away from her neck. He found the latch to Amber's necklace and took it from her neck. "The heart came with this chain when I bought it." He took the charm from Amber's hand and put it on the chain. Then he put the necklace back around Amber's neck. He kissed her neck before he sat down. Then he pointed to the four frames in the heart, still opened, but now next to Amber's heart. "There are four spaces: one for you, one for me, one for Gabe and one for little Annie. Now, I know I'm not their biological father, but I want to be their dad if you will allow me to be."

Amber began to cry. She touched the precious gift and then touched Damian's face. "I don't know what I did to deserve you, but I thank God for you. I would be honored for you to help me raise my children. Maybe we can even create one more."

Damian put his hand on Amber's. "I want to create a baby with you, Amber Ellen Adams. I want a little girl that looks just like her mother. We will call her Ellie Mae Adams, after you and your mom."

Amber giggled. "You are crazy."

Damian laughed and kissed Amber's hand. "I know. There's this woman who keeps telling me that."

Amber and Damian looked into each other's eyes, fed each other cake, and drank champagne.

Damian asked the waiter to begin bringing their meal and another bottle of the bubbly. They ate and danced together for several hours. It was the most wonderful evening of Amber's life.

When the third bottle of champagne was gone and the dishes were cleared, the waiter came back one last time to the happy couple's table. "Will there be anything else for you, Mr. Adams?"

Damian found his wallet in his back pocket. He pulled out a credit card and handed it to the waiter. "No, I believe that will be all. Please include a one hundred dollar tip for yourself on that check, and can you call us a cab. We will be staying at Caesars Palace tonight."

"Very good, sir. I will be right back with your receipt. We have also put the remaining wedding cake in a box for you to take with you."

"Thank you. That will be terrific."

Amber looked at Damian. "Thank you for marrying me. I'm so happy."

"Thank you for marrying me today. I'm the happiest man alive."

◊◊◊

"Hey, Shades, this is Joey. I just got a text from one of my girls. She thinks she just spotted Amber in Vegas…getting married…tonight."

"Is she certain it's Amber?"

"No, but I should be able to find out from the Little White Chapel tomorrow if it was her."

"They won't give you that information. You'll need to check with the courthouse to see if a license was filed. Be sure and send a couple of men to the truck stop and watch for a blue Pete, if for some reason you can't find out the name of the girl that got married. Watch the truck stop. If it's her and she's with the dumbass I think she left with, they probably parked their truck there and will eventually come back for it."

"All right, boss, I'll get on it first thing. What do you want me to do if it turns out to be her?"

"Call me first, and get all the information you can off that truck."

"Yes, sir."

Shades leaned back in his chair. He had been looking for Amber for two weeks, and this was the first clue he had received that might pan out. "You've been a busy little lady, Amber Nichols."

◊◊◊

Damian opened the door to the hotel room. "Allow me, my gorgeous wife." He picked Amber up off her feet, pushed the door open wider with his foot and carried Amber into their suite. "Now, we are officially man and wife."

Amber giggled. Damian put her down on the bed. "You are the most romantic man." She kissed Damian. "I'm so glad you love me. I'm so glad we are married."

Damian took his phone out of his pocket. He aimed the camera lens toward his wife. "I want you to show me that pretty smile." Amber smiled, allowing her husband to take a photo of her. He went to the bed and sat next to her. He turned the phone around and took a selfie of them on their wedding day.

He got off the bed and handed the phone to Amber. "Now, take one of me. I want to remember this day forever. I want our children to see pictures of this day."

Amber took a few pictures of Damian before she gave him back his phone.

Damian took off his suit coat and untied his tie. He took the box with the cake and bouquet of flowers from Amber and placed them on the dresser. Then he knelt in front of Amber on the bed, lifted up her right foot, and removed her sandal. He rubbed her foot before removing the left sandal. He looked into Amber's eyes and kissed her with soft kisses. "I love you and I want to know every part of you. I want you to be a part of me. I want to make love to Amber Ellen Adams."

Damian put his hand gently behind Amber's back and lowered her to the bed. He kissed her passionately as he found every part of her face and neck with his lips. Amber returned his passionate kisses to his face and neck, gently rubbing his back. With a soft whisper in his ear she spoke, "Help me take off this dress and let me help you out of your clothes. I want to feel your skin next to mine."

Damian moved from his position next to Amber on the bed and stood. He offered her a hand so that she could join him at the foot of the bed. Amber stood in front of Damian as he kissed her lips while removing the straps from her arms, allowing the dress to fall to the floor. Amber stepped out the dress and moved it to the side. Damian continued kissing Amber's neck and chest. With ease, he unhooked her bra and released her breasts. Damian fondled the soft small mounds of flesh, which made Amber arch her back slightly in wonting passion. Damian continued to touch and kiss Amber's breasts and nipples. He gently sucked and caressed the now hard peaks that had formed. Damian whispered. "I love you."

She unbuttoned Damian's shirt. "I love you more than I can ever say."

Damian broke away from Amber's body and helped her remove his shirt. She unbuttoned his pants and they fell to the floor. Skin to skin, Damian pulled Amber close, he gently helped Amber once again to their bed. Now face to face, Damian found his body formed perfectly to Amber's as they kissed and touched and came together.

Amber felt the love and passion that she had longed for from Damian. He was gentle, giving, and patient with her. Her feelings and her pleasure was more important to him than his own. He loved her with his body and she loved him with hers, in a way that only two people can when they love one another.

Amber realized that sex was just an act of animal-like gratification when unconditional love was not present. Damian had given her the one thing that no other man had, or could ever give her again: true love.

◊◊◊

"Here, this is a picture of Shades. His given name is Terence Ronald Wilson, black male, age forty-three, six foot-four, two hundred twelve pounds." Detective Olson gave the picture to Angelica.

"Pretty big guy."

"Yep, and pretty well connected in the drug world." He handed Angelica several other photos and mug shots. "These are some of the men he has working for him. Some are handlers, some are enforcers."

"Can I have copies of these?" Angelica looked through the pictures.

"Sure. Some of those photos are old, so I can't guarantee what they look like now. That picture of Shades, however, was taken just a couple of months ago. One of the detectives in homicide took it while on surveillance outside Dante's estate. They were photographing everyone who went in or out of Dante's place and Shades was seen going in." He looked at the file and said, "He was seen entering and leaving Dante's estate twenty-four times in a seven day period. There was only one day that he did not go to the house at all."

He handed the photo to Angelica.

"He's definitely working for or with Dante. He's insulated though, just like Dante."

"Well, too bad for Shades. I want him and I'm not too busy to notice him. I think I will go directly after him, and let the other agents deal with Dante."

"Come on, let's go down to the print shop on the second floor, and copy these." Angelica grabbed her things, and followed Detective Olson down the hall.

"The clerk will bring you the copies. I hate to go, but I haven't seen my old lady and kids in a couple of days," Olson said.

"Oh no, please, Detective Olson, go home. I'm so sorry that I've kept you from your home life."

"You don't need to apologize. Being a cop and doing all of this is my job, which you know sometimes overlaps into family life. My family is used to my unpredictable hours. If they wanted me home every night for dinner at five, I'd be a businessman wearing a suit and carrying a briefcase. But I'm not, I'm a man in a suit carrying a gun." He laughed. "My kids think I'm cool."

"Well, thanks again. I'm going to be leaving here tonight. I'll get some rest in my hotel, and then climb into my big truck that's waiting for me at the truck stop off the twenty. I think it's the one we visited tonight."

They shook hands.

"Well, I'll put the word out to law enforcement—watch out for the female DEA agent behind the wheel of an eighteen wheel truck."

CHAPTER TWENTY-EIGHT

Damian brushed Amber's hair back from the side of her face. He leaned over her body from his side of their bed and kissed her. Amber moved and reached her hand out to touch Damian's arm that was positioned around her head. "Good morning my sweet and gorgeous wife. How about I call for room service and we have breakfast in bed this morning?"

Amber turned her naked body over so that she faced her husband. She moved her messy hair with her hand so she could see. "Oh, yes! I could use coffee."

Damian kissed Amber's forehead. He removed his naked body from the bed where he and Amber had made love all night. "Your wish is my command, my sweet angel."

Amber sat up like something startled her.

Damian stopped in his tracks. He looked at Amber with confusion.

"Don't Damian. Don't ever call me that! Ever!"

"Don't call you what, baby?" Damian went to the bed and sat with Amber. Amber had her head in hands. He gently pried her hands away from her face. "Amber, don't call you what?"

"Please, don't ever call me 'angel.' Paul called me that all the time. Please, just not that."

Damian took his wife in his arms. Amber buried her face in Damian's chest. "I promise, I will never use that word again." Damian lifted Amber's chin. "I promise. Now, can I get you some coffee?"

Amber nodded.

Damian broke away from Amber and ordered breakfast for he and Amber.

Damian went back to the bed and lay gently on top of his wife's body and kissed her face. "It's going to be a little while before they bring us some food. Would you like me to make you feel good again?"

Amber turned over under her husband's body. She pulled at the sheet positioned between them and with Damian's help, removed it from the bed. She felt the warmth of her husband's skin against hers. She could tell without looking that he was ready to be with her again. "Yes, Mr. Adams. Mrs. Adams would like you to make her feel like she was in heaven again before breakfast."

Damian kissed his wife and lowered his body gently between her legs. He found the warm spot of her body that was waiting and willing to let him enter her. The spot that would bring them together into the oneness that they had shared several times during the night.

Amber felt her husband's manhood throb with each gentle thrust into her body. She moved her body willingly in complete rhythm with Damian's. The feeling of his body moving with hers made the feelings inside her stronger with each thrust. She felt the pulse of her own orgasm coming close. "Damian, I'm almost there! I want us to climax together again."

Damian moved his body faster with the rhythm of Amber's body. They continued in that perfect rhythm for a few more seconds.

Amber's body gave way to the feeling of complete, warm peace. She felt Damian climax the very second that she had given way. They held the feeling together for a few seconds before falling into each other's arms. "I love you so much, Amber. You make me whole."

Amber just held Damian. She couldn't speak. She only wanted to continue feeling him inside of her body. She didn't want him to leave.

◊◊◊

Angelica grabbed the keys out of the envelope that had been delivered to her a couple of days earlier and looked at them in her hand. She hadn't been in the cab of an eighteen-wheel truck since Mexico. *Will I remember how to drive the monster waiting for me at the truck stop? Well, time to find out.*

She picked up her cell phone and dialed Shelby's number.

"Hello?"

"Hey, girl, it's Angelica. Just wondering what you're doing?"

"Well, I'm rolling down I-20 right now, headed into Meridian, Mississippi."

"Are you headed west bound or east bound?"

"Oh, I'm headed west after I drop this load a little to the south. I'm taking this load to Hattiesburg, then I'll head west to pick up another one. Why? What's up?"

"Well, how would you like some company?"

"Sure, you can ride with me anytime."

"No, I have a truck. I would just like to roll with you. I won't be carrying any loads or anything. The agency decided it would be less expensive than getting involved with trucking companies again. I'm just going to work the case as an undercover driver. I figure if we roll together, it will be easier for the girls out there to believe I'm a driver, and not a cop. We have other agents working as drivers too, but they will be in different territories."

"Well sure, Angelica, you can roll with me. It will be a blast seeing what trouble we can get ourselves into this time." Shelby laughed. "I don't know that Jack's going to be too happy about it, but he'll get over it."

"I don't want to get Jack angry at you, and I don't want him mad at me either."

"No, he won't be mad."

"Well, you won't be in any danger. We're just going to be out there looking for witnesses that can give us some evidence against Shades. Plus, I need to do what I can to help Damian keep Amber safe."

"Amber? I thought she was away from Shades now. Damian told me just a couple of days ago that Amber was with him and they were going to get married."

"Yeah, she's with him, but I didn't know anything about the marriage. Damian knows that Shades is looking for Amber and that they post all marriages in newspapers, on the computer, and in the public records. He was supposed to be keeping her hidden. I guess I will have to call him and see what's going on."

"I'm sorry, I would have let you know, but I just figured you already did."

"No, I didn't. Damian doesn't realize just how big a reach this Shades guy has, I guess."

"Do you know where they are?"

"No, he hasn't told me that. I think he thinks they are safer that way.

"I can see I'm going to have to make a few things clear when I call him later. He didn't by any chance tell you where they were getting married did he?"

"No, but I'm sure he was smart enough to get married in a small town somewhere."

"I hope so."

"Where do you want to meet up, partner?"

"I'm on my way from the hotel to my truck in Atlanta. How long will it be before you finish your delivery?"

"I'm not sure. I'm taking it directly to location. If they unload me right away, I can be back in Meridian sometime tonight. But if they don't, it could be sometime tomorrow before I get back here."

"Okay. Will I be causing you any problems if you wait on me in Meridian if you get done tonight? I think I can be there in about five or six hours. It's 290 miles to Meridian from Atlanta."

"Of course, that won't be a problem at all. But if I don't get done and have to wait to unload, you might have to wait for me."

"That won't be a problem, it will give me some time to check out the girls at that big truck stop there in Meridian."

"Sounds good, partner. I will see you in a few hours, hopefully."

"Thanks, Shelby. I just hope I remember how to roll a big truck. I had the keys in my hand a little while ago and I was a little nervous just thinking about it."

Shelby laughed. "It's like riding a bike, Angelica, at first you have to get your balance and then you remember. You'll be okay. See you soon."

Angelica laughed. "I know you're right, see you soon."

Angelica hung up and immediately called Damian.

"Hello?" Damian sounded like he was asleep and it was afternoon.

"Damian, this is Agent Dillon, I was just talking to Shelby and she informed me that you have plans to marry Amber. I don't have a problem with you two getting married, but this probably isn't the smartest time to be doing that."

"Too late, Agent Dillon. Damian kissed Amber who was next to him in bed. "We got married yesterday, and we're on our honeymoon."

"Well, congratulations, but Damian I have to ask, do you think this was the wisest time to do all that?"

"I don't know why not, Agent Dillon. I love Amber. I had to show her just how much by marrying her."

"But what about keeping her safe, Damian? Do you have any idea how much information Shades can get if he finds out you too got married? They post marriages online, in newspapers, and they are a matter of public record. If by any chance, he hears that you've gotten married, he can look it up online and find out exactly where you are."

Damian sat up in his bed. "But that's a small chance, right Agent Dillon? I mean, who would have seen us get married? It was just me and her at the chapel."

"Well, the chances are pretty high dealing with Shades. You forget he has girls and people that work for him all over the country, and he's not stupid. I'm sure he has sent out texts and calls to all of the people who work for him. Think about it, Damian. Just with the little bit of information you gave me just now, I figured out that you got married in Vegas and all you told me was 'chapel.'"

"Wow, how'd you know that?"

"That's not important, what is important is that you and Amber get out of there as soon as possible. You need to keep rolling and keep her out of sight. Or, find somewhere that Shades won't look, which is probably nowhere. I'm out on the road now, so maybe we better meet up somewhere and she can ride with me."

"Yeah, I guess she can ride with you."

Amber shook her head.

"Amber doesn't want to do that, she wants to stay with me."

"Well, okay, but you'd better start being more careful. It shouldn't take me to long to get enough evidence against Shades for an arrest, but in the meantime, you can't stay in one place too long."

Damian threw his legs over the side of the bed. "Okay, Agent Dillon. I'll get her out of here now."

"Damian, if they see you together and they spot your truck, it won't take them long to track you down. Be smart. Your new bride's life, and your life are on the line here."

"I know; we'll be careful."

"Go back to work and keep hauling until I let you know we have Shades in custody."

"Okay, Agent Dillon, we will."

Damian ended his call with Angelica. He turned and looked at Amber. She was now sitting up in their bed. Damian leaned over and kissed his new bride. "I'm so sorry, baby, we have to end our honeymoon tonight. Agent Dillon seems to think I've made a mistake in marrying you here in Las Vegas."

"We have to leave right now? This is our honeymoon."

Damian looked at Amber and reached for her. "I know, baby, but Shades will find out where we are since our marriage is public record."

"Seriously, Damian, think about it. Shades would have to check every newspaper and courthouse in the country. They have no idea we got married in Las Vegas, let alone that we got married at all."

"She did mention the internet. Shades could find us that way."

"*If* he's looking for a marriage between us. Shades is a creep. He's been with his top girl Crystal for years. He's never once offered to marry her. He's not one to think that anyone from his world would do anything moral."

"I understand, Amber, but what if someone has seen you here?"

"I doubt that."

"Maybe, but it's still possible. How did Shades find other girls that took off?"

Amber thought for a few minutes. "He would send out a text and photo to everyone."

"So, it's possible one of the girls or handlers in this territory might have seen you, seen us?"

"Yes, it's possible, Damian, but most of the girls like me don't give a damn about those who try to get out. In fact, I actually felt glad for them.

Most of them end up dead, but I felt glad that they at least tried to get out. Those girls and you helped me make the decision to get out. Shades might find me, and he will kill me if he does finds me." Amber moved closer to Damian and put her arms around his neck. "For now, I don't want to think about that. I want to finish the last night of our honeymoon."

Damian pulled his wife close. "No one is going to touch my wife. No one is going to take away the last night of our honeymoon. We will figure things out and leave tomorrow."

Amber smiled and kissed Damian. "Good, now I think you need to make love to me again."

◊◊◊

"I want something, Joey." Shades yelled through the phone.

"I know, boss, I got the guys and the girls keeping close watch on the truck stops. There are several blue trucks at trucks stops here in Vegas, but only two of them have left since Friday. Neither of them had anyone remotely looking like Amber aboard."

"What about public filings or the internet?"

"Nothing yet, boss, it's the weekend. Most of that stuff won't show up until Monday or Tuesday. There's nothing posted on the net, but we are monitoring it."

"If they are in Vegas, I want them found."

"I know, boss, but my girl did say she wasn't sure it was Amber. We might be barking up the wrong tree."

"Maybe so, but I want proof it's not her before we call off the dogs."

"Yes, sir. We will keep looking."

"Give me something soon, Joey. I want this bitch bad. No one betrays me and lives."

Shades hung up his phone.

Crystal was sitting next to him at the dining room table. She was picking at her food. "Any word?"

"Nope, not a sign of her." Shades looked at Crystal with suspicion. "Look at me."

Crystal looked up at Shades with fear in her eyes.

"You'd better be telling me the truth about her. You knew her the best; you spent time with her. She never once told you about some guy she was seeing?"

"I swear, Shades, she never mentioned anything to me about having a guy. She never talked to me about anything personal except her family and her kids."

"Kids, that bitch has kids?"

"Yeah, two. She said her family was taking care of them for her."

"Well, that's good to know. If I can't find her, I will use the rug rats to bring out the big rat."

"Shades, you can't use children like that. You can't hurt kids."

Shades slammed his fist on the table so hard that Crystal jumped. "I can and I will do anything I please. You'd just better hope it doesn't come to that. After all, you're the one that just told me about her kids."

Crystal tried to eat but she couldn't. She didn't like this side of Shades. She picked up her plate. "Excuse me, I don't feel well."

Shades huffed, "Whatever."

CHAPTER TWENTY-NINE

ngelica hugged her old friend. "Hey, girl, you're looking good."
"Thanks, Angelica." Shelby looked at Angelica. "Looks like marriage is good for you."

Angelica laughed. "He's been terrific. We don't get to see each other as much now, since they transferred me to another handler. But, when I'm in the office and not working a case, we spend a lot of time with each other. How are you and Jack doing?"

"Better and better every day, I still have pings of mistrust when I have to be away from him for long periods of time. Other than that, we are great."

"That's good."

"I'm sorry it took me so long to get off that location."

"It's not a problem, in fact, it was good. It gave me a chance to find out a few things about the girls here. I even found out some helpful information without even asking any questions."

"Good. Let's go find us some coffee and you can tell me whatever you think you can share."

Angelica and Shelby walked into the truck stop, got coffee, and sat at an empty table. There were only two other people in the entire store, common for three o'clock in the morning.

Angelica yawned. Shelby noticed. "Hey, if you want to forego the coffee buzz, we can get some rest."

"No, I really want to bounce some stuff off of you first."

"Okay, so what's happening with the case? What's the plan?"

"The case wasn't really going anywhere until I got here. I didn't really have a clue how to nail Shades. He's so insulated, and has his patsies doing his dirty work. At first I didn't know how I was going to pull him out of the shadows. Then I got here and started snooping around. I talked to a couple of girls around here, and I hung out in the bathroom." Angelica pulled out an older type cell phone from her pocket and put it in the middle of the table.

Shelby picked up the cell phone and looked it over. "Man, this phone is some kind of relic. Where'd you get it?"

"Well, even though I'm not usually a pickpocket, I lifted it off the counter in the bathroom. One of the girls I was talking to had it sitting next to her on the counter. I was washing my hands and well, I pushed it off into the trash with my paper towels. She got ready to leave the restroom with her friend and freaked when she couldn't find it. I helped her look for several minutes in the bathroom, knowing all the time where it was. When she couldn't find it, she went outside to look. I told her I would continue to look for it in the bathroom and let her know if I found it. Well, I just fished it out of the trash. I opened up the text message and phone log. I sent everything to my phone. I also looked at the photos. Look at them."

Shelby looked at the photos. "Oh no. There's a picture of Amber on here."

"Yeah, and just like I suspected—he's sent that photo to everyone who works for him. Look at the text messages."

"He's offered a reward for information from anyone that might have seen her? Oh, God, Angelica, Amber is in real trouble."

"I know, especially if someone sees her before we can get there to protect her."

"Have you told Damian?"

"I told him yesterday to keep her hidden, but I didn't have this information until just a little while ago. I don't even know if he's going to follow my instructions."

Shelby put the phone in the middle of the table. "He'd better, otherwise, he's going to get Amber killed."

"I know. I wish they both would have just waited for me. I could have put Amber in protective custody, sent Damian out on the road doing his job, and they both would have been safe until I could build a case."

"But, they couldn't wait."

"Right, they couldn't wait. Something happened to Amber to make her run. I don't know exactly what that was, but something happened to make her turn stupid."

"Love?"

"Maybe, but more than likely, that was only part of it. Shades probably did something to push her over the edge. Regardless, now it's my job to save both their lives."

A young woman walked over to the table that Angelica and Shelby were sharing. "Is that my phone?"

Angelica, picked up the phone out of the middle of the table and handed it to the girl that had lost it in the bathroom. "I don't know, I found this in the trashcan in the bathroom. I went looking for you outside earlier, but I couldn't find you. Is it the one you lost?"

"Yes, thank you. I could have been in real trouble with my boss if I couldn't find it. You didn't make any phone calls or anything on it did you? I mean I wouldn't care if you used it, but my boss is real picky about that kind of thing. He keeps records of all our calls. I just don't want to get in any trouble or anything."

"No, not at all. I looked at it when I couldn't find you, hoping to find your name. But I couldn't get past your entry code. I'm glad we found it."

"Thank you."

"I don't know what you do, but you need to find a better job. If my boss treated me like yours does, I'd quit."

The young girl held the phone tightly in her hand. She put her hand and the phone in her pocket. "Wish I could."

Angelica looked with compassion at the young girl. *She can't be more than a few months over eighteen—if she's even eighteen.* Angelica put her hand out for the girl to shake. "My name is Angelica and this is my friend Shelby, she's a driver, too. Like I told you earlier, if you ever need a ride, let us know."

The girl shook Angelica and Shelby's hands. "Okay, I'll keep that in mind. Right now, I'm waiting for a call from my boss. I'll look you two up when I find out where I'm headed. Maybe one of you will be going in my direction, and you can give me a lift."

"Sure, we'd be glad to."

"Well, I'd better go, thanks for finding my phone."

"No problem."

The young woman left the store.

"Wow and to think Shades has hundreds of those same kinds of girls working for him."

"Yep, and besides sex and human trafficking, they are transporting hundreds of pound of drugs all over this country and using the trucking industry to do it."

"Pretty smart business plan, really."

"Yeah, I guess, except that it's all illegal business."

Shelby laughed. "Just saying…."

"I know." Angelica and Shelby got up from the table. "Let's go get some rest. Where you picking up at?"

They walked to the door.

"Where else? Back in Odessa."

The women walked out of the store and toward their trucks.

"Lots of miles between here and there. Could get interesting, my friend, could get interesting."

◊◊◊

Damian buttoned his shirt and looked down at Amber asleep on their bed. He had gotten out of bed and showered, hoping to let Amber sleep for a little while longer. He leaned over and kissed his beautiful bride and whispered in her ear. "Time to get up, sweetheart. We've got to get going."

Amber turned her head over and moaned. "Oh, Damian, I don't want to get up. I want you to come back to bed and stay here with me forever."

Damian leaned over and kissed her other cheek. "No can do, princess, we have to get on the road. Not only do we have a madman looking for us, but I need to make us some money. We just spent a shit load of it here at this fancy hotel." Damian finished buttoning his shirt.

Amber moved and moaned again under the sheet. "Oh, all right." Amber turned over and slid her naked body out of the bed. She kissed Damian on her way to the bathroom. Damian gently smacked Amber on her naked butt. "Better get some clothes on or I might want to spend another day in that bed."

Amber turned in the doorway of the bathroom and faced her husband, bearing her entire naked body to his full view. "I don't mind." Amber looked down at the bulge now appearing in Damian's pants. "Looks like that's what you want, too."

Damian laughed and then turned on the television. "Might be what I want, but isn't what we have time for. We will have plenty of chances to break in that sleeper of ours. You get in that shower, we need to get out of here. I told Agent Dillon we were leaving last night, but someone talked me out of it. We can't delay the inevitable anymore; we have to hit the road."

Amber went into the bathroom and turned on the shower. "Okay, but you can't say I didn't offer."

Damian walked into the bathroom and grabbed his wife by the waist.

Amber giggled.

He turned her around and kissed her deeply. "You are too hard to resist." Damian took off the clothes he had just put on. He climbed into the shower with his wife. They spent the next few minutes making love in the shower.

◊◊◊

Shelby listened to the rings as she waited for Jack to answer. A sense of relief came over her when Jack answered. "Hello, baby."

"Hi, sugar. What are you doing?"

"Well, right now, I'm going to the store to get some laundry soap. We were out, and I know my sweet darling is going to be home in a couple days."

"About that, I will be home, but I'll be bringing someone with me."

"Really, what stray are you bringing home?"

"She's not a stray, Jack, she's my best friend."

"Angelica? Shelby you promised not to get involved in that case."

"I'm not, Jack, Angelica is just running with me for a while—in her own truck."

"For now you're not involved, but I know you."

"Come on, Jack, you know how important Angelica is to me."

"Just come home, baby, and be careful. I'm making chicken enchiladas for dinner when you do get home. I'll make extra and make sure the spare room is fresh for Angelica."

"Thank you, sweetheart, I love you."

Jack was a little annoyed. "I love you too, but I mean it, watch out for yourself while you're out there."

"I will, I promise. Bye, baby."

"Bye."

The girl sitting in Shelby's passenger seat smiled. "Sounds like you really love your husband."

"Yeah, he's a keeper, but sometimes he is a little too protective."

"So, your husband doesn't like you out here on the road?"

"Oh, he doesn't mind it now, but it wasn't always that way. We have been through some pretty rough stuff over my driving a truck. He bought me this new truck, so I think he's changed his mind a bit."

"You're so lucky. I wish I was doing something else with my life instead of delivering packages."

"So, why don't you find another job like Angelica suggested last night?"

The girl looked out the passenger's side window. "It's complicated. I can't, that's all."

Shelby looked at the girl in despair. She wished she could just take the girl off the road and help her start her life over. "Well, hey, no pressure from me, but if you ever want to talk, I'll give you my number."

The girl never turned to look at Shelby. "Sure."

The girl had approached Shelby and Angelica before they left the truck stop. She wanted a ride to Dallas. Angelica knew that she had to deal with some touchy stuff so she offered Shelby the opportunity to give the girl a ride.

Shelby thought about Amber and immediately agreed.

◊◊◊

Damian and Amber gathered up what they had in the room. Damian kissed Amber before opening the door that had been closed for the last two days, except for a few deliveries from room service. "It's been a wonderful honeymoon."

Amber giggled. "It's been the best. I love you." Amber went through the door to the hallway. "Wow, this is strange, seeing people again. It feels like my world stopped inside that room."

"Same for me, baby." Damian took hold of Amber's hand and they walked to the elevators.

Once they got to the bottom floor, Damian had second thoughts about Amber going with him to the truck stop. "Baby, I'm thinking maybe I'd better put you in a cab and have you meet me at another place outside of town. I'm not sure taking you to the truck would be smart. If Shades put out a text on you, then they will more than likely be looking for you at the truck stops."

Amber didn't like the idea of being separated from Damian. "I don't want to be away from you, Damian. Where would we meet?"

"I feel the same, but I just think we'd better be safe." Damian thought about it for a moment. "I know—there's a casino off I-15, they have truck parking in there. I will have the cabbie take you there and I'll pick you up."

"No, Damian. I don't want to leave your side."

Damian took Amber in his arms. "Look, it's only going to be for a little while. If by chance anyone were to see you, they could put us together. Please, Amber, just take a cab to the casino and wait for me there for just a little while."

Amber hugged Damian. "All right, but please don't take too long."

"I promise." Damian grabbed Amber's things. "I will take these things with me to the truck." He then walked with Amber outside and hailed a cab.

A cab pulled up to the curb. Damian gave the driver money. "Take her to the Oasis Casino off I-15."

"Yes, sir."

Damian kissed Amber, shut the door, and watched her disappear down the street. *It feels so strange that she's not next to me.* He quickly turned around and went back into the hotel. He went to the front desk. "I need to check out of my room please."

After he checked out, Damian walked outside and flagged down another cab. Damian opened the door of the cab and climbed in with all of his and Amber's things before the cabbie could get out of the car. Damian gave him the address of the truck stop. "I know the place." He pulled away from the curb. "Been here gambling?"

"Yeah, something like that. Can we just hurry, please? I have to get somewhere soon."

"Sure." It didn't take long before the cabbie had Damian at the truck stop. Damian paid the driver, grabbed his and Amber's things, and got out of the cab. "Thanks for the lift."

Without looking around, Damian went straight to his truck. He unlocked the truck that had been sitting for two days. Las Vegas was hot and the trapped heat of two days came at him when he open the driver's side door. Damian ignored the heat and climbed into the truck with all of the things in his hands. He placed all the bags on the sleeper before returning to the driver's seat.

Without doing a pre-trip on the engine, Damian started up his truck and turned on the air conditioner. He opened his door and stepped out to check out the exterior of his truck while the truck was airing up. He quickly checked all the necessary hoses and tires. After finding everything in order, Damian got back into the driver's seat. As he waited for the truck to completely air up, he began to have second thoughts. *I hope sending Amber to the casino was the right thing to do.*

The air finally topped off and Damian moved his truck out of the parking space and out to the street. His mind was only on Amber as he fought his way into traffic. *I have to get to her now.*

◊◊◊

The cabbie stopped near the entrance of the Oasis Casino and let Amber out of the car. Damian had given the driver money for the ride but still put his hand out for money. "Nice try, my husband already paid you." The cabbie pulled his hand back annoyed that the young woman didn't fall for his trick. He sped off right after Amber closed the door, not even allowing her to get up on the curb. Amber put her finger up in the air at the cab driver and yelled, "Thanks, asshole, you could have run over my foot."

Amber looked around and noticed a large parking lot to the right side of the casino. She walked toward the trucks that were parked at the back of the lot. She passed several women who were sitting on a stone wall that separated the casino building from the parking lot. Amber didn't recognize any of them, but did the best to conceal her face from them just in case some of them might be working for Shades. She located a quiet unoccupied spot by a tree and trash can near the trucks. She hoped that no one would bother her or proposition her before Damian arrived.

◊◊◊

Joey called his boss. "Shades, I think we might have a lead. One of the girls at the truck stop noticed a man arrive by cab a little while ago. He was carrying a whole bunch of bags. She said some of the bags were from a dress shop on the strip. It's a long shot, I know, but he drove away in a blue truck."

"Did he have a girl with him?"

"No, but I did find out what direction he went and the guys are looking for the truck now."

"Did the girl get a tag number, an MC number, anything off the truck besides the damn color?"

"Yes, she got the name and the tag off the truck."

"Good, give it to me." Joey read the name and numbers into the phone.

"I want to know the minute you locate that truck. Check everywhere in that city where trucks park. If it is the guy Amber is with, he might be keeping her hidden somewhere else."

"You got it boss, I will let you know."

◊◊◊

Amber was getting nervous. She kept looking at the watch that Damian had bought for her. "Please, Damian, hurry."

CHAPTER THIRTY

"**H**ey, Joey, I think we located the truck, he's headed south on two fifteen. I'll bet he's headed to the truck parking at the casino there at the fifteen."

"Stay with him. I'm calling Leo. I'll have him check the casino and parking lot. I bet that little bitch is waiting for him somewhere in or around that casino."

"Leo, check your parking lot and casino for that girl."

"I already did, Joey. Randy is in the lot now with the girls. We've been watching all weekend for her. She ain't here, Joey." Leo leaned back in his bar stool and took another sip of his beer.

"You get your lazy ass off that bar stool and check again. I'm headed to the casino now. There's a blue truck headed that way, too. We think it's the blue truck that the girl's been riding in. Now go and check the fucking parking lot and that casino again or I'll blow your head off."

Leo, slammed his beer down on the bar. Several of the men who worked for him had been sitting with him at the bar. Each had had several beers. "Look," Leo said to the others. He pointed in different directions around the casino floor. "Checkout every corner of this place—inside and out. Joey thinks that girl he's looking for might be around here."

Leo made his way through the crowd of gamblers, watching as he went to see if a small figure of a woman fitting Amber's description was anywhere in the room. He checked around every slot machine and walked by every blackjack and craps table. His companions checked the buffet, the hallways, and the food court. They met up at the front of the casino. "Anything?"

"Nothing, boss."

"Let's check the parking lot. I told Joey she wasn't here. The girls would have told us if she was in the lot."

Leo found his girls and two of his men near the stone wall at the back of the parking lot passing a joint. Everyone perked up when Leo and his other men approached them. "You been watching this parking lot like I told you?"

"Yes, sir, ain't nobody been around but a couple truckers going into the casino."

One of the girls high on something other than marijuana giggled and fell into another girl standing next to her. "Yep, there ain't been nobody around, 'cept that girl over by them trees. She's just standing there like she was one of them trees." The woman giggled again, unsteadily pointing toward the trees and trash cans.

Leo and his men noticed Amber standing against one of the trees. They didn't however, notice Damian's truck as it pulled into the driveway at the back of the lot. "There she is, boys. Shades is going to give me a medal for this one. Let's don't spook her. She might run, and I don't feel like getting sweaty."

The men moved toward Amber. A couple of them went around the wall and worked their way toward her from the tree side of the parking lot. Leo approached Amber straight on with one of his hands in his pocket.

Amber soon realized that someone was approaching her. She knew without knowing the man that he was one of Shades's guys. She looked around and saw the other men moving in on her. She wanted to run, but she was surrounded.

Leo slowed his pace, when he realized that Amber knew his guys were coming for her. "I'm with the casino authorities and I was just wondering if you're okay or if you need any help."

Amber clutched her purse and moved further away from Leo. Her only way of escape was to run straight east. Her heart was pounding—sheer panic had swept over her entire body. The only thoughts in her mind were of Damian. *Where is he? Why isn't he here to save me? Should I run?*

Amber didn't respond to Leo, she listened to her last thought. She ran, she ran east as fast as she could. Leo and his men followed.

Amber was breathing hard and knew from the sounds of the running feet behind her that the men pursuing her would soon have her in their hands. Amber ran faster, and then she saw it—Damian's truck coming straight for her. Amber ran even faster to meet the truck that was there to save her.

Damian saw Amber running toward him. The men who were chasing her were within arm's reach. He sped his truck up to meet Amber. When he reached her, Amber jumped onto the steps of the truck and hung onto the mirror on the passenger side. There was no way to stop and open the door for his wife. The men in pursuit of Amber would catch her for sure. Damian rolled down the window of the passenger side door. "Hang on, baby. I will get us out of here. Hang on tight."

Amber held on for dear life as Damian sped through the parking lot. Several of Shades's men tried without success to grab Amber off the side of the truck. One managed to grab her leg. Amber let go of the mirror with her right hand for a second and punched the man running along the side of the truck. She almost swung off the truck before grabbing the mirror with both hands again, as the man willingly let go of Amber's leg and fell to the ground.

"Damian, they are getting closer. Hurry!"Damian sped the truck up again until he was at the driveway entrance to the truck parking lot. He knew that he couldn't stop and hoped that traffic was clear enough or would stop as he moved into the street.

Several cars put on their brakes, their tires screeching as they avoided the large truck that was in their way. Damian sped on through the stalled traffic, thankful that he had not hit anyone. Amber still hung onto the side of the truck. The men who had been chasing were bent over in the driveway, trying to catch their breath.

"Hang on, baby, let me get a little further down the road."

Amber was done with hanging on. She grabbed hold of the inside of the door panel and pulled herself up into the window. Damian saw what Amber was trying to do. "Amber, stop! You're going to fall. Hold on and I'll stop in just a minute."

Amber ignored her husband's request. She grabbed the handhold inside the truck near the door, climbed, and then pushed her little body through the open window. Damian watched as his new bride fell into the passenger seat of their truck. He smiled. "Damn, baby, you got some skills."

Amber smiled, although she was still in a panic and scared about what was still ahead. "Just keep driving, Damian. If they found me at that little truck stop, they will find me again."

"I'm sorry, Amber. I didn't figure they would be looking there." Damian grabbed his wife's hand.

Amber looked at her husband with compassion. "It's not your fault, Damian. I'm the one that got myself into this mess. Now they know who you are and I've got you involved. Shades won't stop until we are both dead. We need to get out of here and find somewhere to hide. Not that it's going to do much good. Shades is too well connected and he will find me no matter where we go."

Damian thought as he drove down highway fifteen. He kept looking in his rear view mirror, but couldn't tell if anyone was following them. "Amber, I'm going to head down to Texas. My folks have a little ranch is South Texas, and I think we will be safe there. I would take you to my little house, *our* little house, in Junction, but I'm sure Shades knows this truck now. If he has the numbers off my truck, it won't be too hard for him to find out where our house is. My parents don't live there. They live outside of Junction on a little ranch."

"I don't know, Damian. I really don't want to get them involved in all this. Let's just stay away from the main truck stops and work for a while."

Damian picked up his cell phone and found Angelica's number. "I'm calling Angelica. She will know what we should do."

◊◊◊

"Damn it, Leo! Why didn't you stop him?"

"We couldn't, Joey. He was driving through the parking lot like a madman. The girl hopped onto the stairs and held onto the truck. What about the guy who was following him? Is he still behind them?"

"No, you asshole, he lost them when they pulled out into traffic. Shades is going to have both our asses for this shit."

"I'm sorry, Joey, we tried."

"Save it, if you hadn't been sitting up in that bar, chugging down beers, you guys would have had her before that guy driving that big blue truck arrived. Shades is going to kill you. I hope you enjoyed those beers, they might be the last ones you'll ever drink." Joey punched in Shades's number on his phone.

"Shades, its Joey. That blue truck is the truck Amber's mystery guy is driving. He was headed toward the casino on highway fifteen and the girl was here."

"So, did you get her?"

"No…not exactly."

"What the fuck does that mean, not exactly?"

"Well, Leo and his men almost had her, but then the truck driver showed up. She jumped on the truck and he got away with her."

"Did you dumbasses follow them?"

"We tried, but the guy I had following him got messed up in traffic and lost them. The last sighting of them was headed south on fifteen."

"You idiots! I can see that I am going to have to come out there and do this job myself. I want you guys out on fifteen, I want them found, and I want them found now! It's obvious they can't keep traveling without fuel. Get on the horn and make sure every damn truck stop east of the Mississippi is watching for that truck. I'm going to head to Dallas. That shithead driver's name is Damian Adams. He's from some little podunk town named Junction, Texas. I'm going to Texas."

"Yes, sir. I will get on it right away."

"You'd better get it done, Joey. Your life and the lives of all those dumbasses under you depend on it."

"Yes, sir." Joey hung up. "Thanks, Leo, that was fucked up—now Shades is getting personally involved. If we don't find that girl before he does, he's going to blow all our brains out."

"Sorry, Joey."

Joey hit Leo in the face. "Shut the fuck up and find that bitch. She's out there somewhere on highway fifteen."

◊◊◊

"Angelica, this is Damian."

"Damian what's going on? Are you and Amber okay?"

"Well, for now, but Shades's men almost got a hold of Amber this morning at a casino parking lot in Vegas."

"What? I thought I told you guys to leave last night?"

"I know, Angelica, but we wanted to finish our honeymoon. Besides, it wouldn't have mattered if we would have left last night or today. They were watching for us and they found us. They definitely know my truck now."

"Shit. Where are you guys at?"

"We are rolling down highway fifteen, headed toward California. But I was thinking of going to Texas, instead. I think I'll take Amber to my folks' house in Junction."

"Heading to Texas is the right move. Shelby and I are headed for Odessa right now, but taking her to your parents' might not be wise. If Shades knows who you are, like you said, then it won't take him long to find out where you're from and who your parents are."

"Well, I'm sure he knows by now."

"I think you and Amber need to meet me and Shelby in Odessa. The best way to keep both of you safe is to have you in my custody. I will have some of the undercover drivers working for us, in the central area, help you get to Odessa without trouble. It won't take me long to make the phone calls. You guys keep rolling to Texas."

"I'm going to need fuel, Angelica, about the time we get to Albuquerque. I won't take a break anywhere, but it's going to take at least fourteen or fifteen hours for us to get to you. Assuming there's no more trouble."

"Okay, so according to my map, you're going to break off the fifteen and grab the forty. Is that right?"

"Yeah, I can take the back roads if you want, but once they figure out where we are, which they will, it won't really matter if we're on the back roads or not. Plus, it's hard finding fuel on the back roads."

"No, you're right about that, just stay on the main highways. Have you seen anyone following you?"

"Not really. If they are, they haven't showed their ugly heads."

"That's good, you've probably lost them for now. Once you guys stop for fuel or if one of Shades's girls sees you from one of their rides, they will be on you like flies."

"I know of an out-of-the way fuel spot in Albuquerque. That might keep us from being noticed when we get there."

"Okay, great. I will get a hold of a couple of my guys out there; they will be watching for you. Shelby and I are about ten hours out of Odessa. We aren't taking a break either. Let's pray that the DOT don't stop any of us."

"All right, Angelica, be sure and let me know who these guys are that are on our side. Amber and I are real skittish about everyone. Please, Angelica, I know we haven't done things the way we should have, and didn't listen to your advice, but please, do not let anything happen to my Amber."

"I'm going to do my best, Damian. You guys just need to watch yourselves. I will call you back and let you know who to make connections with when you get to Albuquerque. I also have a couple of drivers in Phoenix. I'll see if they can meet up with you in Flagstaff. They can escort you on into New Mexico."

"Okay, Angelica, get back with me as soon as you can."

"I will, Damian."

Damian handed his phone to Amber. He saw his exit off fifteen. "We're going to take highway one-sixty-four to highway ninety-five. Ninety-five will take us down to interstate forty. That highway will take us to Flagstaff. Angelica is trying to get two of her agent drivers in Phoenix to meet us there. They will give us protection into New Mexico."

"Good. I'm really scared, Damian. Shades has people everywhere."

"I know, baby, but we will be safer when we get to Odessa."

"Odessa? Why are we going there? My family lives there—Shades might try to hurt them if we go there. He might think I'm trying to get protection from them and he might kill them. Damian, we can't go there."

Damian grabbed Amber's hand again. "We have to, Amber. We have to meet Angelica and Shelby there. She's going to protect us. Right now, Shades doesn't have a clue where we are headed. She's sending help to get us there. We won't be there long, just long enough for you to be put into Angelica's protective custody."

"No, Damian, I'm not going to be put into the custody of anyone."

Damian let Amber's last words go unanswered. They were both stressed and now was not the time to make Amber see reason.

CHAPTER THIRTY-ONE

"Shades, we went all the way to the California line. The guys came up from Barstow and nothing. It's like they just disappeared."

"Did you idiots check out the roads off of fifteen?"

"As many as we could. A couple of the guys went down highway one-sixty-four. They said they didn't see anything."

"Fine. I'm going to be in Dallas this afternoon. Keep your eyes peeled; maybe that driver will try and go back to Vegas."

"Okay, Shades. I'm sorry we couldn't find him."

"Shut up, Joey, this isn't over. When I finish with Amber, I'll be making a visit to Vegas. I'm tired of the incompetence coming out of there. I think we need a change and I'm going to start with you and Leo."

◊◊◊

"Damian, this is Angelica. Where are you guys at?"

"We're about thirty miles from Flagstaff on the forty."

"Sorry, it's taken so long to get back to you. I have two guys from Phoenix. They will be at the Little America Travel Center. Do you have a CB radio in your truck?"

"Yes, but I hardly ever use it."

"Well, I don't want you to go into that truck stop, I want you to continue going on down the forty. Get on your radio and call for Shiner or Rig Baby. Both of them will have their CB's on channel nineteen. When they answer, pretend you're friends. Let them know you're headed eastbound. Then, just keep going, lower your speed by about ten miles per hour. My guys will catch up to you. Shiner will be in a green flat top with an empty flatbed. Rig Baby will be in a red and white Pete with an empty box trailer. These guys are going to escort you to New Mexico."

"What happens once we get into New Mexico?"

"I have two more guys who will pick you up in Albuquerque. Same procedure, except you said you needed fuel. So, call for them when you finish getting fuel. They will be at the TA off twenty-five."

"The place I'm getting my fuel is in Grants. It's a smaller place, and I doubt any of Shades's people hang out there—at least I hope not."

"That will be okay. Just call for Mr. D. and Rising Sun when you get into Albuquerque. Mr. D. is rolling in a deep blue Pete, and Rising Sun is in a yellow and orange Kenworth. Both of them have empty flatbeds. They will escort you to the Texas line outside Eunice, New Mexico."

"Okay, Angelica. You think this is going to work? These guys will protect us if any of Shades's guys find us?"

"Yes, they are DEA agents. They've got your back. Just listen to them if you get into trouble."

"Okay, Angelica, see you soon."

Angelica used her radio to call Shelby. "Hey, Barbie, you want to stop for a cup of coffee?"

Shelby came back on the radio. "Ten-four on that, Cover Girl. I need to rest my butt for a while."

"How about Monroe?"

"Sounds good, little sister."

Shelby's little rider wasn't as upset as she had been earlier. "We're going to stop for a break?"

"Yeah, just a food break. We'll be driving on through to Dallas."

"Good, I really need to use the bathroom."

"Why didn't you say something? We would have stopped."

"I never ask a driver to stop. He might leave me and then I'd be in trouble for not making my delivery on time."

Shelby did her best not to pry, but she was curious if the girl would open up to her. "I told you my name, but you never told me yours. What's your name?"

"Laura, but don't tell anyone I told you, please." The girl looked a little scared.

"Don't worry, I won't tell anyone."

Shelby wanted to ask the girl more questions, but she felt that she'd better just ask one question at a time.

◊◊◊

"How about you, Shiner?"

"You got Shiner, who's this?"

"Prince Charming and Cinderella."

"Where you headed, Prince Charming?"

"Eastbound on the forty."

"Ten-four, Prince Charming, we'll catch you on the fly and put you in the cradle."

"Ten-four, Shiner."

Damian looked at Amber who was almost asleep in the passenger seat. "Baby, why don't you climb into the sleeper and get a little rest? The two drivers Angelica ordered to protect us will be here in a few minutes. We're safe. Get some sleep."

Amber stretched. "Maybe I will rest for a little while." Amber took off her seatbelt, kissed Damian on the cheek, and went into the sleeper.

◊◊◊

"Shades, over here." Shades handed his computer bag and coat to the two men that had been waiting to pick him up at the airport. The three men walked through the terminal to the exit. Shades was escorted to an SUV that was waiting for him. "Let's get out of here. Take me to the stops off the forty-five."

"Yes, sir."

◊◊◊

"Okay, Prince Charming this is as far as we go. You can pick up your next ride at the cross of twenty-five and forty. It's been clear and easy so far, hope it remains the same for you all the way to your destination."

"Thanks, Shiner for the escort. We will catch you on the flip side."

"Ten-four, watch your back."

"Ten-four."

Amber was in the passenger seat of the cab again. Damian passed through the New Mexico checkpoint and drove toward Grants. "I'm going to stop at the old truck stop up here in Grants. Truckers use it, but it's not a real hot spot, except for locals. I'm going to get fuel. I think it will be secure enough for you to use the restroom and get us something to eat."

"Okay, I will do my best to stay out of sight of anyone who might be working for Shades. I don't know the girls in this area, Damian, but I can watch for the types of activities that I did."

Damian pulled into the truck stop fuel island. He leaned over and kissed his wife. "Watch yourself in there, and be careful. I'll be right out here until I finish fueling the truck."

Amber opened her door. "I will. Hurry and come inside so that we can get something to eat together."

Damian climbed out of the driver's side door. "Be there in a few minutes."

Amber felt uneasy as she walked toward the store. She was relieved when she didn't see anyone standing against the walls, the way the girls did when they were scoping out rides. Amber entered the store and made her way to the restroom. Her unnerved feelings welled up inside her belly when she opened the restroom door and found several women congregated there. Amber ignored them and went into a stall. She heard them whispering, which made her nervous.

After using the restroom, Amber went to the sink and washed her hands. She didn't want to give the women a full view of her face, so she wiped her face with the paper towels on the way out of the restroom. She wasn't sure they were Shades's girls…but it was possible.

Damian had finished fueling the truck and was coming into the store just as Amber was leaving. "Baby, what's up?"

Amber fell into Damian's arms. She whispered into Damian's ear. "I think some of Shades's girls are in that bathroom."

Damian pulled Amber away and looked into her face. "Are you sure?"

"No, but they seem like the type, and they were whispering while I was using the restroom." Amber was shaking.

Damian pointed toward the truck. "Go get in the truck, I will get some food, get my fuel ticket, and use the restroom. I'll be back to the truck in a minute. Lock the doors and don't open them for anyone but me."

Amber let go of Damian and ran toward their truck. "Okay."

Damian went into the store. Several girls in a group passed him as he walked to the fuel counter. Damian watched them leave the store and head toward the fuel islands. Still keeping an eye on the girls, Damian grabbed a few snack items, paid for them, and got his fuel ticket.

The girls looked at Damian's truck in the fuel island. One of the girls pulled out her cell phone and punched in a number. The other girls watched as the girl with the cell phone waited for an answer on her phone.

Damian knew he had to do something. He took his change from the clerk, grabbed his bag of snacks, and left the store. He sped up and ran directly into the group of girls, knocking the girl on the phone to the ground. The phone in her hand went flying across the sidewalk. The other girls spread out in different directions, surprised by what had just happened.

"What the hell, mister?" the girl with the phone said.

Damian stumbled slightly, pretending to retain his balance. "Oh, hey, I am so sorry."

Damian put out his hand to help the girl on the ground up to her feet. She rejected his assistance. "Get away from me, you crazy person."

"I don't know what I was thinking, I was just in a hurry." Damian reached out to help the other girls in any way he could. They all moved quickly away from him as if he was contagious.

"Get away from us, you creep."

Damian ignored the insult. His attention was on the girl's phone, which he spotted the on the ground. He backed up slowly, wobbled and then caught himself by stomping down on the girl's phone, causing it to break into several pieces. He turned to see the damage he had done. "Oh wow, I'm am so sorry."

The girl gasped when she saw her broken phone on the ground.

Damian bent down to pick up it up, but the owner of the phone shoved him out of the way, bent over and picked up the mangled pieces. "Get the hell out of here and leave us alone!" she screamed with hate in her eyes.

Damian backed away, muttering, "I truly am sorry."

"Asshole!" another girl yelled. "She's going to get her ass beat because of what you did to her phone."

Damian knew what she said was true, but he had to protect Amber at any cost. He wasn't sure they were Shades's girls, or if the call she was trying to make was about spotting his truck, but he couldn't take any chances. "Sorry," he said and bolted for his truck.

"What happened back there?" Amber asked as they pulled out of the parking lot.

"I saw them eyeballing the truck and one of the girls started to make a call. I just had to do something. They could be Shades's girls."

"I saw you step on the phone. That was good thinking, but all of Shades's girls have phones."

"At least we got away from the truck stop. Hopefully, they're so busy with the broken phone I bought us some time to get away. I don't think anyone else thought of taking a photo."

Amber looked in the bag of snacks. "Yummy, junk food. I think I'll eat the crackers and peanut butter."

"I wanted those."

Amber laughed as she ripped open the cracker package and put one of the crackers in her mouth. Damian reached for the pack.

Amber jerked it away.

"Give me one."

"Not a chance," she taunted.

Damian grabbed a cracker and put it in his mouth.

Amber laughed. "I love you, Damian. Thanks for protecting me."

"It's my job. I'm your husband. I will always do my best to protect you."

◊◊◊

Angelica and Shelby pulled into the truck stop in Dallas where Laura wanted to be dropped. "Hey, Cover Girl, let's get some coffee after we get some fuel here at my little partner's stop."

"Sure, Barbie, no problem." Angelica and Shelby pulled their trucks into the fuel Islands.

Laura looked around and saw some of the girls on her team. She put on her backpack and waited for Shelby to bring the truck to a stop near a fuel pump. She looked at Shelby and smiled. "Thanks so much for the ride. I sure appreciate it."

"Sure, no problem. Do you want to have something to eat together before you leave?"

Laura opened her door. "No, thanks. My friends are waiting for me."

"Okay. Well, if you need anything, call me." Laura was gone before Shelby could get the words out of her mouth.

Shelby watched Laura run across the parking lot and gather with her friends. She wondered if she would ever see Laura again. She got out of her truck, put on her gloves, and started to pump fuel into her tanks.

Angelica spoke across from the islands. "Hard not being able to help them, isn't it?"

"Yeah. It just makes me so mad that creeps like Shades control their lives. Why do they let him manipulate them?"

"Most of them had nothing when he came across them. They still don't have much, but they have a lot of fear and Shades has made it impossible for them to leave. He's good enough to them to keep them loyal, but cruel enough to kill them if they betray him."

"Damned if they do, damned if they don't."

Both women finished fueling, moved their trucks, and went into the store.

Laura was with the group of girls who all looked at the two women as they passed by. They whispered among themselves and then Laura said, "Thanks again, driver, for the ride."

Shelby turned and acknowledged Laura. "Anytime."

Once both women got their fuel tickets, Shelby said, "I'm going to the restroom."

"I can use a restroom break, too," Angela said.

When they were sure no one else was inside Angelica asked, "So, did your little rider give you any information?"

"No, but she seems breakable."

"You mean if she was put through a real interrogation?"

"I think if her supply line was severed and Shades were under arrest that she would sing like a bird."

"Wow, Shelby, you should be an agent. You've even got some of the lingo down." Both women laughed. They left the restroom.

It was after midnight, so they got some coffee and sat down at a table to relax. As Angelica sipped her coffee, she scanned the room, checking out the other customers. Suddenly, she gasped, almost choking on her coffee. She bent over the table and whispered. "Don't turn around, but I think Shades is sitting in that booth over there with some of his men."

She pulled out the picture she had in her pocket and looked at it. "Yep, that's him."

Shelby was nervous and wanted to look, but knew it would be suspicious. "Shades is here in Dallas? What the hell is he doing in Texas? Do you think he knows that Damian is meeting us in Odessa?"

Angelica grabbed her coffee and got out of the booth. She walked quickly toward the door that led to the fuel island. Shelby followed. "I have no idea, but we have to get to Odessa before that asshole does."

◊◊◊

Shades's phone rang. "Yeah, this is Shades."

"Boss, this is Juanita, one of my girls just told me that they might have seen that girl you're looking for here in Grants."

Shades pointed for one of his men to hand him a state map off the rack near the table they had been using for their meeting. "How do they know it's her?" He looked through the road atlas until he found the map he was looking for.

"Well, she came into the bathroom at the truck stop. Several of the girls agreed that she looked like the girl in the text message. Then when she left the building, she just kind of disappeared. They didn't see where she went from the store. They did mention that there was a blue truck at the fuel island. I guess there was some confusion because some guy ran into the girls while they were checking things out and stepped on one of their phones."

"No one saw which direction the truck was going?"

"No, but if they were coming from Vegas, like the text messages said, then they are probably headed east on forty. Wish I could give you more, boss."

"Good job, Juanita. Thanks for keeping watch. We will take it from here."

Shades ended his phone call. "I think we just got another sighting of the mysterious blue truck and Amber. Looks like they are in New Mexico. Curtis, contact Rodriguez in Albuquerque, have him and his guys watch the forty for that blue truck. If they locate it, have them call me."

Shades got up from the table, went to the coffee machine, and filled his cup. Two of his men followed him. "Something, wrong boss?"

"Yeah, I wish I could figure out where this asshole is headed. I thought maybe he might take her to his place, but now I'm thinking maybe he's going to take her to her place in Odessa. Once I know for certain that the blue truck in New Mexico is the truck we're looking for, I want a tail on that bitch. I was considering taking them out on the highway, but now I'm thinking fewer fireworks will be best."

"Rodriguez is watching the forty for us. He will call the minute he has an ID on the truck."

"Good. Let's go to the hotel. Tomorrow I want you to take me to Odessa. If, it turns out that he's headed to that place called Junction, we can head that way, too. I'm going to find Amber and that truck driver…and they are not going to be happy when I do."

CHAPTER THIRTY-TWO

"How about you, Mr. D.?" Damian waited for a response on the CB. "You got the Rising Sun, Mr. D. is taking a leak."

"This is Prince Charming and Cinderella, looking for a little look out."

"You got it, Prince Charming. Mr. D will be available in a few minutes. Continue on your route and we will locate your rig."

"Ten-four, taking it down a few, waiting for the look out."

"Ten-four."

◇◇◇

"Look, check the numbers on that blue truck that just went over the overpass."

"I can't see it from here."

Rodriguez pointed toward the on ramp. "Get up there on the forty. Get close to the truck, but don't spook them. I can check the numbers against the ones Shades gave us and see if that's our truck."

Rodriguez got on his phone. "Wesley, stay here near the on-ramp. Keep your eyes open for any other blue rigs. Check the numbers if you can. We're going to go check out the one that just crossed the overpass on the forty."

"Got it, boss."

Rodriguez and his men followed Damian's truck for several miles. When they were finally able to get close enough without spooking the driver, Rodriguez matched the numbers. "Back off a little, we got a match."

Rodriguez's driver backed down and pulled in behind Damian's truck.

Rodriguez called Shades.

"We got the truck, boss. It's headed east on forty."

"Good. Stay with it; I want to know exactly where that truck is headed at all times. Do not approach it, and don't lose it."

"Yes, sir."

"Shit, the boss wants us to follow these bastards. I have stuff I need to do. I'm not babysitting these guys." Rodriguez picked up his phone and called his man Wesley. "Wesley, I need you to get up on the forty and head toward two-eighty-five. When you find us, I want you to take over the surveillance on this truck."

"You found the truck Shades was looking for?"

"Yes, but he wants us to keep following it. I have things I need to do back in Albuquerque, so you have to follow these guys. I'll send a couple of other vehicles to help you out but, I can't keep doing this."

"All right, we are on the way."

◊◊◊

"How about you, Prince Charming?"

"You got Prince Charming."

"Charming, Rising Sun is on your tail behind a four-wheeler, Mr. D. is coming up on your six."

"Ten-four, Mr. D. I got you in my mirror, come on around."

"Ten-four, Charming, coming around."

Amber watched as the DEA agent moved the big rig around Damian's truck. "Angelica is really a terrific person to do all this for us."

"Yes she is. We need to help her by getting you somewhere safe."

"I know everyone is doing everything they can to protect me, but Shades is a sadistic son-of-a-bitch. He won't stop 'til I'm dead...or he's dead. And we know who's got the upper hand on that scenario." Amber looked out the window and into the mirror.

"Don't talk like that, Amber. You're my beautiful wife and we have a future together. No one, not even Shades, is going to take that away from us."

"I hope you're right." Amber looked at the car that was behind their truck. I don't mean to be paranoid, but that car behind our truck has been following us for a while."

"Yeah, I've noticed that; he won't even let Rising Sun get in between us." Damian keyed up the CB. "How about you, Rising Sun?

"You got Rising Sun, go ahead."

"Rising Sun, looks like we got some company on my tail. I can't seem to shake them no matter what I do."

"Yeah, I've been watching the leach. I'm not sure what's up his ass. Don't let it spook you; I'm keeping an eye on him. If he's unwanted company, we will quietly ask him to leave, or we have ways of helping them leave. Just keep rolling."

"Ten-four, Rising Sun. Thanks for the backup. We'll be turning off on two-eighty-five and heading toward Artesia, is that cool with you guys?"

"Yeah, that's cool. Mr. D, our little visitor here at the back just pulled out."

"That's good."

"Good, yes, but another one just took his place. I think we got two more four-wheelers going along for the ride now. Charming, when we make the exit off on two-eighty-five, just keep going. Mr. D. and I are going to make some evasive moves on them to find out if they are tailing you. If these clowns are flanking you, we will know it. If they decide to play with tons of steel, we can help them out with that, too."

"I got it, Rising Sun. We will just stay straight on our path and let you guys do what you do. We are taking the exit now."

"Right behind you, and it looks like our visitors are hanging with us. All except the first four-wheeler. He took the exit, but it looks like he went back over the forty. Must be going back home."

"Stay cool, Charming. We got your back and we will deliver you safely to Cover Girl."

"Ten-four."

◊◊◊

Angelica keyed up her mic. "How about you, Barbie?"

"You got Barbie, go ahead."

"Barbie, you remember that channel we used to go to when we were in Florida?"

"Sure do, Cover Girl."

"Can you go to that channel?"

"On my way."

"Did you make it, Barbie?"

"Yep, what's up?"

"Shelby, I just got a text from one of my men escorting Damian and Amber out of New Mexico. They are still several hours out of Odessa, and I have plenty of drivers out here to protect them. But if Shades finds out where they're headed, there is going to be a real showdown. My agents tell me that they aren't making any moves on Damian's truck, but they are definitely hanging with him. When we get to Odessa, I want you to go home and be safe."

"Seriously? Not a chance, Cover Girl. I want to see this thing through. I was even thinking that maybe I should take Amber with me. No one knows me; she would be safe with me."

"That's an idea, but I can't put you in that kind of danger. Plus, Jack will have my ass if I let you get involved."

"Don't worry about that. I want to help, Angelica."

"I know. I'll think about it. We got about a hundred miles left 'til we reach Odessa. Let's camp out at the truck stop near the one-twenty-six."

"Got you on that."

◊◊◊

Wesley sent a text to Shades, letting him know that they were now headed southbound on two-eighty-five. It wasn't long before a text was returned to him. "Where's Rodriguez?"

Wesley sent back: "He's back in Albuquerque. I'm watching the truck with two other teams."

A long delay.

"Stay with the truck and don't let it out of your sight. Do not communicate with Rodriguez any further. He is being removed from his position."

"I understand."

One of his other men contacted him. "Shades, the truck is headed south toward Texas. I'm thinking we should head west as soon as possible.

If they are headed to that town called Odessa, they will arrive there in about three hours. We can be halfway there by the time they arrive."

Shades thought for a moment, and then said, "They may arrive in Odessa in three hours, but they haven't slept. Plus, we don't know if they will head that way or continue south. Let me sleep on it. They can't possibly get away from me now. You'll have my decision in the morning."

"Okay, boss."

"Don't fuck this up. I want to be done with Amber and back in Atlanta by Friday. Do you understand me?"

"Yes, sir."

◊◊◊

Angelica and Shelby pulled into the truck stop off the one-twenty-six. The parking lot was crowded.

"Well, looks like the only parking place here is on the back line. Damian and Amber will be here in about three or four hours. Let's park these babies and grab a few winks, Barbie."

"Sounds good to me," Shelby said.

"We will go back to the nineteen after I tell you a few things."

"Okay."

"That's the channel they will be running on until they get here. Damian and Amber and my agents are going to be tired when they get here. So we need to let them get some rest. Then we will transfer Amber to one of our trucks. I'm thinking you might be right about letting her roll with you for a while."

"I'm game."

"I know you are, but Jack's going to kill me."

"Oh, he won't be too mad at you. But me? Maybe a little." Shelby laughed.

"Well, I will talk to Jack after we settle things with Shades. The guys I have with Damian and Amber are going to take out Shades's guys at the Texas State line, off the one -seventy-six. I have other agents waiting to bring them on into Odessa."

"That sounds like a good plan."

"I hope so. I really don't think Shades knows exactly where Damian is headed, but with the four wheelers he's got following the truck, he will soon enough."

"Are you sure they are Shades's men?"

"My agents have done a number of evasive moves on the four wheelers, and they haven't been deterred yet. They are definitely Shades's guys. It's going to be a long day tomorrow. If Shades and his men stayed in Dallas for the night, they won't be here until around noon. That will give everyone some time to rest and time to get Amber out of here. I've got a couple of ideas to send Shades on a wild goose chase. I just hope we can keep things together and everything goes according to plan."

"I don't want to be a downer, but aren't you the one who says that all plans need a backup, because things never go according to plan?"

"Yes, Barbie." Angelica laughed. "I remember, and I have another one waiting in the wings."

"That's my girl. Now let's go to nineteen and take a nap."

"Right behind you, Barbie Doll."

◊◊◊

"Damian, this is Mr. D. Are you doing okay?"

"Yeah, Mr. D. I'm tired, but I still got a few more miles in me."

"Okay, Damian. We will be on the one-seventy-six in just a few minutes. Rising Sun and I have orders to take out the three four-wheelers hanging with us. We plan to do that around the Texas state line. I want you to stay straight and not worry about what is going on around you. Two trucks are waiting at the line to take you on in to your destination. They changed the drivers on the trucks. You will be rolling with Tony Tiger and Ace. They are both rolling in Pete's. I don't know what trailers they are pulling, but they probably have flat beds. Stay with them and don't look back."

"Thanks, Rising Sun and Mr. D. We sure appreciate your help getting us this far."

"No problem. Get that little girl to her destination."

"I will."

"Ten-four, here we go."

Damian spotted the two trucks coming onto the road. He backed down in order for them to get in front of Mr. D. Mr. D. pulled off the road just long enough for the new agents and Damian to get by. Then Mr. D. pulled out in front of the four-wheeler directly behind Damian's truck. The four-wheeler tried to stop and avoid the impact, but couldn't. He slammed into the side of Mr. D.'s tractor. The four-wheeler behind the first one slammed into the vehicle crushed between the cab and the trailer. Rising Sun put his brakes on hard, causing the third four-wheeler to try and go around him. The driver of the third four-wheeler lost control and took the ditch. The car rolled over several times until it landed on its top, smoke billowing from the undercarriage. Rising Sun pulled up next to Mr. D.'s truck and stopped. Mr. D got out of the passenger side of his truck and ran to get into Rising Sun's truck. "Let's go."

Rising Sun put his truck into overdrive and headed toward Odessa. "The DEA will deal with the DOT on that mess. It went down a lot better than I thought it would. Those jackasses had no idea what hit them."

"Oh, I think they do, about forty thousand pounds of steel."

"Yeah, you're probably right."

CHAPTER THIRTY-THREE

"Tell Shades we lost them off one-seventy-six, right about the Texas state line."

"Shit, Wesley, he's not going to like this."

"I know, but it wasn't our fault. That driver had two trucks running with him. One of the trucks is still at the crash site. They used it to take us out. There were also two other trucks just inside the Texas line. It looked like they were waiting there for the blue truck. A couple of us managed to get away before the police arrived. We are headed back to Albuquerque."

"So, what direction do you think they are headed?"

"They were headed eastbound on one-seventy-six. Other than that, I have no idea where they went. The car we are in is about to fall apart from the accident. We have to stop in Hobbs and get another one from Larry. There's no way we can continue following that blue truck in this piece of crap."

"I'll tell Shades, but don't be surprised when the hammer comes down on all of you out there."

"Frankly, right now, I don't care. I'm pretty sure most of the others feel the same way."

Shades's man hung up his cell phone. He dreaded the next call he had to make "Shades, I'm sorry, sir, but Wesley just called and apparently that blue truck is getting some help. Several trucks just helped the blue truck get away from Wesley and his men. All the vehicles were destroyed except one, which is about to fall apart. They are making their way back to Hobbs, but the trucker got away. They last saw it eastbound on one-seventy-six."

"Shit, can't anyone do anything without me having to hold their damn hand?" Shades got out of bed. "I'm going to get a shower, then we'll head to

Odessa. I want those assholes near and around Odessa, Lubbock, and even Big Springs. I want them looking for that truck. I want it found—and I want it found, NOW!"

◊◊◊

Damian pulled his truck into the truck stop off highway seventeen-eighty-eight and interstate twenty. The trucks that had picked him up at the Texas state line pulled into the truck stop with him. Amber had fallen asleep in the passenger seat. She suddenly woke up as Damian parked the truck at the fuel Island. "We're in Odessa, baby. I'm going to fuel the truck and then we will park. I need to get some rest, so do you."

Amber looked around the truck stop. It was still dark outside, but the dawn of the new day was trying to break through. "I need to use the restroom, I'm not feeling so good. I think those snacks have upset my stomach."

"Are you okay?" Damian was worried.

"Yeah, just a little tummy ache."

"I think it will be okay. Just avoid making eye contact with anyone. Be sure and hurry."

Amber got out of the truck. "Okay, I will."

The truckers that had picked up Amber and Damian at the Texas line were fueling their trucks, too. Ace followed Amber into the truck stop. "Wait, Ms. Nichols, I need to go with you."

Amber stopped for a moment and looked at the driver. "It's Mrs. Damian Adams. I have to pee, so if you have to go with me, you'd better hurry up."

The agent followed Amber to the ladies room door. He went into the men's room.

After using the restroom, Amber washed her face, hoping the water would make her feel better. She wiped her face dry and then went into the store. She found Agent Ace waiting for her by the coffee machine. "It's not bad; you want a cup?"

"Yeah, Damian told me not to stay in here too long. I think I'll get him a cup, too."

Damian and Tony Tiger walked through the door just as Amber was filling the coffee cups. Two more men followed close behind them into the store. All four men walked directly toward the agent called Ace. The men all shook hands with each other and Damian. Damian broke away when he saw Amber. He motioned her to bring the coffee. "Come over here, Amber, I want you to meet the guys who have been protecting us."

Amber handed Damian his coffee as he led her to the men. "Guys, I would like for you to meet my wife, Amber Adams."

All the men shook Amber's hand. "Nice to meet you."

"Nice to meet ya'll, too."

"Angelica is asleep here in the parking lot somewhere. We have several other agents around as well. I don't think it will be a problem for all of us to get some rest."

"Good, I'm really tired." Amber sipped at her coffee. She squeezed Damian's hand, letting him know that she wanted to go. Damian took the hint. "I'm going to pay for our coffee. We'll go park our truck on the back line and get some rest."

"All right, Damian. We know what your truck looks like. We'll be out there in a few."

Damian and Amber went to their truck.

After Damian had parked the truck he turned to Amber, who was staring out the passenger side window. "You ready to get some rest, sweetheart?"

Amber turned to look at her husband. "Yeah, I'll be there in a minute."

Damian was concerned; he touched his wife's shoulder. "Everything okay?"

Amber smiled slightly. "Yeah, just thinking." She paused momentarily to reflect on her thoughts. "You know what tomorrow is?"

"No, baby, what's tomorrow?"

A couple of tears ran down Amber's face. "My baby Annie's birthday. Then next Saturday is Kami's wedding. I told Mama I would try and make it home for both events. Doesn't look like that's going to happen."

Damian knelt down by his wife and kissed her hand. He wiped the tears from her face and held her close. "I'm so sorry, Amber. We have been so wrapped up in keeping Shades from finding you I completely forgot about the wedding. You just told me recently when your birthday was, you haven't shared with me the babies' birthdays."

Amber put her arms around Damian. "I know. There is still so much we have to learn about each other. I just want all of this to be over with. I just want to be free."

Damian picked Amber up out of her seat and took her to their sleeper. "Let's get some sleep. We can talk more about things after we've had some rest."

"I love you so much, Damian. You have been the best thing that has ever happened to me. My life meant nothing before I met you. I will always love you. Thank you for loving me."

Damian kissed his wife. "I love you too, Amber. My life is complete with you in it."

Damian wrapped Amber in his arms and they fell asleep.

◊◊◊

Bam! Bam! Bam! Damian was jerked awake. He remembered going to sleep with Amber in his arms, but now she wasn't in his bed. He quickly pulled open the curtain, expecting to find Amber in the passenger seat.

"Bam! Bam! Bam! "Damian, wake up!"

Damian got out of the sleeper and looked out the passenger side window. A woman was standing at the bottom of the steps. "Damian, it's me Angelica. I need you and Amber to come out here. We need to talk."

Damian again looked around his truck. Amber was nowhere to be found inside the truck. Damian opened the door so Angelica could enter his truck. "She's not here, Angelica. She was here when we went to sleep, but now she's not. I didn't even hear her leave, I guess I was just really tired."

Angelica got into the truck and took a quick look. "Shit. She didn't tell you she was going to the bathroom or to take a shower?"

Damian rubbed his hair. "No, we fell asleep together."

"I'll go inside and see if she's taking a shower or something. You clean yourself up and call her cell phone."

Angelica motioned for two of the agents in the parking lot to follow her. "Amber isn't in that truck. Did you guys see her leave?"

"No, Angelica, we all agreed to get some rest." The agents ran into the truck stop store.

"I sure hope she's in here and she didn't do something stupid, like try and go see her family." Angelica went into the restroom—Amber was not there.

Angelica and her agents went to the store counter. They asked the woman at the register if someone fitting Amber's description was taking a shower. "No, there isn't anyone in the showers right now."

"Did anyone like her take a shower earlier today?"

"No, I've been here since six-thirty, and I ain't seen anyone like that take a shower."

"All right, thank you."

Angelica and her agents went back out to the parking lot. Just as she was walking past the fuel Island, she spotted Shades in an SUV rolling into the parking lot. "Shit, that asshole Shades is here. That's all I need."

Angelica got on her phone and called Shelby. "Shelby, you see where Damian's truck is parked?"

"Yeah, just down from ours a little ways."

"I need you to take your truck and park it in front of Damian's truck. I need you to block anyone's view of Damian's truck. Shades is in this parking lot and he's looking for it. I'm out looking for Amber right now. She's disappeared."

"Damn. Yeah, sure, Angelica. I'm on it." Shelby took her truck and pulled it in close to the trucks park on the back row. She blocked in several trucks beside Damian's.

Damian was in his truck still trying to get Amber to answer her phone. There was no answer. "Where are you, Amber? Where are you?"

When Shelby was finished doing what Angelica had asked her to do, she got out of her truck and went to Damian's. She pulled open the passenger side door and asked, "Damian, where's Amber?"

Damian was in a panic. "I don't know, Shelby. She was here when we went to sleep. When Angelica woke me up just a few minutes ago, I realized she wasn't here. I've tried to call her cell phone but she won't answer. Angelica is inside looking for her. God please, please don't let Shades have her."

"Calm down, Damian. Shades doesn't have her, at least not yet. That's the reason Angelica had me block your truck from view. He's driving through the lot looking for your truck. Angelica just called me and she's on her way back here. I don't think she found Amber in the store either. Where else would she have—?"

Shelby didn't complete her question, she and Damian answered it together. "Her parents."

"She was talking about it being Annie's birthday today. I bet she went home to see her little girl."

"I'll bet you're right. Did she know how dangerous it would be for her to go there? Not just for her, but for her family?"

"Yes, she knows. I think she just wanted to see Annie."

◊◊◊

"Hey, Mama, I hope you don't mind, but I came to see Annie for her birthday."

Elsa Mae opened up the door. "Of course not, Amber, come in." Elsa Mae hugged her daughter. "It's so good to see you. Annie will love seeing you. Katie brought her over just last night. She needed time to set up for Annie's birthday party, so Annie came home last night and slept in her bed. She's in the bedroom playing with toys right now, go on in and see her."

"Okay, how's Pops?"

Amber followed her mother into the house. "He's doing a lot better. He's in the shop with Gabe right now. I will go out and let him know you've come home."

Elsa Mae walked with Amber to Amber's old room, the door was ajar. Elsa Mae opened it all the way. "Annie, your mama is here."

Annie smiled and walked to the door. "Mama!" She grabbed Amber's legs and then looked up into Amber's face. The smile on Annie's face disappeared. The child looked at her grandma and then at Amber again. Confused, the child let go of Amber's legs and went back to her toys.

Elsa Mae saw the hurt on Amber's face. "Go on in and sit with her; she just doesn't remember, Amber. It will take time."

Amber brushed away a tear that had escaped and went into the room. She sat on the bed. "I know, Mama."

Elsa Mae shut the door.

Amber put her purse down on the bed. She scooted onto the floor and picked up a doll that Annie had just put down. She tried handing it back to Annie. "Do you like baby dolls, Annie?"

Annie took the doll and hugged it. "Baby." Then she threw it down and picked through the other toys. She found a block and handed it to Amber. "Block."

Amber couldn't believe her little girl was talking. "You like blocks?"

"Yes, blocks." Annie picked up several more and handed them to Amber. Amber took the blocks and started to build a tall stack with them. Annie joined in by finding more blocks and bringing them to Amber or putting the blocks on the stack by herself.

Soon the stack was too tall and fell. Annie laughed. Amber laughed with her. "Should we build another one?"

Annie grabbed the fallen blocks and started stacking them again.

Amber spent almost an hour with Annie in the room playing. She hadn't noticed if anyone had come to check on them. But no one had come to interfere with their time together. Annie had even given Amber a couple of hugs during their playtime. Amber knew that Annie didn't really know her anymore. She hoped for Annie's sake that Katie and Josh would be good parents to her little girl.

Amber's thoughts were interrupted by her daddy's voice. "I hope I'm not interrupting anything."

Amber got off the floor and hugged her dad. Gabe had come through the door as well. He went straight to the toys on the floor. "Papa, Annie is playing with my cars."

Amber turned to her children. "It's okay, Gabe. I was playing with them, not Annie." Amber got down on her knees with her children. She handed two cars off the floor to her son.

Gabe pushed the cars across the floor. "You were playing with my cars, Mommy?" Amber was shocked to hear that Gabe still remembered her. Annie came close to Amber, took her hand, and pulled her toward the blocks again.

"Blocks, Mama, blocks."

A few tears left Amber's eyes as she began to stack blocks and play with her children. Her parents watched as their daughter enjoyed the special moment. Amber got what she had come home for—her children's forgiveness.

◊◊◊

Angelica reached Damian's truck. "She's not in the store, shower, or anywhere that we can see on the lot." She looked at Damian. "You know where she's at don't you?"

Damian nodded. "Shelby and I figured it out at the same time. Today is Annie's, her little girl's, birthday. She mentioned it to me last night before we went to sleep. I had no idea she would take off and go to her parents' house. She knows the danger involved if Shades gets wind that she might be there. I don't think she was thinking straight. I think she just wanted to see her little girl."

Angelica stepped back to think. She put her hands on her hips and walked around for a few minutes. She came back over to Damian and Shelby. "How did she get there?"

Damian was confused as to why Angelica cared about how Amber got to her parents' house. "By taxi, I guess. We took a taxi there when we came to see her dad."

"Okay, chances are the only way she's going to get back here is in a taxi—if she comes back at all. The only problem with her arriving in a taxi now, is that Shades and his men are scoping out the truck stop. I think I saw them leave a few minutes ago, but he will be back. We have got to continue trying to get a hold of her on her cell phone. She had to know that Shades is in town and he's looking for Damian's truck. I'm thinking maybe we need to go get her from her parents'. I'm going to send Shelby after her. Damian, I know you don't want to leave your truck, but you are going to be safer in my truck.

Once Shades finds your truck, and sees that you have abandoned it, he will start looking for you somewhere else."

Shelby spoke up. "That's all fine and good, Angelica, but the first place he's going to look is Amber's parents' house. We can't leave Damian's truck in this parking lot. He will go straight to them, thinking they are hiding there."

"You're right. We need to get this truck somewhere else. I hate to keep you driving around, Damian, but I think maybe we should take your truck north. Maybe Lubbock, that would keep Shades chasing you. Shelby can then take Amber in another direction or keep her on her truck until I can get my agency to give me a warrant to arrest Shades."

Damian shook his head defiantly. "That's a great plan, Angelica, but Amber isn't here, and she has no idea Shades is. Besides, she won't go for being separated from me like that."

Angelica, finally pushed to the limit, yelled. "Well, she doesn't have a choice here. Not if she wants to live!"

◊◊◊

"Boss, I don't see that truck anywhere in this parking lot."

"Keep looking, Rico. There are eight truck stops in this Midland/Odessa area and I want every one of them checked. Have you heard from any of my other people?"

"No, sir."

"Get on the phone and find out if they found that truck yet. Rico, check every truck stop. I just know that bitch is here somewhere, I can feel it."

"Yes, sir."

◊◊◊

Amber kissed her little babies and hugged her parents on the front porch. The taxi had arrived. "We are so glad you came home to see us. Are you sure you can't stay for the birthday party?"

"Oh, Mama, I would love to, but I have to get back. Damian is waiting for me." Amber took her time giving hugs and kisses to her parents and her children. She hadn't mentioned that she and Damian had gotten married.

She wanted to wait for Damian to tell them the news in person. "You know that I love each of you so much. I am sorry for all that I've put you through."

Amber's father took Gabe in his arms and Elsa Mae took Annie from Amber. Charley kissed his daughter's forehead. "We know, Amber. We love you very much. We will always be here waiting for you to come home."

She stepped off the porch, crossed the lawn, and put her hand on the handle of the taxi that waited at the curb. Elsa Mae yelled across the yard. "Amber Ellen Nichols, will you be here next weekend for your sister's wedding?"

Amber smiled and turned to face her mama. "I'll give you a call, Mama. I'll let you know if I'm coming home."

Amber opened the taxi door and got in. She sat in the back seat, shut the door, and waved goodbye as the driver took her down the street and out of view of her parents and babies.

CHAPTER THIRTY-FOUR

"Take me back to that truck stop across the street. I can't help but thinking we missed something there."

"Yes, sir."

Shades and his men went through the intersection and pulled into the truck stop parking lot near the front of the store.

"Well, what do we have here?" Shades looked at the young girl getting out of the taxi in front of the restaurant. He pointed to the young woman and his driver maneuvered the SUV toward the woman who was now walking around the building. "There she is, get her!"

◊◊◊

Damian's phone rang. "It's Amber." He answered the phone quickly. "Amber where are you, baby? I've been so worried."

"I'm sorry, Damian, I had to see my family. I promise, I was very careful. No, one saw me."

"Are you still there?"

"No. In fact, the taxi driver is just now dropping me off in front of the truck stop. I am walking around the building now. I'll be there in a minute."

"Wait, Amber, stay where you are. Shades is out here looking around. Don't move. Angelica is sending some of her men up there to get you."

Angelica pointed to several of her men. "Go, she is up front. Go now!" The men ran as fast as they could to the front of the building.

Amber still felt the contentment of seeing her children. She looked around half-heartedly. "Don't worry, Damian, I'm almost to the truck. I don't..."

Amber's phone went dead. Damian jumped out of his truck and ran toward the front of the truck stop. "They got her, Angelica, they got her!"

Angelica, Shelby, and the rest of the agents ran to the truck stop store. Just as they rounded the corner of the building, Damian spotted a black SUV speeding out of the driveway. Damian ran toward the SUV and tried to catch it before it got away down the highway.

Angelica, reached her men who she'd sent to get Amber. They were breathing heavily. One picked up Amber's cell phone off the ground. "I'm sorry, Angelica, they had her in the car before we could get to her."

Angelica and Shelby ran over to Damian who was now on his knees in the parking lot. He screamed out in pain. "They have her, oh my God, they have her!"

"We will get her back, Damian." Angelica said.

Angelica and Shelby forced Damian to stand and walk with them out of the drive. He was so distraught that they couldn't comfort him as they walked him back to his truck. "I promise, Damian, we will find her and bring her home," Angelica reiterated.

Angelica had already taken her phone out of her pocket and was making calls.

Damian cried with deep sobs. "She's gone. That fucking bastard has my wife. He has my beautiful Amber."

Without thinking, Damian broke free from Angelica and Shelby. He ran straight for his truck. He opened the door to the driver's side and jumped into the seat. Shelby's truck was still blocking his truck. "Move your truck, Shelby, we have to go after them."

Shelby got up on Damian's truck. "Stop, Damian. Angelica is on the phone right now. She is talking to the local police and sheriff's departments. We have a description of the SUV that took her. They have more resources and manpower. They will find her and Shades, I promise. You can't do anything in this big truck. Let me go to my house and get my four-wheeler, we can use it to go look, but Angelica is talking to the local FBI office, too. Since this is now a kidnapping, they will start looking right away. They aren't going to get away, Damian. They will find her, I promise."

Damian burst into tears again. "Please, Shelby, move your truck. I have to go look for her. He's going to kill her. I know he will, he said he would."

Shelby didn't know what to say to Damian. She just stayed with him and let him cry.

◊◊◊

Screaming and scratching Amber tried with all of her might to get away from Shades's men. "Let me go! Let me go, you bastard! I don't want to work for you anymore. I want to be with my husband and my family. You can't do this. The police already know who you are and they will get you, Shades!"

Shades laughed. "I heard you got married. Now I'm hurt you didn't invite me."

"Shut up, you son-of-a-bitch and let me go! I wouldn't want you at my wedding. I wouldn't invite you to watch me shit in the toilet."

Shades was incensed. He turned around and hit Amber in the mouth with his fist. "Now, shut the fuck up."

Her mouth filled with blood from her split lip. "You've already done this to me before, you bastard. There isn't anything you can do to me to make me go back to work for you. I hate you. You are evil, and the worst kind of monster on the face of the earth."

Shades turned around from the front seat and hit Amber in the mouth again. "I don't want you to work for me anymore, Amber. I just don't want you to work at all. You have such a big mouth, you're a liability."

Shades pointed to a dirt road off the highway. It looked like an oil lease road. "Take this road and find me a nice secluded spot." His driver did exactly what his boss demanded. They drove several miles out into the oil fields. The sun had set, and the dark field was illuminated only by the SUV's headlights.

Amber started to cry. "Please, Shades, let me go. I promise I won't tell anyone what I did for you. I don't care about your business; I just want to go back to my husband and make a life with him. Please, just let me go."

Shades saw a dirt pit off to the right of the oil field and pointed. "There, pull over there." The driver pulled off the lease road and stopped near the caliche pit. "Get her bloody ass out of my car."

Amber begged and screamed and pleaded as the three men with Shades dragged her out of the SUV.

"Stop, Shades! If you kill me they will hunt you down; they will find you! They know who you are! Please, let me go!"

Shades pulled his pistol from his holster. "Let her go."

Shades's men shoved Amber to the ground. Then they stepped back behind their boss.

Amber struggled to get to her feet. Her face hurt and her stomach cramped. She knew she would be leaving the earth tonight. "There, I let you go, Amber. Now run!"

Knowing that she could never outrun Shades's bullets, Amber peacefully and without tears faced Shades. "Shoot me you fucking coward—shoot me while I'm facing you."

Shades took aim and hit Amber in the middle of her head with a single bullet from his gun. Amber fell backwards and hit the ground. Her hand landed on top of her belly. The dirt from the ground mixed with the blood that now flowed from the back of her head.

To make sure that his target had been eliminated, Shades and his men moved toward Amber's body. Shades looked at Amber's lifeless body and put another bullet into her head. Amber's head jerked and turned to the other side from the impact of the close shot. "There I shot you, you stupid bitch."

Shades put his gun back in his shoulder holster and walked toward his SUV. "Let's get out of here. I want to go back to Atlanta. This oil patch shit smells."

Shades and his men left Amber's body exposed, alone in the dark, foreboding night. The ground continued to be saturated with the blood that seeped from Amber's body.

Amber looked down at her body as it lay still and lifeless as her spirit disappeared into the light.

◊◊◊

Shelby honked the horn of Jack's pickup. "Damian, come on, get in." Damian lifted his head off the steering wheel of his truck. He saw that Shelby had gone to her house and brought back her four-wheeler. He opened his driver's side door and exited his vehicle. He slammed it shut and locked it.

"Come on, we have to go now," Shelby said. The sheriff and his deputies have Shades and his men stopped somewhere off highway three-eighty-five."

Damian jumped into the passenger side of Shelby's pickup.

"We have to pick Angelica up near the front of the truck stop. Hurry."

"Is Amber okay?" Damian asked—his eyes filled with hope.

"I don't know. My husband Jack just told me what he saw on the news— the sheriff and his men are in some kind of standoff with some suspected kidnappers off the three-eighty-five. I called Angelica and she confirmed that it was Shades and his men."

Shelby rounded the corner of the truck stop store—her tires, screeching. "There she is." Shelby rolled up fast on Angelica and one of her agents. She sped up and then came to an abrupt stop. "Get in!" Shelby spun her tires, left the parking lot, and headed westbound on interstate twenty.

Angelica had jumped into the back seat of the pickup with Mr. D. "Head toward three-eighty-five and go south. They have Shades stopped somewhere about five or so miles past the loop. They are on the northbound side though. I guess Shades tried to outrun the cops, but they put him and his men in the ditch around there."

"Is Amber okay?" Damian turned to look at Angelica in the back seat.

"I don't know, Damian. They didn't say anything about her. Let's just get there and find out."

Damian turned back around and sat somberly in his seat. He touched his cheek. He knew he'd felt Amber earlier—she wasn't going to be at the crash scene. Damian knew she wasn't anywhere on the earth anymore. Shelby raced down the highway, passing every vehicle in sight. She slowed down only long enough to make the exit off the interstate and go south on three-eighty-five. After passing the west loop, the clear night sky illuminated the flashing blue and red lights in the distance. Shelby pointed at the lights. "There, that's where they are."

At the speed Shelby was traveling, it didn't take her long to each the outer perimeter of the crash scene. Shelby had to slow way down to avoid contact with the other traffic that had been stopped by the police. "I can't get any closer in the truck, Angelica. The cops have everything blocked off on both sides of the highway."

Damian jumped out of the pickup, Angelica and Mr. D. weren't far behind him. Shelby found a place along the road to park Jack's pickup. She put on the emergency flashers, jumped out of the still-running vehicle, and followed the others to the yellow taped off area.

Angelica reached Damian's side just outside the tape. "Damian, wait, you can't go past that tape, the cops will put you in cuffs." She grabbed his arm and attempted to keep him from going any further.

Damian pulled his arm away. "I have to see if Amber is okay."

"I know, Damian, but let me talk to the cops." She touched Damian's arm gently. "Please, let me talk to them first. They aren't going to let you anywhere close to the action. I might be able to find out more with my badge."

Damian backed off and let Angelica move toward the state police officer near the tape. Damian stood behind Angelica as she showed the officer her badge. "DEA Agent Dillon, I'm the one that asked for your help in apprehending that suspect over there."

The officer looked at Angelica's badge and then let her pass under the yellow tape barrier. The confrontation between Shades and the officers who had him surrounded was across the highway median. Angelica walked through the tall grass in the median and found a secure place behind one of the sheriff's unit's parked sideways in the road.

The officers all had their guns drawn behind their cars. One deputy was standing out in front of his unit, gun down to the ground, trying to talk to a single man who stood behind the open back seat door. The man had a small amount of blood on his forehead, but appeared to be communicating without difficulty with the deputy.

Angelica could see that there were two other men still seated in the car. They were shifting around, but not leaving the vehicle. Another man was lying on the ground in front of the wrecked SUV, he was not moving. From the looks of the accident, Angelica figured the man may have been thrown from the vehicle.

"Look, sir, I need you to walk toward me. Do you have any weapons on you? We aren't here to hurt you. We want to get all of you to the hospital. Come out from behind the vehicle and let us help you."

Shades laughed. "We're fine; just go on about your business and I will take care of myself and my men."

"We can't do that, sir. You've been involved in an accident with the Sheriff's Department and we have to investigate the accident."

Shades laughed again. "You're the dumbasses that ran us off the road. I will call my insurance company and you call yours. We can have the insurance companies deal with this."

Angelica showed her badge to the officer as she came up behind the police unit. The officer let her come close. "What've we got?"

"A crazy asshole who won't give up."

"Is there a young woman with them?"

"No, not that we can see. They might have her down in the back of the SUV, but we can't get close enough to tell."

Shelby, Mr. D., and Damian had followed Angelica across median, behind the taped off perimeter. They couldn't get close enough to hear what was being said, but they could see the vehicle, the man on the ground, and Shades standing behind the vehicle for protection.

"Can you see her, Shelby? Can you see Amber?"

Shelby looked into the shadows of the SUV. There was no sign or silhouette of Amber's body anywhere visible around the vehicle. Shelby turned to Damian and shook her head. "No, Damian, I don't see her."

Before Shelby knew what was happening, Damian broke through the yellow tape and ran toward the SUV. Two deputies near the yellow tape took off after Damian and tackled him within feet of Shades. The police forced Damian's hands behind his back, cuffed him, and brought him to his feet.

Shades had seen the advancing man. The cop and Angelica's attention had been drawn to Damian, so they did not see Shades pull his gun from the holster. The cops who'd had their weapons drawn on Shades moved them to Damian when he broke through the barrier. They quickly moved their guns back in Shades's direction when he produced the gun.

The deputy in charge of the scene held up his gun and hands in the air. "Settle down. Hold your fire! Everyone just hold your fire! Shades… May I call you Shades? Just calm down, that's just an excited bystander. My men have him in custody."

Damian yelled at the top of his lungs at Shades. "You son-of-a-bitch. Shades, where is Amber? What the hell did you do to her, Shades?"

The cops who had been pulling Damian back toward the barrier stopped. "Tell me where she is, Shades! You are an evil monster. Give her back to me, you demon. Give her back!"

Angelica spoke to the man next to her. "That's the kidnapped woman's husband."

The cop motioned for the cops to stop forcing Damian out of the crime scene.

Shades laughed and came out slightly from the protection of the SUV door. "So you're the dick Amber has been chasing." Shades laughed again. "You don't look like much to me. She was a fool to leave our family for you."

"Shut the hell up, Shades. You didn't offer her a family—she was your slave. You bastard. Where is she?"

Damian fought against the force of the cops who were holding him back from the SUV. "Let me go. I want to see if Amber is in that vehicle. Please, let me go!"

Shades mocked Damian's words. "Please, let me go. Please!" Shades laughed. "Mister, whoever you are, those were the same words Amber said to me tonight." Shades laughed again and in a mocking tone said, "Let me go! Let me go!"

Damian rammed forcefully again against the officers who were holding him back. He leaned toward Shades's taunting words. "You fucking bastard…what did you do with her? I want my wife back."

Shades laughed. "She was brave. She didn't even run." Shades who had not relinquished his gun, pointed it directly at Damian. Before he was able to take a shot, the officers with their weapons trained on Shades, emptied their weapons into his body.

CHAPTER THIRTY-FIVE

Damian walked through the familiar screen door at Amber's parents' home. Katie was holding Annie as she held the door for Damian. "Come in, Damian. Mama and Pops are in the living room."

When Damian entered the room, Elsa Mae got off the couch and came toward him. "Oh, Damian, we are so glad you're here. Come in, sit."

Shelby and Angelica were standing with their husbands among the crowd that had gathered in the dining room. Shelby whispered into Angelica's ear. "Damian's here." The two women, followed by their husbands, took the glasses of tea they had in their hand into the living room.

Angelica reached for a hug from Damian; Shelby followed suit, holding his hand. "We are so sorry for your loss, Damian." Damian didn't know how to respond. He simply nodded without saying anything and walked over to Amber's father.

Angelica's cell phone rang. Embarrassed, she and Rex slipped out to the front porch. Shelby and Jack followed.

"What do you mean 'that wasn't Shades?'"

Shelby listened intently to the surprising conversation.

Angelica switched her phone to her other ear. She looked at Rex. Shelby saw the lines on her forehead reveal the anger that was building as she spoke with the agency. "Seriously, how is it possible they shot the wrong man? I'm not telling Damian right now. We are at the funeral, and he's not ready to hear that his wife's murderer isn't dead."

Shelby couldn't believe what she was hearing. Angelica hung up her phone.

"He's not dead?" Shelby asked.

"Nope, he's not dead. I was looking forward to arresting Dante and shutting down his operation. Now, I have to go out and find that murdering bastard Shades, too. I hope when I find him I can save myself a lot of paperwork with a bullet."

"We can't tell Damian, not right now. He's crushed that Amber is gone. Knowing this might make him do something really stupid."

"I agree, Shelby."

"Let's give him some time to grieve," Rex said.

◊◊◊

Damian had found a seat next to Charley. Charley stared off through the big picture window in the living room. His family and wife were huddled close, ready to serve the man if he should ask for anything. Damian leaned in to Charley and whispered. "Would you like to get out of here for a few minutes?"

Charley got up off the couch, surprising everyone except Damian who had made the offer. Damian was already up helping the man walk to the back door.

"Charley, what are you doing? Dad, sit back down. We will get you whatever need," Katie said.

"I'm going outside with my new son-in-law. I can manage for myself. I need some time with him." Charley walked with Damian past everyone in the house.

In the backyard, Damian and Charley sat at the old, weathered picnic table. "How are you doing, son?"

Damian put his elbows on the table and rested his head in his hands. "Taking one day at a time, sir."

Charley nodded. "Me, too. I miss her, Damian. I look at little Annie and I see Amber when she was a little girl."

Damian fought back the tears. "I miss her so much, Charley."

Charley put his hand on Damian's arm. "She's safe now, Damian."

The tears fell from both men's eyes. "I know, sir."

Damian pulled the necklace he had bought Amber out of his pocket.

The silver heart shaped charm followed as he put it on the table. Damian opened the heart, revealing two of the small picture frames filled with photos and two left empty. "I gave this to Amber before we got married. She wore her ring that I had given her around her neck on the chain. She didn't want Shades to see it. After we got married, and I put that ring on her finger, I gave her the heart part of the necklace. I put Amber's face and my face from our wedding day in two of the frames."

Damian stopped to compose himself. "Sir, I want to give this to you. I want Katie and Josh to give it to Annie when she gets older. I want Amber's children to always know who their mother was and that she loved them. And that I loved their mother very much, too. Especially Annie, because Amber always worried that Annie wouldn't remember her. Maybe this necklace will help Annie to remember her mama."

Charley took the necklace and clutched it in his hand. "I will make sure that she gets it, Damian. But I think Amber would want you to stay around and get to know her family and her children."

"I would be honored, sir, to come and visit with you and your family whenever possible. Right now, I just need to get back out on the road. I need to get some miles between me and all that has happened."

"I understand, Damian."

"I promise, sir, I will come back. I want to know everything about Amber and her life."

Charley let a few tears fall. "Thank you, Damian. Thank you for loving her and wanting to keep her memory alive."

Damian and Charley sat in the cool air. Amber came by and touched their faces with her hand. Charley and Damian both felt the gentle breeze across their faces. Both men touched their faces and smiled at one another.

"She's here."

"I feel her." Damian smiled.

THE END

ACKNOWLEDGMENTS

I would like to thank Danielle H. Acee, Mindy Reed, Douglas Brown, and all those involved in editing and perfecting the text. Their guidance made the book release possible.

I also can't forget all of the individuals who supported me with their encouragement—my daughter-in-law, Cydney and my friends, Tina, Tamra, and Tammy. To so many others (truckers, friends, family members) who helped me in this endeavor, sometimes without even knowing it, thank you.

I will always remember all those who helped make this dream a reality.

With all my heart forever.
　—Robyn Mitchell
　robynmitchellauthor.com

If you or someone you love is contemplating running away, please call National Runaway Safeline, 1800runaway.org

The NRS listens to those who are thinking of or already have runaway. Their services are confidential and nonjudgmental.

Truckers Against Trafficking (TAT) is a 501(c)3 that exists to educate, equip, empower and mobilize members of the trucking and travel plaza industry to combat domestic sex trafficking.
http://www.truckersagainsttrafficking.org/

ABOUT THE AUTHOR

Robyn Mitchell left the comforts of teaching in a classroom to explore the open road in an 18-wheel sandhauler. Her experiences and time on the road birthed Mother Trucker, a series of suspenseful thrillers based on the trouble and happiness Shelby Mathews—a well-educated, gorgeous blonde, wife, and mother of three grown men—finds while trucking.

Read More
Mother Trucker Book Series
Mother Trucker
Trucktress
Outlaws
Jumpers
Terror West